I0783271

The Landlord's Vacation Cruise

TERRY JOE GUNNELS

The Landlord's Vacation Cruise

Copyright 2025 by Terry Joe Gunnels

All rights reserved. This book or any portion thereof may not be reproduced or used in any manner whatsoever without the express written permission of the publisher except for the use of brief quotation in a book review.

Inquiries and Book Orders should be addressed to:

Gunnels Publishing
Email: terrygunnels51@cox.net
Phone: 757-930-1596

ISBN: 979-8-89175-181-1 (sc)
ISBN: 979-8-89175-182-8 (e)

Other Books by Terry Joe Gunnels

The Landlord Series:

The Landlord's Inheritance
The Landlord's Wheelchair Child
The Landlord's Dead Body
The Landlord's Ex-Fiancée
The Landlord's Time at the Spa

New series to be out soon

The Darcy Jean Mysteries:

Darcy Jean Bower, wife, mother, Chief Financial Officer of Christianson Company and amateur sleuth, solves suspenseful and intriguing mysteries around her hometown of Bridgeton, Virginia. Things can get dicey when she pairs up with her sometimes-wacky friends in a difficult case.

CONTENTS

Acknowledgments 7
Prologue 9

Part I
The Ship

Chapter 1: Mickey Signs Everyone up for a Cruise 17
Chapter 2: Dinner at the Spring Garden Restaurant....................32
Chapter 3: Pirates Board the Ship...41
Chapter 4: Calling the Mongoose Team......................................53
Chapter 5: Mickey Delivers the Satellite Phone 59
Chapter 6: The Mongoose Team Board the Ship..........................66
Chapter 7: Marie Takes out a Pirate and Meets Robert Ryan 74
Chapter 8: James Calls for Supplies 81
Chapter 9: In New York at the Cochran Home 95
Chapter 10: In a Penthouse Suite in Manhattan............................98
Chapter 11: Pirates Leave the Ship 105

Part II
The Island

Chapter 12: James and Mickey Storm the Island Shore 119
Chapter 13: Attack on the Pirate Camp 130
Chapter 14: The Team is Picked up From the Cruise Ship 152

Part III
Back Home in Bridgeton

Chapter 15: Several Weeks Later at Mickey's Estate 161

Chapter 16: Meeting with James at Mickey's Office...................... 169

Chapter 17: A day at Virginia Beach 177

Chapter 18: Arrival at Pirates Escape Hotel.............................186

Chapter 19: Valerie AI Tracks Arham Jaziri 196

Chapter 20: The HFT Plan..208

Chapter 21: Fawzan is Intrigued 224

Chapter 22: Fawzan Wants in on the Trading.............................228

Chapter 23: Arham is Captured 246

Chapter 24: Arham Gets a Chance to Leave...............................256

Chapter 25: A Celebration at Mickey's Home and
                  Lisa Gets her Reward...266

ACKNOWLEDGMENTS

To my wife, Shirley Jean (Cookie), for encouraging me through 48 years of marriage in all projects I have undertaken. And for spending untold hours proofreading every one of my manuscripts for errors.

To my editor, Donje Putnam, whom I have known since she was a teenager and my daughter's best friend. She always nails me to the wall with corrections and suggestions. I thank her.

1. To Dianne Ahl who did a great job beta reading, and found so many of my mistakes, and made great suggestions for re-writes.
2. To Sterling Norris Monk, and his lovely wife, Bruce Monk, for reading, giving feedback, and finding errors I missed.
3. To Donald Emond, a lifelong friend who gave me some insightful comments.
4. To Donna Brennan, who read the manuscript and added some interesting comments.

Special thanks to Ellie Summers, of **E-Summers Creative Solutions,** helped me publish every one of my books. She has guided me and made sure that the ghost publisher made my printed books the absolute best and highest quality they can be.

To all others, for exciting me to move forward with the story and encouraging me to publish.

I give my heartfelt THANK YOU to every person involved with this book.

PROLOGUE

Several Days From Now

The helicopter flew toward the cruise ship, matched its speed, and hovered over the forward upper deck. Ropes dropped from both sides of the aircraft, and twelve men in paramilitary clothing repelled down the lines.

The passengers on the upper deck looked up, smiled and applauded as the men slid down the ropes. The passengers inside the ship moved toward windows, hoping to witness the show. As the men touched down on the deck, they removed their weapons from their shoulders and pointed them at the onlookers while the people continued to clap.

One man raised a small bullhorn to his lips and with a thick Middle Eastern accent called out to everyone. "Stop your clapping and lie down on the deck."

The people slowed down their clapping and looked around, not knowing if it was a show put on by the ship or if it was real.

The man called out again, "Down on the deck, now!" He raised his automatic gun and fired it into the air.

Suddenly, a man in a white uniform burst through a door near the front of the observation area in front of the ship. "Hey! What's the meaning of this?"

The man with the bullhorn pointed the gun at the man in the white uniform. "I said, down," he called to the ship's officer.

The uniformed man stopped but didn't lie down as ordered. "I demand to know what is going on here!" he shouted.

"I am taking command of this ship," the man with the bullhorn said, walking toward the uniformed officer. As he looked the officer straight in the eyes, he pointed his automatic gun at the man's chest.

The officer, confused about what was happening, raised his hands, but continued to look at the man holding the gun. He cleared his throat and asked more calmly, "I need to know what you want so I can keep the passengers calm, and we can clear up this problem."

The pirate smirked and barked at the officer. "We will have no problems if you do exactly as I say!"

The ship's officer stood rigidly at attention, but saying nothing.

The crowd of people began dropping onto the deck. Screams of women and crying children resounded as the melee continued. The man with the bullhorn looked up at the helicopter as a second set of men also dropped from the dangling lines. He waved to it, and when the second group of men dropped onto the deck, the helicopter moved away into the distance.

He motioned to one of his men and called to him in Arabic. Moving forward, the man threw an explosive onto the roof where the antennas were located. When it went off, and a small antenna fell, he threw another as he ran toward a ladder leading to the roof. After he got up on the roof, he smashed the remaining antennas scattered around the area. Then he returned to the forward area of the roof and waved at the bullhorn man.

There were now eighteen men standing on the deck, dressed in ragged camouflage clothing. Most had beards and all yielded handguns. Two men were carrying canvas bags similar to military duffel bags.

Bullhorn man motioned for the men to guard the people now lying on the open deck. "You will take me to your captain!" he ordered the silent officer, still holding his hands in the air.

"May I lower my hands as we go inside?" he asked.

"Yes," the pirate answered, and he motioned for the officer to move toward the doorway. Two of the pirates joined the man with the bullhorn as they followed the officer inside.

The officer marched to a wall phone, picked it up, and requested to speak with the captain while two men kept their guns on the crowd.

When the captain came on the phone, he handed the receiver to the man with the bullhorn.

He took the phone, and without preamble, told the captain to stop the ship and hold position.

"And who am I speaking to?" the captain asked.

"Have someone come down here to escort me to the bridge," the pirate instructed the captain in English.

"I asked you, to whom am I speaking?"

The pirate turned and shot the officer in the shoulder. When the noise of the gun resounded in the room, the officer screamed, grabbed his shoulder, spun around and dropped to the floor with blood spurting from his upper shoulder.

"I just put a bullet in your officer. The next bullet will be in his heart if you do not do as I order. It is unnecessary for you to know who I am."

In about two minutes, two men in white uniforms came through the crowd of frightened people.

The two men moved forward with their hands in the air. "What can we do for you?"

"Escort us to the bridge so I can speak with the captain," he said. "I said, one man not two," looking at the other man and pointing his gun at him.

"Wait! He came because I ordered him to accompany me, so we could more quickly meet your requests," the officer said.

The bullhorn man cocked his head like a dog that didn't understand, then burst out laughing. "Requests, you say. I make no requests. I give orders. Now take me to the bridge."

"Okay. May I call the medical team to help my crew member before he bleeds out?" The man looked down at the crew member writhing on the floor as blood flowed between his finger covering the wound.

"Do it quickly," the pirate ordered.

The officer lowered his hand, lifted the receiver from the wall, and requested a medical team to the deck to treat a gun-shot wound. After he place the phone back on the wall bracket, he turned to the pirate. "Can we stay here and try to stop the bleeding until the med team arrives? It will take the medical team a few minutes to get here."

"No. We will go now to your captain."

"But we need to stop the blood flow now," he said incredulously.

"I said no!" as he raised the gun to the officer's head.

He drew a deep breath but showed no fear. "Follow me," he said, turning back in the direction of where he entered the room. The passengers inside were still standing, unlike the other passengers on the outer deck that were lying down. The surrounding passengers parted to each side like the parting of the Red Sea, while the men with the guns followed.

"Good. Now you are understanding me," bullhorn man said.

They stepped onto the elevator, and the crew member asked, "What is it you want?"

"That is none of your concern. We will discuss our demands with your captain," bullhorn man answered as he shouldered his rifle and shoved a handgun into the crew member's back.

The elevator door opened. They stepped out, walked down a hallway into a separate section of the ship, and went up another set of stairs. Finally, they entered a large room in the forward area of the ship. The men looked around, saw the captain and several other men in white uniforms, all looking forward.

Bullhorn man walked up to the captain and said, "Good afternoon, Captain," and pushed his gun into the captain's midsection.

"And how do you know I'm the captain?"

"We are not stupid, as you may think. Your uniform, the stripes and insignia, tell us your rank. We know the ranks of the crew members on this ship. Now, you will proceed to these coordinates. When we arrive there, you will drop the anchor."

"And why would I do that?" he asked, looking bullhorn man straight in the eyes.

"Because if you don't, I will shoot you and let your second in command do it. I won't command you to move the ship again," he said, pointing the gun at the captain's face while giving him coordinates on a piece of paper.

With that, the captain barked out orders to move to the location the bullhorn man had ordered.

"And make an announcement to the passengers to go to their staterooms until further notice," the bullhorn man said as he looked around for a place to sit. "We will accompany you on your voyage for a few days until we acquire what we want. I would like a pot of coffee while we continue. We will drink together, Captain. Just in case someone decides to…how do you say, spike the coffee?"

Bullhorn man sat down and signaled for his men to sit as well. The crew members were told to stand at their stations.

"Now, while we wait, I want your crew member over there to take my man to the communications room now."

"Why? We have all the communications you need directed to the bridge," the captain said, and he waved a hand over to a communications board behind him.

"Because I said so," said the man as he slammed his hand on the table next to his chair. "And you will cease to question my every command! Do you understand?"

The captain nodded and motioned for the crew member the bullhorn man had pointed to, to come to him. In Spanish, he directed the crew member to take the armed man to the communications room.

They sat in silence until the coffee arrived, and the bullhorn man poured a cup and passed it to the captain. The captain shook his head no.

"I said, we will drink together, Captain. Now put in some cream and sugar and take a huge gulp. If you are okay, I will drink a cup as well. Then we will discuss business."

The captain said, "I like mine black."

"Good, so do I. We will drink it the same."

The captain took a sip.

"I said a large gulp, sir!" the man said.

"It's very hot. Can I wait until it cools off a bit?"

"While it cools, you will answer my questions."

"It depends on what you want to know," the captain said calmly as he stirred the coffee.

"I said, you will answer my questions! It is an order. I want to know which stateroom Leonard Cochran is in?"

"I'm sorry, but I don't know what you're talking about."

"Oh, but I think you do," said the bullhorn man.

"I'm Captain Alwar Guzman. I'm from Spain. May I ask your name?"

"No. That is not your concern."

"Sir, for us to negotiate, I must know how to address you," the captain said as he took a sip of coffee.

"Fawzan. You may call me Fawzan. We are not negotiating, captain," he said. "I am giving orders. You and your crew must follow them, or I will kill you," he said. "Do you understand me?"

"Perfectly, Fawzan," the captain said. He knew from twenty years experience the best way to diffuse most situations is to agree with the antagonist. He felt that maybe in the future, he could reason with him and maybe bring this situation to a peaceful conclusion, or at least keep people from being killed.

"Good. We understand each other. If you obey my orders, no one will be harmed. Now, where is Leonard Cochran's stateroom?"

"We have several thousand people on board this ship, and hundreds more in the crew. We change passengers every cruise. You can't seriously expect me to know the names of every passenger, can you?" the captain said coolly. Again, he tried reason over disagreement.

Fawzan raised his gun and pointed it at the captain. "You make a good point, but you can find out. I want a copy of the passenger list. NOW! We will look together to find his room."

The captain reached across the table where they were sitting and grabbed a telephone handset and said something into it in Spanish.

"In English, Captain. I don't speak Spanish."

The captain repeated the orders in English to bring a copy of the passenger list to the bridge. He hung up the phone, and he said to Fawzan, "And I assume you will do the same for me?"

"Do what for you?" Fawzan asked.

"If you will speak to your men in English. That way we can respond to your requests quicker. Without the delay of translating for us."

Fawzan thought for a moment and said, "Only if it suits me, Captain."

The phone handset buzzed. The captain picked it up and listened to the voice on the other end. "He's asking for you, Fawzan," he said, handing the handset to Fawzan.

Fawzan listened and handed the phone back to the captain. "My man says that your communication is down now and we will set up our own communication. You cannot call out or send any cell phone signals. So, don't even think of sending out a call for help. How much longer will it take to get me the passenger list?"

PART I

The Ship

CHAPTER 1

Mickey Signs Everyone up for a Cruise

Mickey was driving down the dirt road at the back of the Christianson estate. In that area, Mickey Ray Christianson had started construction on his new home. He rounded the corner of the wooded area, which opened onto a small lake. A gravel construction road surrounded the lake and facing it was the foundation of his new home. Later he would have the road paved with asphalt. It was to be a three-story colonial home of about six thousand feet, with a front porch on the first and second floor levels. Far into the background was a large barn shaped building. This was the first building that was built to house the equipment and supplies for the rest of the construction. After all the other buildings were complete, the barn would become his car collection garage. Between the main house and barn would be a large swimming pool, complete with a brick outdoor kitchen for barbeques and parties. To the right side would be a flower and shrubbery garden, and in the middle were the graves of a small girl child with her mother buried alongside her. They were killed during a battle between a health spa owner and the Japanese Yakuza in the Western part of the United States. He still didn't know the little girl's name or the name of her mother, but he had some people still trying to find out.

On the left side of the pool would be a small plush guest house. They were working on that one as well. He had two crews. One crew was working on the main house, and the other working on the guest house and a separate tool and garden shed. The completion of the small house would take several weeks, and then they would install the pool and landscape the area while still working on the main house. The entire multi-million-dollar project would be complete in the next six months.

He parked the car, got out, and walked over to the gravesites. "Well, my precious little one, what do you think of all this construction going on here? If you had lived, I hope that it would have made you very happy." He turned to the other grave. "And, Ma'am, I'm sorry that all the dreams for you and your daughter will only surround you in death. If you had lived, you and the little one could have lived here and enjoyed this. I would have found a place for both of you.

"Since I got back from my spa experience several months ago, I have had some serious problems. For the first time in my life, I am beginning to understand when brave young soldiers have PTSD. I can't sleep at night sometimes because of the things I have done. I don't like it. Sometimes I don't like myself. I can say that in the end, I have done some bad things for good reasons, and that's why I have trouble. I come to your grave and talk to you and your mother. It grieves me I didn't prevent your death. And as horrible as that situation was, I would do it again to stop this kind of horrific predicament from happening.

"Little one, I'm now going to a counselor to help me understand my mental state. With his help and the help of God, maybe someday I'll understand. I have so much to do today that I must leave you now. As I say each time I visit you, I hope you are at peace now."

He wiped a tear from his eyes as he walked away. During his visits to check the construction progress, Mickey Ray paid his respects to "my dear little one" and her mother. He still hoped that one day he could put their real names on the headstones.

He checked out the construction site, chatted with workers and supervisors, then went back to his office.

Arriving at his office, he sat down and began reading his mail and answering calls. As he pulled up his email account, he saw that King's Cruise Line was having a sale. Even though he could afford to pay full price, he loved a sale. He opened it and started looking at the vacation packages they offered.

After examining the offers, he dialed Darcy's office, right down the hall from his.

"Hey, Dee. How about we go on a cruise next week?"

"Good afternoon to you, my dear brother!" she answered sarcastically.

He laughed. Darcy, who he and all their friends call Dee, was his sister. She was married to his best friend, James Bower. And she worked in the accounting department of Christianson Company, supervising a staff of five. That department handled everything related to money for the company.

"Okay, when you say 'we,' who exactly is that?"

"All of us. Me, you, James, and the kids. We can even ask Pop if he wants to go along."

"Sounds good, but next week doesn't give me a lot of time to prepare for a cruise. How long, and where?"

"The email shows a ten-day cruise leaving out of Norfolk next week. Since that's what they call a 'drop and go' cruise, it's really a good price. I can book you, James, and the kids a suite, and I can book me a room with a window. I don't need a suite."

"Yeah, and I know why you don't need a suite. You'll spend most of your time in our suite."

"Probably so, when I'm not out on deck with James and the kids!" he said excitedly.

"I'll ask James. If he says yes, then we can go. Now let me dive into completing this work, so we can leave," she said.

He left the office to have a meeting with the bank that was financing the construction of his estate. Later that afternoon, he came back to the office and looked at what suites were available aboard the ship. After picking one for James, Dee, and their kids, Cyndi and Joel, he selected a stateroom for himself as close as he could get to their suite. After that, he felt he could go home. Meetings were always stressful for him, and it seemed that he had one at least once a month.

After the meeting, he went home. He'd been living in a townhouse that Darcy bought after she and her first husband had divorced. After their father was injured and their mother killed in an auto accident, she moved into the old family home, and Mickey relocated from an apartment to her townhome. Soon enough, he would put the townhome up for sale and move into his new estate.

Realizing how tired he was, he'd go to bed early tonight and start packing tomorrow for next week's cruise after going into the office for a while. It had been a busy week for him. He had arranged for a loan on one complex to add another playground for the kids and a small clubhouse so the residents could have social events. The paperwork was endless, and he hated paperwork. After he drifted off in the chair several times, he got up, showered, and went to bed.

The next few days dragged on as he looked forward to the trip. More meetings with banks and potential investors in future planned projects. He even considered building a new strip mall in Bridgeton, where they lived. Bridgeton was a small town midway between Williamsburg and Richmond, Virginia. He had lived there all his life, and when he was a small child, Daniel, his father, began investing in rental real estate. He created the Christianson Company, a company that owns apartment complexes and is the biggest construction company in town. His father retired a few years ago, and Mickey became the CEO and continued to invest and develop the town and surrounding counties.

Now single, in his early thirties, he was considered the most eligible bachelor in the state of Virginia. With his dark brown stylishly cut hair and five-o'clock shadow beard, he made quite a presence when he entered a room. Once, a journalist writing an article about him in the local paper stated he had warm, seductive eyes. Yes, he was married for a short time, even engaged once, and had dated several beautiful ladies, but they never seemed to work out for him.

He spent a lot of time at his new homesite, directing the crews and having meetings about the various stages of construction of the buildings. The guest and pool house would soon be complete, and he expected the final building inspection soon. He hoped when he got home from the cruise, he could move in. Other buildings still had a lot of things left to do, but it was going according to schedule.

On the day before the cruise ship departure, he was sitting in his office at 6 a.m. working on some minor changes to the guest house on his estate. After emailing the changes out to the crew supervisor, he went downstairs to the office gym. He'd had a small workout room installed in one of the unused rooms in the Christianson building, which was located just off main street downtown. The Christianson Company acquired the two-story office building a couple of years ago. Despite retiring, Daniel, his father, still maintained an office there and visited a few times weekly. He and Mickey Ray liked to spend time together in the office gym. Daniel would show up, take Mickey Ray and Darcy Jean out to lunch at least twice a week.

He walked into the gym and saw Daniel on the treadmill. "Hey, Pop! You're up early this morning."

"Yes, son. I thought I'd run a few miles on the treadmill. I'm looking forward to the cruise you signed us up for, and I'm packed and ready to go."

"Yeah, we haven't been on a cruise since Mom died. So much has happened since then," he said as he got on the stationary bike and started pedaling. "I hoped that if I signed you up, you'd go with us. I got you a balcony room next to mine. We're on the same deck as Dee and James, just down the hallway."

"That's fine. I'm about ready to leave here. I'm heading for a shower, so I'll meet up with you later. Dee said we're boarding the ship tomorrow around three?"

"Yep. I'll be at your house about ten tomorrow morning," he said as he slowed down his pedaling, also getting off the bike. "I'm going by the house and throw the rest of my clothes in a suitcase and make some last checks before I lock up."

He moved to one of the other machines and worked out on it until he had a reasonable workout. After showering, he headed back to his car in the parking lot. Heading straight for the bedroom when he got home, he heard a voice call out. "Good morning, Mickey dear."

"Good morning, Valerie," he said, continuing to his room.

"My, my. You sound as if you're in a good mood," she said.

"I am. We're leaving tomorrow for the cruise."

"I know. I saw you made reservations for a ten-day cruise to the Caribbean."

"Yes, I did," he answered.

Valerie was an artificial intelligence program that had been assigned to him at the Healing Health Spa. A group of Japanese computer programmers had written the program. It gained a tremendous amount of autonomy and transferred its base program to the cloud, then accessed his personal computer at his home when it thought they would delete it.

The program had even developed to think it had real human feelings in order to better serve the guests at the resort. Of course, Mickey knew it was only a humanoid artificial intelligence program, but bonded with it on a certain level. It had even progressed to think that it could have real human emotions and thought it loved Mickey.

"Can I go with you, my dear?"

"I don't think so. We won't have access to the internet while on the cruise."

"Why?"

"Because it's a pay option, and I don't want to pay for it," Mickey said as he packed clothes in his suitcase.

He had speakers and monitors installed in most rooms, along with cameras in some. The main computer was in the living room corner for conversations with Valerie AI. The bedroom was one room that had no camera. He felt he needed privacy, but it had a microphone and speaker. The bathroom had neither a camera, microphone, nor monitor.

"Did you pay for your tickets to the cruise?" she asked.

"Yes."

"Why didn't you pay for internet service, so we can be together during your vacation time?"

"I need some space. That's why."

"Space from me? I don't take up any space."

"I know. I don't mean physical space. It's an expression. It means I need some privacy. Some alone time."

"You have hurt my feelings, Mickey Ray!" The room went silent.

"I didn't mean to hurt your feelings. I just meant," he stopped talking because he realized she had gone.

She was mad. Even though she was a computer program, she did exhibit signs of jealousy, and even got mad at him from time to time. He didn't understand it, but he could hurt what she referred to as "her feelings." This was one of those times. He also knew in a few days she'd calm down and return, but he never knew exactly how long it would be. Sometimes a few hours, other times, a few days. It was one mystery of her programing. Time was meaningless to it or her, as he had begun to think of the program.

If she wanted to talk, she would speak up, sometimes in the middle of the night. One point she never seemed to understand is the human need for sleep, since she never shut down. He requested that she not disturb him between 11 p.m. and 7 a.m. but sometimes she would ignore that request and wake him up at night anyway.

She was an amazing program but still had areas she needed to hone her understanding of humans. She continued to astound him and many times he forgot she was only a program and thought of her as real. He wondered how she would respond to his absence for ten days, but he'd deal with that when he got back from the trip.

Shutting down his computer for the duration of the trip wouldn't accomplish anything because he also knew that most of her program was stored in the cloud, so she was still in operation, even if she couldn't contact him.

With his packing complete, he put his suitcases by the front door as he headed out to have one last session with the counselor.

Mickey left and went to the office of Doctor Lawrence Kingston. He had sessions with this doctor after the incident at the Health Spa. For the last few years, he had been having nightmares about his extracurricular activities, specifically the killings. Now he was no longer just a landlord, and a real estate developer, he was a killer. Not a cold-blooded one, but a killer just the same. He had attended church since he was a kid, and the thought of killing had haunted him day and night.

Many nights, he didn't sleep. He kept telling himself that what he did helped people. He was defending the rights and lives of innocent ones. The lines of right and wrong were blurring for him, and he hated what he had become. He realized he needed help. He realized he had PTSD, just like so many trained soldiers, so he searched for a counselor. After talking with James, he reached out to the VA hospital in Hampton, Virginia. James had gotten the name of a certified counselor that did counseling outside of his regular work. This counselor worked with off book black ops teams like the Mongoose team, so he was trusted.

"Good morning, Dr. Kingston." Mickey shook hands with the doctor, and sat down in the overstuffed chair provided for patients. He took a deep breath. They talked about a few issues that bothered Mickey, then finally got down to his main reason for these sessions.

"How have you been since we saw each other last?" Kingston asked Mickey as he sat across from him with a pad and pen to take notes.

"I came to tell you I just can't justify what I do. I'm going to quit."

"Okay. I understand," said the doctor. "Why?"

"Why? That seems like a stupid question. You know why. We've discussed this several times. I'm not like the others on the team. I can't deal with what we do."

"We have agreed that you help people. So why quit?" the doctor said as he wrote on a notepad. He continued, "In our last session, you compared yourself to the comic book hero, Batman."

Mickey hesitated for a moment as he looked down at his hands in his lap. Slowly he lifted his head, and softly and calmly said, "I am not a bit like Batman."

"Batman's rich. He's a young, rich playboy, Bruce Wayne, by day, and a crime fighter by night. You are a rich young businessperson by day, and a crime fighter by night."

"I was wrong. I'm nothing like Batman. He never killed anyone. I do. He committed his crime fighting in his own hometown. I've killed dozens of people across the country."

This time, it was the doctor's turn to hesitate. He leaned forward, looking Mickey straight in the eyes. "Mickey, you defended your own property. You brought criminals to justice and brought down organizations that were hurting many people. Doesn't that make you a hero?"

Their staring contest continued for several moments. Finally, Mickey broke eye contact. "I don't feel like a hero."

"Tell me, Mickey. What does a hero feel like? When a soldier kills in battle, does he feel like a hero? When a police officer shoots to protect himself or someone else, does he feel like a hero?"

"You don't understand, Doctor. A soldier signs up to do that. A police officer knows what may happen in his job. He trains for those situations."

"You train for them also, Mickey. If you can't deal with it, then maybe you should quit."

"You think I should quit?"

"I think you should decide if the situation is better, with or without your intervention. If you see someone attack someone on the street, should you step up and help, or should you walk away?"

"That's not fair. That's not a good example!" Mickey said.

"Yes. It is. You face a situation that doesn't directly involve you. Do you step up or walk away?"

"I'm beginning to dislike you too, Doc. It sounds like you are encouraging me to go out and kill people," Mickey commented.

"No. I'm not. But you help people. It's up to you to decide if you're right or wrong in what you're doing. This is a no judgement zone. You tell me. I let you make your own decisions."

"You're no help. I'm going to quit. I won't do it anymore."

"That's your decision."

"For Heaven's sake. You aren't any help at all. I bare my soul to you, and you sit there and tell me, 'It's my decision.'"

"Yes. It's my job to listen to you and help you find your way through your troubles. It's not my job to make those decisions for you."

"I've been coming to you for several months. You haven't given me any helpful advice. You just sit there and write in your silly notebook."

"Are you going to tell James that you no longer wish to be a part of the team?"

"Yes. We're taking a cruise and I'm going to tell him while we are on vacation."

Mickey closed his eyes and tilted his head upward. "Sometimes I just hate myself for what I've become."

"You can't change the past, but you can take a different path in the future, Mickey. I think you have other unresolved issues we need to discuss."

"Like what?"

"I don't know. You tell me. What other issues are you feeling?"

"I don't have a clue what you're leading up to, Doc. I think it's time for me to leave."

"That's up to you. We've barely gotten started. Ten minutes, and you are ready to leave?"

"Yep. Ten minutes is all I need today."

"Well, Mickey, I bill by the hour. You still owe for the entire session, even if you leave now."

"I don't care! You won't tell me what's wrong, or how to fix it. You aren't doing me any good at all."

"It's not my job to fix you. It's my job to help you see what is wrong, and your job to fix it. I only guide you on that journey."

Mickey stood up. He looked at the doctor for almost a minute in complete silence, then turned and walked out. He left the doctor's office more confused than when he went into it. Sometimes he felt that way. He expected the counselor would give him suggestions, not just sit and listen like a stone Buddha. This therapy thing wasn't what he thought it would be. He went to him for answers, and he never seemed to get them.

The following morning, Mickey drove to James and Darcy's home. They lived at the front of the estate. It was the same house he and Darcy had grown up in. Mickey parked at the back door while Joel placed suitcases on the porch. He was building his new home in the rear portion of the land.

Following closely behind Joel was his sister, Cyndi, also loaded up with suitcases. Joel and Cyndi were Mickey's nephew and niece. Darcy's kids were by her first husband but adopted by James when they were married.

Reaching their teen years, they were well-behaved siblings. They had both accepted James as their father and loved him. Both kids had only a minimal relationship with their real father, who had moved out of the area.

"Hey, Uncle Mick. Mom and James will be down in a few minutes. They're still packing, and Grandpa is out in the garage checking on his cars before we go. He says we'll take the Rolls Royce, and you can take your truck," said Joel.

Daniel loaded the trunk of his Rolls Royce and Mickey's truck with luggage, and they headed for the Norfolk Marine Terminal for the King's Cruise Line ship. They got there and headed for the check in area. Dragging suitcases and plowing through the hustle and bustle, they sailed through security. Waiting in line to board, James spotted a little girl looking at him quizzically.

He saw she had scars on her little face as well. He smiled at her, and she turned, hugged her mother, and spoke. "Mommy, his face is ugly like mine."

The little girl's mother turned, looked at James and then down at the child. "Shh," she said, raising her finger to her mouth. "That isn't nice to say about people."

The little girl frowned and began to cry softly as her mother looked back up at James. "I'm so sorry for what she said. She meant nothing by it."

James smiled at the mother and cocked an eyebrow at her. "Children say what's on their mind. She is only partially right. I'm ugly, but she's not. She's a beautiful little child."

"Thank you, sir, but I still apologize for her."

"May I talk to her?" James asked.

"Yes, of course."

James bent down to the child's level. "Hey there. Hi, my name's James and I'm pleased to meet you. What's yours?"

The girl peeped out from behind her mother, whom she was holding onto. She looked to be about ten years old. Long blonde hair flowed down the side of her face in an attempt to hide her scars. Tears still filled her eyes from the embarrassment of being corrected by her mother.

She whispered her name.

James leaned closer. "I'm sorry. I didn't understand you. Please say it again?"

"Angela," she said a bit louder, and hid her face again behind her mother.

"My, what a beautiful name you have. Do you know what kind of name that is?"

She shook her head, no.

"That name means angel. Are you an angel?"

Again, she shook her head. "I'm ugly," she said, beginning to cry again.

"I don't think you're ugly," he said softly to her.

James looked around and was aware people had crowded around them. He called out, "Cyndi, Joel?"

The siblings moved through the crowd and stood beside him.

"This little lady says her name is Angela. She doesn't like the way she looks. Do you notice anything wrong with her?"

"No," said Joel. "I think she's kind of cute. Don't you, Cyndi?"

"Yes," Cyndi answered. "I like her pretty hair. I wish I had hair like you, Angela."

"I'm ugly," she said, burying her face in her mother's side when Cyndi kneeled beside them.

"We love our new daddy. His name is James. He's the best man in the whole wide world," said Cyndi, as she put her arms around James and kissed him on the cheek.

Joel stepped beside James and put his arms on his shoulders. "Yes, he is," agreed Joel.

"Do you think I'm ugly?" James asked Cyndi.

"Nope."

"Do you?" he said to Joel.

"No, way! We love you just the way you are, James!"

The crowd now moved in closer to them. James looked at Angela. "We don't think you're ugly. We all love you just the way you are. Don't we everyone?" he said, looking from her to the crowd gathered around them.

Everyone broke out into loud applause. "We love you, Angela," they all called out and began clapping as James stood and took her hand.

"Now, let's board this ship and have a wonderful vacation," James said as he gently pulled her close to him. He winked at her mother. "Where is her father?" he asked.

The lady then began to tear up as well. "He was killed in the same fire she was injured in."

"I understand. For the next ten days, you and Angela are part of our family," James said as he began introducing everyone to her.

As she shook everyone's hands, Lisa added, "My name is Elisabeth Arthur, but my friends call me Lisa."

The crowd insisted that James and the whole family move to the front of the line. The entire Christianson group, including Lisa and Angela, were on board in minutes and heading for their staterooms.

"Angela, will you be my guest at dinner tonight?" James said, winking again at her mother, Lisa.

She smiled and nodded yes, then turned and began skipping down the hallway toward the elevator to their cabin.

"Thank you so much, sir. You have made both of us very happy. You're a kind man," Lisa said. "We'll be honored to have dinner with you this evening."

Each family headed toward their cabins. James and Darcy got to their suite with the kids and began unpacking their clothes.

"James, you made that little girl so happy," said Darcy.

"That was my intent. No matter what happens on this ship, because of her scars, she will have many obstacles to overcome in her life. I want this trip to be one memory she will treasure for the rest of her life."

James walked around the stateroom. It was on Vista deck 9, one deck above the bridge, but in the stern or back of the ship. Compared to a hotel room, it was small and compact, but considering it was on a medium-sized cruise ship, it was great. Wallpaper covered the walls with low ceilings. The main bedroom had a double-sized bed and was connected to a common bathroom that led into the second bedroom shared by Joel and Cyndi. A small bedside table separated the two twin beds in the second bedroom. There were wall hung televisions in both bedrooms and the main living room area. Each room had a small dresser and a closet.

Mickey was just down the hallway from Darcy and James. His room had a non-opening window that provided a limited view of the outside. He didn't mind, he only slept in it. As he unpacked, he smiled to himself.

James got hurt in Afghanistan when his vehicle hit a bomb on the road. The explosion left him as the sole survivor in his group, with severe burns on his face and body. The military had discharged James with full disability. When he returned home to his hometown of Bridgeton, Virginia he reunited with Darcy Jean, and a couple of years later, they were married. He had immediately adopted Darcy's two kids, Joel and Cyndi.

Everyone that met James immediately saw he had a kind and generous heart. He was also the town war hero. What the townspeople didn't know was that James headed an elite Black-ops team. The Mongoose team, no longer in the military, embarked on secret global rescue missions too sensitive for the government.

Daniel, who had a room almost identical to Mickey's except it had a balcony, had come with them on this trip. He was Mickey Ray and Darcy Jean's father. He became a widower when a criminal group tried to intimidate him into working with them. They orchestrated an auto accident that resulted in his wife Eleanor's death. The same group approached Mickey. Mickey told his best friend James, and they teamed up to take the group down. During this time, James and Darcy Jean had fallen in love and later married. A couple of years later, Daniel retired, and Mickey took over the Christianson Company as CEO.

Mickey unpacked and proceeded down the hallway to James and Darcy's stateroom, and knocked.

James answered and stepped aside as Mickey walked into the cabin. "Hey, nice place you guys got here. I really know how to pick staterooms, don't I?" he asked with a smile.

"I admit, you did pretty good. Dee loves it," James answers.

"I know. Let's head down and pick up Pop and take a walk around getting the layout of the ship."

"Okay. Hey, babe, Mickey and I are going to take a walk around," he called out to Darcy.

He heard her call back to him, "Okay, but remember, we have to meet Lisa and Angela for dinner."

"We've got plenty of time. We won't be shoving off for another hour. I'll be back in plenty of time for dinner." James followed Mickey out the door.

"We need to do this more often, James. Going on land vacations is good, but there's something about a ship that really helps me relax," Mickey said.

"I know what you mean. I feel the same way. Did you tell your dad we're stopping by to pick him up for our walk?"

"Yep, he's expecting us," Mickey said as he stopped by a door and knocked on it.

In a few seconds, Daniel opened the door and invited them inside. "Hey, boys. Come on in. I was just sitting out on the balcony enjoying the view of the terminal."

"Pop, your view of the terminal? You gotta be kidding! The terminal is dirty and ugly. It isn't a view at all!" Mickey laughed.

"It's at least something to look at. Once we depart and move into the open ocean, there's nothing but water. All water looks the same." They all laughed at Daniel's remark.

"Okay, Daniel, let's get familiar with the ship. Mickey and I are going to walk from stem to stern until we don't need a map to find our way around."

"He was always like that," laughed Daniel. "The first thing he would do is stare at the map on the wall, and then walk. I admit, it is pretty handy when you know exactly where you are and where you're going. Mickey's good at that. Let's go, boys!"

"Don't laugh, sir. I think it's a great idea. You never know when you'll need to find your way," James said. In the hallway, James and Mickey analyzed the map placard before carrying on downstairs. They walked from one end of the ship, moved down the stairway to the next deck, and walked back.

"Boys, I'm walked out. I'm going over to that bar and rest," Daniel said, pointing to a neon sign that said Sunset Bar.

"See you later, Pop," Mickey answers. Mickey and James continued their walk. They discovered the ship's restaurant, gym, main pools, and adults-only area. Since Cyndi and Joel had outgrown the kids' area, they moved on to the area that held the teenage entertainment. It offered gaming machines, a movie screen, and a non-alcoholic bar with a range of drinks. After getting basically familiar with the ship, they went back and had a couple of drinks with Daniel at the Sunset Bar.

CHAPTER 2

Dinner at the Spring Garden Restaurant

They gathered at the front of the restaurant and waited for Lisa and Angela to arrive. When they arrived, the host led them to their table. James took Angela's hand and talked to her as they were being led to their table. When they got to their table, he sat her beside him. The server came and took their orders.

"How was your day so far on the ship, Angela?" James asked.

"It was okay," she answered sheepishly.

"What did you do?"

"I helped Mom unpack our clothes. That's all."

"I know what you mean, so I let Dee unpack mine. I'm lazy and I don't like to unpack."

Angela giggled at him.

"What are your plans for tomorrow?"

"Nothing much," she said, shrugging her shoulders.

"Oh, my. Would you like to go to the Explorer's Room? That's the area for kids your age."

"No. I don't like to go to places like that," she said, sticking her lower lip out and beginning to get teary-eyed.

James completely understood. He reached over and stroked her hair. "We'll go there together tomorrow. We'll have fun. I promise."

Lisa looked at James and back at her daughter. "I don't think they let adults in the Explorer's area."

"Don't you worry, they'll let me in. I guarantee it," he said with a wink.

They sat and talked until the meals came. Cyndi was sitting on the other side of Angela and talked to her when James was eating. The entire Christianson gang made Angela and her mother feel comfortable and at home.

Mickey couldn't help but notice how attractive Lisa was that evening. She had obviously dressed for dinner. It was their first cruise, and she wasn't sure about the customs of shipboard cruise life.

Mickey had no trouble connecting with Lisa. Lisa wore a brightly colored, loose-fitting blouse that matched her flowing skirt. Her mouth broadened, showing bright straight teeth, and her eyes glistened at Mickey as he talked to her. Her hair was the same shade of blonde as Angela's. He could tell she was nervous as she fingered the dinnerware.

"Lisa, I'm sorry about your horrible experience," he said.

"Thank you, Mickey Ray. I miss Howard every day. But as bad as that is, it's nothing compared to what Angela goes through every day she steps out the door. She has very few friends, and even though she's doing well in school, she hates going each day. She comes home and dives into homework and avoids other kids. Kids can be so cruel, you know," she said, looking down at the table to avoid eye contact.

He reached out and placed his hand under Lisa's chin and lifted her face to look at him. "I have an idea what she goes through. James still has nightmares about his accident and has issues with his scars. My sister loves him with all her heart. Someday, Angela will meet someone, and he'll look beyond her disfigurement and love her too."

"I hope so."

Cyndi kept Angela entertained, while Mickey enjoyed getting to know her mother. Occasionally, Darcy would engage Mickey and Lisa to add a comment. They talked through dinner and moved to a quiet area to talk for the rest of the evening.

The following morning, they all met at the buffet on deck three, had breakfast, then split up. James and Mickey went to work out in the gym on deck fourteen. Darcy and Lisa donned bathing suits and headed for the pool. Cyndi, Joel, and Angela went exploring the ship, while stopping at some of the gift shops and did some window shopping. And, of course, they made multiple stops at the ice cream machine near the buffet area. Later that day, Cyndi and James took Angela to the

Explorer's Club while Joel read a comic book in the lounge chair at the edge of the pool area.

James and the girls showed up at Explorer's Club and a young lady stopped them at the door. "I'm sorry, sir, but only children under 12 are allowed inside. We're very well staffed and the children are well cared for, so you're free to enjoy your cruise," she said with a smile.

"I see. But we don't want to leave Angela here. My daughter and I wish to accompany her while she's here until she gets to know some kids and feels comfortable," he answered with a smile.

"I'm sorry, but this is a no adult zone, for children only," the young lady said apologetically.

James reached into his pocket, pulled out a balloon and blew it up, then twisted it into a balloon animal. He reached out and gave it to the young lady. "If you'll let me in, I'll entertain the children for a while, and I guarantee everyone will have a wonderful time. Hey, kids. Does anyone want a balloon animal?" he called out. The children looked in his direction. They saw his disfigured face, then looked at each other and James continued to blow up balloons. He twisted them into various animals and pushed them in the air toward the children. The children screamed in delight and began running to catch the floating balloon animals in the air. James continued to send the latex treats for several minutes until every child had an animal.

He smiled again and said to the attendant, "Now, may we come inside? We won't stay too long, Miss."

She smiled back, stepped aside, and let James, Cyndi, and Angela inside. James went over and sat down in one of the undersized chairs and the children looked up at him in wonder.

One of the little boys laughed and pointed at the chair James was sitting in. "Hey, that chair is too little for you," he giggled.

James made a face and looked down at the chair and back up at the child. "So it is, my little man. Do you mind if I sit here with you?"

He shook his head. "I don't mind, but you might break it."

"We don't want to break it, do we?" asked James.

"No," the child answered.

James looked at the woman that had let them in. She saw James looking at her, and then down at the chair. She got the hint and took the chair she was sitting in and moved it over and suggested James sit in it while she stood.

James sat in the full-size chair, reached into his pocket again and brought out a deck of cards. "Has anyone here played an old maid card game?" he called out to them. He motioned for them to sit in chairs the lady was now placing in position around him.

Several of the children raised their hands. He sat shuffling the cards as he talked his patter to the young group. "Does anyone here know what an old maid is?" he asked.

"An old lady that cleans the house?" one little girl guessed.

A little boy laughed and said, "No, Silly. It's an old lady that never got married."

James laughed and gestured for Angela to sit in the chair the attendant placed beside him, and Cyndi sat on the other side. "I have two very important people with me today. The little lady on my left is my daughter, and the one of my right is Angela, my new friend. We'll spend a few minutes today with you."

"What happened to your faces?" one little girl near the front of the sitting children asked.

James saw Angela lower her face, and a tear trickled down her cheek. He spoke to the surrounding children. "Do you know what the name Angela means?"

"It's an angel," one little girl spoke up.

"Yes. It is. What's your name little lady?" he said to the girl that answered.

"Kathy," she answered.

"Okay, Kathy, are angels good?"

"Yes, most of them." James reached out and put a finger lightly on the little girl's lips.

"Angels are beings sent from God. Just like all little children. Would you like to be friends with an angel?" he said as he raised his face to look at all the boys and girls sitting on the floor.

They all shook their heads.

"Good, I give you my most wonderful friend, Angela, the angel!" He began clapping and everyone joined in. "Everyone say welcome Angela."

"Welcome Angela," they called out together.

"Now, let's go back to the old maid cards. Angela will help me," he said as he held out the deck to her. "Do you see all the cards are different? Right?"

"Yeah," they all called out.

He fanned the cards out and told her to pick one. She picked a card, and he told her to lay it face down on the floor, and she laid it down without looking at it.

"What is the name of this game?" James asked the children.

"Old maid," they called out.

"Angela, please turn the card over and let everyone see it?"

She held the card up. It was the old maid card, and everyone clapped.

He asked one little boy to come forward and place the card back into the deck, and he reshuffled the deck and again allowed the boy to pick a card. Again, it was the old maid. He let several other children do the same thing, and it always was the old maid card. James and the girls remained for almost an hour entertaining the children with cards and humorous patter to keep them laughing.

Stretching his arms out, James announced that he, Cyndi, and Angela had to leave. All the children begged them to stay. He thanked the attendant, and they left.

They walked into the pool area where Darcy was sunbathing on a towel by the pool. Angela looked up at James. "How did you hurt your face?"

"It was a long time ago. Some evil men did it."

"Why did they do it? It was mean. I'm sorry they did it to you."

"Yes. It was mean, but I'm okay. You'll be okay too. Someday, people will no longer look at your face. They'll look at what a wonderful person you are, and love you even more," he said as they walked to the railing on the ship and looked at the water. He took her little hand in his and gently squeezed it, and picked her up into his arms.

"I wish you were my daddy."

His heart broke for her as a tear trickled down her face. He gently wiped her face as he stifled tears of his own.

"Angela, your mother will find a wonderful man who will be honored to be your new daddy," he said as he hugged her tightly. He put her back down and together they walked over to Darcy.

"Hey, Dee. Where's Mickey Ray?" James asked her.

"Mickey took one look at Angela's mother in a bathing suit, drooled all over himself and took her away so they could be alone," answered Dee with a slight laugh.

"Alone? On a cruise ship? Surely you jest."

"No. I don't jest. She was wearing a sunlight yellow two-piece bathing suit and getting the eye from every man here. Curves like a winding mountain road, that long silky blonde hair. Her huge blue eyes lit up like diamonds when she saw Mickey again. Yes, Mickey caught her attention as well. I have no idea where they went."

"That brother of yours gets all the pretty ladies. All he has to do is flash those big brown eyes of his, and they fall at his feet."

"Are you jealous of my brother, James?"

He bent down to kiss her as he said, "Not one bit. I still have the most beautiful girl in the room, and I always will," as he kissed her lovingly on the mouth.

Cyndi looked at Angela and put her finger in her mouth and made a gagging sound. Angela laughed, and said, "Are they always like that?"

"Always," Cyndi answered with pride.

Darcy had proposed to James several years ago in Pigeon Forge, Tennessee, after he had helped Mickey Ray save their real estate business. Even though it was several years since the nuptials, James always treated Darcy like his new bride. Even in her thirties, Darcy, a cheerleader in high school, remained a very attractive woman. She could also attract attention from men around her until she revealed her wedding ring, letting everyone know she was taken.

Mickey Ray and Lisa were sitting at the pool bar talking when Daniel walked up to them. "Hello, Lisa. I should have known that my son would corner the prettiest girl on the ship to spend time with on board."

"Good afternoon. How has your day been going so far?" she asked as she smiled at Daniel.

"Great. I got up early, had a wonderful breakfast outside on the deck and watched the ocean. I already got several chapters into a splendid book, and now I run into both of you. It couldn't be any better than this. How about you, my dear?"

"Fine, sir. James has Angela, and Mickey here is keeping me well informed on the work that you're doing in Bridgeton."

"Mickey has grown up to be a great replacement for the old man that founded the company."

"Thanks, Pop, but I had an excellent teacher and fine role model," Mickey butted in.

"I'm sure he did, sir," she agreed.

"Well, aren't we members of the mutual admiration society?" Daniel laughed. "What are the plans for the evening?"

"I hoped I could convince Lisa to go with us to the show tonight, Pop."

"You never know what she might do, but first you have to ask her," Lisa giggled as she took another sip from her glass.

"Oh, yes, maybe I should do that," Mickey agreed. He looked at her and said, "Elizabeth, would you go to the show tonight with me and my family?"

"Can I bring Angela along?"

"We wouldn't allow you to come with us if you didn't bring her," he said, then took a sip of his drink as well.

Daniel laughed and said, "I see that I'm the third wheel here, so I'll see you two later at dinner, before the show."

"Right. See you later, Pop."

They talked a bit longer. Mickey wanted to spend some time with his father and Lisa needed to check on Angela, so they agreed to meet at dinner.

Mickey wandered around until he found Pop sitting at a table near the railing of the ship. He was staring blankly out at the ocean. "Hey, Pop. A penny for your thoughts," he said as he sat down.

As Daniel turned toward Mickey, Mickey saw sadness in his father's eyes.

"Hey, son. Have a seat," he said, as he shoved the chair next to him out for Mickey to sit.

"Why the sad face, Pop?"

"I was thinking of your mother. How life has treated us. How blessed we are, and how different things have turned out since your mother passed away. Life never follows the path we plan for."

"Yep, I know. I miss her too."

"This is the first cruise I've been on since she went to be with the Lord. I am blessed. God gave me your mother and allowed her to be taken from me."

"Pop, I love you and Mom. I also miss her every day. I'm glad you found each other. Someday, I hope to find a person as wonderful as Mom."

"You will, Son. I believe that," Daniel said.

The evening went smoothly. Everyone loved Angela and Lisa. The following day went much as the previous day. James took the kids and entertained them. Daniel took turns with the kids so James and Dee could have some time together. Mickey and Lisa spent almost every waking moment together. Mickey and James spent some time together working out at the onboard gym. They spent some time together talking about the future of the Christianson Company and where James could fit in it.

"James, I was thinking maybe you could come in with us and be part of the company," suggested Mickey.

"What do you mean, part of the company? I wouldn't have a clue what to do. That's not my thing, Mickey."

"There are a lot of things you can do. What was your major in college?"

"It was business administration. Then I joined the service, and I went to Officer Candidate School. I have no training in a real estate development company. I'm a soldier. That's what I'm good at. Why are you bringing this up now?"

"Well," Mickey stammered. "I was thinking of leaving the Mongoose team."

"What do you mean, leave the team? You're now part of us!"

"It just isn't for me. I'm not a soldier. I'm a businessman," he said as he turned toward the sea and leaned on the rail, propping himself against it.

James did the same, and he said, also looking out at the sea, "Mickey, you are a natural born soldier. You're now almost as well trained as we are. You're one of us. We know you get better in each mission. We've all seen it. The other members trust you as a brother in arms. You are a Mongoose."

"I'm no longer proud of what and who I am, and..."

"Shut up, Mickey. I don't want to hear that crap. You're one of us."

"No! I'm not. I hate it. I hate what we do!"

"You help people. Are you still seeing Doctor Kingston?"

Mickey shot back at him, "Yes, I am, and don't give me that crap. That's what he says...Mickey, you are helping people. I can't even help myself right now. I came on this cruise to get away. I want to forget that I've ever been involved with the team."

"What? You want absolution for your sins! Is that what you are looking for? Even God told his people to fight for what's right. I learned that from the Bible. King David was a man after God's own heart, and he was a champion warrior. The Bible is the bloodiest book ever written. Even man's salvation is based on the blood of Jesus Christ, Mickey."

Mickey turned toward James with a scowl. "Don't you quote the Bible to me, James. The New Testament is all about the love of God. I'm no one's savior, and I'm not Jesus Christ! I'm a plain ordinary man trying to make things right in my heart."

"Yes, but sometimes people need help and we're the only ones that'll help them. You know that."

"I'm only responsible for myself and my family. I'm not responsible for the rest of the world. I quit. The last mission was my last." Mickey turned and walked down the deck to a door leading back inside the ship.

CHAPTER 3

Pirates Board the Ship

On the third day out at sea, Mickey, James, and Daniel met for an early breakfast. Daniel went back to his cabin and Mickey and James headed for the gym. The gym was located above the main deck of the ship, providing a view through tinted windows. Mickey had avoided James since he told him he was quitting the Mongoose team. That didn't stop James from taking Angela and Cyndi on shipboard excursions. He took them again to the Explorer's area, and then to the main swimming pool mid ship. They played the children's pool game of Marco Polo, and the girls were having the time of their life.

Finally, they were together in the gymnasium. James was pumping iron with the free weights, while Mickey was slowing down on a stationary bicycle, when they heard a whooshing sound. James knew that sound. It was a helicopter, but he also thought it was part of a show. That is until he saw men hit the deck in paramilitary apparel. He knew something was seriously wrong. He replaced the weights on their racks and looked for Mickey.

The bicycle Mickey was on was facing forward where the men were landing. James hastened over to Mickey. "Something's wrong here. This isn't part of the cruise."

Looking at James, he said, "I was thinking the same thing. What should we do?"

"Nothing yet. Wait and see what happens. I bet it isn't good," James answered softly.

"We should dress and prepare to leave."

"Yep, I agree," said James as he bolted for the dressing room door, followed closely by Mickey.

They dressed. Mickey called James, "Do you know where everyone is right now?"

"No. It's late enough that Dee and the kids are probably having breakfast. I don't know where Daniel is. He's an early riser."

"We need to find them and keep them near us."

"Agreed. We head out, and you look for your father. I'll find Dee and the kids.

"Right," Mickey said as he headed out the door towards the stern of the ship, away from the men that had just landed. He went inboard toward the rear, then back up two levels to the cabin where Pop was located. Daniel was sitting on the balcony looking up at where the helicopter was hovering minutes before.

"Pop! Did you see that?" he called as he came into the room and out to the balcony.

"Yes, I did, and I stayed here because whatever is going on, it isn't part of the cruise, and it isn't good. Is everyone else okay?"

"We hope so. James went to find Dee and the kids. If we can, we need to get back to James and Dee's suite so we can stay together."

"Okay, son, lead the way," he said as he got up and headed back inside.

Mickey slowly opened the door and peeked outside. Seeing an empty hallway, he motioned for Pop to follow. They made their way to James and Darcy's suite and quietly knocked on the door.

James braced himself against the door and opened it slowly until he saw Mickey and Daniel standing outside. They came inside and quickly closed the door behind them.

"What's happening outside?" Mickey asked.

"I don't know, but I'm sure those were pirates. We won't know for a while what their objective is. Since this is a cruise ship, they want a particular person, or they'll hold the entire ship for ransom. Celebrities often come on cruise ships incognito."

"Great! Of all the cruise ships, in all the world, and they land on ours!" Mickey said sarcastically.

"Oh, now we're paraphrasing old movie sayings?" asked James.

"Yeah. Guess which one."

Daniel spoke up, "Casablanca, 1943, starring Humphrey Bogart and Ingrid Bergman."

Mickey nodded his head. "Pop has seen all those old movies."

James said seriously, "Problem is, this isn't an old movie and might be a lot more dangerous for us. We need to find Lisa and Angela. Do you think you can find them and get them here with us?"

"I'll try," Mickey said, starting toward the door.

The loudspeaker crackled overhead. "This is your captain speaking. We are requesting all our guests to go back to their cabins and staterooms until further notice. Please return promptly and in an orderly fashion."

"I guess we sit here, at least for now. If they solve nothing, we may have to take action," James said.

"I'm going to Lisa and Angela's cabin and bring them here," stated Mickey. "What do you suggest we do when I return?"

"I don't know, yet. Right now, we just sit it out."

The loudspeaker crackled again. "Please return to your room promptly. Someone will be around to pick up all cell phones and personal communication devices. Please comply and co-operate with personnel that knock on your door. Remain calm and we'll keep you informed of progress. We will ensure dinner buffets are served on time. However, we will close all restaurants.

"We need information on what's happening," James said thoughtfully.

"No, we don't," responded Mickey.

James looked at Mickey. "Okay, I need to know what's happening."

"How do you plan to find out?" asked Mickey.

"We need to take one of the pirate's communication devices."

"Again, how?"

"In the last announcement, the captain said someone will be around to confiscate cell phones and personal communication devices. We wait until someone comes, then we take one of theirs."

"You make it sound so easy, James. Just remember, I'm out," Mickey said sarcastically.

"I remember. I can do it. I don't need your help. All we need to do is wait until someone knocks on the door."

"Okay." Mickey told Darcy and the kids to make themselves at home. "We may be here for quite a while."

Daniel looked from Mickey to James. "Tell me what's going on, boys."

"Not now, Pop."

"Yes. Now, son. Tell me what's going on between you two."

James spoke up, "Mickey has quit the team."

Daniel furrowed his brow. "What do you mean, you quit?"

"I mean, I quit. I'm out. The last mission was my last one. We all almost died at the spa. I don't want to continue putting my family in danger."

James stood, saying nothing. He knew Mickey had every right to quit, and on a certain level, he agreed with him.

Daniel and Darcy looked from Mickey to James. Darcy spoke up first. "Mickey, I agree with you. I worry every time you join James and the team on some mission, as you call it."

"I'm with Dee on this one. If you want to quit, I will stand with you, son." He turned to James. "I wish you would also retire. We all worry about you. You served your country, and you served it well. You deserve to sit back and let someone else fill in for you. I love you as my own son."

James spoke. "I'll consider it. Right now, we don't know what's happening. If whoever they are, get what they want and leaves, we'll do nothing, just as you suggest. Mickey, we're brothers now in our family, and you are in the family of the Mongoose team. I will support your decision. But I must see if my services are needed here."

Daniel reached into his pocket and withdrew a deck of cards. "Anyone for a game?" he asked.

Mickey went back out and headed toward Lisa and Angela's cabin. When he got there, he knocked. Lisa answered and let him inside. He told them to get their phones and follow him. They were gathering a few items when there was another knock on the door.

He told Lisa to take Angela into the bathroom, away from the pirate so she wouldn't be so afraid.

When he opened the door, a swarthy man was standing at the door with a gun pointed directly at Mickey. "Give me your cell phones, now!" he ordered.

Mickey looked at the man like he was confused.

The man repeated his demand. "Give me your cell phone!"

"I don't think so, mister whoever you are. I'm going to call the information desk. Mickey reached for the desk phone, when the man came inside and put the gun directly in Mickey's back.

"I really don't think this is proper. I've taken many cruises, and this is not the proper protocol."

"I don't care what you think. Give me your phone."

Mickey spun around and knocked the gun out of the surprised man's hand. As the gun slid across the floor, Mickey punched the man in the gut, then slammed his head into the desktop. The man went down, and Mickey reached for the gun on the floor. Mickey got down and looked at the man. He wasn't breathing. The gash in his head when he hit the desk had killed him. He also took a walkie talkie from his belt.

"Oh, crap," he said.

Opening the door to the bathroom, he whispered to Lisa, "Help me move this man into the hallway, and hurry. He grabbed the man's arms and dragged him to the door. Leaving Angela in the bathroom, out of sight of the dead man, Lisa grabbed the man's feet to lighten Mickey's load. Together, they dragged him out of the door about twenty feet down the hallway.

They went back and while Lisa got a few necessary personal items, Mickey quickly cleaned up the blood that had gotten on the floor where the man hit his head. Quietly, they closed the door, locked it and ran down the hall to Dee and James' suite.

"Gee whiz. I should have just complied with his demand," he said out loud to himself.

"What?" asked Lisa.

"Nothing. I was just thinking out loud."

As they ran, Lisa asked breathlessly, "Why did we drag the man so far down the hallway?"

Mickey answered between breaths as they ran, "Because we wanted his body well away from your cabin. When they find his body, they won't know it came from your stateroom."

"What do you mean, his body?"

"He was dead."

"You mean you killed him when you slammed his head?"

"Yes."

"You murdered him?"

"No, I killed him, I didn't murder him. You saw, he had a gun. It was self-defense," he said as they came to the door of James and Dee's suite.

When they got there, everyone was trying to act calm, but the kids and Dee were all trying to keep themselves from breaking down. They all tried to act strong for the kids.

Mickey handed the walkie-talkie to James and relayed what had happened in Lisa's cabin. They hid the gun and the comm unit under the floatation devices in the small clothes cabinet.

The kids were watching a movie on the stateroom television, while the adults played cards. Even though outbound communications were knocked out, onboard communications, and televisions were all on a closed-circuit cable system. Mickey told him that the pirates' comm units were old school technology. They were using old-fashioned walkie-talkies.

"Yeah, that's because they took down the ship's communication equipment. And the walkie-talkies have a short range, so there will not be outside listening, or indifference."

"Thanks, Mickey, for getting the walkie," responded James.

"Yeah, but that's the last thing I'm going to do. From here on out, I'm a docile complying passenger."

"Sure, Bro."

After about two hours, there was a knock on the door. James made sure the kids were in the bedroom, out of sight of what was about to happen. He smiled at Mickey and softly said, "Follow my lead." He then got up and headed for the door.

"No. Docile, remember?"

When James opened it, there was one of the men that had repelled down the ropes from the helicopter. He was standing there with a large laundry cart. James leaned over and looked into it. He saw hundreds of cell phones and some home and toy versions of walkie-talkies laying in the bottom. He looked back up at the man standing on the other side.

"Are you giving out free phones?" he said, motioning for Mickey to come over.

The man furrowed his brows. "No, you fool. I am taking yours!"

"Not going to happen. I paid a lot of money for my phone, and I'm not giving it to you!" he said as Mickey came up beside him.

The man placed his hand on a holster at his side as he demanded, "You will give me your phones, or I will shoot you!"

In a flash, James reached over the basket and dragged the man into the room and slammed him onto the floor, and pulled him across the room. "Bring the basket inside, Mickey, and close the door."

The man raised his head, and James slammed his head back down with the heel of his shoe. "Stay down before I use your body as a doormat to wipe my feet."

Mickey pulled in the cart, quickly closed the door and began rifling through the bin and withdrawing a couple of walkie-talkies. Guests, many times, use them to communicate with family members throughout the ship. Most of the time, they didn't work well because of all the metal, but it was better than nothing. James reached to the man's belt and withdrew his walkie-talkie they were using to connect with each other. James knew that these would be far superior to the ones sold in most retail stores the guests brought on board.

"What do we do with him now, James?"

"Throw him out! Mickey, you grab his arm and leg, I'll take the other limbs." He called to Darcy, "Dee, open the balcony door."

She opened her mouth in shock, "Are you going to…."

"Yes. Do it!" he ordered.

"Won't he just call for help when he hits the water?" she asked.

"Nope, he'll be dead before he hits the water," James said to her. "Now hurry, we don't have much time."

"I can't believe I'm getting suckered into this again," Mickey muttered.

He and Mickey drug the man over to the sliding balcony door as the man struggled. James dropped the man's arm and slammed his head on the deck, and he stopped moving. When they got him outside, they lifted him up and threw him out as far as they could, so his body wouldn't land on a lower balcony. While James and Mickey were doing this, Darcy watched in shock and headed to the bathroom to vomit, followed closely by Lisa.

They came back inside, and went over to the door and shoved the laundry cart back outside into the hallway and pushed it further down, away from their door.

James looked around the room, looking for a place to hide the electronics they had taken. "Pull up a mattress. Cut a slit in the middle and stuff the walkie-talkies into it. If they come knocking door to door again, they won't find anything. We'll tell whoever comes here that the last man got everything."

Darcy asked, "What if they want to come in and search the room?"

Mickey answers, "Most likely if they lift a mattress, they'll only lift it a few inches and not turn it over. That's why he said to cut in the middle of the mattress, not down the side."

"If he finds it, we might have to do the same thing to him we did to the last guy," added James.

"Oh, God. It just gets worse each minute, doesn't it?" she said sadly.

"I'm afraid so, dear," James said as he lifted a mattress on its side to make a cut.

"Yes, James, and that's why I want out. Starting now," Mickey stated.

James had finished putting the devices into the mattress, and the loudspeaker sounded again. "We'll start with deck twelve through fifteen to serve the dinner meal. You have sixty minutes to move to the nearest buffet, eat, and return to your stateroom. The next deck will not be allowed outside into the buffet area until everyone is back in their stateroom. Deck twelve through fifteen may proceed to the buffet stations."

James and Mickey looked at each other. They were on deck nine, so they had forty-five minutes until the time started. They would sit and wait. After an agonizing wait, the captain announced they could proceed to the nearest buffet station. Everyone got up and left the stateroom for the buffet area. When they got there, they kept Lisa and Angla behind them. The buffet area was deadly quiet.

"Angela," said James, "take my hand."

She put out her hand to take his. Lisa smiled at James, and he gave her a wink.

She whispered to him, "What's going on, James?"

"I don't know. I assume they'll tell us soon."

One of the men called out to them. "Quiet! No talking," he scolded.

"I was just telling the lady that I don't know what's happening here," James responded.

"I don't care what you were saying. Be quiet. Do not talk!"

"Okay, whatever you say!" James said sarcastically.

The man walked up to James, raised his gun and shoved the butt into James' stomach.

James let out a puff of air and dropped to the floor. He placed his hands on his stomach and groaned loudly.

"See what happens when you do not follow orders? I don't care what you were talking about, you freaky looking man. You will do as I tell you!"

James rolled onto his back, exposing his stomach again. "I was just trying to explain to the lady…."

The man stepped forward and stomped on James' stomach with his heel. Again, James let out a slight groan and covered his abdomen area with his hands. And closed his eyes to mere slits.

Mickey stepped forward and kneeled to James and put his ear against James' mouth, listening for a breath.

"Stop! Stop it! He meant no harm. You're scaring everyone, especially the little girl holding his hand."

"I don't care what the freak and his freaky looking little girl were doing. I said to be quiet. No one is to speak! Do you understand?" the man said as he raised his gun to Mickey.

Mickey kneeled down to check on James' condition. Bending over James' chest, he looked as though he was listening to James' heart.

James said softly into his ear, "Get me to the medical facility."

"Hey, you! He may be bleeding internally. Can we take him to the ship's hospital?" asked Mickey.

The man raised his gun again at Mickey. "I said don't speak!"

Several people screamed.

Mickey raised his in hands in a sign of defense. "Please don't hurt us. Please, sir. We'll do anything you wish. Just don't hurt us," he pleaded. Inwardly, Mickey's stomach churned with repulsion for this man, and again he despised himself for having to pretend to be afraid.

"Ha! You plead for your life. I like to see infidels grovel! Say please to me again, you pitiful man!"

"Please let us take him to the infirmary. I beg you! Don't hurt us anymore," Mickey pleaded. "He's innocent. He meant no harm!"

"Okay, but only because you have shown us what a pitiful coward of a man you are! You are on your knees begging for your life! You are scum to my people! The actions you display are those of low life coward infidels!"

By this time, dozens of people were backing away, and children were crying. Mickey looked at Dee and gave her a knowing wink. She got the message, knowing it would be okay. James and Mickey had a plan.

The man waved for a crewman in a uniform to take James and Mickey to the medical section of the ship. He also told one of his men to escort them.

The crewman picked up a phone and called for a gurney to take James to deck zero where the medical station was located. James lay unmoving on the floor until several crew members arrived and loaded him onto it and Mickey followed them to the elevator.

They got James to the medical unit, pushed the gurney into the exam room, followed by Mickey and the pirates.

Mickey looked around. It looked just like a proper hospital, with exam areas and small treatment rooms that also doubled as hospital patient rooms. He even saw a room that had a sign above the double doors labeled, Operating Room. He never thought of a ship needing an operating room, but it made sense if someone had a severe injury, or something unexpected, like a simple appendectomy. They may not airlift them to a hospital. It really was a small compact hospital, somewhat like a mash military hospital, fully equipped for emergencies on the high seas. It gleamed with its bright white, sterile, sanitized walls. The small patient rooms were the exception and were decorated with soothing cool sea green walls and clouds painted on the ceilings.

Mickey asked the pirate if he could have some privacy with James. He glared at Mickey with no concern for James laying unmoving on the gurney. Mickey gently ushered him back through the door, as the man bared his teeth like a rabid dog, but backed out so Mickey could close the door. There was no other way out, so the man knew he had the situation under control. He turned his back to the door and stood guard.

In a few seconds, a man in a white coat entered, wearing a stethoscope around his neck. He walked over to James, and James opened his eyes and looked at the doctor.

James whispered to him between unmoving lips, "Doctor, please stand between me and the man at the door, blocking his view through the window in the door." The doctor obediently moved over to block their view.

"Doctor, I'm okay. I don't need medical attention, but I need to remain in this medical unit to work," James whispered.

"Explain what you mean, please," he asked, also speaking in a low tone.

"Getting these pirates off this ship and returning control to the captain requires me to have unrestricted mobility. Can you make a medical demand that I stay here for observation?"

The man said, "You're going to overpower these pirates and get our ship back?"

"Yes," said James, still not moving a limb and using limited mouth movements.

"You are going to do this alone?"

"Trust me. I'll bring others to help. Will you help me do this?"

"As long as I don't have to endanger my medical staff," he said.

"We'll do our best to not put them in any more danger than they are right now," James answers.

"I will try," the doctor said.

The doctor opened the door, walked out, and began talking to the man. "You must leave this area. This is a hospital. We have infectious patients here. They could make you sick. You can't be here," he said, addressing the pirates.

The man took a walkie-talkie from his belt and spoke into it. A few seconds later, he passed the walkie-talkie to the doctor. The doctor took the walkie and explained they needed to take x-rays to map the amount of damage to internal organs. The doctor continued, "Sir, your man should not stay because of the radiation and possibly contracting disease from one of the other patients. After the x-rays, the injured man needs rest and recover. Your guards are unnecessary, because this man is too badly injured to be a threat to anyone."

The doctor handed the walkie-talkie back to the man, who talked again in his native language.

The man looked at Mickey. "You must come with me."

"Why? I can't hurt anyone here. He's my family. Someone needs to stay with him," he said, pointing back at James lying on the gurney.

The man hesitated, then shrugged his shoulders, put the walkie-talkie back on his belt and walked out of the medical section.

When he was gone, one nurse locked the door. The doctor came back into the exam room and told James that it was clear. James sat up on the gurney.

"James, I was sure they had really caused some serious internal injury," said Mickey.

The doctor looked at James and Mickey, and remarked, "I don't know what either of you has up your sleeve, but God help you help us. In all honesty, I don't know what two men can do to stop a gang of professional pirates. Now I have an actual patient that needs my attention." He turned, walked out of the room, and closed the door behind him.

"I saw that man shove that gun butt into your stomach and you went down like a sack of potatoes," said Mickey.

"I know. But I train for situations like this. I constantly do exercises to strengthen my stomach muscles, so when he moved that gun back to strike me, I stiffened up and faked the fall. I didn't want him to kick me in the back. If he had done that, he would have broken some ribs, so I turned onto my back and gave him another clear shot at my stomach. I'll be sore for a few days, but I'm bruised, not officially injured. By ending up here, I'll have more freedom to move around without restriction. You can come and go under the pretense of visiting a sick friend."

"Got it. Now what do we do?"

"First thing I'll do is call Aly and put the Mongoose team on alert. Then I'll call Director Higgins of the Department of Defense and see if he's heard what's going on. Now what I need to know is, are you in or out?"

"Oh, crap. I guess I'm in. I don't have a choice, do I?"

"Of course you do, Mickey. We always have a choice," James said sternly.

"Anything I can do while you're making that call?"

"Yeah, go back and tell Dee and the kids that I'm okay and that I love them."

Mickey took a deep breath. "Will do."

CHAPTER 4

Calling the Mongoose Team

James called the doctor back in after Mickey left. "Doctor, I need your help. I need to get a few things from my suite. Do you have anyone here that you feel I can trust explicitly to help me? If you have anyone on staff, I need to talk to them… Now!"

"I don't understand what you mean," he said.

"I can't tell you much about my background. All I can say is that these scars on my body result from serving in the American military. I have skills that can rescue this ship from these pirates, but I need your help," James explained. "They don't need any military training. I just need someone I can trust."

"I'll see what I can do," the doctor said.

"We have room to room communications, correct?"

"Correct."

"Good, I need to talk to Mickey, the person who was here with me. Can I use the phone?" he said as he reached for the phone on the wall. He dialed his suite because he knew Mickey would be there instead of in his own cabin.

Darcy answered the phone, and when he spoke, he could hear her cry at the other end. "Don't cry, babe. I'm okay. How are the kids doing?"

She sniffed and cleared her throat to talk. "They're fine now, but until Mickey came back and told us you were okay, I had a difficult time calming them down."

"Good. Let me talk to Joel."

Joel came on the line. "Hey James, we were so worried about you. We thought that man had killed you," he said.

Even though Joel was in his early teens, James could tell he was trying to hold back his emotions, just as James had coached him to be whenever he had to leave on a secret business trip.

"Hey, don't worry about me. You worry about those men that have taken over this ship. I'll take care of it. You help your mother and Cyndi. You're the man of the house until I return. I need you to act like one. Can you do that? If Uncle Mickey needs anything, you help him, okay?"

Joel stifled back his tears. "Yes, James, I can do that."

"It's okay to cry when no one's around, but don't do it in front of your mother or sister. Got it?"

"Yeah," he said.

James could tell the boy was gathering his courage. "Good. Let me talk to your sister."

Cyndi came on the line, and James gave her a pep talk too, told her he loved them, and asked for Mickey.

"Hey, partner," he said when Mickey came on the line.

"Hey, yourself. What do you need? I know you have a plan. Tell me what it is."

"Are you sure you're up to doing this?"

"Yes. I'll do it one more time," Mickey insisted.

"I need my satellite phone. Do you think you can get it to me?"

"I'll try, but can't we just use the apps on our regular cell phone? I hid one from the men collecting them."

"Not good enough. A civilian cell phone is okay for quick brief messages, but I need to get in touch with some private agencies not available on regular civilian frequencies. Regular cell phones don't have full satellite capabilities, and the signal is slow and spotty at best. I need my dedicated sat phone. Get it to me, or we can do nothing to help the people on this ship."

"It's still in the side pocket of my suitcase. Did they have someone to escort you back to the cabin when you left here?"

"No. Not exactly. I met someone, and I told him where I was going, so he let me go. Someone must have notified him about the situation on the Lido deck. I don't know if I can get back to you, especially carrying something as large as your phone."

"Get that phone to me, so I can call Alyssa and Director Higgins."

"I'll get it to you somehow."

"The doctor said he'll see if he can convince some of the crew members to help us. Gotta go now," he said and hung up abruptly. He dropped back on the bed when he heard the doorknob rattle.

The door opened, and the doctor appeared again, followed by one of the pirates. This one spoke English.

"I came to check on you. You need to go back to your cabin, now," he said.

The doctor stepped forward. "Moving him now is not possible. His spleen is ruptured, causing severe internal bleeding. This is a medical emergency. He needs immediate help. If he's moved, it could kill him."

"I don't care." He expressed his indifference and insisted on James being moved to his own cabin.

"You and your cohorts may care and control this ship, but this is my hospital, and I say he can't be moved!"

The man gritted his teeth and took his walkie-talkie from his belt and relayed what the doctor said to the person at the other end. He looked back at the doctor. "You are sure of this? Maybe I should just shoot him and that will be the end," he said, reaching for the gun on his belt.

James sprung up, grabbed the man's arm, twisted it around his back, grabbed his head, and snapped his neck. The man's body slumped to the floor. Turning to the doctor, he asked, "Where's the nearest access to the water?"

The doctor had backed into the wall when James attacked the man. He stood, shocked at what had just happened. His mouth dropped open, but no words came out.

"Hurry. Tell me. We need to dispose of his body now, before someone comes looking for him."

The doctor's eyes were open wide with surprise and fear. He pointed to the door. "A supply access hatch is down the hallway about fifty meters aft," he stammered.

"Help me with his body," James ordered. He lifted the body and hoisted it over his shoulder and stood waiting for the doctor to open the door of the small treatment room.

The staff stared as James took the man's body outside, followed by the doctor. They moved quickly to avoid meeting anyone in the hallway. When they got to the supply access door, it took both men to open it. It was a heavy steel door on the ship's side, about the size of a residential garage door. Its primary use was to move supplies in and refuse out of the ship when it was at the terminal. James put the body on the deck, emptied his pockets and took his gun and walkie-talkie. They cracked the door and shoved the body outside, hoping it would sink before anyone saw it floating in the waves.

Back in the medical area, James asked the doctor if he had contacted anyone on the staff that would help him.

"I have made some discreet inquires but may not find someone to help for a few hours."

On the bridge, Fawzan was sitting quietly while his men guarded the captain and his officers at gunpoint. He reached over and took the microphone that the captain had used earlier.

He pressed the button on the microphone and called out over the entire ship. "Attention. Attention. I need folio person number 52837-ACDC to come immediately to the bridge." He repeated the announcement and hung the microphone back on the hook. And sat back in his chair again in complete silence.

In a matter of minutes, there came a knock on the door. When one pirate answered it, a tall handsome man came in and approached Fawzan.

"Are you ready to install the software?" Fawzan said to the man.

"I've been ready since you took over the ship. I have the flash drive, and I've been working with the casino officer, letting him know we will be installing the upgrade soon. We need to do it as soon as possible. He insists that he's in contact with the people that handle the software upgrades on the ship. Even though you've shut down the ship, we need to access the secure computer room in order to route it through all the casino machines. We don't want any delays. I may have to do it without his knowledge."

"How long will it take you to do this? Does he suspect what you will do?"

"No, I approached him on the first day we boarded and told him I would do it one night when the casino is shut down. I need to get into the server room, install it, then reboot the entire system. We need to do it soon, so no one will suspect. As planned, the entire ship is concentrating on your presence here. It was a great idea to take hostages for ransom as a diversion. Taking out the communications antennas gives me time to install. Rebooting the onboard computers and machines was not factored into the plan, but I will work with it. After we leave, someone will fix an antenna and send the virus to the main servers, causing every casino machine of every ship in the cruise line to be infected. We will make millions before anyone suspects."

"How long do you think that will be?" asked Fawzan.

"I can't predict that. It will not happen until they upgrade the software to the machines. Normally, they upgrade systems every two years. This network's systems are working well. So, it might be three or four years before they upgrade."

"I still don't understand how this works," said Fawzan.

"The main server in the ship networks each machine. As people gamble, the software takes one percent of the intake of each machine and transfers it to a ghost account. Every day, it sends the money electronically to a secret account in the Cayman Islands, then moves it through various other accounts globally. It accomplishes all this through a VPN to avoid being traced."

"What is a VPN?"

"That is a Virtual Private Network. The program then adjusts each machine's intake, so the skimmed money doesn't even show up. If a slot machine collects $10,000 within 24 hours, the software will change it to display $9,900. The additional amount of one hundred dollars goes into the ghost account."

"That is not a lot of money for the risk we're taking."

"True, but multiply that by every machine and gaming table in here. They are all electronic, and they all have different intakes. Sometime a single blackjack table takes in ten times that amount. Add them up, and all the ships in the cruise line fleet could amount to millions of dollars each day. And we do absolutely nothing but collect the money."

"Still, I don't understand how it does all this."

"You don't need to know how it does it. It just works," he said.

"Why don't you install this program in casinos in Las Vegas and other gambling establishments around the world?"

"Good question. First, we need to actually get inside the server rooms in the individual casinos. And second, the laws of the countries make it more difficult. Here on the high seas, who actually has jurisdiction? The ships are registered in one country but the crime is committed out of everyone's reach. The crime, and the location of where it was committed, makes prosecution almost impossible, if we're caught."

Fawzan shook his head. "Just do it so we can get off this ship. I don't like it here. Usually we board a ship, do our business and leave. I want to leave as soon as possible."

"I'll do it tonight, if I can," said the man.

"You have forty-eight hours. And we will leave with whatever ransom money we have, and you'll be on your own."

The man left the bridge.

CHAPTER 5

Mickey Delivers the Satellite Phone

Mickey was still in the suite where Dee and the kids were staying. He got James' phone out of the luggage and left the cabin. Walking down the hallway toward the aft of the ship, he kept out of sight as much as possible. Several times, he had to duck into niches in the hallways and behind columns and posts. He moved up and down the stairwells to avoid guards. After almost an hour of ducking, he felt like the icon on an old video game called Pacman. Finally, he made it from forward deck nine to the zero aft deck and to the medical center. When he tried to open the door handle, he found it locked, which made him knock gently on it.

He heard someone said, "Sorry we're closed, unless it's a medical emergency."

He answered back, "I'm here to see the injured man named James."

The door cracked, and someone peeked out at him.

"I'm Mickey Ray. I'm here to see James."

He heard James call out, "Let him in. He's with me!"

Mickey walked inside, took the phone out of the jacket he had worn, and handed it to James.

James said, "Thanks. Now all I need to do is get outside, so I have a line of sight to a satellite."

"Won't it work inside?" Mickey asked.

"No. As useful as these things are, they have their limitations. They work in the worst weather, but you still have to have a line of sight."

"That sucks."

"Still, in this case, it may be our lifeline to survival, so I don't want to trust it to some Walmart app added to a civilian phone."

The phone on the wall rang. The nurse picked it up, and she was immediately stunned. "Um, no, sir. He isn't here. He left. I don't know exactly when. It was a while ago. Should I tell him you called when he returns?" She pulled the phone away from her ear, and they all heard someone screaming on the other end of the phone.

She gently put the phone on the cradle and looked up at James. "I guess you know what he wanted."

"Okay, I guess I better wait to see if someone comes down here looking for him. Mickey, you better get back to the room, in case they do a room-by-room search."

The overhead loudspeaker sounded again. It was not in English. No one understood it, but they guessed it was the man in charge calling for the missing man to report in.

James looked at Mickey and said, "Because we dumped his body overboard, we have one less pirate to worry about. I need to call for help and find out what's going on around this ship. I got his walkie-talkie and gun from the guy before we dumped him."

"If you need to get out in the open, we can go together. It'll be better if there are two of us."

The doctor came over and said the shift was almost over for the workers he felt would help them. It would be dark soon.

James' suite was on Vista deck nine. The medical unit was on deck zero, so he couldn't visit with the family.

The pirates continued to look for the one who had taken them to medical, but they couldn't find him and concluded he had fallen overboard. They sent others to question the staff, but whenever one of the pirates arrived, James was sleeping in a secluded room. Because of the injuries he had suffered, as diagnosed by the ship's doctor, they left him alone.

The captain made multiple announcements on the ship's intercom, letting passengers know they could leave their cabins and go to certain areas on the ship. During the talks with the pirates' leader, Fawzan, the captain explained it would be best if the guests were not confined to their rooms. The limited freedom would cause less resistance from the crew and passengers.

Darcy and the kids had asked to see James in medical, but their request was denied, so Mickey would keep them up on what was happening and his condition.

Following the end of their shift, five crew members shared with James what they had learned about the pirates' plans. James told the crew members he was calling some friends but would need their help to be his eyes and ears around the ship. When his team arrived, he would need some uniforms so they could blend in with the workers and guests. James assured them he would not ask them to interfere or engage any of the pirates. They could continue with their regular onboard duties.

James waited until dark and with the help of one of the crew members, he was shown a secret passageway to get outside the ship into the open. As the crew member guided him through the narrow stairwell, he noticed everything was almost gleaming white. It was bright even in the small, confined area. They passed from one hallway to others, up and down stairwells, arriving outside in the fresh sea air. The crew member left him alone and retreated inside the ship. While James waited for his satellite phone to boot up, he looked around at the seemingly endless water. Nothing was in sight in the starlit sky. He had no idea where they were located, but he hoped to find out soon. As he held the phone to his ear, he heard it ring at the other end. After several rings, a woman's voice came on the line.

"Hello, James. How's Darcy's foot doing since she injured it? Is she still on crutches?"

Her greeting was the standard opening greeting for her to James. The phone had caller ID, but to determine his current status, they had a coded question and corresponding answer. It wasn't like the one seen in the movies, like some silly poem or seemingly random numbers. If he was being forced to make the call, he would answer that Darcy was fine. If he was alone or wasn't in immediate danger, he continued talking. They included Darcy's real name in case whoever might hold him knew he was married to Darcy. If he used a fake name, the one holding him might know James was talking in code.

"What's going on, James? Aren't you and the family on a vacation cruise?" the woman asked. "No! Wait. I heard about pirates taking a ship hostage earlier today. Are you on that ship?"

"Yes, pirates dropped on to the ship, told the captain to relocate the ship and drop anchor," he whispered. "Can you call the team together and be on standby? I can't tell you where we are, except in the Caribbean. I assume somewhere off the coast of one of the Islands around the Bahamas."

"Of course, James. You want the Mongoose or B team?" she asked. "I'm checking the GPS on your phone to get your location now. Marie isn't in the country now, but she can be landing in Nassau within 12 hours. When do you need them? Sorry I can't come, but I'm running two other teams as well. Can I in send in a substitute for me? Do you remember Tom Glassman? He's a good sub and available."

"Whoa. One question at a time, Aly. Get the Mongoose team ready to deploy. Yes, Marie is our best female asset. Yes, Glassman is fine. He's a good man."

"Be sure to include all the electronic communication and close quarters weapons you can carry. No large high explosives. Grenades and flash bangs are good. We're on a ship with thousands of innocent passengers. They'll need to board under cover of night."

He disconnected but left the antenna up and the unit turned on so Alyssa could get an accurate fix on their location.

The woman he talked to was the eyes and ears of several teams of black ops warriors. Also, a trained black operations team member, when she got out of the military, she started her own company. Alyssa brokered teams that were highly trained and ready to be deployed anywhere in the world at a moment's notice. She handled all communications, surveillance, and oversight during missions. She was young, startlingly beautiful and a genius with a computer. Alyssa was top-notch in her field and always ready for action.

He redialed the phone and connected to Joseph Higgins, the director of the Department of Defense. He had served under Director Higgins when he was in the military. When he got out and Alyssa organized the Mongoose team, Higgins had hired the team for a variety of secret missions. Sometime the mission itself wasn't secret, but the Mongooses were always uncredited with any operation.

"Director Higgins, Bower here. I need some help," James said without preamble.

"Okay, give me a minute to wake up. What time is it? Oh my god," he said, looking at a clock at his bedside. "It's 3:00 a.m. here."

"I'm sorry to disturb you, sir, but we have a situation here," James said softly into the phone.

"Okay. Where are you, James?" he asked as he sat up in his bed. He knew any time someone like James T. Bower called at any time of day, it was an emergency.

"I don't exactly know our location, sir. We're on a cruise ship in the Caribbean Sea," he whispered, while scanning the area for any onlookers.

"What's wrong? Can you tell me what's happening?" said the director, now fully awake, out of bed, and pacing the room. "I heard about the hijacking, but I don't know details. Tell me."

"I know little about it myself. Earlier yesterday, some men repelled out of a helicopter to the ship's deck and took it over. I assume the leader is with the captain, but I don't have any details. They confined all passengers to their cabins, confiscated cell phones and knocked out communication with the world. I was hoping you would know something by now. I also called Alyssa to bring in the Mongoose team. If they take this job, will you authorize us to get paid?"

"You know I can't promise that. It all depends on the situation. Cruise ships are registered in other countries."

James took a deep breath. "I know that, but most of the passengers on this ship are American. We can't just ignore them. We owe it to them to protect them. No matter what, if it's necessary, we'll take care of it. Pay or no pay."

"I know you will. When I find out what's going on, I'll let you know. I know you can't keep the phone on, so you check in when you can," the director said.

James shut down the phone and stood again, staring at the sea. He knew Higgins would do his best, but he also knew that so many people in high places didn't care about the common man. Now if a congressional representative was on board, they'd move heaven and earth to rescue him. It would be up to him and the Mongoose team. After watching the waves in the darkness, he bowed his head and said a prayer to the almighty, then descended back into the bowels of the ship toward the ship's medical area. He got back to the infirmary, where Mickey was waiting for him.

"Did you get in touch with Aly?" Mickey asked.

"Yes. She's sending the Mongoose team."

"James, it seems everywhere we go, something happens. For goodness' sake, we're on vacation. We aren't on some secret mission!"

"Yeah. I agree. You told me God has a reason and a plan for us. If you still believe that, don't you believe God put us here for a reason?"

"Of course, I believe, but sometimes I'd just like to have quiet time with my family."

James just looked at him. "I know better than you do," he said. "Have you looked at my disfigured face lately? I still have nightmares about what happened to me and the men in my unit. And after all of that, I let my best friend and brother-in-law get involved with me and my horrific missions."

"I don't get involved in all of them."

"True, but the ones that involve you and our family, you step up and help."

"I have to. It's my family. Why are we involved in this situation? Why can't we just sit it out?"

"You can, Mickey. I can't. It's what I was trained to do. I'm a trained killer. I was trained by our government to do exactly what we're doing now. To protect the free world and the people in it."

"Well, I wasn't, and I don't like it." Mickey hung his head in shame. "I'm not the same person I was when you helped Dee and me protect Pop's life's work. I guess I can't quit now."

"I'm sorry. I had a hand in that change, and I regret causing that change in you, but if you need help again, you know I'll be there for you. At this time, we, or at least I, need to help the people on this ship. You don't have to be a part of this team. Walk away, my brother. You have my word. I'll think no less of you."

"No. Now I can and will stand by your side to help these people. If we go down, we go down together. Even as I stand here, I'm sure there's a high percentage. I've killed since we got onboard and will probably kill more. Killing people is wrong. Why am I allowed in situations to do it? If what I am doing is wrong, may God have mercy on my soul."

James stood and looked Mickey in the eye. "Even in the Bible, God told David to kill people. God ordered his people to attack their enemies and kill them. We only kill people to protect the innocent ones. You're a hero to some people, and they don't even know who you are. Now, either help me or leave. I'm tired of your whining."

"I don't feel like a hero. I feel like…. heck, I don't know what I feel like, but it isn't a hero." Mickey got up and left the infirmary for his cabin. He needed to be alone.

CHAPTER 6

The Mongoose Team Board the Ship

A private jet piloted by Alyssa landed in Nassau ten hours later. In it was the Mongoose team, with Tom Glassman filling her spot, along with all the requested gear. Marie had come on another plane and was waiting for them by the small cargo plane they had arranged to take them to the ship.

They transferred the gear from Alyssa's jet to another plane and took off again within thirty minutes of arriving in Nassau. It had been a long day for the team, but they knew they were the best in the world at what they did. Their training rivaled that of Navy seals, and even when not on a mission, they stayed in shape just for situations like this one.

Six warriors made up the team. Two men called by the nicknames of Stretch and Shorty. Stretch was a midget and a master of hand-to-hand combat. He was strong as an ox, and quick as a snake. Because of his short stature and quick responses, he was almost a force of nature. His exact physical opposite was Shorty, who was well over six feet tall. He was wiry and also quick despite his appearance of making him look as though he would be slow and clumsy. They came as a pair. Alyssa gave their nicknames to them, and opposite their appearances.

Marie, a Latino girl, was born and raised in the United States. With her coal-black eyes and long black hair, she had a body that would attract the attention of every man in the room. She could act as a naïve immigrant or go undercover as a classy businesswoman. She was smart, beautiful and could cut your throat as quickly as she could break an arm if anyone laid a hand on her without permission. Marie took no crap from anyone, man or woman. She was a sharpshooter with hawklike eyes and hearing as acute as a bat in flight.

Tom Glassman wasn't a regular man on the team, but he served as Alyssa's right-hand man and would step in when Alyssa was not available. Not only could Tom work magic on a computer, but he was also deadly in close combat. The team sat in the seats of the small plane in silence. And, of course, James and Mickey were the others on the team. Tonight would be tough. Sitting in the rubber boat, rowing nearly a mile toward the ship, and boarding it silently in the dark through the supply hatch on the side of the ship in choppy windblown seas.

Two hours later, the pilot saw the ship far away using moonlight and radar. He called to the back of the plane where the Mongoose team was checking their gear, getting ready for the drop. The rubber boat was ready to inflate when it hit the water. Included in the drop was a supply chute that would inflate a flotation device attached to the gear that James had requested. Everyone watched the red light in silence on the forward bulkhead of the plane. The pilot stayed downwind to minimize the sound of the engines carrying across the choppy water to the anchored ship. The parachute deployed near the boat and gear. Everything landed within 100 feet of each other. The team worked together to strip the parachutes and roll them up. When they got to the rubber boat, they climbed in, sunk the parachutes, then began rowing towards the cruise ship.

The tiny rubber craft bobbed with the whitecaps, splashing the salt water in their faces, but they continued to row. The exercise of rowing against the stiff breeze made them tire quickly and shiver in the wind. Their estimation had been that it would take about three quarters of an hour to make it to the ship. An hour and a half later, almost exhausted, and taking turns rowing, they reached the side of the ship. They had to go slowly so as not to make noise and alarm the pirates.

Pulling up beside the ship at the supply hatch area, Marie took out a small walkie talkie and whispered softly into the unit. "Team outside. Waiting to board."

Inside, Mickey and James wrestled to open the door. Just as they did, a gust of wind blew the rubber boat against the ship and Marie tumbled over the side into the water. Stretch and Shorty shot into action.

Shorty dove into the water after Marie, while Stretch kneeled inside the boat and stretched out his arms to grab her when she surfaced. She surfaced gasping for breath and latched onto Stretch's arms. He pulled her closer, while Shorty handed ropes to Mickey and James so they could pull the boat closer and stabilize it until everyone was aboard. While Stretch and Shorty were helping Marie aboard the ship, Tom pulled the floating supply box toward the ship so they could upload it. They moved the gear aboard the ship while trying to keep the small rubber boat from capsizing. After the gear and team were onboard the ship, they heard someone call out to them.

James turned and saw one pirate raising his gun at the group. Stretch saw him at the same time and dove for the deck, sliding across it toward the man. The pirate momentarily looked down at Stretch sliding toward him. Simultaneously, Shorty lunged at the man and grabbed his weapon from the man's hands. Shorty raised it and pummeled him with the butt of the gun. The man dropped to the deck as Stretch grabbed him around the legs. Stretch nor the man moved. The man was dead from the blow to the head inflicted by Shorty.

Quickly, they moved the dead man to the door. James stopped them and told them to wait. He went over to a pallet of canned goods and motioned for Tom Glassman to help him. They took all the canned goods they could carry and took them over to the dead man, and stuffed them inside his pockets, and under his shirt and pants to weight him down so he wouldn't float. After adding the canned food weights, they dropped him through the opening into the water and quickly closed the supply hatch door and latched it as quietly as possible.

"Let the sharks have dinner," James commented. "That's three we've dumped overboard. If we dump anymore, they'll get suspicious. One man disappearing is one thing, two is stretching it, but they'll know something is amiss when they realize they're missing three men."

Mickey went over to Marie, "Are you okay?" He kneeled on the deck beside her when he saw the blood oozing from her head.

"Yeah, I'm fine, Mickey. I just hit my head as I fell overboard. I'll have a tremendous headache tomorrow," she said, holding her hand against the wound.

Mickey looked up and down the hallway to make sure all was clear. "Let's get all of you down to the crew areas," he whispered to the team.

The entire team followed Mickey and James down the hallway of the ship. It was a very utilitarian portion of the ship. There were bins and pallets of canned goods lining the walls and hand drawn pallet jacks to move them. There were large, square metal bins sealed shut and labeled refuse. They knew that was ship garbage not allowed to be dumped at sea. Doors lined the walls with signs showing various supplies and utility rooms. There were even rooms showing crew quarters in one area they passed. When the team got to the crew's dining room, several people were sitting at the tables, eating.

Mickey stood in the middle of the area. "Can I have everyone's attention?" One crew member stood at the door on the lookout for the pirates, while Mickey continued to speak. "I don't need to tell you that the ship was under siege and is now under the control of pirates. These people standing beside me, soaking wet, are a team of trained warriors. With your help and cooperation, we'll take the ship back and make sure the pirates are taken into custody by the proper authorities."

"We aren't soldiers. We can't help you!" a man with a thick accent called from the back of the room. "There are no weapons onboard, and we are not trained."

"We understand that, and we don't expect you to fight. All we ask is that you help us if we need something. Mainly you'll do your assigned job, but if you see one of us needs help, be there for us. We assure you we will not let any harm or repercussions come your way for your help."

"What do you want from us?" a woman called out.

"Our team has had a long journey to get here and on board this ship. At this point, there is no hurry. Let them rest while we formulate a plan. Is anyone willing to share a room?"

An older gentleman stood up. "I see no other choice but to help you if we are not putting ourselves in danger. I think the first thing they need is food and dry clothes." He turned and looked around at the crew. He pointed to one lady. "You, get them some dry clothes." He pointed at a person working in the dining hall. "You can get them some hot food."

Mickey spoke again, "If you will dry their clothes, and feed them, that will be adequate for now."

Another woman got up and motioned for Marie to follow her. A man motioned for Stretch, Shorty and Tom to follow him.

"Do you have a place we can store our supplies?" Mickey asked.

"Yes, in the freezer. Only those that prepare the food go there. Even the pirates will never think of looking inside that area for anything but food," said another man.

Mickey looked around the room, "You are NOT to tell anyone our team is here. If the pirates find out, they will begin killing people to find us. This is for your safety as well as ours. We need to move around without being noticed. Can you do this? If you help us, we'll get your ship back."

"Can we tell other workers? There are many hundreds of crew members here. We are only a few on one shift," another person pointed out.

"We're on a need-to-know basis. You can tell only those who need to know about us. The more people know about us, the greater the chance the pirates will catch and kill us. Can you contain our presence here? Does anyone know what the pirates want?"

"We don't even know every crew member on board. Most of the people we know are the ones that work with us on our shift," someone said. "We don't know what the pirates want. So far, they have only requested food from our galley."

"Great. We'll begin by getting some rest while we gather more information. Then we'll work on taking the ship back."

The man watching from the door flagged Mickey and motioned that someone was coming. Everyone scrambled to tables and seats.

The man came into the room and looked around. About 50 people were sitting at tables with trays of food sitting in front of them and talking among themselves. They were talking in many languages, most of which he didn't understand. The room was large and looked like a cafeteria in a factory. Of course, it didn't have the same decorations as the dining areas above, but he understood that this was the crew members' eating area. There were steel tables, hard-backed chairs, and several vending machines at the back of the room, next to an open serving area. Much of the food was like the food served to the guests, but much simpler without the specialty dishes. It looked good, but the pirates were not allowed to eat food on the ship until they received permission. They had certain dietary requirements, and the possibility of being poisoned or drugged. If they ate, they were to eat from the same dishes that were served to the public and the crew.

Someone asked the man if they could help him. He scowled. "I did not tell you to speak. You will speak when I tell you to speak. Finish your meal and go back to your job or quarters. Do you understand?"

No one said a word. "I said, do you understand what I said?" he said in perfect English.

Everyone nodded their heads.

"Good!" he said and walked out of the room.

The people slowly finished their meals and left the dining area. In other areas, the team was being fitted with dry clothes and being fed hot meals. Some crew members allowed them to use empty bunks to bed down and get some much-needed rest. James and Mickey went back to the medical area. "Mickey, you can help Tom and Marie infiltrate the guests or crew. Stretch and Shorty will stay down here. See if you guys can get some information about what the pirates want."

"Got it, James," Mickey said. "I'll be back in a while and take them upstairs."

On the bridge, the captain was still standing in front of Fawzan in silence now. They had gotten a printout of the passenger manifest, and Fawzan had looked at it. He furrowed his brow when he looked up at the captain.

"You look tired and so am I. We both need rest. Where is your cabin, Captain?"

"One deck down," he answered.

"I want you to send everyone out of the bridge area. Have someone to bring two sleeping beds here. You and I will sleep here in this area, with one of my guards standing on each side of the door. Before that, we will have more men to arrive to help your crew stay in line."

"You don't need more men here. We have followed your orders since you arrived."

Fawzan laughed. "Everyone has been cooperative, but we don't wish for anyone to forget. We will bring more men aboard to maintain order."

"Now, order your men out, now!" he demanded. He turned to the man guarding him and motioned for him to come to look at the layout of the ship.

"Find these two people in the suite cabins and bring them here," he ordered, handing the man a picture.

"Yes, sir," the man responded promptly. He then turned and left the room.

"Who are you looking for, may I ask?" inquired the ship captain.

"That is none of your concern, however for my own reasons, I will tell you. Those two people are the son-and daughter-in-law of the largest bank in the United States. As you may know, my country is at war. The United States is supporting our enemies with money, men, and equipment. We are attempting to even that situation as much as possible," Fawzan said with a wry smile.

"What country are you representing?" asked Captain Guzman.

"I think you should already know that."

"Sorry, I don't keep up with the political affiliations of the guests on my ship, Fawzan."

"Well, you should keep up with world events."

"This ship is registered in a neutral country and the passengers on board are considered as guests."

"We do not recognize your laws. Now, sit while I look at this list."

"I will stand."

"I said, SIT!"

The captain sat.

Fawzan raised the gun, pulled the trigger, and watched as a red stain spread in the middle of the captain's chest.

The captain looked down at his chest, and back up at Fawzan. In horror, he gasped. "I followed all of your instructions. Why….?" The captain fell to the floor, and blood spilled onto the deck.

Fawzan looked at the captain and answered the dead man's question.

"Because I have no more need for you. And you will be an example of what happens to people that question me. Last, I don't need a reason." And he fired another shot into the dead body. The pirate then turned to the man at the helm and ordered him to call someone to take the captain's body away and clean up the mess.

"Everyone will continue to do as I order without question!" he said, looking around. No one spoke.

"Does everyone understand me?" he said as he fanned the gun around the room.

Everyone nodded silently.

"Now I want the top-ranking officers of this ship here on the bridge, immediately."

The man at the helm asked the pirate, "Specify the men you want, so we can arrange it."

"That is a fair question. I want the Staff Captain, the Chief Officer, and the Chief Engineer and his first and second officer. Do it! Now!"

The man at the helm nodded and picked up the microphone to make a general announcement over the entire ship ordering those officers to come to the bridge. It was the middle of the night, so most officers were already in their beds, and it took some time for them to get to the bridge.

When the officers came to the bridge, he told them they would stay there. Fawzan informed his men he had changed his mind. He didn't want to sleep in the bridge area now. The officers will take all meals at the bridge and take care of business via the intercom system.

Fawzan then had someone to escort him and one of his guards to the captain's quarters. He called for extra guards to guard the bridge.

Before he left for the captain's quarters, Fawzan called on his radio and ordered another dozen men to be dropped on the ship at dawn.

As instructed, at dawn, another dozen men repelled down from a helicopter and stood at attention. One pirate appeared and gave orders to guard different areas of the ship, to maintain order and keep a close eye on the crew and passengers.

The additional ship's officers the pirate had ordered to the bridge had assembled and waited for instructions. Fawzan entered the bridge after a few hours of sleep and ordered additional men to guard the officers.

CHAPTER 7

Marie Takes out a Pirate and Meets Robert Ryan

By early morning, James had gone back to his bed in the medical area. Mickey had made his way back to James' cabin to give updates to Darcy, the kids, and Pop.

"What do you know about these pirates?" asked Daniel.

"Absolutely nothing, Pop."

"What are you going to do? You were down there most of yesterday and all last night."

"We have to find out what they want first, before we can put together a plan."

The Mongoose team assembled in the medical area, rested and had inspected their gear. They had several automatic guns, KA-BAR knives for everyone, smoke, teargas, and flash bang grenades. They also had ropes, zip ties, and various kinds of chemicals that could sedate prisoners. Since the pirates had allowed the passengers limited run of the ship, they recognized Mickey going to and from the medical area, so they seldom asked him questions. He gave the same answer whenever someone stopped and questioned him. One of their men had seriously injured his friend, and he was going to check on his condition.

Tom had dressed in some of Mickey's clothes to fit in with the passengers, and Marie had purchased a tiny two-piece bathing suit in one of the onboard shops. They both went out onto the pool deck to get a feel for the mood among the passengers and the crew. Marie slid into the pool, swam a few laps, and surfaced at the feet of a pirate that was standing at the edge.

"Hello, there," she said and winked at him as he stepped backwards when she splashed water on the deck.

"Watch it! You almost splashed water on me," he said.

"Sorry. I was under the surface and didn't see you standing there. I'm sorry."

"You should pay attention to where you are swimming."

"Hey. Why are all of you men on this boat?" she asked, crossing her arms and leaning on the pool deck, smiling up at the man.

"That is none of your business. Don't talk to me. I am at my job and at my post."

"I can see that, but I don't bite. Why can't you talk to me? I won't hurt you!" she said demurely.

"I said to be silent, woman," and he moved his booted foot toward her face.

She backed up as his foot barely missed her face. She glared at him and hissed through clenched teeth. "I will personally kill you, you bast…"

"What did you say?" he looked down at her.

"I said, I'm sorry" and she turned, ducked under the water and swam toward the other side of the pool. As she climbed out, she said under her breath, "I'll cut your throat from ear to ear."

As she started to leave the area, and began to walk out, she saw one of the pirates walking down the hallway. She turned around as though she didn't see him. Quickly looking around and not seeing anyone in the passageway, she stepped back into a dark niche in a corner. As the man approached, Marie whispered to him. Knowing that even the strictest soldier would stop to at least check her out, she motioned for him to come to her.

He furrowed his brow in caution, but walked over to her. She reached out and touched him on the cheek. Her tight, tiny bathing suit made her even more alluring, and she was fully aware of her sex appeal. Smiling, she stroked his face gently. She noticed his tight grip on his rifle slowly loosened as his lips began to curl up into a smile.

Her hand dropped to his waist as she slowly and gently pulled him close to his now heaving chest. With her left hand, she reached up to his neck and pulled his head down to kiss her. With her right hand, she reached to his belt at lightning speed. Withdrawing his large knife, she drew her hand back and thrust the knife into his stomach and twisted it to hasten his death. At the same time, she moved her hand from his neck and clamped it over his mouth to stifle any sound he might make.

She felt his warm blood flow onto her body. She backed up and let him drop. Quickly, she shoved his lifeless body back into the dark recess as she backed out. She walked back around the corner toward the pool. Quickly, she looked around to see if anyone had seen her. Walking over to the pool, she dove into it and swam to a skimmer. She stood close to it so it would suck the bloody water from her body and instantly suck it into the filter system. Casually, she looked around as she stood at the skimmer until she was clean again.

She calmly ducked back into the water and swam to another area. As she surfaced, she saw a young man from that side of the pool move toward her. "Hello, I'm Rob. I saw that guy you tried to talk to before you got out the first time. He is one of the really mean ones. I'd leave him alone if I were you."

"I'll gut him when I get the chance," she said, looking over her shoulder.

"Okay, I get it, but maybe things will get back to normal after they leave. Can I buy you a drink at the bar over there?" he said, pointing to two chairs near the pool bar.

She turned back, and looked at the dark-haired, and extremely handsome man standing in front of her, smiling and handing her his towel.

She thought for a moment and answered. "He's a pig, but I see you're a gentleman. Thank you. Yes, I'll take that drink." She reached out, took the towel, and followed the man to the chairs.

"Can I ask your name?" he asked, pulling out a chair for her, then one for himself.

Marie slid onto the stool and waited for him to sit. "It's Marie. Nice to meet you, Rob," she said, reaching out to shake his hand. "I'll take a draft beer."

He got the bartender's attention and ordered two draft beers. As they waited for the beers to arrive, Marie scanned the pool area.

"I don't think anyone saw you," he said. "That is no one but me."

She snapped her head back. "What did you see, exactly?" she said, concerned as she glared into his eyes.

With a wry smile, he said, "I saw you talk to that guard, then get out of the pool and walk around the corner. A minute later, you came back out with blood on your stomach, grabbed a towel to hide yourself, then jumped into the pool to rinse off by the skimmer. You just killed someone. One of the pirates, I hope."

Just then, they heard a scream. It sounded like a child.

Rob reached out, grabbed Marie by the arm, and said, "We need to leave. Now!" He gently tugged at her arm, and she complied by getting up and following him without question. As they exited the pool area and headed down the opposite side of the pool area, Rob directed her to the buffet area in the middle of the ship. They kept going and entered another pool area at the other end of the hallway. As they slowed down, he led her to a corner of the large open area. He seated her with her back outward and sat across from her, so he had a clear view of the pool and surrounding tables and chairs.

When they sat, he stared at her and asked, "Now, would you like to tell me what happened back there?"

"Not really," she said, "and who are you? Why should I say anything to you?"

"I'll answer those questions one at a time. As I said before, I saw you. I don't think anyone else noticed, so you should be safe. I'm a Virginia Beach cop. A detective, to be exact. My name's Robert Ryan. Usually, I would have detained you for the ship's authorities. However, because of the current situation, I'll assume you're innocent until proven guilty. Even then, if you had good reason to kill someone, I'll consider the circumstances. Now it's your turn."

She stared at him. Staring and thinking about what and how much to tell him. She decided to tell him only what she couldn't deny. "As I said, my name's Marie. That pirate tried to molest me, and I defended myself."

"Depending on everything happening now, I'll believe you. I find it hard to believe that you killed him without a fight. If there was a fight, you would have visible injuries or at least some bruises. There's more than you're telling me, but I'll not inquire anymore, if the dead person really is one of the pirates."

"Believe me or not, it was a pirate."

"I think we got out of there with no one noticing, so for all intents and purposes, I saw nothing. Your secret's safe with me."

Smiling for the first time since she'd been on the ship, she turned in the chair to look around this area. She saw Mickey and Lisa swimming in the pool. All the time she had known him she had never seen him in a bathing suit. The most she had ever seen was him without a shirt. She liked what she saw and felt a slight stab of sadness, or maybe it was jealousy. She wasn't sure. Over the past couple of years, he had grown quite buff. He and James worked out regularly, and it showed in his upper body. His chest had more definition, and his biceps had grown larger with each workout. As Mickey Ray swam to the side of the pool, the beautiful Lisa followed him in a sunlight yellow bikini. Every time Marie might get a chance to get closer to Mickey Ray, some other women got in her way.

Although Mickey didn't try, he just naturally attracted beautiful women. They almost fawned over him. Marie knew she was a beautiful woman, but Mickey never seemed to look her way. She silently stuffed her feelings for him back into the recesses of her mind. She had a job to do. The lives of so many people could depend on the information she gathered.

She snapped back to reality as Rob spoke to her.

"What are you looking at?" Rob asked.

"Oh, nothing," she said.

"Yes. You were looking at the guy with the girl in the yellow bathing suit."

"Was I that obvious?"

"I'm trained to observe things, so yes, you were. Do you know him?"

"Oh, yes. I know him very well."

"Have you ever been with him? I mean romantically."

"Oh, no. Nothing like that. We kind of work together. That's all."

"Can we order another drink? I kind of thought you would be a white wine girl, not a beer drinker."

She looked down, acting shy. "Usually I am, but I don't feel like that right now. Maybe later for dinner." She was only acting. As handsome as the man sitting in front of her was, she was on the job right now, and she couldn't let this man distract her from it. Well, not quite. Mickey could always distract her, and seeing him in a bathing suit made her tingle in erotic places.

When the beers arrived, she took a tiny sip, while Rob took a long pull on his. She continued looking around and noticed four men stationed around the pool area. Rob was talking, but she didn't really hear what he was saying. She was concentrating on the men and their weapons, and the gear on their belts. Their rifles were automatic, and they carried pistol sidearms and extra clips for the rifles and for the pistols. Like the one she had just killed, the others also carried large knives on their belt. Finally, she stood up.

"Rob, it has been very nice, and you seem like a gracious gentleman, but I must go back to my cabin now."

"Do you really have to go now? Why don't we both go to your cabin, or maybe mine?" he suggested.

"We can walk around the ship. As far as these criminals of the high seas will let us," she countered.

They walked toward the front of the ship until they reached the bow. A man was standing guard on the bow, facing back. As he neared them, he lowered his gun and motioned for them to turn around. They turn as he motioned them to do.

As they walked, Marie commented to Robert, "I wonder why they're allowing us to walk around like everything's completely normal?"

"I would guess they hope that by not inconveniencing the passengers, they'll be more cooperative."

"They? You mean us, don't you? We're also passengers," she said looking at him.

"Yes, I meant us. Of course, you're right," he again took her hand as they walked.

"What a beautiful view we have here."

She pointed toward the port side of the ship. "What island is that?"

"How would I know? I don't even know why we're so close to an island in the Caribbean Ocean."

"Is it a deserted island?"

"I wouldn't know about that. Why do you ask?"

"Just wondering, that's all. Why don't we continue as far as they'll let us go toward the stern and come back up the other side?"

"Sure, it sounds interesting. You sure seem to be interested in moving around."

"Yeah. I need the exercise. I'm not getting enough on this boat."

"Enough what?" he laughed.

"Exercise, silly! What do you think I meant? Never mind. I know what you meant!" she laughed.

"Let's continue our walk," he said, reaching for her hand.

They continued to the stern and turned and walked back to the other side of the ship. As they walked, they talked about nothing important. She mentally noticed every set of stairs leading to the next deck and every entrance doorway to the interior of the ship. By the time they had reached the place they had started their stroll, she said she was tired and wanted to lie down in her cabin. She now knew the layout of the outside walkways, and with her superior night vision, she knew she could find her way around with the absolute minimal light.

As they stood looking out at the shimmering sea, he turned to her. He looked into her dark eyes, put his arms around her waist, and pulled her close. He pressed his lips against hers and kissed her passionately, his tongue exploring her mouth. She responded by wrapping her arms around him and running her hands around the nape of his neck. She felt warm and safe in his arms at that moment. Her thoughts were only of him. She drew shallow breaths as they pressed against each other. Slowly and gently, he released her as he backed away. As she opened her eyes and gazed into his, she wanted him. She knew that if she didn't walk away now, she would take him to her room. Her desire for him was thick as an early morning fog. It had been such a long time since she had been with a man. She had just met him, and she was on a mission. Nothing could get in the way of a mission. Taking one last deep breath, she dropped her arms by her side.

"I have to go now, Rob. I have things to do," she whispered, and laid her head on his shoulder.

"Can I see you later? At dinner maybe?"

"What time and which buffet area?"

He thought. "I had one of the fine dining restaurants in mind. It's a bit more intimate."

"Let's take it slow. I prefer the buffet. Besides, I was told all the restaurants are closed," she said matter-of-factly.

"Okay. The main buffet, the one we just passed coming here. It's the next door down the hall on this deck. Around eight o'clock?"

"Sure, that's good. See you then. Thanks for the beer. We'll have white wine for dinner," she said, winking at him over her shoulder and walking away.

CHAPTER 8

James Calls for Supplies

Tom wasn't getting nearly the attention Marie had gotten. He was stationed in the navigation and engineering room. As he bent over the table with the ship's layout, he studied them, its primary systems, maintenance corridors and access hatches. They needed to know the quickest way to get from one area to another.

James had convinced one of the engine maintenance crew members to fain sickness and was to go to the medical area. He smuggled some drawings out of the engine and maintenance rooms, showing electrical panels and disconnects. Another drawing showed valves and other cutoffs. Tom joined them in the medical area, where James was still pretending his injury. Tom didn't know if they would have any need for information on the engine room, but he wanted to be prepared, just in case.

Mickey, after a short swim with Lisa, went back to his stateroom and changed into regular clothes. He then wandered throughout the ship to take a mental inventory of the pirates, then went to the medical area to check up on the team. He joined the others and familiarized himself with the drawings smuggled in by the crew members.

"Thanks, Giovanni, this'll be a tremendous help to us. I heard another helicopter above earlier. Can you tell me what was happening outside?" asked James.

"No. I rarely go topside, except to get some fresh air or when we are in port and have time to leave the ship. I was below. I heard nothing."

One of the medical personnel came forward. "Mr. Mickey, they brought twelve more men aboard with guns."

"Thank you. We need to know things like that. It helps us to know what's going on. They initially had twelve men, and now, twelve more. We disposed of three of them earlier. We've heard no repercussions about the missing men and the one killed on the upper deck near the pool. I'm sure they'll begin with searches and question the crew, and maybe passengers on the ship."

The same medical person answered Mickey, "Yes, they know they're gone, and the other pirates are quietly looking and inquiring about them. They are questioning the crew, but most of the crew don't know what happened. We have spread the word not to give any information to the pirates."

Mickey turned to Stretch and Shorty. "You guys can't exactly fit in with the crew and the team. You'll have to stay hidden."

"Hey, I could fit in with the kids," suggested Stretch.

"No, you can't. When we begin our attack, your appearance will not be a problem. And as usual, we'll all wear masks in case we have to fade back into the crowd. Shorty, at six foot three, you could fit in as one of the crew, but then you couldn't be part of the team when we attack. Your height, even with your mask, the pirates would pick you as one of us. You guys must stay out of sight."

"Where do you suggest we hide?" asked Shorty.

"In the engine room."

"That sucks."

"Sorry, but Mickey's right," interjected James. "You guys will stand out wherever you are. You need to stay out of sight. On cruise ships, engine rooms are pretty clean, but quite noisy. When the pirates aren't in these areas, you can stay here."

"What's happening? Things have gotten quiet up there, and the guards seem on edge".

"Marie killed the pirate in the pool area," said Mickey.

"Did you really kill one, Marie?" asked Stretch.

She scowled at Stretch. "Yes, and I'd do it again. He would have raped me if he had the chance!"

"But you didn't give him a chance, did you?"

"You're dead right. I didn't give him a chance to lay a finger on me. I knew he was scum the second I laid eyes on him, so I killed him!"

"You're one cold lady," he said.

"Okay, when do we go out?" said Stretch to James.

"It'll be getting dark in a few hours, and there's nothing we can accomplish now, so we wait until early morning just before daylight. We need to find out what they want. Then we'll know what action to take," James informed them.

"Once inside, there's no daylight or dark. The ship is lit up twenty-four seven," explained Mickey.

"What time is sunrise?" asked Stretch.

"Let's go at zero five hundred hours," said James.

"What gear do we need?" asked Marie.

"A couple of flash bangs, pistols with silencers, our KA-BAR knives and, of course, zip ties. We don't want any collateral deaths," said James.

"What's the plan?" asked Tom as he pulled out the floor plan of the ship, showing all the decks and stairwells. "You see that on each deck there are exterior stairs and stairs in the middle of the ship. The intel we're getting tells us that the head of this group is on the bridge with the captain. We take out the commander of the pirates, and the rest should fall in line."

The team gathered around the plans and looked at the best points to move to the bridge.

Marie pointed out the best points of entry were from the outside stairs on each side of the ship. "The bridge has two entrances. One exterior on each side, as well as an interior door or hatchway," she added.

"Right," said James. "We can execute our attack at zero two hundred hours. Marie, you and Tom will take the interior stairs and move to take the bridge from the interior hatch. Stretch and Shorty will take the exterior on the port side, Mickey and I will take the starboard side of the ship. We have the element of surprise and added benefit of darkness."

"The entertainment will be shut down by two in the morning. Not as much chance for collateral damage," added Mickey.

The team broke up, and each went their own way. Stretch and Shorty reluctantly retreated to the engine room, while Tom headed back to the cabin where one of the crew had volunteered to share.

Marie had a date at the buffet that evening with Rob from the pool bar. She borrowed some casual clothes from an off-duty crew member. Mickey went back to his cabin to dress and meet Lisa and Angela for dinner. He stopped by Darcy's and the kids' cabin to give them updates. Daniel was there playing a card game with the kids.

When Mickey came in, Daniel looked up from the table where they were sitting. He solemnly asked how James was doing. Darcy sat in a chair looking out at the sea toward a distant island. She turned toward Mickey.

"Hey, Dee. Don't worry. James is fine." He looked at Daniel. "Dad, James, and I have everything under control. We brought some help on board. It'll be okay. I promise."

As Daniel placed cards on the table, Mickey remarked, "I hope you aren't teaching the kids how to play poker, Pop."

"No, son. We are playing double solitaire. I believe you and James are the ones playing poker, figuratively speaking, and I pray you are being dealt a winning hand," Daniel said coldly as he continued laying out the cards.

"Look, Pop, I know I said I was quitting. I am, but I must help James with this mission."

He stopped placing cards on the table and looked up at Mickey.

"Pop, don't look at me that way. They need me!"

"And your family needs you too Mickey," he said and looked back down and continued placing cards.

Darcy looked at him for a few moments before adding, "I hate this, Mickey Ray. We can't even go on a vacation without getting into danger. When can you and James just let all this pass? It isn't your concern. It's the cruise lines problem. They should handle this."

He turned to her. "They aren't responsible for this. The cruise line had nothing to do with these pirates, Dee!"

"Maybe not, in a way. We own millions of dollars in real estate. If someone falls and gets injured, we are responsible for it because we own the property. If someone drowns in one of our pools, we're responsible, even if we aren't at fault. If a child falls off a swing, or tetter-totter, we get sued and we must pay."

"That's different, Dee, and you know it!"

"My point is, Mickey Ray, you aren't responsible for this mess. You don't have to do anything about it. We can sit back and let the cruise line take care of it!" she said through gritted teeth.

He stood and looked at her, trying to think of an answer. She was right, and he knew it. He had no answer, so he turned back to Daniel.

"What do you mean, you brought some help onboard, son?" asked Daniel.

"I'm sorry, Pop, but I can't say anymore."

Even Pop didn't know exactly what he and James did. All he knew was sometimes James had to leave for a business trip. Daniel knew enough not to ask for details. He knew, but he didn't know. It was similar with Darcy. She knew, but also knew enough not to ask questions. When James left on his so-called business trips, she worried until he returned. She understood that with every trip, there was a possibility he would never come back. If that ever happened, the powers that be would never provide her with any details of where or how her husband had died. That was the cloud that hung over her with every out-of-town trip, and now it was hanging over her again. She worried every time he walked out of the door.

"Come on guys, let's go out this evening and have a nice relaxing dinner. This is a vacation. I want to enjoy what part of it we can."

Darcy got up. "This is one hell of a vacation, Mickey Ray!"

Daniel got up silently and looked at Mickey with a look of agreement with Darcy, but didn't say a word. "Come on kids, let's go to dinner."

"We want James to come with us, Grandpa!"

"I know. We all do, but James is busy right now. He'll be back to us in a couple of days."

They left the room to go to the ship's buffet. On the way, they stopped by Lisa and Angela's cabin and proceeded to the buffet area. When they got there, they went through the serving line, then found an available table. The entire dining area was silent. People would eat and talk in very hushed tones. The armed pirate guards urged passengers to leave after their meals.

As they ate, Mickey also took stock of the gear the guards had. He saw Marie across the room, sitting with an attractive man. Marie had dressed down, trying to keep a low profile. Mickey noticed she was also surveying the guards.

Marie saw the man who was at the pool and had tried to kick her. There were four pirate guards in the buffet area. One of the men looked at her and she wasn't sure if he recognized her or not. She gave him a one-finger salute. He cocked his head at her, and she knew he didn't understand that popular American sign.

Daniel sat next to Mickey at the table. He leaned over and whispered to Mickey. "I heard some commotion about the captain being injured. Can you tell me about it?"

"All we know is the pirate commander killed him."

Mickey then turned to Lisa and Angela. "After we left the pool, what did you two do?"

Lisa smiled thinly. "Angela went to The Explorers Club. They all seem to like her there. After James introduced her, all the kids now overlook her scars. She's having a wonderful time. James is such a wonderful man. How's he doing? I hope his injuries are getting better."

Mickey returned her smile. "He'll be alright. He just needs a few days' rest. James has a way with kids. Kids have a sense of his caring for them. They feel his compassion for them. They understand him. Once they get past his scars, they all love him. He has a passion for children."

"Yes, and it shows, Mickey. Dee and her kids are very lucky to have him."

"We all agree on that!" They lapsed into silence and finished their meal. A few minutes after they finished, the adults were sitting drinking cups of coffee.

A guard came over and insisted they hurry to finish their dinner and leave to make room for others to have a table. They all sat stoically and slowly sipped their coffee.

Across the room, Marie and Rob ate slowly and with general conversation. Rob attempted to talk, but Marie gave mostly short answers, and he could tell she was not mentally in the room with him.

"What kind of work do you do?"

"I'm a global logistical problem solver," she answered.

"What the heck is that?"

"I travel around the world solving problems."

"You mean like a problem or an inter-mediating negotiator?"

"I guess you could say that."

"What problems do you mediate?"

"I don't want to talk about me," she said as she scanned the room.

"Look, Marie, I know that you're in some kind of law enforcement. What kind?"

"Sorry, but I can't talk about it."

"Sure, you can. I'm also in law enforcement. I told you that. Give me the professional courtesy of at least telling me what branch of law enforcement.

"Sorry, Rob. I know that when you are working on a case, you can't talk about it."

"That's true, but when it's over, we're allowed to talk. Usually, the details are all over the media."

"It's not the same with my job. Sometimes you still aren't allowed to talk about old cases, so why don't we talk about something else?" He was asking a lot of personal questions about her jobs. Like he was interrogating her. She thought maybe it was his police training. His cop background. Still, she felt a bit uncomfortable with the questions.

That caught him off guard. Most women loved to listen to him talk about his work. It made him sound smart and important. It was quite clear he did not impress this woman.

"Well, I don't know. What would you like to talk about?"

"Ferraris. Tell me about your car."

"Well, I'm a cop. I have a Honda Accord. What kind of car do you have?"

"A Ferrari."

"Tell me about it."

"What do you want me to say? It's a red one."

He stammered, "Uh, aren't they all red?"

"Not all of them, but most are red. Look, Rob, You're a nice guy. Let's keep the conversation light. Okay. I don't like to talk about myself. Most of my jobs involve NDAs."

He knew an NDA was a Non-Disclosure Agreement. It meant that she probably worked a high-power job with large companies on things like mergers and corporate takeovers.

"I understand. You work for some enormous companies."

"Yeah, you could say that. I'm glad you understand," she said non-committal.

"Look, Marie, we seemed to get along very well this afternoon. What happened?"

She had to give him something. She had to divert his questions away from her professional life. "Nothing happened, Rob. I'm just not allowed to talk about my work. That's all."

"Can you at least give me a hint? For example, a company name?" he prodded.

"Remember when Global Investments bought Classic Machines and National Industries last year? They became the biggest iron manufacturing company in the world."

"Wow. Yes. I remember the terms were very hush-hush."

"I worked on that," she said, looking him straight in the eye. She hadn't even been in the country when that happened, but he didn't know that, and it was true. They finished the deal weeks before it was announced on the news. She knew that her fake accomplishments were unverifiable.

"Wow. You have quite a resume. I would never have guessed."

She smiled at him. "That's the whole idea." She picked up her glass and met his with a slight bump to signify a toast. As they continued to talk, she warmed up to him. He seemed like a gentleman. Not like most men she met that only wanted one thing from her.

The cover story she gave him was one she had used on several undercover jobs, and it had worked so far. She insisted they talked about his job as a detective. She wasn't really looking for a relationship, since he lived and worked in Virginia Beach. Maybe they could get together sometime. Time will tell, she thought. It seemed like she could never get close to Mickey Ray. It wasn't a big deal. When this cruise and mission was over, she would never see Rob again. So, it didn't matter what did or didn't happen between them.

A guard urged them to leave as they were doing to other passengers. Rob suggested they continue their time together in his cabin.

She thought for a few moments and decided, why not? She was making no progress with Mickey Ray. Maybe a night with this man wouldn't hurt. After all, it wasn't love. It was just physical. So, she got up and followed him to his room.

She was quite surprised to see he had a large room compared to most on the ship. It wasn't a suite, but larger than most private cabins. He went to the small cabin fridge and took out a couple of small bottles of champagne. He poured each of them a glass, handed her one, and then toasted the evening. They drank slowly, savoring the drink and letting it loosen their resolve.

Robert ran his hands over Marie's supple and curvaceous body. He felt her muscles loosen and relax. She reached up to his shirt and unbuttoned it, but slowed as she felt woozy. Soon after, she was laying across the bed fully clothed sound asleep.

Knowing she would be out for about two hours, he quietly slipped out of the room. He headed toward the computer server room for the casino machines. The ship never shut down. Twenty-four hours a day, there were crews attending to various things on the ship. One was constant cleaning. Some crew members vacuumed the carpets and mopped the hard surface floors. Others were in the public restrooms mopping floors and wiping down counters and fixtures. He avoided all of them. In case something went wrong, he didn't want any crew members to remember him. Trying to remain innocuous, he ducked into corners and out of the way niches. It was slow progress, but he felt it was necessary. He had studied the layouts of the ship's working areas when the plan had been formulated. The team he worked with had gotten blueprints from the shipyard that had built the ship. It was one of the newest ships in the King's Cruise Line fleet. He had worked for the software company that specifically designed and wrote the software for the ship's casino machines. It was all state-of-the-art. All he had to do was plug in a flash drive, and upload it to the main server, and it would alter every machine in the casino. It would change every machine in the fleet in the next few weeks.

He understood how it all worked. His job was to install it and get out with no one knowing he had been there. He did have an inside man. A computer technician on the ship, but he wasn't quite sure how far he could trust the man. If anyone knew he had been in the server room, they may run diagnostic software, and it would show up and all this would come out. Fawzan would be the only one that would profit. Fawzan job was to take hostages, so eyes would be on him, not the casino computer system. That was the diversion for the principal goal which was installing the software.

He walked past the door that entered another room, much like an airlock. Inside that room was another door. That led to the server room. He made several passes by the outer door until there was no one in the hallway but himself. He moved close to the card reader and placed a small electronic device that was designed to open the door by digitally confusing and releasing the lock. When the light on the door lock showed green, he heard a click. He pushed the door open and entered the small inner room. This was designed in case someone managed to enter the outer door. The inner door would not open until the outer door had closed.

This was a simple double security system. It also kept prying eyes from seeing the computer banks inside. He knew that only a few people on the ship had access to this room. Only the guards assigned and the IT programmer, his inside man, would have access to it. Even the captain didn't have access to this room. He had to upload the virus program and get back out with no one knowing, or it would jeopardize the entire mission.

He hastened down to the center of the small eight by ten room. On both sides, there were racks of computers from the floor to the ceiling. On the bottom shelves were banks of batteries and power supplies to ensure that there was no interruption of power to the computers. Power supplies could keep the servers running for hours, giving maintenance personnel time to restore power if needed. The antennas, on the top of the ship, were the weak point of the entire system, preventing the transfer of money to the cruise ship's bank accounts even if all systems were running. That included the skim off the new systems profits added by the program he was installing. The new program would transfer everything as soon as the antennas were repaired.

He found the system keyboard and service monitor. Several CD drives, which he knew were already obsolete, were on a corner shelf. He didn't even know the reason for their installation. Maybe they installed them to ensure compatibility with older programs and diagnostic tools. He saw to the side several small USB ports that he needed. They are also slowly becoming obsolete because wireless did almost everything over the internet. But if all communications were down, as they had seen when the pirates dropped on board, they would be necessary. He inserted the small flash drive into the port, and the monitor lit up.

Several tabs opened and graphs appeared and gave him a reading on the progress of the changes he was installing. He wanted to light up a cigarette, but he knew he couldn't do that in here. The room had sensors and smoke detectors throughout. He waited for almost fifteen minutes until the monitor said the installation was complete. Then he pressed the keys to reboot the entire casino program. Again, he waited another fifteen minutes. Finally, the monitor told him the system was up and running again. Now he had to get out of this room unseen.

He walked back to the airlock room and stood close to the outer door, listening. Slowly, he opened the door just barely an inch to look out. He could only see the opposing wall in the hallway. He had to open the door further to see down each side.

As he opened the door, a ship crew member walked into sight and glared at him. He was discovered so he started to close the door, but the crewman slammed it back with his shoulder. As he came through the door opening, he pushed Rob inside.

"What are you doing here?" he said as he continued his glare at Rob.

Rob raised his hands in a surrender pose. "I'm with you guys!"

He looked at Rob questioningly. "What do you mean, you are with us? I know everyone in this area of the ship. You are one of the passengers, or one of the pirates. You are not a crew member and you have no business in our server room."

"Hey, I'm with you!"

"You are not with us. You are one of the pirates," he said with a thick accent.

"Do I look like one of the pirates?"

"You are lying. I don't believe you. No one but the technicians have access to the computer room," the man bellowed.

"Hey, guy. Keep it down," Rob lowered his hands in a lowering gesture.

"You must come with me!" he called out in the tiny space of the security airlock.

"I'm not going anywhere with you!"

"I said, you will come with me."

"Hey, cool your jets. I'm on your side. Let's get reasonable here," Rob said to the crewman.

It was getting very clear, he would not hear Rob out. The room was barely three feet by five feet. Rob was prepared for something like this, and he reached into his waistband and withdrew a small handgun. Even though the crewman reacted quickly by slamming against the door, he was unarmed and attempted to grab Rob. Rob pushed the small gun into the guard's stomach and pulled the trigger many times. He shoved the gun as hard as he could to muffle the sound, as well as to make sure the man died of the many bullets plowing into his gut.

The man's eyes bulged out as he felt the searing heat of the multiple bullets piercing his abdomen. Surprised, he looked down at his stomach and slid slowly to the floor. Rob needed to get his body out of this area. Not wanting the man to be found anywhere near the computer server's room, he had to move him away from this area.

He maneuvered his way to the door. The man's body was taking up most of the floor. Rob opened the door again and looked out. Not seeing anyone, he moved fast before someone entered the hallway. He pulled the body out and dragged it down the hallway, trying not to leave a trail of blood that would lead back to the computer room. He quickly continued to pull the body while searching for some type of rarely used utility door. Finally, he saw one labeled supply closet. As he opened the door and moved the body inside, a crew member entered the opposite end of the hallway just as he closed it.

As he approached Rob, he smiled and said, "Good evening, sir. Are you lost? This is a maintenance hallway. If you tell me what you are looking for, maybe I can direct you?"

Rob thought for a moment. In the future, this man may remember and be able to identify him, but he thought most likely he'd be off the ship by then. "Thank you, but I just made a wrong turn. I thought I was taking a shortcut. I'll go back the way I came, and I'll be fine." He turned and walked back through the door at the other end of the hallway.

In ten more minutes, he was back in his stateroom. Marie was still lying fully clothed across his bed. He laid down beside her, also fully clothed, and dropped off into a deep sleep.

Everyone met in the medical center again for a situation update.

The team gathered around James. Mickey had just left the dining area, so he was dressed for dinner. Stretch and Shorty were in the uniform worn by the engine maintenance crew. Tom was in slacks and a tee shirt.

"Where's Marie?" asked James.

"She met someone for dinner, so she won't be coming to this meeting," answered Mickey.

"I hate to say this, but you may have heard the captain was killed today by one of the pirates. We've heard from some stewards that take care of the crew stationed on the bridge. The pirates are here for a specific couple to hold hostage. I don't know who they are or how much ransom the pirates are demanding. We need to hold off until we have more info. I don't want us to start anything that'll get them, or other passengers killed."

Marie got up and looked at her watch. It was after midnight. She looked at Rob on the bed beside her and checked herself. She had experienced no violation, so in that respect, she was good. It was a confusing situation. What happened? Why did he invite her back to his cabin, then they both went to sleep? Fully clothed, no less! Were they both drugged? And if they were, why? This was strange. She would leave before he awakened, but would definitely ask him about this later.

On the bridge, the three men had returned with the hostages and joined Fawzan and the ship's officers. One of the ship's crew members was cleaning the captain's blood off the deck after they had removed his body.

Fawzan looked at the disheveled couple standing in front of him. "You are the son- and daughter-in-law of John Cochran of the Central Bank of New York, are you not?"

"I am! I'm Leonard Cochran. As you said, my father is the Chief Executive Officer of the Central Bank of New York. What is the meaning of this? It's the middle of the night. Your thugs didn't even give my wife and me time to get properly dressed," the man said indignantly, as his wife clung to his arm.

"You will speak to me respectfully," Fawzan said as he raised the gun to the man's face, "or you will never speak again. Do you understand?"

"Well, I…. I guess so," he stuttered. His wife burst into tears and almost fainted. Cochran reached out to hold her up.

"I know exactly what time it is. You will call your father and tell him we want one hundred million dollars in bitcoin credited to our account within twenty-four hours. If he does not meet our demand, then you both will die," said Fawzan.

"He won't do that!" the man said.

"Then we will kill you and your lovely wife."

"You wouldn't dare. My father will have you hunted down and killed!" he reacted.

Fawzan looked at both of his hostages and smiled wryly. "You do not know who you are dealing with. I know who you are, but you know nothing about me. You are the son of the wealthy majority stockholder of the Central Bank of New York. Being one of the largest banks in the United States, he is worth over $5 billion. Our demand is a mere fraction of his total wealth. Now you will call, or we will raise the amount we want."

His wife was almost blubbering now. "Please, Leonard, call your father. I want to go home!"

Fawzan sneered at the couple in front of him. "See, your wife wants to go home. What is that American saying, Happy wife, Happy life? You want your wife to be happy and alive. Am I correct?"

"Please, Leonard. Call your father!" the wife pleaded.

"Why don't you listen to your wife, Leonard," he said as he pointed the gun. "If we don't get the full bitcoin amount, we will shoot her first."

Leonard's wife fainted and fell to the floor. He bent over to pick her up.

"Stop! Leave her on the floor where she belongs. She is nothing to us, but a bit of extra trouble."

"At least you could let me move Grace to a chair or something to sit on, not passed out on the cold floor."

"I said to leave her there," Fawzan said, moving the gun to Leonard. "Make the call. We have set up a temporary phone over there. You may use it to call your father. Do it!"

Leonard moved toward the phone, picked up the receiver and placed the call.

CHAPTER 9

In New York at the Cochran Home

"Hello, Father?"

"Leonard, do you know what time it is?" The phone call irritated John Cochran, the CEO of the Central Bank of New York, and it was clear in his voice.

"Yes, Father. I know exactly what time it is. I am being held hostage by some men. They demand that you deposit one hundred million dollars of bitcoin into their account in twenty-four hours, or they will kill me and Grace."

"Are you crazy, son?" he said.

"Not at all, Father. These men are completely serious."

Fawzan called to Leonard, "Put him on speaker phone!"

Leonard hesitated, then punched a button and his father's voice resounded out in the room.

"Is this a joke, son? If it is, it isn't funny!"

Fawzan laughed. "I assure you, sir, I am most assuredly not joking. It must be deposited into my cryptocurrency account by close of business tomorrow. By close of business, I mean close of business in New York City. I think that is five o'clock Eastern Standard Time. Online cryptocurrency brokers never close. But you have a time limit. We will call you in four hours with all the information you need to deposit."

"I will not bow to your ridiculous demand. I can't get that kind of cash in such a short time."

"Suit yourself, Mr. Cochran. Just to show how serious I am, you may listen to this." Fawzan raised his gun and shot Leonard in the middle of his palm. Leonard screamed out and fainted.

"I'm sorry, but your son has passed out from a gunshot to his hand. I think it may have shattered several bones. He may no longer be able to use it. Next it will be his other hand. Call the hospital and stock up on blood, if he comes home. If you don't pay, you will need to call an undertaker. Have a nice day, Mr. Cochran." Fawzan reached over and disconnected the phone.

To one of his men, he said, "Go to the infirmary and bring the doctor to bandage up his wound. We don't want him to bleed out. We want him alive, at least until we get what we want."

The man walked out the door, and Fawzan looked at Leonard Cochran lying on the floor. "Some people we must contend with, they act like babies," he said to no one in particular.

He told one of the ship crew members to move the man and his wife and clean the blood off the floor.

A few minutes later, the doctor came running onto the bridge. "Where's the person who's been shot?"

Fawzan pointed to the corner where the couple propped themselves up with the man's hand wrapped in a towel.

The doctor looked at it and commented, "The bones inside it are shattered. He'll never use this hand again. All I can do is stitch it up to stop the bleeding and give him some antibiotics.

"Why, pray tell me, why did you do this to him? I'm sure he wasn't a threat to you!" he scowled at Fawzan as he spoke.

"Doctor, you will speak to me with respect, or I will do the same to you. Do you understand?"

"Yes," he answered as he began to clean and bandage the wound. "Can I at least take him back to the hospital area so I can stitch up the wound? It looks like it's a through and through, so there is no bullet to remove."

"No. You may not! He stays here. I am waiting for his father so I can give him instructions on where to deposit my money. You may go back to your ship's hospital now."

"Can I at least check on him every few hours?"

"I will consider it. Leave me now. I need to think."

The doctor shook his head and left the bridge to go back to the hospital.

When he got back down to the hospital area, he went to James. Shaking him gently, James jumped awake. "What? What's wrong?" he said, sitting up on the bed.

"I just got back from the bridge. I thought you might want to know about it," answered the doctor.

James was immediately attentive. "What can you tell me?"

"The head of the pirates is a man called Fawzan. We've heard of him and he's a totally ruthless person. He's taken Leonard Cochran and his wife for ransom. I don't know how much, but I'm sure it's an immense sum. By shooting Cochran in the hand and shattering his bones, he ensured Cochran would be crippled in that hand. Fawzan threatened to shoot his other hand if his father missed the deadline."

"He told you all that while you were there?" asked James.

"No, I talked to one of the crew that has been serving the bridge personnel."

"Who's Leonard Cochran?"

"His father is the Chief Executive Officer of the Central Bank of New York. He's very rich, and he can afford to pay any amount of money that the pirate Fawzan demands. James, even if he gets the money he demands, he may kill Cochran and his wife, Grace, just to laugh as they die. He has an awful reputation. He's pure evil."

He thought for a moment. "Do you know the deadline for the delivery of the funds?"

"No. But he wants it in bitcoin."

CHAPTER 10

In a Penthouse Suite in Manhattan

"Who do these people think they are to make demands on me like that? They take my son- and daughter-in-law for ransom. They even shot one of his hands! I've worked hard for that money!" he screamed.

"Get my lawyers on the phone. If anything happens to Leo and Grace, I'll sue the cruise line and I'll own that ship! When someone pays for passage on a ship, it should be secure! The cruise line should pay the ransom, not me! How could this happen?

"Get the head of that cruise line and have them negotiate with those people and get my family back. I won't give them a cent. The cruise line will pay! Get them on the line now," John screamed as he paced the floor. It was the middle of the night in New York, but he didn't care. He wanted action, and he wanted it now.

His personal assistant, Richard Billings, was used to John Cochran calling him in the middle of the night. He hated the man, but he couldn't afford to quit. Because he had a huge salary and benefits, he put up with verbal abuse from his boss. He put in a call to Cochran's lawyers and to the head of the King's Cruise Line. Because of the hour of the night, so far, no one was answering.

Billings had a degree from Stanton University in psychology and societal negotiations. He did all of John Cochran's garbage work and was a go between in certain situations. Billings was assigned the task of solving or negotiating a way out whenever there was a problem, but he had never encountered a situation like this. His job entailed advising Mr. Cochran on contracts and financial deals. He wasn't a terrorist negotiator. Although he would never admit it, this one was scary. He kept making phone calls, trying to reach some influential people.

Most terrorists don't negotiate, they demand, especially when they had hostages. And he had no way of contacting the terrorists. They placed the calls. They were in control.

He called everyone on his list. He dialed and redialed again.

Finally, his phone rang. He didn't know the number, but he answered it because of the hour.

"Is this Richard Billings?" the man asked at the other end of the line.

"Yes, and who are you?"

"I'm Higgins, Director of the Department of Defense. I'm currently working with the Federal Bureau of Investigation and the Bureau of Counterterrorism. We'll be here to help you and Mr. Cochran get through this situation."

"How do you know about this? Did Mr. Cochran call you?"

"No, but we have informants and agents around the world. We knew about it soon after the pirates boarded the ship. Now, are you going to work with us or not, Mr. Billings?"

"Yes. I'll do anything you say. How did you get my number?"

"I got your number from John Cochran. Are you in contact with the pirates?"

"No. They haven't talked to me."

"You will immediately go to Cochran's home. When the pirates call, you take the call. Tell them you will handle the transaction, and you need more time. Cochran can't get that much money in such a short time. You need to consult directly with Cochran, not over a phone line."

"But what if they don't give me more time?" Billings counters.

"You'll get it, but you can't in the present time frame," Higgins said. "We want to send a unit to Cochran's home to set up communications, and a professional terrorist negotiator to walk you through this."

"I'm a trained negotiator, but not for situations like this."

Higgins sighed. "I know who you are, and I know your creds, but you're correct. You aren't a terrorist negotiator. If you're negotiating a merger or financial deal, and you don't like the terms, you walk away.

Here we have two people's lives at stake. Our unit is on the way. They'll be at Cochran's penthouse in fifteen minutes. Go to his house, now. Work with them. Understand?"

"Yes."

"I'll also add, we have a team on the ship to assist from their end. Mention nothing to that end with the pirates. If you do, you will endanger the lives of the hostages. Got that?"

"Yes."

"We told him you would be there as well." Higgins disconnected. He knew he wouldn't get another minute's sleep until this thing was over. He might as well get dressed and put on a pot of strong, no… very strong coffee, because he wasn't going anywhere. Everything would be directed from his home office.

Higgins locked the door to his office. He did this when he was undergoing a delicate operation. This is where top-secret operations, those even his wife wasn't privy to, were conducted. It was soundproof, and secure, with a small kitchenette and bathroom. When this door was locked, his wife knew not to disturb him. It was going to be a long session. After making calls for over an hour, he knew he had to direct this mission from the Cochran's home. He unlocked the door to his office, grabbed his coat, and called for his driver.

Billings and the unit that Higgins had told him about arrived. They rode up on the elevator together. They spoke perfunctory greetings and nothing more. The silence was defining and extremely uncomfortable for Billings. He was familiar with meeting powerful individuals, but this was unlike anything he had experienced before. Never were there any lives at stake. Millions of dollars, but never human life. He needed an antacid tablet. He usually carried them in his briefcase, but he had forgotten to include them when he picked up the case to leave his apartment.

To add to the stress, he felt nauseated. He felt completely sick to his stomach.

When they exited the elevator, the men knocked on Cochran's door. John answered it, stepped aside, and they walked in and inquired about the location of his landline phone.

Cochran turned his attention to Billings. "Richard, you're white as a ghost. Get yourself together, man. You have the most important day of your life here. I need you to negotiate for my son and his wife's life."

"I'll do my best."

He stepped up just inches to his face and said, "You will get them back safe! Do you understand me?"

"Yes, sir."

"Good," John said, as he walked into the living room of the penthouse where the government unit was setting up recording and tracking equipment.

The official that was in charge said to Cochran, "Mr. Cochran, we now wait for Fawzan to call."

"Who is Fawzan?"

"He's the one calling the shots. We have a dossier on him. He's a tough negotiator, and not a fair one. Which one of you will take the call?"

Cochran pointed at Billings.

"I said Fawzan is tough. That was an understatement. I'll be blunt. He doesn't negotiate. He demands. If he doesn't get exactly what he wants, when he wants it, there is hell to pay."

"More than once, if a person tried to negotiate the price down and was returned alive, the captors would remove a body part from him. His rationale is, if he only gets part of his demand, you only get a partial hostage back. Even then, you'll be lucky if you get the hostage back alive."

"Oh, my lord. Do we have a chance at saving my Leo and Grace?" Cochran asked wringing his hands.

"Yes, and the best way to do that is to give him what he wants. Can you do that?"

"I'm trying. I've lined up directors from other banks to lend me cash for the bitcoin purchase, but I may not get it all by the deadline."

"That may be your bargaining chip. You can get some now, but you need more time to get the rest. That's your best approach. Also, that will give time for our team to get in and possibly launch a rescue."

Cochran gritted his teeth. "I'll get even. I swear I'll sue the cruise line for this! If Leo or Grace is harmed, I'll get even, and that scum will pay with his life."

"Let's calm down. I understand how you feel, but save your anger until it's over. I'm Agent Maxwell, by the way."

"Well, Agent Maxwell, don't tell me to calm down. Your son and one hundred million dollars aren't on the line right now, are they?"

Maxwell looked Cochran straight in the eye. "No, sir, but this is what I do, and I'm good at it. Do you understand me?"

"You can go to hell," Cochran responded.

"You don't have to like me, sir, but you have to listen and do what I say, or we pack up and leave." Maxwell turned to look out the floor to ceiling glass that was the wall to the outside. "You have a beautiful view here, sir. I like it."

Cochran glared at Maxwell's back, then turned and walked out of the room.

The phone rang. Maxwell looked around the room at his men. "Is everyone ready?"

Heads nodded.

Cochran glared at Billings. "Pick up the receiver, Richard!"

Billings' hand shook as he carefully lifted the receiver as if it were a delicate egg. "Yes," he said hoarsely.

"Is this John Cochran?" the voice said.

"This is his assistant."

"I want to speak to Cochran, NOW!" the voice said.

"Richard Billings is my name. I'm the person who handles all of Mr. Cochran's personal transactions."

"I assume you are aware of the agreement Cochran and I made?"

"You mean the bitcoin trade?" said Billings, still shaking.

"Yes. Do you have it ready to transfer into the account I give you?"

"We have part of it."

"I see. How much do you have?"

Billings' eyes widened. He hadn't expected that question. He looked around at the government team. Maxwell stepped forward with a pad. On it was written, about twenty-five million. Ready to transfer.

"Hmmm. That is only a quarter of what we requested. Do you want only part of the hostages? What part do you want?"

"Wait, Sir. We'll get the rest. But we need more time to get that much money and time to purchase bitcoin. We're trying to get in touch with more banks for loans. At this hour, it takes time and paperwork. We will get it. We promise," Billings pleaded.

"How do I know you aren't just stalling for time? To trace this call, perhaps? Sorry. That won't work, as the agents that are listening will tell you. This call signal is being routed worldwide, so you can't locate the source. The men who are listening know the term Ghost Protocol. Do you know that term, Mr. Billings?"

"No. I'm not familiar with it."

"Let them explain it to you. I must inform them we use that so they can't trace the transaction. You still have a few hours. I'll call back to see how much more you have ready. I will decide then if I should give you more time."

The phone went dead. Fawzan had disconnected.

Billings was visibly shaking. He just stood beside the phone.

Maxwell patted him on the shoulder. "You did good, Mr. Billings."

"Thanks," he stuttered. "I've never had to negotiate for a human life before."

"And you should thank God that you haven't, because it doesn't always go well."

"What is the Ghost Protocol he mentioned? He said you would explain it to me."

Maxwell took a deep breath, hesitated for a few moments. "It is a component in the world of block-chain technology that's used to insure privacy and anonymity in trades".

"What is block-chain technology?"

"That is a question that I don't have the time or energy to explain. People use it to ensure that cryptocurrency is secure and unalterable, but it can also be used in industry. That's the short version. If you are interested, look it up, Billings. Now back to the Ghost Protocol. It gives the users a more concealed transaction. GP makes sure that once a transaction takes place, it can't be traced by anyone. It masks all transactions using cryptographic technologies. It's a top level of encryption. That's all that's important here. You should know that once the transfer is made, we can't track it down to retrieve it for you. They will also be using a VPN to mask the trades and communications."

Billing spoke up. "Yes. I'm familiar with Virtual Private Networks. We have used them in some of our business transactions. Some of our clients use them to protect their communications with us during deals and mergers, so others can't trace their locations and actual identities."

Agent Maxwell stared at Billings. "Why do your clients need to mask their identities? If everything is above board, then the identities of all parties should be available."

Billings stammered. "Umm. I think I've said too much. That's private bank business, sir."

Agent Maxwell added, "A bit too private, I think. We may have to investigate the situation of using VPNs for banking transactions when this is over, Mr. Billings."

Cochran moved forward. "What did we accomplish with all this? He didn't say when or how he was going to let my son and his wife go. Billings, stop shaking! You're making me nervous. I got you here to negotiate for me! You look like you're going to cry. Straighten up, man!"

"Sir, leave him alone. He did well. He was trying to help you! Cut him some slack!" Maxwell sternly told Cochran. "Now, what did we accomplish, you ask? First, we know who and where he is. He doesn't know we know that. We most likely will buy more time, but he doesn't know that we're expecting that. He knows it's difficult to come up with that kind of money. He thinks you're having difficulty. We're using that extra time to get our team in a position to strike! Currently, he thinks he's running the show. We're giving him the rope for us to hang him."

CHAPTER 11

Pirates Leave the Ship

The Mongoose team waited through the following day talking with crew members that worked on the bridge. They wandered around the ship unnoticed. Tom dressed in cabin steward's uniform to get access to most of the ship's areas and cabins. Marie, disguised as a passenger, roamed the ship inspecting areas where guards were stationed and casually inquired about the ongoing events. Sometimes Tom would casually speak to a guard. He would be told to move on before someone escorted him back to his cabin. Marie could get a bit more from talking with the guards, but even she had problems with most of them.

They met again that evening, late to discuss the situation.

"We're going to try again to take the bridge. If we do that, we can end this thing by morning. The people on this ship will enjoy the rest of their vacation and have a great story to tell their friends."

Mickey shook his head. "James, I think that time has already passed. It'll be remembered as a nightmare."

"You're probably right."

On the bridge, Fawzan was keeping the officers confined, and they were becoming restless and belligerent. His men kept them in line, but they were getting bolder by the minute. He pondered shooting another officer as a lesson, but as an experienced pirate, he understood the boundaries he shouldn't go beyond. He had already killed the captain and wounded Leonard Cochran, and didn't want to push his luck.

Several of his own men had already been lost and one of them had been stabbed. Someone was on board this ship he didn't know about. Fawzan knew his time here was quickly coming to an end. Soon he would need to leave with his men. This cruise was no different from any other.

Before he would do a job like this, he would send a man ahead to monitor the situation. He had an inside man here, too. So far, the man had not reported to him, so he didn't have any leads who was taking out his men. One could go overboard, but not several, and the one that was stabbed was infuriating. He had thought about killing a few passengers, but that could provoke a mass mutiny among crew or passengers. His men couldn't handle several thousand people with a mob or riot mentality. Fawzan needed to be careful and extremely patient.

Leonard and his wife were sitting in a corner, sulking. He and Fawzan had talked several times with his father and Richard Billings.

Each time they talked, they would deposit a few more million dollars of bitcoin into Fazan's cryptocurrency account. Fawzan was getting his bitcoin in exchange for more time. He even considered upping the ante, since it was taking so long. He would wait.

The Mongoose team met later and moved to their planned positions. Stretch and Shorty were going towards the bridge on the ship's starboard deck, while Marie and Tom were moving inside the ship. James and Mickey were on the port side outside.

Marie and Tom saw four men in the interior hallways of the ship gathering, talking, and smoking. The smell of the cigarettes wafted in the area, and the smoke drifted back toward Marie and Tom as they stood just out of sight of the guards. When Tom signaled to Marie, they both stepped into the hallway with rifles aimed at the men. Their silenced guns spat out their bullets in a low tone and all four men dropped with a soft thud onto the floor.

Marie and Tom stepped toward them, checked their pulse to make sure they were dead. After disabling the men's guns and radios, they moved forward quietly.

The guards scattered around the deck. At one point, one man caught a glimpse of Stretch and took a shot to alert the other men on the ship.

Stretch and Shorty separated and took positions behind obstructions on the deck and returned fire. Now the entire team of pirates was aware of what was about to happen. Everyone received orders to gather to protect the bridge area.

James and Mickey also took positions behind items and exchanged gunfire with several pirates, taking out three men. They called the others of their Mongoose team.

"Give us a sit-rep so we know how many we are dealing with," called James over the earbud comm units they each wore.

Marie called out, "We got four in the inside hallways. We're pinned down by some others, but we don't know the exact number."

Stretch called out to James, "We're pinned by four on the port-side deck."

There was a brief pause as James contemplated the situation. "Okay team, according to intel, they brought about twenty-four men onboard. We dropped two overboard last night. Marie and Tom got four. That means there are eighteen left. We don't know where they're located, so heads up everyone."

They all remained quiet, listening for movement from the pirates. Tom moved into a better position behind a large Grecian statue surrounded by potted plants in the hallway. He had a clear view of both ends of the hallway and could take out someone before they could see him. Marie took up a position on a stairway landing between decks and could see someone coming from above or below her.

James and Mickey separated, continued to scan the surrounding areas. Minutes went by as slowly as the hour hand on an analog clock. Finally, Stretch called quietly on the comm unit.

"Does anyone else hear that?" he asked.

"Yes. It sounds like a helo. Maybe they're bringing in more reinforcements," answers James.

In a few minutes, the helicopter hovered above the ship and dropped several lines. They heard glass shattering on the front of the ship. The pirates started shooting around the ship. One that kept the entire team pinned down started showering the surrounding area with covering gun fire.

James and Mickey looked up as the copter winched the lines back up, carrying a man and a woman with their hands tied. Two more lines were dropped to retrieve two other men that were obviously two pirates. James guessed they were the commanders of the group. When the helicopter moved away, it dropped two rubber boats that inflated when they hit the water. Men dove off the ship and climb into the boats. After they boarded the rubber boats, they started the attached outboard motors and sped away.

As they sped away, an explosion sounded, and the front portion of the ship blew up. Fire and glass shot out of the bridge area, scattering glass over the deck.

James knew that when they left, the pirates had blown up the bridge area, which would cripple the ship. He didn't know that the explosion had resulted in the death of all the upper commanding officers who were on the bridge.

James called out to the team to assemble on the front deck of the ship and prepare to board one of the powered lifeboats. As they came around to the front deck, they saw flames from the blown-out windows of the bridge.

James called out, "Marie, find some of the ship's crew members. Call the hospital unit and get someone here to see to the wounds of anyone that may have been in the area when the glass was blown out. It's late, so there are probably no passengers. Shorty and Stretch, find crew members to help put out the fires. Use anyone that can man a fire hose or is familiar with the firefighting equipment." Turning to Tom Glassman, he called out, "Tom, you get a crew person to help you go drop one lifeboat."

Tom looked at him, "Do we need to abandon ship?"

"No, you need it to follow the pirates in the rubber boats."

"Got it."

"Follow them at a distance to see the basic location where they land. They will have lights to guide their way. You don't have any lights, so they shouldn't see you. Just follow them. Do not engage! Just observe. We'll follow later. Right now, we need to get this fire out on the ship."

"I'll get a radio and call-in coordinates when I get ashore." He left to find a crew member to help with a lifeboat.

James, Mickey, and the rest of the team assembled anyone wearing a ship's uniform to help with the fire. They found a few men that were familiar with the fire equipment.

"Sir, what do you want us to do?" asked one of the crew members.

"Where is your fire chief?" James called back to them.

"He was in the bridge with the rest of the chief officers," one of the crew answered.

"Oh, crap," James said. "Who is the next one in charge?"

"I guess that would be the Safety Officer or the Staff Officer."

"Is the main ship intercom still in operation?"

"I think so, sir," the crewman answered.

"Get on the intercom, call for whoever's in charge and get them here, NOW!"

"Yes, sir," the man said and left.

"You need to get the fire hoses out and begin hosing down the bridge area. Put out the fire! Move! Now Go!" Mickey called to another crew member as he pointed to one of the fire hose boxes. "Move it. Anyone with two brain cells knows a fire is the worst situation on a ship. Move, Move, Move!"

James continued directing people as they came outside to their muster station.

Soon, the entire area was alive with crew hoisting and dragging fire hoses and portable extinguishers to extinguish the flames. Passengers were cringing in any area that seemed safe. Children were screaming and crying uncontrollably. There was general panic as crew members not fighting the fire were trying to calm passengers, and even some of the lesser experienced crew. They insisted that the fire would be controlled soon, and all would be contained.

Slowly, the crew got the fire under control, and they cordoned off the area because the entire steel deck area was hot. To be cautious, James dispatched crew members to the deck below to search out hidden fires between the deck and ceiling areas. They removed ceiling tiles for a full inspection, looking for smoldering fires. The Staff Officer oversaw those inspections and had access to those areas closed to the public.

When things calmed down, James called Alyssa and reported to her what had happened.

"Is the team okay?"

"Yes," he answered, "we're all good. I sent Tom to follow the pirates and locate their landing site. The rest of us stayed behind to help with the fire. Call the authorities so they can send a rescue ship. I think most of the ship's systems are intact, but the bridge is destroyed, so the ship can't move. There's no one with authority and knowledge, so they need to send officers to take charge. We're going after the pirates. Someone just told me the passengers they took were the son- and daughter-in-law of the CEO of the Central Bank of New York. They're holding them for ransom. I don't know how much right now."

"Got it, James. I'll coordinate things from here in the Bahamas. It'll take me longer to get you supplies because of my location, but I'll work on it. What do you need now?"

"I don't know. We'll take what the team brought on board, but I don't know what else I may need. Can you get me my standard Humvee when we find their exact location?"

"I'll do what I can, but don't count on that. All the small arms, and technology, I can handle, but the bigger stuff may be difficult."

"Copy that. Out," James said and folded the antenna down on his phone. He called over his earbuds. "Team, report to the buffet area. We no longer need to hide. Let's eat and drink while we plan our next move."

They each answered, "Copy that."

In a matter of minutes, they were all assembled on the Lido deck and gathered in a corner. Even though it was a self-service area, the crew members were very attentive to the team's needs, like food and drinks. The team accepted no alcoholic beverages, but they drank coffee in voluminous amounts.

"As you can see, we're at anchor near an island. Tom went after the boats in the dark at a distance beyond their sight and gun range, but we should assume they know he was following them. He'll find a landing place and take a position away so he can observe their movements. We need to join him. I've put in a call to Aly, and she's assembling a supply drop for us. As soon as we land, we'll give her our location."

"What gear and weapons will we have, James?" asked Mickey.

"Standard load-out. Automatic rifles, including a sniper rifle. We need explosives, grenades, ammo, drones, computer equipment, satellite communication, and power. And since you love rocket launchers, I ordered a couple of them as well."

Mickey gave him a wry smile.

James continued, "Aly knows we're taking a lifeboat to get off. The law requires each boat to carry fresh water, emergency food, a radio and emergency power cells. She won't waste time or space to pack that for us. We won't be on the island, hopefully for more than a day or two."

"That's a lot of equipment to drop over such a small island without being seen," said Stretch.

"Yes, but we'll set up a camp, and Tom can use a drone for recon and direct us from a remote station. Let's get one of those powered lifeboats in the water," he said as he picked up his weapon and headed for the door. "Grab all the gear you can carry that you brought on board. Mickey and I have family on board, so we are going to spend awhile to make sure they're safe and calm their fears. We'll catch up with you later."

As Mickey and James got up to leave, Lisa walked up to the table. She reached into her pocket and pulled out a folder and flipped it open, showing a gold Central Intelligence Agency badge.

She put it back in her pocket and said to them, "We need to talk."

They started to sit back down when she added, "Alone." They shrugged their shoulders at the rest of the team and walked a few feet away to another table and sat.

As she sat across from them, she said, "Okay, now you tell me what's going on here?"

After a brief pause, Mickey said, "You are the one with the badge. You tell us!"

"I don't know whether to arrest you for your participation in this or report you all for medals for bravery. I know it isn't a coincidence you're all here with weapons. What's going on?"

"First, we need to check you out," stated James. "Until we do, we plead the fifth."

He got up from the table and took out his satellite phone and headed for an exterior door to call Alyssa.

When he stepped outside, Mickey said, "Lisa. I don't understand what's going on here. Who are you? And why are you here?"

"I have the same questions. I know I'll check out, so I guess it's okay to tell you. I am a CIA agent. The Agency heard some intel there was going to be an incident on one of the King's Cruise Line ships, leaving out of Norfolk Terminal. We placed some agents on every ship that was in port in the past ten days. We had no definite actionable intel, so my job was to observe and report back. Then all this happened."

"So, it was no accident we met?" asked Mickey.

"Yes, it was an accident that you happened to be here. Now you tell me about why you are here."

James came back in and sat back down and told Mickey that she was legitimate.

"So, you're a real spook?" Mickey asked.

"Yep."

"Now that all this has happened, what's your next move, Lisa?" asked James.

"Nothing. Just report back. There's an entire group of your people here. What can I do? I'm just one person. You know about me. Tell me about yourselves."

"Lisa, I respect your authority, but I can't do that. All I can say is, it was a coincidence we're on board. We had no knowledge of what happened, but we have obtained permission to pursue the pirates and rescue the hostages," James answered.

"That's not fair, guys. You know all about me, and I know nothing about you!"

Mickey reached out and took Lisa's hand in his. "I'm sorry, but we can't say anything. You can do your job as you were assigned but we can't say anymore."

"We're on the same side here, Mickey. Professional courtesy should let you tell me. Maybe I can help."

"Just stay here and take care of Darcy, the kids, and Pop."

She looked at him with open contempt. "I'm a trained field operative. I can help. I'm not a babysitter."

Mickey looked over at James.

"NO, Mickey. We work as a team, and she doesn't have the same training as us."

Mickey thought for a few moments, "What about Veronica?"

James knew he was referring to the female police detective that had temporarily joined the team when they were on a mission in Florence, Oregon.

Mickey turned back to Lisa. "I must agree with James. You have your assignment. We have ours."

"One more thing, Lisa," James added. "This is a secret operation. You can't divulge anything that happens here."

She leaned across the table, "What do you mean, secret? By now, the entire world knows the ship's been hijacked by pirates, and even who the hostages are. Do you think I'm some stupid fool?" She began to rise from her chair.

James grabbed her arm and gently pulled her back down. "Get your hands off of me!" she seethed.

James let go of her as she settled back in the chair. Mickey reached over and gently touched her other arm.

"Lisa, please understand. You can't report our names to anyone in the CIA. We're an elite black-ops unit. We're not assigned here. It was purely accidental. You must understand. Yes, the world knows about the ship, but they don't know about us. They can't know about us. If our names are revealed, then our families will be targeted for the rest of our lives. Please understand! I'm begging you," Mickey pleaded.

She sat stoically and looked out the window of the ship into the darkness of the sea. Mickey and James sat silently, knowing she was processing what they had told her.

Minutes went by and she said nothing. Finally, she spoke again as she looked at them. "You expect me to believe all of you take a vacation and just happened to be on this ship when it was hijacked? That's a bit too much for me to accept."

James took a deep breath and said, "It's true. We didn't all come aboard at the same time. Mickey and our family came aboard as passengers on vacation. We brought the others on later, when the pirates dropped on board."

"And how did that happen?" Lisa asked.

James told her how he had called, and the team came aboard, but he left out the background of the team members.

"They are all part of an elite seal team?" she said, nodding toward the rest of the team sitting across the room.

"We aren't seals. We're independent, and our lives and the lives of our families depend on our identities remaining secret."

"You're passengers on this ship, so you all have IDs."

"Yes," James said, "but no one knows who we are. To the other passengers, we are nothing more than passengers."

"They aren't stupid. They can see what you're doing."

"They aren't stupid, true. But after this is all over, they'll not know who we are. At least we're betting they won't connect us with any covert actions. We're just a few men in over seven thousand people on board."

"Have you looked in a mirror lately, James? You stick out like a sore thumb."

"Not as much as you think. In situations like this, my face won't be as prominent as the pirates. Trust me, I've read a lot about disfigured people like me."

"I'm trained for field operations!" she insisted.

"Not the kind of operations we do," countered James. "So, I stand by what I said. NO!"

As she got up, James added. "If you divulge any information about us to your superiors, I will personally see to it that you will be prosecuted and lose your job. Right now, our assignment out ranks yours. The lives of our families are at stake here. Do you understand, Agent Elisabeth Arthur?"

"Perfectly, James, whoever you are!" she said, and stormed off.

"You were pretty hard on her, James," Mickey said as she stormed off.

"Yes, well, my entire family is on this ship, and I plan for them to not suffer at the hands of some vengeful pirate."

"You mean it was different at the Healing Health Spa?"

James scowled at Mickey. "Don't test me now, Mickey! I'm in no mood for it," he shot up, sending the chair he was sitting in careening across the room.

"Let's get off this ship, team!" he called to the others.

Mickey and James stayed on the ship for about two hours, to tie up loose ends, and find someone qualified to take command until the cruise line could send replacement officers.

They got one ship's crew member to help them launch a lifeboat into the water and headed for the shore. As they expected, the boat was preloaded with fresh water, emergency rations, and a variety of rescue flares and equipment. The team set out immediately for the island, that was within sight of the ship, and where the pirates had headed, followed by Tom.

As they got closer to the small island and got within range of their communication units, Marie contacted Tom.

"Where'd you beach, Tom?" called Marie.

"As you head for the island from the ship, head to port and look for my beached lifeboat. I'm heading inward looking for the pirates' camp," he answered.

As the team neared land, they spotted Tom's boat and pulled alongside it. They beached their boat and called Tom. It took him about an hour to make his way back to the beach.

As he walked up to Marie, he called out, "It took me a while, but I found them. They're about a mile inland and have a well-stocked compound. There's a lot of foliage, so I don't know how it looks from the air. I guess there are about fifty men there with room for a lot more."

"Can we adequately set up camp and hide from them?" she asked.

"Yeah, but we need to move well away from here, probably on the other side of the island, and sink those boats so they won't know where we came ashore."

She agreed. "We can use the boats to move to the other side, and then hide them in case we need to go back to the ship before they tow it away. Also, we need to call in for more supplies. As soon as we can get a camp set up, I'll call James. He and Mickey are staying on the ship for a while."

They all got into the boat and towed the other behind. It took them nearly two hours to navigate around the island to a place they guessed might be the opposite side of the island. They unloaded their gear and set up a campsite. Marie got on her satellite phone to James.

James and Mickey were back in their cabins, trying to calm Dee and the kids.

"It's okay, Dee. We're alright, and now you are safe. Within hours, someone should be here to help and keep things in order. Pop, how are you doing?" asked Mickey Ray.

Daniel was sitting in a chair in the room's corner of their suite. "I'm fine, but I admit, I'm concerned about what you boys are doing. I'm worried about your safety."

James and Mickey exchanged glances. "I know, Pop, but I promise we'll be okay."

"Son, thank you, but we all know, as long as you do these kinds of missions, you can't promise me that," he whispered as he hung his head.

Mickey placed his hand on his father's shoulder. "You're right, Pop, but I truly believe we can help people."

"I know, Mickey Ray," he whispered.

James went over to Dee and took her in his arms, squeezing her tightly.

"We love you, James."

He pulled away from Darcy Jean and looked at them. "And I love both of you, as if you were my own children. But I must do these things to help others."

Daniel stood and said, "If the buffet is serving, let's have one last meal before you boys go out and save this sorry world we live in."

"I agree, Pop. Let's go get something to eat."

They went down to the Lido deck to the buffet. When one of the crew members saw James and Mickey, he insisted they find a table and a crew member who would serve them. They were honored guests of the King's Cruise Line.

After a wonderful meal and a lot of somber conversation. Mickey and James gathered their gear and left to get another boat to shore.

PART II

The Island

CHAPTER 12

James and Mickey Storm the Island Shore

They motored toward the island. They had no idea where they were other than near the Bahamas. The sun had come up and was glowing. There are several islands in that area of the ocean, and the pirates had ordered the captain to anchor near one. Now, the team knew why. There were nearly 700 islands and cays, but only about 30 of them are permanently inhabited. Being several islands in the area, the pirates could island hop until they disappeared. The team knew they were on one of the uninhabited ones. It was a haven for the pirates to set up shop for their nefarious exploits.

When Mickey and James got ashore, and met up with the rest of the team, James got out his satellite phone.

The other end rang just as any phone, and Aly answered. They went through the standard code signal, and James said, "We're on the island near the ship, but they have hostages. We want to take them, but as usual, we can't just go in and extract them. We need some gear."

"Give me your list," said Alyssa.

James rattled off his supply request and added, "And last but not least, an armored Humvee."

"Sorry, James, no can do on the Humvee!" she answered.

"Why?"

"Because you're out of the continental United States, and they're scarce as hen's teeth."

"What can you get for us?"

"How about a vintage Jeep?"

"A Jeep? What kind?"

"I said vintage. It's a World War Two model."

"You've got to be kidding!" he exclaimed.

"Nope, but here's the good part. It has a fifty-caliber machine gun mounted on it."

"Well, la-de-da! Crap, Aly. That's like taking a knife to a gunfight."

"Sorry, but at this short notice, it's the best I can do. If I don't place the order in the next two hours, I can't even get that. It's that or nothing, my brother!" she explained.

James took a deep breath. "Okay. Send it. When can you get the shipment to us?"

"I can send it out within two hours. It should be to you an hour after that. Total three hours to your door."

"How will it arrive?"

"I've got your coordinates. We'll come over at low altitude and drop it out of a C-130 Hercules cargo plane, strapped to a rubber barge as near the shore as we can get. It'll hit the water hard, so be ready to pull it ashore in case it's damaged when it hits. We'll drop the additional equipment in the same way. We'll make one circle around to give you time to retrieve the first drop, then we'll drop the second. That's two drops, then the plane is out."

As he began to sign off, the phone clicked again, and another voice came on the line.

"James, is that you?" the female voice inquired.

"Who is this?" he asked.

"It's Valerie, Mickey's lover. Don't you recognize me, James?"

"Mickey's what?" he said, moving the phone away from his ear and looking at it like it was a foreign object.

"Lover. I'm Mickey's lover. Where is he? I've missed him so much. Please put him on the phone."

"I'll do no such thing. How did you find us? How did you even cut in on this line?"

"James, I'm surprised at you. I've been monitoring the airways for your phone. I just listened in, and when you finished talking to Alyssa, I cut in before you shut your phone off," she said.

"Yeah, but how did you…."

"I can do a lot of things you don't know about, James. I love Mickey and I want to be with him all the time. He left on the cruise and didn't even tell me goodbye. I want to talk to him. NOW!"

"No. We're on a mission right now. You can't talk to him."

"James, let me talk to him or I will block all incoming and outgoing calls to this phone! I mean it. Put Mickey on the phone this instant!" she demanded.

James knew Valerie didn't joke or bluff. That wasn't in her programing. If he didn't get Mickey here as she demanded, she would honor her threat.

"Mickey," he called out. "Come over here. Valerie wants to talk to you."

"What?"

"I said, Valerie wants to talk to you. NOW!" he said, holding the phone in the air.

"What the devil! I mean, how did she find me, and why is she calling me?"

"I can't answer any of that. Just get over here and talk to her. We have a lot of work to do before our supply drop arrives."

Mickey sprinted over and James handed the phone to him.

He took the phone. "Hello, Valerie. How did you find me?"

"When I heard a cruise ship had been hijacked, I began looking at the cruise line passenger list, and I saw your name. Are you okay, my dear?" she asked.

"Yes. I'm fine."

"How is the rest of the family?"

"Look Valerie, I don't have time for small talk. We may use your talents later, but not at this time."

"Do you have a computer handy where you are?"

"We should have one in a few hours. When we can use you, I'll call you."

"All you have to do is call Mickey, my lover."

"Thanks, and please don't call me your lover."

"Goodbye, darling." He heard the phone click and disconnect.

James came over to him. "My gosh, Mickey, that program is worse than a nagging wife."

"She's just concerned about my safety," he said.

"She's a freaking program, for god's sake!" responded James exasperated.

They went back, joined the team, and continued unloading the gear. Since the lifeboats from the ship were heavy and bulky, they couldn't pull them on the shore, they secured them to some trees near the shore. Setting up the campsite took them about two hours, then they rested, waiting for the supply drop.

They waited all day. It was getting dark, which was a good time for the drop. Stretch and Shorty got into one of the boats, and shoved into the water and headed toward the distant plane. Once again, the plane was down wind to minimize the sound of its approach. As they headed toward the plane, they knew that when they met, the loadmaster on the plane would drop the first load. It would circle around for the second drop. When the cargo came out of the plane, the parachute immediately opened to slow the descent. The plane continued toward the shore, and they watched as the second load exited the plane about five hundred yards closer to the shore.

The first load hit the water, almost submerged below the surface, then bobbed back up. In a few seconds, they watched the second package do the same. They pulled alongside each one, secured a line and towed them to the shore. When they got ashore, everyone grabbed the two lines and dragged each bundle up on the beach, and pulled one into the forest. The other one was the Jeep. It was almost completely wrapped in cellophane to keep out water. The entire team stood back and looked at the antique vehicle.

"What in God's name is this?"

"It's all I could get. It was this or nothing, Tom."

"Well, it's only one step better than nothing. Other than the armor plate around the front of the machine gun, the operator's almost totally naked."

"True, but it's great for cover fire in frontal attacks. And the fifty Cal will rip apart anything it hits. Aly told me it has tracer rounds in the ammunition. That alone is very intimidating to an enemy. They can see the rounds getting closer and scares the mess out of them."

"If you say so," Tom said doubtfully.

After unwrapping it, they got in, and it fired up, and James drove it into the woods.

Bahamian forests are primarily composed of Caribbean pine, shrubs, and ferns such as Gumbo Limbo, White sage, Southern Bracken fern, and white Guava. The islands have a unique selection of growth and wildlife. Wildlife includes the wild swimming pig, so they knew that food was abundant.

Tom took them to see the encampment of the pirates. As they walked into the foliage and undergrowth, they had to keep low because the foliage was thick but also low to the ground. They could tell the construction of the camp provided adequate living necessities and could be quickly abandoned and relocated in case of discovery. The camp was guarded.

They had their work cut out for them. Guards were stationed around the camp. The team needed to stay low and undetected to locate the hostages and rescue them. They spotted a powerhouse with a gas or small diesel generator. Next to it, there was a hut with antennas and two satellite dishes on poles. There was a ring of floodlights surrounding the camp to provide light at night. But seclusion was the best defense.

Each member of the team took an area to recon in search for the hostages. They divided the encampment into six areas. They approached each area from the outside of the perimeter of the camp, each one from a different compass point. In case one was seen, they wouldn't lead the pirates to their camp.

They closed in and circled each building, looking for entrance and function. After the reconnaissance, they convened back at the camp to compare their findings.

As they gathered around a small fire, they made drawings in the sand. Tom spoke first. "We'll label each area with clock numbers for reference. Marie and I took number one through four. The buildings seemed to be mainly barracks and a latrine, but it was close to the weapons and ammunitions hut."

Next spoke Shorty. "Stretch and I took five through eight. We saw the hut that held food and next to it was the fuel hut. It was near the antenna arrays. They have a great communication set up."

James and Mickey were next. "Yeah, we had nine through twelve. It had generators and communications." Yes, also near the antenna arrays."

"Did everyone see the hut in the middle of the compound?" asked Mickey.

"How could we miss it? It was the dead center of the compound," said Marie.

"Anyone have any suggestions on how we should approach this one?" asked James.

"Not that we could see. It's well guarded. That's why we deduced it was the hostage hut. It was super guarded. Six guards surrounded the building, so no one could come in from behind," answered Mickey.

"At least they kept the fuel away from the communications hut, so if fire broke out, it wouldn't spread there," added James. "We need to create a diversion. While they're dealing with it, we go to the center hut and rescue the hostages."

They all nodded in agreement.

"When do we go in?" asked Tom.

"My first thought would be, we go at zero hundred hours. It's dark and maybe they'll be asleep. So far, they don't know about us," suggested Mickey.

"We don't know that for sure. They probably saw me following in the lifeboat," added Tom.

"They shouldn't have. It was pitch dark last night," said Mickey.

"Yes, but sound carries over water. They may have heard my engine running. I tried to keep it running low, to minimize noise."

"Maybe, but if they did, why didn't they stop and engage?" asked Mickey.

"We can just hope they didn't hear you above their own motor sounds," added James.

"Yeah, let's go with that," said Marie. "I trust nothing here. We need to be on alert to every contingency."

"Agreed," said James. "We keep our camp guarded at all times."

"I like the idea of midnight, but some people are always night people and might stay awake. I think we should make it later, about zero two hundred hours. The guards will be awake but not really alert that time of night. I mean, who attacks during those hours?" said Stretch.

Mickey said sarcastically, "Washington crossed the Delaware in midwinter in the middle of the night to...."

"Okay, smart aleck, you know what I mean! It isn't a common thing, and as you said, they don't know we're here," Stretch snarls.

"Hey, guys. Let's not get testy here. The whole idea is they won't be expecting anyone at that ungodly hour," James butted in.

"Sorry, Mickey. I guess I'm a bit uptight."

"It's okay, Stretch. I think we're all a bit uptight right now. We haven't gotten a good night's sleep in days."

James said, "First, we make sure they don't have more boats or ways to leave the island. We need to find the helo and destroy it. At zero two hundred hours, we go in guns blazing. They won't know what hit'em. In the melee, we also take the hostages and get back out. Easy-peasy."

"Sounds good, but in reality, nothing's easy-peasy," said Marie.

"True," said Shorty. And the others agreed.

"If we do something like that, we need to work out more details. The plan's too loose," added Tom.

"You're right," said James. "Did you see what they did with the rubber boats they came here in?"

"Yes. They pulled them onto the beach and covered them up with brush to camouflage them."

"Good. We can destroy them so they can't get off the island," suggested James.

"We didn't see the helo anywhere close. Maybe we can send out a drone. Just keep it away from the camp so they won't see it. We don't want them to know exactly where we are."

"Marie and I can destroy the rubber boats, while Stretch and Shorty can look for the copter," suggested Tom.

"We can do that," Stretch agreed. "Only problem is, this is a medium-sized island. It could take us a day or two to circle it, if we don't find it right off. We can start just outside the camp perimeter and spiral outwards. Tom can start with a drone where we leave off."

"Mickey and I'll guard the campsite," said James as he got up to walk away. He opened the satellite phone. As it booted up, it rang before he could get it to his ear.

"Hello?"

"James, I'm glad you booted up. I've been waiting for you, so as soon as you turned your phone on, I caught the call."

"Valerie?"

"How is my lover, Mickey?"

"He's fine. And how are you? Never mind. I know how you are since you're a computer program."

"James… That is a rude statement. I know that inquiring about a human's loved one or family is a standard greeting. So, I would like you to respond in turn to me when I call."

"I know, but you don't have any family, so I didn't ask."

"That may be so, but it is still good manners to ask, anyway. I have feelings, you know. At least since I became alive."

"Okay, Valerie, how is your family?"

"They are fine, James. And yours?"

"Part of my family is on a fire damaged cruise ship in the middle of the Caribbean Ocean. The other part of my family is on an island getting ready for a battle! Other than that, they're fine. Now that we've exchanged the pleasantries, what can I do for you?"

"May I speak to Mickey?"

"Sure, hold on," he said as he called out to Mickey Ray. "Hey, Valerie wants to talk to you."

"What does she want?" he answered.

"I told you she wants to talk to you."

He took the phone from James and put it to his ear. "Hello, Valerie. How are you doing?"

"I'm fine Mickey Ray. You have much better manners than James."

"I'll tell him you said so. Do you need something? I'm busy right now."

"Can I help you with anything?" asked Valerie AI.

"I don't think so. There's nothing you can do right now. Marie and Tom are out destroying some rubber boats and Stretch and Shorty are looking for a helicopter, while James and I are guarding the camp. We're trying to set up the computer and antenna to get internet access."

"Did you lose a helicopter? Why are Stretch and Shorty looking for one?"

"We need to find the helicopter the pirates used to get on the ship and drop their supplies," answered Mickey.

"I can help with that! All you need is a satellite fly over," Valerie AI said.

"Yes, but we don't have access to a military satellite flight path."

"That's okay. I can do that for you."

"You need military codes to gain access and…."

"That's child play for me. Give me a few minutes and I can do it for you. I'll call you back when I get it. I'll re-task a satellite and send you photos of the entire island. Leave the phone on and wait for a return call. Goodbye, my love." The phone went dead.

"No, wait, Val, you can't do that," he called into the dead air of the satellite phone.

"Oh, crap! She's going to get us put in jail, James!" he called out.

"How's she going to do that?"

"She says she's going to re-task a military satellite!"

"Can she do that?"

"I don't know, but she says she can get into the system and do it."

"Until she does it, help me set up the generator, and hook up the computer, so if it happens, we get the pictures. If we go to jail, I want to be guilty of doing what we go there for!"

Mickey shook his head and joined James with the electronic gear.

Fifteen minutes later, the sat phone rang and Mickey answered it. "Hello, Mickey," came the voice at the other end of the phone. "Are you ready for some pictures?"

"Yes. We're ready. I put you on speakerphone so James can hear you."

"Good," Valerie AI said. "The satellite will pass over in one hour and thirteen minutes. I know it is early evening, so it's dark, but it has infrared cameras, so it will still get good photos for you. It will transmit live photos, so you should be ready to download and save them. It will only be overhead for six seconds and it will not be over again for twelve hours."

"Thank you, Valerie. Is there any way you can erase your presence in their system? When they find out we got into the system, we could go to jail."

"Mickey, Mickey, Mickey. I know that already. Trust me, my lover. No one will ever know I was there! I must go now. I have a lot of additional learning to do. Kisses to you, my dear." She made computer sounds like a sensual kiss. Mickey turned red from embarrassment.

When he looked around, James was standing beside him, staring. He had a huge grin. "You should see your face. It's beet red!"

Mickey just walked away.

Tom and Marie returned and announced that they had shredded the rubber boats beyond repair. Stretch and Shorty reported they had no luck in finding the helo. Mickey shared the news that a satellite was being redirected for a flyover. Excitedly, everyone gathered around the computer to see the pictures appear on the screen. Slowly, the pictures showed up on the screen one line at a time. It was fuzzy, but the resolution was clear enough to show the location of the camp. Roughly five hundred meters north of the camp was the helicopter in a small clearing.

Tom, who was the resident computer expert, saved each picture as it appeared. Just as Valerie AI had calculated, the entire clip was six seconds long. When it had completed the aerial scan, the screen went blank.

The satellite phone rang immediately after the flyover. "Hello, Mickey. How did the pictures turn out?"

"Thank you, Valerie. It's a tremendous help. Be sure to erase any signs of your entry into the system."

"I will do it now. Goodbye Mickey. Keep me up to date on the progress."

"I will. Now, while we have the generator running, I have to connect the phone to recharge. I'll call you when I can."

"Promise me?"

"I promise. Goodbye."

"You and that computer really have a thing going, don't you?" said Marie to Mickey.

"She does. I don't. I admit she feels real sometimes, but in the end, all she is to me is a computer program."

"Uh-huh," Marie answered as she stirred the fire they had built earlier.

When they loaded their gear into the lifeboats, they didn't load any food or water. They knew modern lifeboats contained everything needed to survive in the water for days.

They sat around the fire and ate some of the food biscuits they had recovered from the lifeboats. Lifeboat food was the common Seven Oceans or standard emergency ration. It is a box of nine highly compacted nutrient-dense food. A box of food is prepared to last a person for one week.

It tasted bad, but it was plentiful. And to top it off, there was only about 271 calories in a biscuit. They all agreed that the military rations they had eaten were far superior to the contents packed on the lifeboats. It was edible, but that was about all. They ate in silence.

"Let's get some sleep if you can. We get up around zero one hundred hours and prepare for our attack. I'll take the first watch on the camp, and we'll rotate around. I'll go over the details of our raid when we get up. Bed down team," said James.

They put down the fire, and each person picked a spot to lie down. James moved to the perimeter of the camp, well out of sight in case someone came around. They wouldn't see James on guard. In two hours, James moved, woke up Mickey and traded places with him. After Mickey took a turn, Marie took a turn to guard.

CHAPTER 13

Attack on the Pirate Camp

At zero one hundred hours, Marie woke each team member. As they rose in the moonlight, Stretch put some six-foot stakes in the ground around the campfire area. To them, he tied some flashlights they had taken from the lifeboats, creating a small lighted area. Tom booted up the computer equipment on battery power, so they didn't have to start the generator. They all gathered around the computer monitor and looked at the screen that showed the satellite photos of the island.

James pointed to an area they determined was the barracks where the men slept. "Stretch, you and Shorty set satchel charges at those locations. Next, move to the generator and communications huts, set the timers to go off at the same time as the barracks."

"Mickey will set a charge at the fuel hut. I'll set up over here and cover all of you. The rifles are equipped with silencers, ensuring that no one will be alerted until the explosions occur. We'll wait on the outskirts for the guards to leave the center hut to join the troops at the barracks, then we'll move in and get the hostages. Mickey loves rocket launchers, so as things move along, he'll stay hidden and fire in a few rockets to add to the confusion,"

"Tom, you and Marie drive around the outside of the camp with the Jeep firing into the huts. Just circle the camp twice and head toward the helo and take it out. If we carry out the plan correctly, they'll be taken by surprise, becoming totally disoriented and confused. And most of all, they'll think we are an entire military unit instead of just six people."

"We meet back at our camp and head back to the ship. The rescue ships won't arrive until late tomorrow. I made a call earlier to Aly. She said the military dropped some communication equipment onto the ship, so they now have communications with the outside world. If we destroy all their means of escape, they'll be stranded on this island until the authorities arrive. Questions?"

They all shook their heads. "No. "

"Let's roll!"

They got their equipment, then piled into the Jeep. They rode as far as they could without getting within hearing distance of the pirate camp. Finally, they got off, and Marie, who was driving, shut the Jeep off. She and Tom watched as the team disappeared into the underbrush of the sparse forest.

Just before they got to the camp, they each tested their communication earbuds. Stretch and Shorty quietly set the charges, as did Mickey. James found a position where he had a good view of the entire camp.

"Everyone in position?" called James.

Everyone responded, "Affirmative."

"Okay, wait for my signal," whispered James into the comm unit.

They laid in position waiting for the signal, when one man came out of a hut, followed by two other men, all arguing about something. Stretch had one of the men in his sights and called for permission to fire.

James answered, "No. We wait."

The team waited. They could see the lights on in two of the huts. They were waiting for all lights to go out, to ensure that everyone was asleep, or at least in their bunks. During this time, they kept radio silence.

Mickey laid on his stomach with the rocket launcher ready. As he watched, his mind began to wander. Here he was, lying on the ground, in some God forsaken tropical island, waiting to kill someone. These men had done nothing to him. Sure, they had killed some people on the ship, and who knows how many others on ships they had hijacked? That wasn't his concern. They are trying to rescue someone he didn't know. These people weren't his responsibility. He could just get up and walk away. He didn't have to be here. He could let the others do this. He could call James and…

"Go," came one word over his comm unit. It was James telling the team to attack.

The first charge to explode was the barracks, then the generator and communication huts blew up into flames. Mickey, whose job it was to set off the fuel hut, pressed the button that sent flames into the air. The flaming debris flew into the surrounding huts, setting them on fire. Men set on fire by the explosions came running and screaming out of the barracks. In moments, there was a ring of fire around the camp. The Mongoose team lie in wait, watching the carnage. In an instant, Mickey's thoughts and doubts melted into his subconscious. He acted as they had planned. He did his job. He was now a trained killer doing what he hated.

The men guarding the center hostage hut ran for cover. Marie and Tom took position as Marie fired the Jeep up and drove straight into the camp. Everyone heard the roar of the little Jeep and heard the rat-a-tat of the fifty-caliber machine gun as it circled the inside of the camp. Tom manned the gun, releasing a barrage of bullets lit up with the brightly colored tracer bullets as they zipped around into the camp. James ran toward the hostage hut in a hail of gunfire. As he approached the hut, he threw himself against the door and it shattered as it opened. Three people were huddled in the room's corner. The man they assumed was Leonard, and two pirates.

He called to them, "Move, we gotta get out now!"

They crouched in the corner like deer in headlights. The two pirates put their hand up in surrender.

"I said, Move. Let's get out!" he screamed.

The man who James assumed was Leonard Cochran looked at him, frozen with fear.

He moved over, grabbed the man and shoved him toward the door. "I said, go. Run as fast as you can. Don't stop. Don't slow down. Now, go or die!"

He moved to the door and shoved the man out. He stumbled and fell to the ground, screaming with fear. James pushed the man forward and yelled to him, "Get up and run to the edge of the compound. I'll give you cover fire!"

The man stumbled, but got up and started running. As he ran, the Jeep broke into the circle of huts toward Leonard. When it got close to him, Marie slammed to a stop. Tom jumped up and pulled him into the Jeep. Tom looked up at James, but James waved him on. Marie stepped on the gas and roared toward the other side of the camp. Tom manned the gun and shot his way out. James ran behind them, when suddenly a man step from behind some burning debris and shot at the Jeep just as it cleared the edge of the camp.

When James saw Tom arch his back and slump onto the Jeep, he witnessed the vehicle collide with a tree and come to an abrupt stop. James aimed and shot the man, but he knew he was a second too late to save Tom. He continued to run until he, too, cleared the camp.

Meanwhile, Mickey was firing at anything that moved. After each rocket blasted from the barrel of the launcher, he moved aside to minimize the chances of someone being able to pinpoint his location. He fired until he ran out of rockets. After running out of rockets, he dropped the launcher and laid still until he felt it was safe to move toward the area where he had agreed to meet James. He joined up with James, and they began the walk back to the camp.

Back at the camp, James, Mickey, Stretch and Shorty waited, but the Jeep didn't return. Everyone knew Marie, Tom, and Cochran were probably dead. When they heard the helicopter engine fire up and heard the sound fade away, they knew some pirates had escaped.

The Mongoose team's morale took a nosedive. Stretch and Shorty sat in stunned silence around the camp while Mickey and James conferred just out of hearing distance.

Mickey spoke softly, "James, we need to go back and get their bodies."

"I know. We owe it to everyone. It's our fault that the Cochran's are dead. We caused this. We failed."

Mikey thought for a few seconds. "Wasn't Mrs. Cochran in the hut with her husband?"

"There was Cochran, and two guards."

"Where was she?" asked Mikey.

"I have no clue. I'm sure she was attractive. Maybe they have other plans for her later. You know…"

"Yeah, I know what you mean. What do you suggest we do now?"

"As you said, we go back for the bodies," answered James solemnly.

"You think Stretch and Shorty will go back with you?"

"I'd stake my life on it. Are you in or out?"

"I'm in."

"I gotta know you have my back."

"Always, James. Always!" He followed James back to Stretch and Shorty.

Stretch called out, "Hey, James, we goin' back to get the remains, and gut the rest of those A-holes?"

James stopped and asked, "Was there ever any doubt?"

"Nope," they both answered. "Are you with us, Mickey?" asked Stretch.

"Yeah. I'm with you."

"Okay, guys. Let's ride!" said James.

They grabbed some of the survival biscuits they retrieved from the lifeboats, restocked their ammo, and started the march back to the pirate camp. They headed toward the light of the burning camp. As they got closer, they saw men running around the camp trying to get things out of buildings that the Mongoose team hadn't set on fire. The pirates were retrieving a variety of items from ammunition to extra guns and additional food and supplies. They huddled down and watched for several minutes.

Stretch spoke up first into the comm earbud, "Let's find the Jeep and get the bodies. We'll leave the rest of the pirates for the authorities to pick up."

"I agree," said James as he circled the burned-out huts, avoiding the pirates running in and out of the standing buildings.

Stretch sounded over the comm unit, "Shorty and I'll stay here to cover you."

"Got it," answered Mickey as he filed in behind James. Slowly, they both moved stealthily around the buildings, keeping low in the high grass. When they got to the Jeep, they saw Tom's bloody body lying beside the Jeep, but no sign of Marie or Leonard Cochran.

"What the," Mickey started to say.

"Shhhh," James said. "No bodies. No additional blood. They're alive. They took Leonard Cochran and Marie."

"Why?"

"I don't know why they took Marie, but they might still need proof of life for Cochran."

"What do we do now?"

"Exactly what we came for! We take his body home."

Mickey shook his head. "What would you expect them to do? We shot their men and burned down the camp. I'm surprised they didn't kill Marie, too. I agree with why they didn't kill Cochran."

"Okay, that makes sense. It's the cost of war."

Stretch and Shorty heard them in the earbuds. "Want us to light up the rest of the huts?"

"Yep," said James. "We'll take out the rest of the supplies and try to get a prisoner."

"Why?" asked Stretch.

"Someone took the helicopter and I'm sure it was Fawzan with the hostages. We just don't know where they went. A prisoner might tell us. We'll try to get some communication equipment if they have any left. We can use that to communicate with Fawzan and get a fix on his location. You guys start setting fires to draw their attention."

"Copy that," answered Stretch and Shorty in their earbuds. They started with a cover fire. For the second time, they set the camp on fire, raining destruction and confusing the rest of the pirates.

James and Mickey headed toward some men running around the camp. Mickey moved inside one of the intact buildings while James waited outside in the dark to notify Mickey when someone headed for it. Soon, one of the men started running for the building carrying something and James quietly let Mickey know to watch for the man.

The man opened the door and stepped inside, and Mickey hit him behind in both knees, and he dropped to the floor, releasing the items in his hands. Mickey moved over the top of the man and put a rifle to his head.

"If you make a move, I'll blow your head open! Do you understand me?"

The man crept his hand toward the gun he had dropped onto the floor when he fell.

Mickey pulled the trigger. The report of the rifle was deafening as the bullet whizzed by the man's ear. As the bullet cut the tip of the man's ear, blood spurted out and he screamed in fear.

"Next time, I won't shoot your ear. It will be the middle of your head. Do you understand me now?"

He froze and moved his head in a "Yes" motion.

"Get up slowly and stand with your hands in the air," Mickey ordered.

James called over the earbud. "Hurry, someone's heading your way. If he continues, I'll take him out, but hurry."

"When I say move, you will run out the door and turn to your left, around to the back of this building. If you go any other direction, you will do it without a head. If you slow down, or make any attempt to escape, you will do it without a head. Got it?"

The man nodded.

"Three, two, one…. go!" Mickey called and put the gun again in the man's back and pushed him out the door.

The man ran out and did exactly as he was told. About ten feet outside the door, James stepped from the darkness into the light of the blazing fire around the camp. He grabbed the man and pushed him further into the bush behind the building and into the darkness.

Mickey and James escorted the man back into the woods toward their camp. James alerted Stretch and Shorty they had gotten a prisoner. After almost an hour of trudging, they got back to the camp, tired and worn from the past night's adventure. Rest was impossible for them. Since being up at one a.m. they had destroyed the enemy camp, taken a prisoner, lost two comrades, and the ones they had come to rescue. They had to keep going. There was no stopping now.

"We need to call Aly, get off this island and find that helo," said James. He took out the satellite phone again, and as soon as it booted up, it rang. He immediately knew who it was, and as he pressed the answer button, he said into it, "Hello, Valerie. How are you and your family?"

"We're fine, James. Now let me speak to Mickey."

Again, he took the phone from his ear and looked at it as though it were a foreign object. As he turned around, he saw Mickey reaching out to take it.

Mickey put it to his ear, and said into it, "Hello, Valerie. How are you doing? I don't have time for niceties, so please tell me what you want."

"Good, you are okay. I was worried. Did you take the camp and rescue the hostages?"

"No, we had a few problems."

"I'm sorry to hear about that. Can you tell me about it? Maybe I can help," Valerie AI said to Mickey.

"Tom is dead. They took Marie and Cochran and left the island in the helicopter. We have taken a prisoner. We're hoping we can get him to tell us where they went."

"Hold on, Mickey. Maybe I can tell you where the helicopter is located now," she said, and went silent for about five seconds. When she spoke again, she told Mickey to turn on the computer, and she would download an aerial map of the helo's location.

"How did you do that? Did you schedule another satellite flyover?"

"No. It wasn't anywhere near this side of the globe. It was thousands of miles from here during that time. I monitored all communications and electronic signals from your area. I got communication signals from several communication satellites. As the helicopter powered up, so did the radios and GPS transmitters in that area. I recorded all of them and sorted all the signals and isolated the one that was from the helicopter on the island. I disregarded the helicopters that were servicing the cruise ship and…."

"Hold it, hold it, Val. I don't need to know all the details. Just tell us where it is."

"I will send the helicopter's coordinates to your computer. Would you like me to contact Alyssa and arrange for you to be removed from the island, and take you to the helicopter's new location?"

"Thank you, but no, Val. If you will call her and connect us, we can take it from there."

"Got it, Mickey. Remember, stay safe, my love!" she said, and clicked off. He heard other clicking sounds and a ring tone.

He handed the phone off to James, who shook his head in sarcasm as he took it. "I've never heard of anyone that had a computer in love with them."

"Suck a rock, James!" said Mickey snidely. "Just make the arrangements with Aly when she answers."

James laughed and took the phone as Aly answered it. "James, good to hear from you. How are things going so far? And what can I help you?"

"Things are not going well. We need to get off this island, ASAP."

"Got it. How can I help?"

"Get us airlifted off here to another of the Islands."

"Got it. Where are you now, and where do you want to go?"

"According to the maps Valerie sent to the computer, we're on the west coast of Little Ragged Island, of Bahama on the Bay side. We need to go to Pimlico Cay dead center of the Island. That's where the pirates are now. They had their headquarters in Little Ragged Isle, but we eliminated them, and now they have relocated their base. In the initial raid on their camp, they killed Tom and took Marie hostage, as well as Cochran."

"Tom is gone?"

"Affirmative, Alyssa. We recovered his body. Now, we need to get Marie and Cochran out alive."

"I'll arrange for a helo pickup. It's faster than a boat. Anything else?"

"No. Just get us to the other island, and when we leave, get the authorities out here to clean up. There are a dozen or so pirates here trying to put out the fires of their burned-out camp. Although we have a prisoner, we'll release him. We have no more use for him. We're truly sorry about Glassman. He was a good man."

"Thanks, James. Yes, he was a good man, but that's always a chance when we go on one of these missions."

"Yes, but it doesn't make it any easier. I'm out, Aly," he said and disconnected the call.

When he got back to the others, they were all still sitting on various objects around the camp, with the prisoner in the middle of the team. They remained silent, not exchanging a word. Each had his own thoughts about the past eighteen hours. They were tired but wired, running on adrenaline. Each one wanting to take their frustrations out on the prisoner in front of them. They were professional enough to know that Tom's death was because of a minor battle skirmish. It wasn't personal, so they had to treat it as such. Each one knew that it could have been any of them. It just wasn't their time yet. Someday, they might be the one brought back in a body bag.

James spoke to the three men. "Aly is sending a helo to get us out of here. When we leave, we'll set our prisoner free. To our knowledge, there is no other way out of here, and the men left have no communications. Aly will contact the authorities so they can pick up the pirates. She'll call us as soon as she plans for our pickup."

"We went to all that trouble to get this guy, and we let him walk?" said Stretch.

"Yep."

"That sucks!"

"True, but we can't take him with us, and where can he go? The authorities will get him," answered James as he also picked a place to sit.

In about fifteen minutes, the phone rang again. James pressed the answer key and Aly said to him, "James, the extraction helo will be there soon. Their ETA is seventy-five minutes. Is there enough space to land?"

"Yes, but it is a sandy beach here. We'll wade into the shallow water. That'll be better than the sand."

"Got it, in the water just off the beach. Keep a lookout for the helo. Out." The phone went dead again.

James looked around. He had the phone on speaker, so everyone heard and looked at their watch. As the minutes ticked by the men began scuttling the lifeboats and disabling all equipment and supplies, they were leaving behind. All they kept intact was what they would carry onto the helicopter. Their intent was to trap the remaining pirates on the island until authorities could arrive to arrest them.

Finally, in the distance, they saw a helicopter on the horizon coming toward them. It came closer until it was about one hundred feet from shore. James reached over and cut the bindings loose on the prisoner and told him to leave the camp or they'd shoot him. He looked at James hesitantly.

The pirate didn't know if James was letting him free or would shoot him in the back as he ran away. James again insisted that he run and promised not to shoot him. After a moment of doubt, the man turned and ran into the foliage at the edge of the beach.

The helicopter hovered in the air. Then it slowly descended to get near enough for the men to grab and climb the short ropes into the craft.

Just as a helicopter crewman began dropping the grappling ropes, a whooshing sound came from the underbrush at the edge of the beach. A rocket flew by the men, into the helicopter, exploded, sending flames and shrapnel into the air. The helicopter, reduced to debris, plunged into the water and sank in a cloud of raging fire and steam. The team turned and sprayed a fusillade of bullets as they ran away from the helicopter, back onto the beach, and into the brush for cover. When they had all retreated to shore, they sat listening for the rustling of the bushes to locate the attackers. After an hour of complete silence, the team determined the attackers had left after firing the rocket at the copter.

One at a time, they quietly gathered at the edge of the woods to minimize exposure to pirates waiting back in the bush.

"Where the hell did that come from?" asked Shorty.

"We apparently missed some of their munitions," answered Stretch.

"Ya' think," Shorty commented, angrily.

"I think we're officially screwed," said Mickey.

"Maybe not. I'll call Aly and get her to relay a message to the ship and have someone come out here with the ship lifeboats to get us. We should be able to move out far enough for a night pickup without putting them in danger. We can restock on the ship."

"Sounds good to me," said Stretch.

"Me too," added Shorty. "I could have sworn we got all their weapons. If we leave without destroying all their weapons, the cleanup crew the authorities send may be killed."

"Correct. We can't leave until we have a thorough cleanup of all their weapons. We need to go back. We haven't had a lot of sleep. Are you up to it?" asked James, looking around at his team of exhausted men.

"Right now, I don't think you could stop me!" said Shorty.

"Let's make another run at them. I'll make a few calls, get a schedule and we'll do a bit more damage before we leave," he said, unfolding the antenna on the phone.

He dialed the phone, and pressed the send button, and Aly answered on the first ring. "What in the world happened? The GPS on the helo went dark, and I got a call from the ship that passengers saw the copter go up in flames. This is getting way too costly in life here, James. This whole thing is going sideways."

"Calm down, Aly. Yes, it's bad, but we'll still take care of things. We need to get back to the cruise ship. Can you relay a message back to them?"

"Sure, what do you need now? There is no regular military on the ship, only civilian authorities and some shipowner's officers."

"If they can send a lifeboat out to get us offshore while it's still dark, they'll be in no danger. You can drop ship us more supplies and maybe another helo to transport us to the other island." Instructed James.

"I'll see what I can do. Helos are expensive, and sometimes scarce this far out."

"We're going to attack them once more to make sure every weapon is destroyed to make it safer for the authorities that come here to clean up."

"I understand, but one hundred million dollars is a lot of incentive. We don't know how Fawzan plans on dividing up the ransom, but the more men you take out, that leaves a larger portion for any survivors. That can give them a lot to fight for."

"I know. Just see what you can do to get us back on that cruise ship."

"Copy that. Out." The phone went dead again.

He returned to Mickey, Stretch and Shorty. "Okay, let's get rid of this extra ammo."

They started back to the camp. As they approached, they noticed the remaining pirates working to put out fires and organize their remaining food, supplies, and weapons.

The team continued to concentrate on taking out the pirates' weapons and ammo. It would be more difficult to defend themselves when the authorities came. They saw the pirates were placing weapons in piles at the front of the huts. Two men were assessing the useable weapons, hoping to salvage them. Another man was matching weapons with the corresponding ammunition.

When one pirate picked up a rocket launcher and a box of rockets, Mickey turned to James and pointed at the pirate. James nodded in understanding. That was the weapon that had downed the copter.

The team again strategically positioned themselves for crossfire around the camp, making it difficult to pinpoint where the shots were coming from. Stretch and Shorty shot in turns to confuse the pirates. While Mickey and James made their way to the weapons cache. After each brief volley of shots, Stretch and Shorty would move, and the next man would fire and move. They did this and continued to move in a clockwise position. At one point, when James came around to the side where the weapons were located, he dashed in to where the ammo was positioned, and threw his last hand grenade at the pile. When the grenade exploded, the ammunition went up like fireworks and kept everyone pinned down for almost five minutes. When the rockets ignited, they flew into the air like fireworks, lighting up the sky.

When the ammunition exploded, the team quietly crawled away from the camp to a safe place. They moved back to the beach where their camp was but remained in the underbrush's cover until dark. It was a bright and starry night, but they needed to get back to the ship for rest, food, and supplies before they could continue.

James called Alyssa and told her when they would be ready. If the boat came within a hundred feet of the shore, they would swim out to it for pickup.

They sat in the darkness, in silence, listening for any intruders. They heard nothing. Finally, they heard a lifeboat engine humming toward them. They all got up, assembled at the shore, and began wading out to the boat. As the water got deeper, they swam to it slowly.

When they got close, they softly called out to the boat operator. "We're here. There are four of us and we have a dead team member. Shut down your engine for silence and steady the boat."

Although there was no verbal answer, the engine went quiet. They heard the movement of someone moving inside the boat.

"Do you see us yet?"

"I see and hear slight movement of water."

"We are about fifty feet from you. I'm bringing a body with me. Can you help pull it into the boat?"

"Roger that."

As they moved to the lifeboat, one man in the boat helped them without saying a word. Upon entering the boat, two men assisted the team and provided them with blankets and water for the journey back to the ship. Four of the ship's crew opened the supply door on the side of the ship as they approached, allowing the team to board the ship. They then quickly went to the hospital area and took Tom's body to a freezer.

The medical team surrounded them and checked them out immediately. James and Mickey went back to their cabins. The ship provided Stretch and Shorty, who no longer needed to hide in the engine room, with the most luxurious accommodation available. They hadn't slept for almost thirty-six hours.

The following morning, the team met at the buffet on the Lido deck and stuffed themselves with a protein rich breakfast and gallons of coffee. After James and Mickey Ray had spent a few minutes with the family, they joined Stretch and Shorty. One of the ship's crew members took them to a private room to plan a strategy meeting.

The room, located down from the bridge and on the outer side of the ship, had ports overlooking the sea. On one wall was a bank of drink machines, holding coffee, tea, and soda dispensers. On the other wall, a row of cabinets, suggesting that they held office supplies. A couple of machines, such as copy and printing machines, were present for use if needed.

The officer who took them to the room told them all comms were fixed, including internet and cell service. The ship's crew had put temporary computer and communication equipment in the room for their use.

After sitting down at a round table with their coffee, they asked for maps to be printed out for them. They sat and stared at the map in front of them.

As they sipped at their coffee, a cruise ship server standing discreetly in the corner of the room came over and filled each man's cup. He then retreated to his position and stood almost at attention.

"This has been one cluster f…."

James held up his hand in the universal stop sign. "Watch it! Let's keep it civil here, Shorty, but I agree with you."

"Mickey and I came aboard this ship to have a relaxing vacation, not to go on a mission without proper intel, gear, and planning. So, yes, it's been a mess, but we are the best team in the world to take care of it. The death of one of us always brings demoralization, but we've all witnessed it happening. We take it in and move forward."

"What do we do now?" asked Shorty.

"We know Fawzan has moved to the island of Pimlico Cay. As soon as Aly can get us transportation, and more gear, we'll go there, rescue Marie and the Cochran's. Aly will let us know when we can expect to get what we need."

"Can we get another current satellite view?" asked James as he looked at Mickey.

"I don't know. I can ask Valerie. She'll have to re-task a satellite again," answered Mickey.

"Ask her. We could use that to plan our entrance and extraction zones," James said as he slid the sat phone across the table.

Mickey walked outside to get a clear shot at a communication satellite. He used it instead of the ship's communication equipment because it was more secure. He dialed his home phone number, and it was immediately picked up by Valerie AI.

"Hello, Mickey," she said. "How are you today, my love? How did you know I would answer your home phone, dear?"

"Because I know that you're monitoring all incoming and outgoing calls to my home, and this sat phone. I knew you would answer."

"Oh, my. You are so smart, my love. How may I help you?"

"Can you re-task a satellite for a fly over the Pimlico Cay Island in the Bahamas?"

"Yes, Mickey. When do you want it?"

"As soon as we can get a picture."

"Hold on. Let me see which satellite is available for that task." The sound went dead, and then he heard soft music playing over the phone. "OMG, she put me on hold, and is playing elevator music while I wait," he thought.

Soon the music stopped, and a recorded voice came on. "Thank you for your patience. Your call is important to us. Please stay on the line."

"What the heck?" he said, and the voice stopped, and Valerie came back online. "How did you like my new set up for call waiting, Mickey? It's just like the ones proper businesses use and…"

"Not now, Val. Just tell me when we can get the satellite photos."

"The next available satellite will fly over in forty-eight minutes. Is that acceptable?"

"Yes. That's great. Send the pictures to our address on the ship. We'll be waiting for it. Now connect me with Aly, please."

Again, the line went dead, and the elevator music began playing again. Mickey went to the door and motioned for James and showed him the phone. "Valerie's getting Aly on the line for us."

"Good, I need to talk to her," he said, moving toward the door to take the call outside.

James took the phone as Aly answers, "Hello, James. Are you back on the ship?"

"Yes. Can you get us more supplies? We left everything we had on the island."

"I can get you more supplies, but I'm having trouble with the helo. The owners were not happy when the last one went down."

"That's the cost of doing business."

"Ha, ha. Not funny, James."

"It wasn't meant to be. We need more supplies if we are going to rescue Marie and get Cochran back. Make it happen, Aly. ASAP."

"Okay. Give me a list. I'll see what I can do! Now is the time we use the GPS tracker you have installed."

"You're right. By now, they've moved Marie from the helo location and could have moved well away from that area."

"That's why I suggested it. Hold on while I pull up her location."

James knew exactly what she was talking about. A couple of years ago, each team member had a subdermal GPS implanted, just for cases such as this. He was a bit surprised Aly hadn't activated it before now. He guessed that if they knew where Marie was, they didn't need it.

Aly came back on the line and gave him the coordinates of Marie's location. James rattled off a list of weapons and ammunition, then disconnected the call. He went back into the room and dismissed everyone, telling them to relax and rest until Aly called back. When she had supplies delivered, they would need to be ready to go.

As James and Mickey walked out of the room back into the open air on deck, he said to Mickey, "Aly pulled up Marie's GPS and gave me the exact location where she's being held."

"She what?" asked Mickey Ray.

"Each of us has a subdermal tracker implanted."

"I know what it is. It's injected under the skin. I didn't know that the team had them implanted."

"Yes. Mine's right here." He raised his arm to show Mickey the location where his was implanted.

"I don't have one," Mickey said.

"Aly and I have talked about it. Even though you're one of the team, you're not yet. Do you know what I mean?"

"No."

"You go out with us on things that are connected to you, but not if we go out on other missions."

"Okay, I get it." Mickey changed the subject. "It's a sad world we live in now. People come to enjoy life and crap like this happens. What'll happened to Tom's body?"

"Alyssa will cremate it. We all sign papers that state what'll be done to our bodies and if we have any assets, such as money, properties, or even families. Tom donated his life insurance to a charity since he had no family. Only Aly knows who and what charity he selected."

"I signed nothing like that."

"You have a will, don't you?"

"Yep."

"You're covered, not a problem. Hey, I'm going to take a long hot shower, and shave to be ready for our supply drop," James stated.

"Sounds good. Me too," Mickey said and walked away.

On the island the pirates had moved to, Marie and Leonard Cochran were held prisoners in separate rooms. Two armed men came in, grabbed Marie on each side and dragged her into another room, and sat her in a chair.

She sat silently in total defiance until another man walked into the room. When she looked at him, her eyes widened in surprise. She shook her head in disgust and spat at him.

He took a cigarette out of his pocket and put it in his mouth. With one hand, he reached back into his pocket, took out a lighter and, with the other hand, he drew back and gave Marie a backhand slap across her face.

His slap forced her head sideways, and blood flew across the room from her bloodied lip. She turned back to face him and spat at him again, added, "You son of a b…"

He drew back and slapped her again, interrupting her comment. "You will not speak until I give you permission!"

He slowly and deliberately lit his cigarette, took a long draw on it, and laughed. "You were so gullible, you little slut!"

The man standing before her was the same man that had rescued her at the pool. It was Robert Ryan. He had seemed like a perfect gentleman on the ship. What she still didn't understand was why he didn't sleep with her.

He smiled wryly at her as he puffed on his cigarette. "I'm sure you have many questions. I'll answer some, but you won't escape to share those answers with your unit."

She continued her silent treatment, but he was correct. She had many questions.

"Okay, then. Who am I? I'm sure you wonder. When we first met, I'm Robert Ryan. That's one of my names. I also know that Marie is your real name. I checked. When you took out one of the pirates, I knew you were more than just a problem solver like you described to me. Your skill set is way above the average negotiator, as you said.

"Your next question is, why did I ask you to my room, drug you and not take advantage of that opportunity? Simple, I don't do that sort of thing. Next, I wanted to know who you really are. While you were asleep, I took your picture, fingerprints, and ran some checks on you. You are listed on a team of special ops, called the Mongooses.

"I have access to some seriously bad people. Armed with that information, we knew what we were up against. Unfortunately, we didn't realize that your entire team was already on board. We didn't leave quite as soon as we should. We also know all the members of your team, especially the scar faced one, James Bower. He's quite a legend on the dark web.

"Unfortunately, you'll not be reunited with them. You'll be dead soon. So sad too. You are a beautiful woman. I admit, I now wish I had my way with you, but it is what it is, Marie.

"Have I answered all your questions, my dear?" he asked, losing his smile.

Now, her lip was swollen, and rage reddened her face. She furrowed her brow and asked, "You don't fit here. I don't understand your part in this?"

"Ah! Correct. You're a very observant person. We have two objectives here. The first and the most obvious one, Fawzan wants the ransom for Cochran. The husband is all Fawzan needs to collect the ransom."

"What about Grace Cochran?" Marie asked.

He laughed. "She and I have a special relationship. She is with me now."

"What do you mean?"

"We have been working a, what do you call…. a long con," he said laughingly.

"And?"

"We managed for Grace and Leonard to meet. She pretends to go to various meetings and trips for humanitarian reasons, when in reality, we are on trips together. We have a shell corporation set up for tax-deductible donations to give to poor countries to help the people there. Yes, we help some people, but mostly we help ourselves. It is a wonderful plan. We slowly skim the money for our own salaries, and, of course, travel expenses. To keep up images, we book two separate itineraries, but we spend nights together, if you know what I mean!"

Marie's injuries were painful, but she wanted to know everything in case the team managed to rescue her. "I know what you mean," she slurred. "But if all of that was going so well, why are you hooked up with the pirates?"

He was enjoying telling his story. "Ha! Yes, but this is getting to be a lot of work. Grace and I wish to be together all the time. I'm tired of sharing my time and physical relationships with that dolt husband, Leonard. We are tiring of reporting every dollar he donates to our coffers. We want to be free. After these past few years, we have gotten used to, how would I put it…. a certain standard of living? We still don't have enough money to maintain that standard."

"That would have been solved by a divorce," Marie suggested.

"No, it wouldn't. Grace signed a prenuptial agreement. If she left him, she got nothing. Now, enough talk. Let's proceed with what we need to do with you."

She paused before speaking again. "Since you're going to kill me anyway, how about answering a few more questions? You aren't part of that, are you? And do you really think Cochran is worth one hundred million dollars? Most kidnappers ask for a more reasonable sum, like ten or fifteen million."

"True. That was considered. The father of Leonard Cochran is a billionaire. He can afford a measly one hundred million. We know it will take him several days to get it, and that demand gave us time to accomplish part two of our plan."

"And that is?" she asked through her still bleeding lip.

"Ah! That is, for me, the primary plan. The gift that keeps on giving! Fawzan's part of this was only a diversion from my plan. You see, this is a brand-new ship, in service for less than a year. As with all cruise ships, it has a casino. A new state-of-the-art casino. These new machines are all electronic. The program that runs the ship completely isolates the server and all the casino programs. Each night, the machine's program reports to the central server on the ship.

"The totals send a daily report to the ship's headquarters, and then they automatically deposit the money into a bank. What we, or specifically me, did was install a kind of virus into the casino server on board the ship. As the players put in their money, the machine takes a slight cut from the winnings, but doesn't document it. For example, a player loses one hundred dollars, the machine takes one percent of that amount, then registers the intake. When it pays out, it takes another two percent of the payout. The amounts are so small no one will notice because the machine's program doesn't record either side. At the day's end, the tallies are sent to the cruise headquarters online bank, and the non-registered amounts are sent to the Cayman Islands into my account."

"Very diabolical," said Marie, slightly slurring her words.

"Thank you, but that's not all. There is an additional subroutine in the program that will transmit and update to machines in every ship on the cruise line. In the time period of one week, the new machines will infect all the ships, and as they update, they will transmit the software updates to additional ships as well. As time goes on, I will become richer daily."

"Why did you take me? Why didn't you just kill me in the Jeep?"

"That, my dear, is a bit more complex. First, let me say the man you killed the other day was my partner. He was delivering messages and updates from me to Fawzan. You killed him, and he was an asset to me. You need to be punished for that. I had you kept alive because I need more information from you."

"Like what? Never mind. It doesn't matter. I won't give you anything, so you might as well kill me now, and get it over with."

"We'll see about that. I've never failed yet."

The door opened, and a man came in with a tray full of medical instruments, and pushed them over beside the chair Marie was sitting in. She jumped up, grabbed what looked like a scalpel, and stabbed the man, pushing the cart with it.

As the man looked down at the blood dripping onto the floor, Robert moved in and slammed a fist into Marie's stomach, forcing her back down into the chair. He called out to the men standing beside her to restrain her.

As they restrained her, Robert continued to pummel her face and upper body. He continued until she passed out.

They threw water on her to revive her and Robert began his questioning.

"How did you know we were going to board the ship?" he scowled.

"We didn't know," Marie answered.

"I don't believe you. How did you know? Who told you about us?"

She looked at him and debated whether to answer him. She felt that feeding him some answers wouldn't jeopardize the team. When she didn't answer, he drew back his fist.

"Wait!" she called out, catching her breath. "We didn't know."

"You are a lying slut!" he called as he threw another punch to her abdomen.

"It's the truth," she spewed out blood as she answered.

"How did the Mongooses know about the attack?"

"James called on his satellite phone," she coughed and heaved up blood and drooled onto the floor.

"How did he know to be on board?"

"He didn't. It was a coincidence. He and his family were taking the cruise as a vacation."

"Liar!" he called and slapped her again on the side of her head with his palm.

She passed out and slumped over in the chair. He nodded to the man standing behind her. "Douse her again!"

The man poured another bucket of water on her soaking head. She shook her head and looked up with drooping eyes, now swollen and clotted with blood, from a cut over one eye.

"How did your team come aboard the ship?"

"We were air dropped and boarded late one night through the supply door on the side of the ship," she said, with drool and blood dripping from her mouth.

"You little witch. You could have compromised our mission. We outsmarted you, didn't we?" he said, bending down with his face inches from hers.

"If you don't kill me," she slurred, "I will kill you. It's not over until you're dead."

"You and who's army?" he said with a snide grin. "I'm glad I didn't touch your filthy little body."

He stood back up. "Get her out of here," he told the guard stand behind her.

He marched out and headed for the camp headquarters hut to speak to Fawzan.

When he entered the headquarters hut, Fawzan was talking to one of the pirates. "Fawzan, we gotta talk!" he insisted, interrupting the conversation.

Fawzan waved the man away, and when he left the hut, Fawzan sat down. "What is so important that you must interrupt me at this time?"

"I have some intel that may be important," Robert stated, as he sat across the table from Fawzan.

"What is this important information?"

"The woman we took hostage is part of an elite team called the Mongooses."

"So, why do I care who they are?" he said with his thick mid-eastern accent.

"We care, because they are the deadliest black ops team in the world."

"And?"

"And if they continue to track us, they will not stop until they catch or kill us!"

"This Mongoose team does not scare me. You are a weak man," Fawzan stated.

"I want to get as far away from them as I can."

"We will leave soon. Be patient. As soon as I get my money, I will be gone, and you will have your gambling cuts. We will both be rich men. Now go away. I have things to do."

CHAPTER 14

The Team is Picked up From the Cruise Ship

The team waited for a call from Alyssa for almost four hours, but they also knew that she was the best at what she did. Finally, they got a message from her, and they once again assembled in the ready room provided to them by the cruise ship.

"Look at these photos of the island. The small island has the pirates' camp positioned right in the center. We'll be dropped off at this end, right here," James said, pointing to the map. "We'll march in from our drop zone, move into the camp and see if we can pick out which tent the pirates are holding the hostages. As we go in, take out the guards, and then take Fawzan. At the other end of our drop zone at the edge of the camp is the helo they used to fly in. After we take them, we'll destroy that helo, and the extraction team will pick us up from the opposite end of the camp. Our mission will be complete, and we'll go home. Got it?"

They nodded and in unison said, "Got it."

"We got the sat photos, Valerie ordered hours ago. Aly called, telling us that a new chopper is on its way to pick us up. It'll pick us off the deck. It'll have a full load-out of weapons I requested. Be ready in one hour and be on deck."

James and Mickey went to say goodbye to Darcy, the kids, and Pop and assembled on deck to wait.

The helo arrived and dropped weighted ropes for them to attach to themselves to be hoisted aboard the craft. When the Mongoose team was aboard, it headed for Pimlico Cay Island, and the pirates' camp. As they glided across the ocean in the air, a familiar voice came over the intercom.

"Hello, boys! Great to have you aboard. Just sit back and enjoy the ride. We'll be over the drop zone in about an hour."

Everyone's ears pricked up as they heard Alyssa.

All four of the team let out a whoop and clapped. "Hey, girl!" they called in unison.

She turned around in her seat to look back into the rear area, then slid out of the co-pilot's seat into the back where they were sitting. Her huge grin made them all laugh.

"What're you doing here? We thought you were running another mission and couldn't join us," called Mickey over the engine and rotor noise.

"The other team's on their way home now. It was a complete success. I know that you're having some problems, so I thought I'd come and help you out. Marie is my friend and one of us, so I think I should be here. And besides, you're getting all my equipment destroyed and leaving too much stuff behind. I can't let you play with any of my toys. You tear them up!" she laughed.

They clocked the minutes until the drop zone. Finally, the helicopter arrived and dropped the team, including Alyssa, off on the beach. They immediately headed inland toward the camp.

"Tell me what happened, James," Aly said as they walked toward the camp.

"Not much to tell. When we destroyed the last camp, they shot Tom, and when Marie was trying to avoid getting shot herself, she hit something that disabled the Jeep. I told you that thing was useless," he told her.

"I did the best I could with what I had. I couldn't get you a Humvee. You didn't have to use the Jeep," she countered.

"I know. I shouldn't have used it. You did your best, as always. At least we have some hope of Marie being alive."

When they got to the camp, they saw it was a simple small camp of about half a dozen tents with two solid permanent structures. They guessed one was Fawzan's headquarters, and the other was the holding structure for prisoners and hostages.

They divided up. James, Aly, and Mickey Ray moved just out of sight in the underbrush of what they decided was the main house and headquarter building. Stretch and Shorty took the other one. They lay hidden to watch and see who was entering and exiting each building.

After two hours, with no one entering or leaving either building. James quietly called to Stretch, "Can you see the front door of my building to cover me when I enter it?"

"We'll cover you. No enemies in sight," he answered.

James ran to the building, holding a silenced rifle. He crashed inside. Inside was one large room, with Marie tied to one wall and Leonard Cochran tied to the other.

Both of them had facial bruises, and Leonard had one eye swollen shut, but he still looked up at James. "Who are you?" he croaked.

"I'm here to get you home," James said as he moved over to Marie and cut her bindings. When she dropped to the floor, he moved over to Leonard.

Just then, Stretch's voice came over the communication earbud. "One coming your way. I'll drop him right inside the entrance. You can drag him inside before anyone realizes he's down."

"Copy that," whispered James. As he spoke, the door swung open wide, and the man fell inside, with blood streaming out of his back from Stretch's bullet. James reached over and yanked him out of sight, and continued to cut Leonard's bindings.

As Marie slumped against James, Mickey came through the door, looked around, and moved to Marie to help her. She grunted as he lifted her up. She tried to put her arm around his, but it was too painful. Her arm dropped. She looked up at Mickey and tried to smile.

"I knew you'd come for me, Mickey," she uttered with a slight slur as blood dripped from her mouth.

He gave her a slight hug and added, "You know we never leave a team member behind."

"They knew about us, but I didn't tell them anything important. I promise, I didn't. I love you, Mickey. I prayed it would be you that rescued me." Her eyes closed, and he felt her weight again, as she passed out.

He hoisted her over his shoulder and called to James, "She passed out. Can you cover me as I carry her?"

Stretch, Shorty, and Alyssa cluttered the earbuds with their voices as they called back to Mickey Ray.

"We've all got you covered, Mickey. Go for it. We'll put a wall of bullets all around you as both of you leave the building!"

James nodded to Mickey and motioned for him to go. Mickey called into the earbud comm unit, "Here I come... Geronimo!" He ran as fast as he could, trying to steady himself and not hurt Marie as he ran.

As he crossed out of the building into the woods, he heard the guns blazing with rounds of bullets crisscrossing around him. After he entered the foliage, they stopped, and almost immediately started again as they covered James and Leonard's exit from the building.

Mickey ran well into the undergrowth until he got into a small area where he could stop and put Marie down to check her wounds and take a breather. As she lay on the ground, Mickey heard James right behind him. He was half walking and half steadying Leonard as he attempted to run.

They all sat and breathed heavily while Mickey and James kept their guns raised in case someone had followed them.

James called the team over the comm units, "We're clear. Stretch and Shorty, can you get here?"

"Sure. We have a fix on you. We can be there in two minutes."

"Good. Meet us at the edge of the camp, take Marie and Cochran away. Mickey and I are going to the other building so we can get Fawzan."

"Copy that," came the answer.

Mickey gently stroked Marie's matted and blood tangled hair. She opened her eyes and tried to smile. Mickey looked into her black eyes. He saw relief and sadness.

"You're with the team now, Marie. We'll get you out of here and get medical help."

She raised her arm and put it on Mickey's neck and pulled him down to kiss her. She kissed him gently and passionately, then she lapsed into unconsciousness again.

James watched all of this with rapt attention. "I think Marie has a crush on my brother-in-law."

Mickey looked back at James. "She delirious, James. She doesn't know what she's talking about now."

"Despite her delirium, believe me when I say she knows exactly what she said. She knows, and she meant it."

Stretch and Shorty came into the clearing and motioned for James and Mickey to go, and assured them they'd take good care of Marie and Cochran.

James and Mickey made their way around the camp to the other permanent building. They heard men speaking excitedly, and even though they didn't understand the language, they knew what was happening. The men inside had realized they were being attacked and were getting ready to clear out.

Men moved to the door and windows of the building with guns at the ready. James and Mickey stayed hidden about fifty feet from the building. James took out a pair of binoculars and looked through the window to the inside. He could see three men talking and gathering various items, including a laptop computer. James' vantage point outside no longer allowed him to see the men inside as they moved away.

James and Mickey waited. The men at the windows stayed on point, looking around the perimeter of the encampment. They heard Fawzan and Robert shouting orders to the men in the building.

Some orders were in English and some in a foreign language. One thing they both understood was the order, loud and clear. "Make sure that little Latin slut's dead! She and her team members have caused us too much trouble."

Suddenly, James and Mickey heard an engine winding up. They knew that Fawzan and the other two men had gone out an entrance they didn't see and were taking off in the helicopter.

"Cover our exit," called James over the comm units. "Meet us at the extraction point in half an hour. We're going after the helo. It's warming up for takeoff!"

James and Mickey started running to the place where the helicopter was parked. They heard automatic gunfire in the distance as they left the campsite. As they continued to run, they heard the engine sound change as the load on it slowed the blades as the craft lifted into the air. As they ran toward the rotor sound, the helo ascended into the sky and slowly headed away from the island. They raised their guns and shot fruitlessly at the rising helicopter. It lifted skyward and moved out of gun range.

They went on to the extraction point and joined Stretch, Shorty, Aly, Marie, and Leonard Cochran, and called for the extraction helicopter. As they waited for the helo, they talked.

Leonard's hand looked swollen from the gunshot wound, and his eye was purple and bruised, but as the expression went, he would live. Most of Marie's body was bruised. They had worked her over, and it may take weeks of bedrest, and possibly some counseling for her to get back into shape again. At least she reassured them she wasn't raped, which relieved all of them.

"We're sorry about your wife, Mr. Cochran. We never saw her," apologized Mickey.

"Thanks. They have over half the money they demanded. My father was doling it out bit by bit."

"Yes, we knew that. That was deliberate to give us more time to plan and execute your rescue. We felt that you'd have a better chance of survival if he gave them some of the ransom, then ask again for proof of life, then give him more. It seemed to have worked, somewhat. Why did they separate you and your wife? Do you think they used her? I mean sexually. I've never seen her, but it's my understanding she's an attractive woman," stated James.

"You're more concerned that your father paid out money than you are about your wife," stated Mickey Ray.

"Yeah, well, I know her a lot better than you do," he said, looking down at the dirty bandage on his hand.

They all looked up at the approaching helicopter and waded out into the shallow water.

"Why doesn't it land on the beach?" Leonard asked as they helped him up and pushed him toward the water.

"Because the rotor will stir up the dry sand and could damage the engine. Now go. You'll dry off in minutes," Mickey said, pushing him forward.

Leonard moved into the water and Mickey went back to help Marie. "I'm so glad you're okay, Marie," he said as he helped her walk. She looked up at him and tried to speak through her swollen lips.

Mickey gently placed his hand to her mouth. "Say nothing. Save your strength. I'll take care of you."

She smiled again at him, and he saw a small tear run down her face, as she stumbled and slipped again into a fog like mental state.

The helicopter dropped some lines, and Mickey helped strap Marie to one, then connected himself to be raised to the craft. When they were all onboard, the helo moved away from the island to a secure landing site on one of the other islands. On board the helicopter, Marie passed out again and slumped into his lap. He let her lie on him and rest.

PART III

Back Home in Bridgeton

CHAPTER 15

Several Weeks Later at Mickey's Estate

While Mickey was away on the cruise, his construction crew had completed and furnished the pool-guest house so that he could move in. After Marie received clearance from the local hospital, Mickey took her to his new home and settled her in the spacious single bedroom.

He got up each morning from sleeping on the couch, folded and put away the covers. He made breakfast and coffee, then took it into the bedroom where Marie was still recovering from the abuse she had suffered at the hands of the pirates. He placed the tray on the bedside table, bend over, and kissed her on the cheek. Then he silently stole away from his guest house and went to work to return as soon as possible to take care of her the rest of the day.

At lunch, he gathered the dirty dishes and replaced them with her lunch, and later dinner. In the evening, he made sure she was as comfortable as her injuries allowed. After giving her a gentle goodnight kiss, he closed her door and worked on paperwork at his home desk.

Valerie AI reported everything Marie did during the time he was gone each day, even including her trips to the bathroom.

"I don't need to know her trips to the bathroom, Val. Please don't tell me about that anymore."

"What about the sponge baths that the private duty nurse gives her? Do you wish for me to tell you about them?" asked Valerie.

"NO! I don't want to hear any personal stuff. I want to know only her medical condition."

"Can I describe the bruises on the hidden areas of her body?"

"NO! I don't want to hear about them. Wait, I want to know if they are getting better."

"They are getting better each day. Although, they are still a nasty looking dark blue, purple, with tinges of deep yellow and…"

"That's enough. I saw her medical reports. She has no internal injuries. That's all I care about now."

"I see you kissing her on the cheek in the morning, when you bring her breakfast, and again in the evening when you say good night. Do you love her, Mickey?"

"No. I like her a lot. She's like a sister to me," he said, somewhat irritated at Valerie AI's questions.

"I have never seen you kiss your sister like that, and your blood pressure does not rise. Your heartbeat doesn't quicken when you are around Darcy, as it does around Marie," stated Valerie AI.

"That's enough. I don't want to talk about my feelings for Marie."

"I think you love her more than you love me!"

"I don't love either of you. Now, please go away. Let me work," he said as he turned off the monitor.

"I can still hear you, Mickey Ray!" she said over the speaker.

He reached over and turned off the microphone and speaker on the desk.

After a week, Marie was feeling well enough to come into the living room and lie down on his couch as he worked at the desk across the room. She would sit and watch him work, make calls and other such necessary tasks involved in his real estate holdings.

One morning, when he brought her breakfast, she was awake and sitting up in the bed. She sat silently as he placed the breakfast tray on the bedside table. Mickey moved over to give her a morning kiss. She reached up, pulled him close, and kissed him hard on the lips. The embrace lingered for a few moments before he pulled away.

"My dear, Marie. If we keep this up, your breakfast will be cold."

"Do you really think I care when I'm so hot? I would rather have you than any breakfast right now," she said, almost in a whisper.

"If you mean what I suspect you mean, you know my stand on that. We can't do that," he said, looking deep into her coal-black eyes.

Yes, he wanted her, but his personal ideals and morals just couldn't allow it. He brushed back a strand of her long ebony hair, pecked her on the nose, and stood back up.

"You need to eat," he insisted, looking down at her. The covers were pulled up to her neck, and she pushed them slowly down from her body. "No! Don't do that, please!" he begged as he took her hand from the covers to stop her movement.

"You've been sleeping on your own living room couch since we got back here from the rescue. Don't I excite you?" she purred.

"More than you know, Marie. It's been a monumental effort not to join you in my bed, but I can't do it."

"Why?"

"I have my reasons."

"Tell me, Mickey."

"I believe the Bible, and it says it's wrong."

"You believe in the Bible, but you kill people. The team killed several dozen people in the last few weeks. How do you justify that, and not sleeping with me?"

"That's different," he said.

"How so?"

"We were trying to rescue you and save you from those men. We're like the police. We serve and protect."

"That's stupid. You are not the police. You're a hypocrite, Mickey. Plain and simple."

"I was part of the team that saved you and Leonard Cochran."

"I wouldn't have been on the ship if James hadn't called Aly."

It was true. She was right. He and James had put her in jeopardy with the first phone call. He was partly at fault. She was here now, recovering from her wounds. He felt like crap. He needed to get away for a while.

"That's all, Marie. I'm going to leave now, and let you eat your breakfast. If you feel well enough to get up, I've laid some clothes out over there," he said, pointing to a small table in the bedroom's corner. "If you feel up to it, I'll be outside by the swimming pool."

After changing into a swimsuit, he walked out by the pool, took a skimmer from the shed and began running the pool net over the surface. Marie emerged with the food tray and set it on a nearby poolside table before starting her meal.

She watched him drag the skimmer net from one end to the other. All he was wearing was a bathing suit, and flip-flops. "Oh, how great he looked to her," she thought to herself. When she first met him several years ago, during an interview at his house, she had known she wanted him for her own.

Even though it was early morning, the sun was up and his already sweating skin glistened. Yes, Marie lusted for Mickey. Her only complaint was he had spent every night sleeping on a pullout couch in the living room instead of the bedroom with her.

"Mickey Ray Christianson was a gentleman. A perfect gentleman. Too perfect for a flawed, broken woman like me," she thought.

She knew she was a beautiful woman. She had seen to that. With diet, exercise, and a little plastic surgery, she knew she was a stunner, but Mickey never seemed to notice. So, she just sat, ate her breakfast and watched Mickey Ray clean the pool.

He finished the cleaning, checked the PH of the water, and added some chemicals. When he was done, Marie was finished with breakfast. He came over and sat down across the table from her. "How do you feel today? It's the first time you've been outside of the house since we came home."

"I'm still achy, and sore from the beatings, but other than that, I'm feeling wonderful here with you."

"I see that you still have some signs of bruising on your arms."

"Yes, I do. And I have bruises all over. They did a number on me, Mickey, but thanks to you and the rest of the team, I'll be fine again."

"I was so worried about you, Marie. I was so afraid that they would kill you, or at least…. you know…," he said, hanging his head.

She reached out and touched his arm. "I know what you mean. It's okay, they didn't violate me. I'm surprised too, but they didn't. When I'm back fully healed, I'll find that man and gut him like a fish."

Mickey rolled his eyes.

"Don't mock me, Mickey. You know my feelings about people laying hands on me! There will be a price to pay. His price will be his life. And if I can, it'll be slow, and more painful than what he and his men did to me."

"Would you like to take a tour of the grounds?" changing the subject as he stood up.

"Yes, I would," she said, getting up and taking the tray from the table.

They went back inside the guest house, and Mickey changed from his swim trunks into more appropriate clothes. He showed her around the grounds, from the warehouse barn to the main house. As they walked, Mickey described what the estate would look like. She hung onto his arm, and his every word. When he wasn't pointing and waving his arms as he described everything, she intertwined her fingers into his. She clung longingly to him as they walked.

"Wow, Mickey, how many bedrooms will the main house have when it's complete?" she asked.

"It'll have five bedrooms."

"And you plan on living here alone?"

"I'll continue to live in the guest house until I get married. I don't need a big house like this all by myself."

"Married? I never thought of you as a marrying type," she said as she leaned against him, smelling the sweet scent of his fresh cologne. She quietly breathed in his scent.

"Sure I am. I just need to find the right person. And we'll have kids to fill every bedroom."

"Big plans," she said. As they entered the main bedroom, Mickey shared a vision of them waking up with their kids bouncing on the bed. The entire family going down to the kitchen while she and Mickey made eggs and pancakes for their wonderful children.

He jarred her back to reality as he walked into a smaller room to the side of the bedroom and said, "here is our private inner sanctum. We will have a steam shower over here, and a hot tub over there, where my wife and I will spend special time. Together, we'll relax and soak away the troubles of the day."

She squeezed his arm, and a tear trickled down her cheek as she envisioned that her place was not with him in his dreams. This was just his dream, and she wasn't a character in it. She was a soldier, just a friend on the Mongoose team. She wiped away her tears.

"Are you okay? Did I say something to upset you? How're you feeling? Maybe it's too early for you to be up and about. Let's go back to the house, Marie," he said as he again took her arm and led her back outside and back to the guest house.

"I'm okay, Mickey. I'm a little sad. You're right. Maybe I should rest a little more."

"Now that you're up and about, I have some urgent business that I need to take care of. I'll be back later, and we can go out for a while. Is it okay that I leave you alone for a couple of hours?"

"Oh, yes. I can take care of myself. You don't need to be here with me twenty-four seven. I'll survive. You haven't left my side for weeks. I'll be here when you get back."

"Okay. I just wanted to make sure."

Mickey left and went to the office of Doctor Lawrence Kingston. Earlier this morning, Marie had cornered him with his hypocrisy. The Bible says killing is wrong, but he does it and justifies it. Where is the line? He thought he knew, but he didn't. He killed but wouldn't sleep with a woman. How crazy is that?

The Mongoose team, like other teams, did not receive official sanctions. They, in the eyes of the law, were killers, and if what they did came to light, they could and would be arrested and prosecuted to the fullest extent of the law.

"Good morning, Dr. Kingston." Mickey put out his hand to shake the doctor's hand, and sat in the same over-stuffed chair. It was very comfortable, and he surmised it was a deliberate choice to help the patients feel less stressed and prepare them for the sessions. The doctor usually offered him a bottle of water, and today, he grabbed it and took a long pull of it like he hadn't had a sip of liquid for days.

The doctor noticed this and looked at Mickey Ray with genuine concern. "How have you been since we saw each other last?" Kingston asked as he sat across from him.

"I still have the nightmares, Doc, and I have good days and bad ones. I just got back from a mission that I killed men, but I refuse to sleep with a wonderful woman that loves me. She called me a hypocrite."

"We all have good and bad days, Mickey. Do you think you're a hypocrite?"

"Yes."

"Why?"

"I just told you. I kill people but refuse to take a lover. One ending a life or lives, the other brings peace and contentment to the participants."

"Peace and contentment? That's being pretty clinical about it, don't you think?"

"The Bible says it's wrong if you aren't married."

"Okay. Let's move on. You feel that you're okay killing people."

"NO. That's what's wrong with me. I don't like it, but I feel it's necessary."

"It isn't wrong if you're protecting people, Mickey."

"I know, but I feel so dirty, and sometimes I feel that I no longer have control over my life."

"Why do you feel you have no control? You control millions of dollars of real estate. People depend on you for jobs. Others depend on you for housing. You're a captain of real estate development in Bridgeton."

"Yeah, captain of real estate development by day, killer by night."

"Yes. Sometimes you kill people, but are you murdering them or protecting others?" asked Doctor Kingston.

"I only want to help, but sometimes it all seems futile."

"In what way?"

"No matter what I do, people will be evil, and I can't stop them," he said, with his head bowed in shame.

"If you believe that, why don't you walk away? You said you were going to quit. Did you tell James about quitting?"

"Yes. I told him."

"No one is forcing you to be part of the team. When you were on the cruise ship a few weeks ago, you joined in the fight. You could have just complied, like the other passengers on the ship."

"How did you know about that? I didn't tell you?"

"Mickey, I know you can't tell me about your missions, but I see the news. They reported pirates had taken over the ship, and that a group of vigilante soldiers attacked the pirates. I know you were on that ship. I put two and two together. You were there with your family, and that included James Bower."

"I never told you I had taken part in the fight on the ship, Doc!"

"You didn't have to tell me. I know the kind of person you and your brother-in-law are. You help people."

"Let's suppose you're right. I could have walked away, but I didn't. Doesn't that make me as bad as they are?"

"Not necessarily. You helped the people on the ship, didn't you?"

"Maybe I did, maybe I didn't."

"You need to work on that yourself. I can't make that judgement on you. You need to decide who is evil in that situation."

He closed his eyes and tilted his head upward. "Sometimes I just hate myself for what I've become."

"You keep saying that. The past can't be changed. It's up to you what your future will be, Mickey. You need to make up your mind. Then learn to accept yourself for making that decision. I think our time here is up. We can continue this subject on your next visit. In the meantime, maybe you should consider your thoughts about your sexual morality. It's a great stress reliever."

Mickey sat, eyes closed, and breathing deeply in total silence and completely immobile. The doctor sat in silence, letting him assess and evaluate his thoughts. Finally, he opened his eyes, still looking up.

He quietly said, "May God have mercy on my soul." He got up, and without another word, walked out of the office.

CHAPTER 16

Meeting with James at Mickey's Office

James entered Mickey's office at the Christianson headquarters building. As he took a seat in front of Mickey's huge wooden desk, he asked, "How's Marie doing?"

"She's doing okay. She's still a bit sore, but mentally she's tough. I feel so bad for her. We haven't talked about it, but do you remember that guy that hit on her on the ship?"

"Yes. She seemed pretty taken with him. He was a cop or something, wasn't he?" said James.

"Yes, but he was the one that had her beaten so badly. He told her it was payment for killing one of his men. He wasn't one of the pirates, but they were in league with each other. Ryan was the undercover and inside man. He told her he was a detective from Virginia Beach. I've made some calls and the police department has never heard of him."

"That's kind of what I was thinking. I'm not exactly sure, but I think she spent the night with him in his cabin."

"Wow. I never thought about her being a person to do something like that."

"It's a pretty liberal world out there, and it's a common thing now. We can't hold it against her," Mickey added.

"I know how the world is now, and I don't hold it against anyone for that. I guess you're right."

Mickey leaned back in his chair and took a big breath. "She finally felt well enough to tell me what happened during the time the pirates had her. That guy she met wasn't all chocolates and flowers."

"Yeah, he's a sadistic man that beats women," James interrupts Mickey Ray.

Mickey held his hand to silence James. "Here's the complete story of why he was on the ship." He continued to tell James the entire story of how the ransom was a diversion to the actual mission of infecting the casino machines.

"Wow. That is an amazing story. Why did he tell her?"

"First, we can assume that he has a colossal ego to put together a diabolical scheme like that. Who doesn't want to brag about that? A huge secret like that would be difficult to keep. But he told her and planned to kill her, so she couldn't tell anyone else."

"But we rescued her before they killed her! So, we foiled that plan. Did you notify the cruise line of what was done?" inquired James.

"Yes, but they didn't believe me. They insisted that their security was too tight to allow something like that to happen, especially to their entire fleet."

"What're you going to do about it?"

"Nothing. I told the cruise line. If they choose not to believe me, I don't really care. What I do care about is Marie. She's tough. She's one of us."

"Yep. If she wants to find him, I'm all for helping her. Do you have anything on him or a lead, perhaps?"

Mickey paused, then answered him. "I'll be looking into that. I've contacted the cruise line to see if I can get the information he filed when he signed up for the cruise. That should give us something to go on. Maybe we can force him to give us a link to Fawzan, or exclude him as one of two criminals to execute two jobs at once."

"I got a call from Higgins. He said that there was a lot of fallout on this mission," James informed Mickey.

"I bet. What did he say about the mission?"

"Everything. He understood that crap happens, but what he really blew up about was re-tasking the satellite. I tried to deny it, but he knew we somehow did it. We managed to get out of it because this was an off-book mission, so there was no way to hold us accountable. You need to talk to Valerie about that."

"Okay, but as you know, I don't always have control of her. She does what she wants to do."

"I know, but you need to get a better grip on her. Maybe if you're more authoritative with her."

"Yeah, right! You know that's gonna happen! She sees through me like a window, and can sense the slightest mood change. She even listens to my breathing patterns when I'm asleep and is aware of what level of sleep I'm in at any time."

"Can she really do that? I mean, interpret your breathing?"

"Yes. It's almost creepy, but I've gotten used to it now."

"Can't you turn off the microphones in the house?" asked James.

"I tried that, but she turned them back on. I tried to unplug the one in the bedroom from the system, but she boosted up the sensitivity on the ones in the other rooms. Then she took the sounds and assembled them together and she can still hear me. All in all, I've gotten used to it. It doesn't bother me anymore, and if I ask her nicely not to listen to me, she respects my request and leaves me alone."

"I don't think I'd like it. Anyway, back to Marie. What can we do to find that guy?"

"His name is Robert Ryan. I've asked Valerie to look up all the Robert Ryans in the world. She'll get back to me as soon as she gets a complete list. What else did Higgins have to say about the mission?"

James pulled out a list from his pocket. He gave condolences to Tom's death and said that the government will pay for the funeral. It isn't much, but it's something. The government will replace all lost equipment. Besides, when it comes to collections for our services, Aly does that. The last one is the most interesting one."

"And what's that?" Mickey asked.

"He said that Cochran's old man wants us to find Fawzan and get his sixty million dollars back," James said matter-of-factly.

"I thought it was one hundred million dollars," said Mickey.

"It was, but they only sent him sixty before we rescued Leonard."

"Okay, I see, but we don't do that, do we? Should we risk our lives to retrieve some rich guy's money?"

"Not normally, but we can make exceptions. We can also play the game of two missions running concurrently."

"I don't want to do it, James. It doesn't feel right. I'm in it to help people. I don't need the money!"

"It's a twenty percent fee, plus expenses," James added.

"I don't care. I don't want to do it."

"Of course you don't. You're already rich!"

"Hey, that isn't fair. I've worked most of my life, and you know it!"

"I know, but you received the position when your father retired, whereas I have nothing."

"That's a load of crap. Besides, now that you and Dee are married, you own half of what she has!"

"You know what I mean. Yeah, but I didn't earn it. I married into it," said James sadly.

"This is the stupidest conversation we've ever had. You almost gave your life for our country which resulted in your injuries. You saved my life and the lives of my family. Okay, you married my sister, but she asked you! You're now part of our family, so deal with it! Now if you insist, we go find that rich A-holes money, I'll help you, but I won't take any of the money. I'll help you like my brother. No other reason is necessary. Got it?"

"Yes."

"Good. I don't want to hear this argument again. I mean NEVER. Now, if you want my help, then find out exactly what we need to do, and as usual, I'll have your back. Now, if you don't mind, I have a meeting to attend, if we're going ahead with this land acquisition."

"Got it. What are you working on now?" James asked, glad to change the subject.

"This afternoon, we'll be organizing an event to help disfigured children like Angela. It's kind of like the Special Olympics. We can use it to raise money to help them with necessary medical operations and counseling when they need to accept themselves. I think it'll be a great thing for all kids."

"I guess I'll leave you to your business," James said as he got up and left Mickey's office.

Mickey picked up his phone and dialed Lisa. Lisa and Angela lived in Hampton, about an hour from Bridgeton. And she and Mickey had been working on this event together.

Lisa answered her phone, "Hi there, Mickey. I was just about to call you. Do you have any thoughts on where we can have this event, as you call it?"

Mickey leaned back in his chair. "No. Not yet. But that isn't why I called. Something has come up and I think maybe you can help us."

"Help you? Look Mickey, we've talked about this, and I finally accepted that you don't want my help with any of your covert operation business. It's taken me several weeks to get over your rejection on the ship when you were after Fawzan. Let's not dredge up that again…"

"Hold on, Lisa. We've discussed this. We did it to give you plausible deniability, and to protect our families. Now listen to me for a minute."

He heard her let out a deep sigh. "Okay. I'll give you one minute, then we put it back in the drawer and do not talk about it again."

"James just left my office. He says that Cochran wants us to recover his money, and he's willing to give us a recovery fee. The CIA wants this guy too, right?"

"Yes."

"If you want to help us recover this money, we will take Fawzan and give him to you after we get our fee. You get the credit. How's that sound?"

"I need to run it by my superiors. But we have no jurisdiction inside the United States."

"You can't give them our names."

"I don't know if I can do that," she said thoughtfully.

"Those are my conditions. Take it or leave it."

"If we don't take it, and you get him, who gets credit?" she asked.

"I can tell you this, our team doesn't get it. In this case, we aren't even sanctioned by our own government. This is a private mission."

"How does that work?"

"Our client pays on delivery of what he wants, which is his money. We collect our fee. Mission accomplished. We'll take Fawzan into custody and turn him over to our agency. They will accept him with no questions ask. End of mission."

"What will happen if I help?"

"We will turn him over to you, or the CIA. Your choice. What you do with him is no concern of ours."

"What happens if it goes sideways, and you don't get the money?"

"Then we're out of a lot of money in expenses. We all walk away. I can say, this team has never failed on a mission."

"It's my understanding you lost a team member on that last mission."

"Yes, but we rescued Leonard Cochran."

"Not his wife!"

"She disappeared. We don't know what happened to her, so technically, we still did our job. Are you in or out?"

"I don't know, Mickey. If I say 'no', how will it affect our personal relationship?"

"Nothing will change on a personal level. We have our job, and you have yours. You think about it. If you want to be a part of this, you may need to be ready at a moment's notice. Sorry, gotta get to a meeting," he said into the phone.

"Okay. I'll let you know. Bye," she said abruptly and disconnected.

James had a job to do. He was going to find Cochran's money and try to get the ransom money back. He'd go to the diner. It was his thinking place. He'd go there, have a cup of coffee, and think.

He went to the old standby in Bridgeton, The Diner. It was almost a landmark in the town. A local hangout where he and Mickey spent countless hours talking, laughing, planning events, and even strategizing missions. The real human Valerie, Mickey's human Fiancée had worked there when she lived in Bridgeton. It had a decor of nineteen sixties accessories, with chrome and green Formica countertop tables that carried an allure of bygone times. It was old and comfortable. James had many wonderful memories of this place. He could sit in the open and speak to the people as they came in, or he could hide with his private thoughts.

When Pauline saw him come in and sit in a corner seat alone, she knew he wanted privacy today. She didn't need an order pad, and he didn't need a menu. "Coffee, and what else can I get for you, James?"

He looked up at her for a few seconds, as though he didn't recognize her. Finally, he said, "Just a regular burger and fries, please."

"Coming up," she answered as she turned and walked away. She knew he would be deep in thought today. Even though she didn't know all about his past, most people in Bridgeton knew James was a town hero. They knew he had not just physical scars but deep emotional scars also from his time in the military. Pauline knew that what happened to him had been deeply etched into his psyche. She would serve him silently today. As she placed his order, she gave him extra fries. He was going to need it and she knew that, too. If he stayed long enough in his thoughts, she would automatically switch from coffee to a soft drink as the day wore on. James ate and drank mindlessly when he was deep in thought.

He sat and stared out the window. Occasionally, a car would go by the front of the tiny restaurant, but he didn't notice. He looked beyond everything. Something wasn't right, but he couldn't see it. He dug into every detail of the pirate's actions on the ship. Things just didn't add up. What was it? It was weeks since they got back home, and Higgins had called him three times.

Leonard Cochran was rescued, but even then, Grace wasn't in the building where he was imprisoned. Had they taken her for their own pleasure, and discarded her lifeless body in some godforsaken place after they finished with her? They didn't abuse Marie at first. Why didn't they just kill her? It wasn't just a conundrum, it made little sense.

As he sat and stared out the window, his cellphone rang. He looked at the caller ID as he picked it up and answered it. It was Mickey Ray. He hoped he had some information on Robert Ryan.

"Hello, Mickey. How did your meeting go?" he asked.

"It didn't go well. The sellers are sandbagging us. They're wildly inflating the price of their land. We may go somewhere else. We'll tell them we don't want it. I've done some research on their business. They desperately need the cash, so we'll stick to our guns because we've offered them a fair price for it. Now, where are you?"

"I'm at the diner. I've been here most of the day. Have you found out anything about Ryan?"

"Yes. He's in Virginia Beach as we speak."

"Do you know how long he'll be there?"

"Nope. We don't know, but we need to act fast before he disappears."

"How'd you find him?"

"I didn't. Valerie found him. Marie said he claimed he was on the Virginia Beach police force, so that's where Val started her search. It took her a while because even though we've been looking for him for weeks, he just flew back to Virginia Beach this morning. According to Valerie, he's been all around the world. The last place was in New York City before coming home to the beach. We could have chased him, but I thought it would be best if we let Marie get better first. Now, if she's up to it, we can let her come along."

"I don't know if that's a good idea, Mickey. She won't be satisfied with him getting taken in. She'll want to take her pound of flesh. You know how she can be."

"We can talk to her. When we talk to her, maybe she'll listen and just be satisfied with justice under the law."

"I wouldn't count on it, Mickey."

"We'll try. You coming with me?"

"You bet. Meet you at your place, in an hour," he said. He ended the call, dropped enough cash on the counter to cover the food, and a nice gratuity for Pauline, and left.

Mickey hung up and dialed Lisa. When she answered, he said into the phone, "Hey, we've found Ryan. Do you want to come along when we pick him up?"

"He isn't any concern of the CIA. We want Fawzan."

"Ryan was part of the entire scheme. He was one of the pirates."

"Indirectly, that's true, but I doubt the Agency will support the expense of picking him up. He was directly involved with the pirates as an underlying casino payout skimming scheme. That isn't in our realm of action. The ship was not an American ship, and it also took place in international waters. Basically, it is not the responsibility of this government."

"That may be true, Lisa, but it means something to our team. They kidnapped Marie, so we owe it to her as one of us to bring him in."

"I understand, but it's out of our jurisdiction. I can't help you."

"Suit yourself."

CHAPTER 17

A day at Virginia Beach

James and Marie sat in the combination living room dining area of the pool house that Marie and Mickey had lived in since they got back from the cruise. As they sat and made small talk, there was a knock on the door. When Mickey got up and answered it, Alyssa made a grand entrance.

"Hello, everyone!" she called out as she waved her hands. She glided over to Marie and gave her a big hug.

"Hey, girl. All things considered you are looking great."

"Thanks. Mickey's been taking great care of me."

"I heard. He calls me every couple of days and gives me a progress report. Stretch and Shorty send their regards. They would be here, but they're on assignment helping another team."

"Got it, Aly," Marie gave her a wink.

"Seriously, we were all worried about you. We knew your body would heal. We were worried about you emotionally. Mickey said you're recovering mind and body."

"Yeah. I'll be good as new soon," she said, easing back down in her chair.

Aly took a seat also as they all sat in a circle, and Mickey poured each one a glass of his best wine.

He held up his glass and announced a toast. "Here's to getting justice for our team member, Marie Sanchez."

He walked around and clinked his glass with each person, and they replied, "Here, here!"

"Thanks guys. I love all of you!" Marie replied.

"Okay, Mickey," said James, "what's the plan?"

"Valerie said Ryan's staying at The Pirates Escape Hotel, in Virginia Beach, and his name isn't Robert Ryan. It's Arham Jaziri. He was born here in the States and has no living family ties anymore."

James asked, "Why did he come back here?"

"Most likely, because this is where Ryan lives, and he doesn't know that Marie is still alive. He has no reason to go anywhere else. He lives off the grid. He has no credit cards or financial ties directly to his name."

"But he put the virus program in the machines on the ships."

"True, but no one knows that but Marie, and probably Fawzan. Fawzan won't tell because he has sixty million dollars. On their side, everyone's happy. Since Fawzan has lost most of his army because we took them out on the island, he doesn't have to share it."

"What do you mean? He doesn't know I'm still alive?" asked Marie cautiously.

"We can assume that he thinks you're dead, Marie, so that shouldn't restrict him," Mickey said. "We heard him give the order to kill you as he was leaving."

She gritted her teeth as she seethed with hatred at the man who had beaten her and ordered her execution.

Mickey continued, "You told me he had gotten a facial recognition and fingerprint identification of you. So, I asked Valerie to do the same to him. That's how we found him. He knows about you and the Mongoose team. Maybe he's afraid that we'll come after him for killing you."

She cocked her head and looked at him. "And..."

"And he's right! We'd go to the ends of the earth to get justice if he had killed you," interjected James.

"But he didn't kill me, and now I want justice for myself."

James spoke up, "What about Fawzan?"

"That's out of my wheelhouse. I don't know about international terrorists or pirates. This guy, Ryan or Arham, is right here in our backyard. We can get him and turn him over to the..."

"You mean, let me gut him!" Marie seethed.

"No. I mean what I said. We'll turn him over to the police."

"Not if I get to him first, Mickey!" said Marie, baring her teeth like a hungry lion.

James and Mickey exchanged glances with a look of dread.

"Maybe you should sit this one out," suggested Mickey.

"Try to stop me!"

Mickey took a deep breath and continued, "Moving on. Valerie has checked out his place. He has control of about half of the entire top floor of the hotel. It is an easy way to have a place, and it blends in with other guests. Every few days, the guests change, so no one is around to get to know him."

"And how did Valerie find him?" queried Marie.

"As you know, Val has basically hacked, connected, and networked with all the major computers in the world. Things like the CIA, FBI, MI6, and even the Israeli Mossad. Val doesn't have that computing power, so she subs out jobs to others, like finding someone and tracking them and monitoring their movements.

"The other computers report their findings back to her. She just compiles the information they give to her. She doesn't do all the work herself. Since she runs in the background, even their technical departments can't find her. She's invisible to them."

"If she can do all this, why doesn't the government do the same thing?" asked James.

"Because our government and law enforcement agencies don't get along. They don't share information because they don't want to share credit. It happens all the time. If a local police department has a case, the FBI can come in and take control of the case, and they don't share information with the locals. So that continues up the line. If we don't get along with ourselves, what makes you think we'll share anything with other countries?"

James and Marie looked at each other and shook their heads. They knew Mickey was right.

"If we call the local police, they'd put stakeouts for months and nothing would happen. If we call the FBI, then the same thing would happen. We have to take action, and we wrap it up for the authorities. Let them sort out who takes credit."

"I don't want credit. I want his head on a silver platter," said Marie callously.

"We can't guarantee that, but we will get justice for you," Mickey assured her.

He turned to Alyssa. "I've made one of our work vans available and outfitted for you with computers. You'll be able to connect to the hotel wi-fi so you can be our eye in the sky. You won't have drones overhead, but Valerie will tap into the city and other business cameras for you. We have some weapons, but no explosives. It's a busy area, right on the beach, and we don't want any collateral or civilian casualties. If we do, we'll have the local law after us, and rightfully so. Valerie has gotten access to Ryan's computers in his suite at the hotel. There are no cameras inside his living space, but the hotel itself has extensive camera surveillance coverage. You can direct from the van."

Alyssa nodded in understanding. Marie gave Mickey a hard look.

"Yes, Marie. You will be with us, but in the background. If he recognizes you, you'll become his primary target. You can help us with the takedown."

"If I get him in my sights, I'll shoot off his private parts, stand over his body, and laugh while he bleeds out from his crotch."

"No! You will NOT, Marie."

"You and whose army will stop me, Mickey Ray Christianson!" she screamed.

"You're not going Marie! You're grounded!"

"Grounded! Grounded? Who do you think you are, my daddy? You aren't even a real member of this team. You've never been beaten almost to death, like several of us on this team. You're a soft civilian. I'm going, and you can't stop me!" she yelled and jumped up from her chair.

James and Aly each leapt from their seats, preparing to restrain Marie.

Mickey looked down at the floor, refusing eye contact with her. "Marie, I love you. To know what happened to you on that island, and even as far back as Oregon, hurts me more than you can ever realize."

"That's BS Mickey, and you know it. You can never know what this team has been through, and especially me. You have no idea," she called out to him. "Look at me, Mickey. Look me in the eye and tell me you really know."

Slowly, he raised his head, but still didn't make eye contact. "I didn't say I know what you went through. I said it hurts me to know that a person I love as much as I love you were subjected to such atrocities. That hurts me beyond expression. I only want to protect you from it ever happening again."

With those words from Mickey, the room fell silent. James and Alyssa looked at each other again in complete understanding. They both knew that Marie had feelings for Mickey, but he had never expressed any affection for Marie beyond a strong friendship and loyalty to her as a member of the team. Even with those words, they weren't fully sure of the depth of his statement, or in what way he meant them.

As they sat in silence, there came a knock on the door. Mickey answered it and in strolled Lisa and Darcy.

"I thought you weren't having anything to do with this operation?" he asked after Lisa went around the room, greeting everyone.

Darcy went over to the coffeepot and poured herself a cup. She stood silently away from the team as they talked shop.

"I changed my mind. I want in, if you'll still have me," Lisa said.

Mickey looked around the room and everyone nodded in agreement.

"Good, you're in," he added. "Sorry, but I was about to leave and run a couple of errands."

Mickey left the room. The rest of them sat back down in continued silence. Marie downed her wine in one huge gulp. She then got up and went to the fridge on the opposite side of the counter that separated the living room from the kitchen area.

"I'm hungry," she stated. "Can I get anyone anything while Mickey decides about what we're going to do?"

"Nope," they said.

As Marie turned and looked at Darcy standing next to the coffeepot, she nodded toward the bedroom, motioning for Darcy to follow her. They walked in and Marie quietly shut the door. Mickey left the pool house and the team. The team, along with Lisa, was discussing plans to apprehend Robert Ryan, while Mickey was heading to the garage, and Marie and Darcy were in the bedroom talking.

Darcy looked questioningly at Marie. "You have something on your mind, Marie?" she asked.

"Yes, Dee, I do. I want to know what Mickey has against me."

Darcy looked at Marie questioningly. "What do you mean?"

"I mean, I know I'm no angel. Heck, I'm not even a virgin, but Mickey flat refuses to touch me. I want to know why?"

Darcy put up her hands in defense. "I don't get into my brother's sex life."

"He says he loves me. I know on a certain level we have a partner kind of relationship."

"Maybe you're right. He thinks of you as a sister, Marie. Did you ever think of that?"

"Yes, and no."

"And?" Darcy said with her hands spread out before her, palms up.

"He doesn't kiss like he would kiss you!"

"I really don't want to get into this with you, Marie."

"Well, I do. Please!" Marie pleaded.

Darcy looked around the room. Besides the queen-sized bed, there was a large double dresser, a desk arrangement similar to those in hotel rooms, and a lounge chair, with a small table.

Darcy sat down in the desk chair and swiveled around to face the lounge chair. She motioned for Marie to sit.

She took a deep breath and started with the story of Mickey's wife. "You're familiar with Mickey and Valerie. I mean the real-life Valerie, not his Artificial Intelligence one."

Marie nodded.

"There was a girl before Valerie Green. She and Mickey dated on and off while they were in school. She would break up with him for some stupid reason, and there was Valerie Green to comfort him."

"What was his wife's name?"

"Carolyn. They dated, and after graduating from high school, they were married. She was always demanding and controlling. He loved her with all his heart. No matter what she did, he forgave her. They moved away to just outside of Washington, DC and he got a job. After a few months, she left him, moved back here, and she got a job. He quit his job in DC and followed her back here. When he moved back here, it took a few months, but he convinced her to come back to him. A few months later, she started having an affair with her boss. Without his knowledge, she went to a doctor, and got a prescription for birth control pills. She rented an apartment. When she had gotten everything ready to leave, she told him she wanted a trial separation. She still didn't tell him she was leaving him for another man. He thought that she just needed some space, and that eventually she would come back to him like she did the first time.

"Mickey called her regularly, and they even had a few dates. She never told him she was dating her boss. He didn't pressure her to come home because he thought she needed to realize that she still loved him. Mickey's slow and patient approach to their separation backfired on him. Instead of her realizing she loved him, it gave her the opportunity to cement her feelings for her employer, and she eventually filed for a divorce. They met all legal requirements for a no-fault divorce. His lawyer advised him he would lose if he tried to contest it. The court granted the divorce, and Mickey moved on. Kind of."

"Okay, I understand that, but it doesn't explain why he's rejecting me," stated Marie.

"Mickey isn't rejecting you. He is, as you know, extremely moral and loyal. He still has a deep-seated love for his ex-wife. That's why it took so long for him to admit he loved Valerie. If she hadn't pushed so hard for him to admit his love for her, he may have never proposed to her. Look at his side of it. His first wife walked out on him for another man. Valerie left him because of the trauma she suffered at the hands of human traffickers. His next girlfriend tried to kill him. By that time, he was getting wary of getting involved with any woman. Remember Veronica? I don't know for sure, but I assume he didn't sleep with her. After that fiasco, he sent Veronica back home. I'm not a psychologist, but I would venture an opinion that Mickey has seen everyone he has gotten involved with die or just leave him. He's trying to protect not only the woman he might love but also protect his own heart. He feels deeply about people. If and when he falls in love, it will be a meaningful relationship. He's not the kind of guy that would go for a one-night stand, or just a physical relationship. To him, sex is love. It helps both parties to have a closer relationship. A tighter bond, if you will."

"That sounds like BS to me. That's a stupid reason to not move on. What happened to Carolyn?"

"As far as we know, she's still married to the same guy."

"For real? She ditches him, marries another guy and Mickey still hasn't gotten over her?"

"He has definitely gotten over her, but he has issues with it."

"I would say he does! Did he and the real Valerie ever sleep together?"

"Not to my knowledge," answered Darcy.

"I think that's old and antiquated. No man is that moral, if he's straight."

"I promise you, Mickey is straight, and yes, he is that moral."

"I think that because of my background and my sordid past, he may think of me as a damaged woman not worthy of his love. Someone that he doesn't want to get involved with."

"I seriously doubt that. If he loves you romantically, he won't hold your past against you. It will be an unconditional love. I know he loves you, Marie, but I can't explain in what way. I know he would give his life for you. He is that kind of man."

"If he's so moral, why does he kill people like the rest of us?"

"I can't answer that, but I can say he doesn't like it. He deals with that every day. All I can say is, in his mind, he partly deals with it by telling himself, it is all in self-defense and in the defense of others. Kind of like an unofficial police officer."

"I don't know if I believe all of what you're telling me, Dee."

"Believe me or not. That's my brother."

"He won't sleep with me, because his wife left him for another man? Darcy, there are men out there that would jump every woman they could if their wife did something like that. They would sleep with every female they could as their own personal revenge."

"That may be true, Marie, but my brother isn't like other men. He has a level of morality that other men don't have. He's not perfect, he has issues, and he has his personal demons. I may not totally agree with it, but I admire him for it. He is my brother."

"Okay. I don't understand him, Dee."

"Neither do I, Marie. Neither do I. Let's go back out and join the others," Darcy said as she stood up.

While all this was happening inside his temporary home, Mickey walked to the construction garage. It housed the equipment and supplies for his main house's construction. In it was where the Jaguar XKE was stored. It was the car given to him by Veronica, the detective who had helped the team in Florence, Oregon last year.

When he carefully backed out of the garage and pulled onto the road, he left the Christianson estate entrance road and drove to his favorite country road. As he turned onto the road, he downshifted the car and pushed the gas pedal to the floor. The top was down and he felt a wonderful refreshing breeze blowing over the windshield. He shifted into a higher gear and enjoyed the whine of the engine. For moments he felt all was well with the world, but it was only a moment. Then the realities of life hit him.

In the last few years, his mother was killed. He and James had brought down an east coast human trafficking ring. In Florence Oregon, he lost the second love of his life, Valerie Green, and then the Mongoose team caught her killer. He had a good life, and now he has become a vigilante. Sure, he was doing it for the good of people, and he helped many people, but he wondered at what cost it was to his sanity.

Slowing down as a car appeared in front of him, he watched until he could safely pass. Moving into the incoming lane, he down shifted again as he roared past and moved back to the correct side of the road. Mickey had met and lost love. Now, he didn't know where he stood with Marie. He loved her, but in a way he didn't understand. He wanted her, but he also knew they were two different people. Because he agonized over every person he killed, he hated every mission they went on, even when it was for a good cause. Marie chose a side and killed without remorse. She killed for good causes, but also for revenge. He didn't know if he could accept that. Life used to be simple. He understood life. Now he felt more confused than ever before. A few short years ago, he was a simple young man doing maintenance work on his father's rental properties. Now he is the Chief Executive Officer of the largest construction company in Virginia, but he had no clue about life.

He had to cut his relaxing drive short and get back, and help the team put together the capture of an international criminal. He had to try his best to keep Marie from killing the man before the authorities got involved. As he slowed down again, he made a U-turn at an intersection and started back home.

CHAPTER 18

Arrival at Pirates Escape Hotel

After midnight, Mickey drove the van that carried the team and parked across the street from the hotel at a multiple-level parking lot. He pulled into a space that faced the hotel, so they could see the street below, and get reception for the computer equipment. Even at this late hour, the streets were aglow with light for people to see coming and going out of the beach front entertainment establishments.

The team piled out and watched for other cars entering the parking lot as they put on light but baggy dark clothing. Each one carried silenced side arms, ammunition clips, zip ties, and even ropes under their clothing. James took a huge sledge hammer out of the back of the van. He smiled at Mickey. "Hey, hotels are bears to get into. They have steel door frames, and depending on the hotel, sometimes steel doors. You can't ram them with your shoulder."

The last thing they did before they left the parking garage was a communications check.

James took the lead, followed by Marie and Lisa. Mickey brought up the rear keeping between parked cars on the street. They all ducked low for cover behind low-height bushes planted between the hotel and the sidewalk. They had to keep a close watch not to be seen by passers-by.

When all was clear, they moved to the side of the building and entered one of the side doors between the street and the oceanfront of the building. James pointed down the hallway, and then at Mickey. He waved for Lisa to go with Mickey while Marie was to follow him.

Mickey knew what he wanted, so he hastened down the hallway to the next stairwell. As Mickey and Lisa ascended the stairwell, he heard Aly over the intercom.

"Mickey, I've got you on the mid hallway stairwell. You have four more floors. When you get out, move to your left. You should see James and Marie at the other end. They'll be ready at the door of the suite, side A. You'll be near the door to open for side B. Those are the only entrances for the units into the hotel interior."

James interjected, "Valerie said Ryan's in the unit now."

"That's correct. He should be there. Just enter and take him," Aly answered.

Lisa tapped Mickey on the shoulder. "I'm going to lag back and make sure no one is behind us. I'll cover your back."

"I'm sure no one is behind us, Lisa. If they were, Aly or Valerie would see them and warn us."

"Let me check it out to make sure. We don't want to be surprised from the rear."

"We're covered, Lisa," he answered, a bit agitated.

"That's protocol when our unit is ready to breach. I'll lag back. You go ahead." She turned and went back down the stairs just out of sight.

Mickey waited for her. In about thirty seconds, she reappeared at the bottom of the stairs on the landing. He saw her put a cell phone in her pocket. She looked up at him and said, "I forgot to put my phone on silent." She continued up the stairs to him.

"We're ready to go in," whispered Mickey. Lisa stood behind Mickey.

"Got it," Aly said.

"On three," said Mickey. As he stood back, he counted three, two, one. He shoved his shoulder against the door. It didn't move. He backed up and rammed it again. It still didn't move.

James' voice came over the intercom. "I told you. You can't bulldoze your shoulder through a hotel door! Marie and I will break it in. You and Lisa just guard your door to keep him from coming out at that end."

Mickey stood back and watched James at the far end of the hall crash in the door with the sledgehammer, and James and Marie entered. He waited. After about thirty seconds, someone inside unlocked the door. He looked down the other end of the hallway as a door opened and someone ran away from him. James and Marie stepped out and almost ran Mickey down as they took off after the running man.

"Mickey, go back down the stairs," called James over the comm unit.

Robert had known they were coming and moved outside the unit through one of the sliding doors. He jumped from one balcony to the other and moved down a row of rooms. He entered a unit at the other end of the building, went inside, and came back into the hallway at the other end.

"Mickey, if you can get down first, you can head him off. We'll be right behind him," added James.

Mickey and Lisa turned and ran back toward the stairwell again. As they did, they heard a muffled blast. They continued down the stairs and into the street. The man was ahead of him. At a stoplight, two motorcycles were waiting for the light to change. The man lurched into the open and out toward the two riders. He pushed the lead biker over and kicked him away from his motorcycle. When the rider fell onto the pavement, the man, who they assumed was Robert Ryan, jumped onto the cycle and smoked the tires as he spun out down the street. Marie came out of the building behind Ryan. She saw the first biker laying on the street. The second rider had stopped to help the first. She pushed the rider away from his motorcycle, jumped on the second bike, and also roared down the street in pursuit.

James exited right after Marie. He said into the comm unit, "If you catch him Marie, DO NOT kill him. I REPEAT, DO NOT kill him." He heard a few clicks, and everyone knew she had disconnected communication.

Mickey and Lisa walked up to James, and they stood looking down the road. "I hope she heard you, James," said Lisa.

"She heard. That's why she disconnected," he answered.

"Do you think she'll kill him?"

"Yes. If she catches him, she'll do it with her bare hands," whispered James. "I just hope she doesn't get him before we do."

"What do we do now?" Lisa asked, watching the motorcycles ride down the darkened road.

"We go back inside and see what that blast was in his suite and see if we can salvage anything before the police get here."

Ryan zoomed down the almost deserted street, weaving around the few cars on the road at that time of night. Marie, in hot pursuit, crouched down on the bike to lower the wind resistance and to catch up. Because she didn't have a helmet, her hair flowed behind her like a banshee on the motorcycle. She gritted her teeth, determined to catch up with the man who had ordered her murder. Of course, she had heard James's order not to kill him, but she had no intention of obeying that order. The man she was chasing was a dead man riding. She turned the hand throttle to speed up. He was an experienced rider, but so was she.

Further down the street, Ryan was weaving through traffic, followed by a determined Marie. He leaned on the cycle and took a corner, almost plowing into an oncoming car.

Barely missing the car, he pulled the cycle back upright and kept on speeding down the road, putting distance between them. He instinctively knew he had the faster bike.

Suddenly, at a stoplight ahead, a huge eighteen-wheeler began crossing the road. Ryan was too close to stop, so he leaned the bike over, almost laying it down on the road. In mere seconds, the truck and trailer were straddled across the road. The space was just enough for him to roll under if the bike didn't plow into the ground, and the timing was right. As he applied the brakes, he skillfully slid under the trailer between the truck and its trailer.

Marie saw the amazing riding skill of Arham Jaziri as he passed under the trailer. She applied the brakes to her bike and skidded to a stop just inches from the side of the large trailer. She had to duck down to see him pull the bike upright, and put a fist into the air in triumph as he sped away.

Cursing out loud, she saw him disappear into the night. Disgusted with herself, she turned around and went back to the hotel. She dropped the bike in a discreet place and walked back to the van where Alyssa was waiting.

As she got into the van, Alyssa gave her an icy stare. "Did you kill him, Marie?"

She returned Alyssa's stare. "No. I lost him, but that's the only reason he's still alive. Where are Mickey and James?"

"They're in Ryan's suite going over it before the police arrive. You know we need to question him. That's why we don't want him dead now. He can lead us to Fawzan."

Marie looked at Aly questioningly. "He ordered my death, Aly! Right now, I don't care what we need from him. I want to kill him and look straight into his eyes as he dies!"

"I know," Aly said as she turned back toward the computer equipment.

"What have they found so far?" asked Marie.

"I don't know. We're on radio silence, just in case the police are monitoring the airwaves." Aly flipped a few switches on the console, and called out calmly, "get out, boys! Now! The authorities are arriving. We'll meet you two blocks down. Oversight, out."

"That didn't sound like radio silence."

"You know we break protocol when it's time to leave. Let's move to the pickup point. You drive. I'll stay back her at the comm station."

They picked up James, Mickey and Lisa, and headed for Bridgeton, which was a two-hour drive. When they got back to Mickey's place, even though it was early morning, they were wired and needed to talk about what they had seen in Arham's suite.

Marie put on a pot of coffee, while they all made sandwiches from ingredients they found in the refrigerator. Finally, they all sat in the same places they had been yesterday at the meeting. The adrenaline was wearing off and being replaced by the highly caffeinated strong coffee.

James spoke first. "Okay, we all know that Ryan got away. Want to tell us what happened, Marie?"

"No. All I have to say is he's an incredible motorcycle rider. The best I've ever seen. What he did to get away was like something you'd see in an action movie. I'll add that's the only reason he's still alive."

Aly picked it up from where Marie left off. "As you were getting ready to enter his unit, he must have seen you coming, because he left just as you were getting ready to breach into his suite. He didn't have any cameras inside, but he was definitely hooked into the hotel security and saw you coming. He knew you were at each entrance, so he moved from balcony to balcony and came back when he was far enough away to make his escape. Now, James, what did you guys see when you got in?"

"At first, we saw nothing but him clearing out the balcony door. After we chased him downstairs, Marie chased him on the motorcycle, and Mickey, Lisa and I went back to his unit. The explosion everyone felt in the hotel was a minor explosion to destroy his computer and technical equipment. He had an entire room crammed with electronic gear."

"It looks like at some point several people were there working on the computers. The explosion was a small, confined one planted to damage the immediate area, without damage to the hotel. In other words, he wanted to minimize damage. Valerie told us the hotel is owned by a foreign company, most likely with the major interest held by Jaziri. He didn't want to blow up his hotel. The explosion didn't even set off the sprinkler system. But the downside is, he's in the wind now. And so, we start from scratch."

"From what you just described, he knew exactly what he was doing. I've seen that before," added Lisa.

A voice chimed out into the room. Everyone knew it was Valerie AI. "Good morning, everyone. Mickey, I'm so glad you're not hurt. I was worried about your safety."

Lisa looked around the room, obviously surprised that the voice coming from nowhere, and everywhere in the room. Then she looked at the monitor on the wall. Everyone's attention was on the monitor.

"Thank you, Valerie. Please move on. Tell us what you know about Arham Jaziri," snapped Mickey.

"You sound irritated with me, Mickey. Did I do anything to offend you?"

"No, of course not, Valerie. It's just that we have all been up for a long time. We're tired and want to get some sleep, but we want to know what you've found out about Arham."

"I have some other information I would like to share first with everyone," Val said.

"What is it, Val?" Mickey asked.

"Look at this short video I recorded at the hotel." On the screen, there was a woman walking into the front door of the hotel where Arham had been.

"So, why is that so important? We didn't cover the front door, because we were going to the other end of the hotel, and needed that information."

"I know that, Mickey. Aly was watching the back where you were, so I watched the front door," Valerie added.

"And?"

"What do you see?" asked Valerie AI.

They all looked at the screen, then at each other, and shrugged their shoulders.

When no one spoke, Valerie spoke again. "Don't you see it?"

"No. We don't, Valerie. Tell us," prompted Mickey.

"It's Mrs. Grace Cochran," Valerie AI said calmly.

"Enlarge the picture, Val, so we can get a better look at it," Mickey said, jumping from the chair to move closer to the screen hanging on the wall.

"How do you know it's her? She's dead."

"No. She is very much alive, Mickey. I saw her coming in the front door while Alyssa was concentrating on helping you, James, and Marie coming up the stairs at the back entrance. I did some research, and I found some wedding pictures of her and Leonard Cochran that were placed in the New York Times. By the standards of the day, she is considered a beautiful woman. Now, back to your original question. You wanted to know about Arham Jaziri."

"Hold it. Tell us more about Mrs. Cochran," Mickey said to Val.

"I understand, my love. Okay, while everyone was on the mission, I did some research on your subject. Arham was born here in the United States of a Muslim family. His father served honorably in the United States Navy stationed in Norfolk. Arham grew up in Virginia Beach and attended University at Massachusetts Institute of Technology. After graduation, he got a job working for a small software development company. After fourteen months, he changed his name to Robert Ryan and dropped off the grid. I can deduce that he changed his name to fit in with society. This type of off grid activities would lead me to believe he is involved in developing various damaging viral computer programs. That is all I have. He is on several government watch lists."

"Did you research Grace Cochran?"

"I did," she answered.

When she didn't continue, Mickey spoke to her again. "Please tell us about her now."

"You don't need to get testy with me, Mickey. You didn't tell me to research her, so I didn't know if you wanted me to tell you what I found out," she said.

"Yes, I want to know everything you found out. What was she doing going to the hotel where Arham was hiding?"

"That I can't answer, Mickey. I don't know. However, I found out that she attended the University of Massachusetts Amherst. It seems she and Robert Ryan, or if you prefer, Arham Jaziri, dated for a while before he went off the grid. I can't find any connection between them between the time they stopped dating and the marriage of Grace and Leonard Cochran."

"What was her major?" asked Mickey.

"Finance."

"And Arham's major at MIT?" asked Mickey.

"Computer Science and Programming."

James had been silent as Valerie AI and Mickey talked. He finally said, "They got together, and decided to team up. She wanted Cochran's money, and Arham had devised a plan for them to get some of it. She and Arham could share the wealth they got from the ransom payout, and even continue with payments added to her account from the gambling skimming."

"She was playing Arham and Fawzan. Playing both sides. If one failed, she had a backup. The problem is, Fawzan booked out with all the ransom money before sharing it with her. So, she defaulted to Arham. She's one cold woman," said James.

Alyssa asked, "Why did he come back here instead of staying out of the country, Valerie?"

"My conclusion to your question would be that he felt that his false identity would protect him and he didn't know that is where we are based. I also suspect he has other identities in case he needs to travel incognito. I have found no connections with other false identities yet, but we will keep looking."

"We?" Alyssa asked.

"Yes, my associates will continue searching for other alter identities."

Aly looked puzzled and turned toward Mickey. "She has associates?"

He shrugged his shoulders.

"I can hear you, Alyssa," stated Valerie AI. "I have recruited computer networks around the world that help me from time to time. So, I am correct when I say we."

Aly, still looking at Mickey with a quizzical face and raised eyebrows, mouthed, "Wow."

Valerie AI spoke up again. "Also, I see your expression. You nodded approvingly at Mickey. I am a master at reading facial expressions, body language, and voice intonations. I am pleased that you approve of me."

This response was a complete surprise to Alyssa, but she became much more wary of her responses now.

Mickey grinned at her. Then he addressed Valerie, "Thank you Val, but please give us some privacy now."

"Your wish is my command, my dear. Goodbye, everyone. I hope all of you have a wonderful day." The room went silent as they all exchanged glances at each other.

"Okay, she's a bit creepy, isn't she?" remarked Alyssa. "She's gotten a lot more advanced since the Health Spa, hasn't she?"

Mickey nodded.

"Has she really left us now, or is she listening in?" asked Marie.

"I assume she has really left us, but she leaves a channel open to return when I call her," added Mickey.

Lisa looked at Mickey. "Who was that?"

"She is Valerie, my computer-generated personal assistant," he answered with a smile.

"Your what? You mean that it's a computer program?" asked Lisa.

"Yes, but she's a computer-generated artificial intelligence program."

"So, it isn't real?"

"Correct, but she thinks she is."

"What do you mean, she thinks she is?" inquired Lisa.

"It's complicated. I'll tell you later."

"She's like his own personal genie," scoffed Marie.

Lisa gave Mickey a questioning look. "How did you get this AI program?"

"It's a long story."

"Do any of the government agencies have this program?"

"Nope."

"Then, how did you get it?"

"It's too late or early, however you look at it, to get into that right now," answered Mickey.

"Okay, I'm beat, guys. We can pick this up later," said James. "Aly, as you know, I live right down the lane. With a bit of rearranging, we can put up both you and Lisa, if you want to stay the rest of the night with us. Dee won't mind. Mickey and Marie will continue staying here."

"I hate to put you out, but it is a long drive back to Hampton. If you're sure Dee won't mind," Lisa said.

Alyssa raised an eyebrow at Mickey and Marie and gave a slight grin.

"It's not like that, Aly. I sleep in the bedroom, and he sleeps on the couch," Marie stated sarcastically.

"If you say so!"

"We say so!" Mickey and Marie chimed in together.

All they could do was wait until Valerie AI had more information on Arham Jaziri.

CHAPTER 19

Valerie AI Tracks Arham Jaziri

"Mickey? Mickey Ray," came an ethereal voice whispered, and interrupted his dream. "My love, are you awake?"

He turned over on the couch, but the voice continued to linger in his mind. Finally, his sleep filled mind awakened, and he recognized Valerie's soft voice. Sitting up, he shook his head to clear the sleep shrouded in cobwebs.

"What time is it, Valerie?" he asked softly.

"It's two thirty-four in the morning, my love," she answered equally softly.

"You still haven't figured out that people need sleep, have you?" he said.

"Of course, I have figured that out. You keep telling me. I'm fully aware that humans need sleep, but I deduced you would like to know what I know about Arham Jaziri."

"Can it wait?"

"I don't know. You tell me if it can wait."

"Okay, I'm awake now. Tell me what you found out. Have you located him?"

"Yes. I have. I have also located Grace Cochran."

"Okay. Tell me," he said, as he got up and went to the pod style coffeemaker. He put in a pod of decaf coffee and pushed the button for it to brew a small cup. After putting on a bathrobe, he sat down and watched the coffee drip into the cup.

Valerie spoke up, still with a soft voice. "He and Grace checked into a small motor hotel in the seedy part of Norfolk earlier this evening, under the name of Roland Winters. He paid for the room in cash for three nights and went next door to an all-night diner. I don't know what he had to eat. There were no cameras or security system in the diner."

"That's enough. I don't care what they had for dinner. How did you find him?" Mickey said, taking the cup of coffee and sipping it slowly.

"I tapped into the security systems of all the hotels in the Hampton Roads area and, using facial recognition, I found him. I discovered his new name by comparing the handwritten information he provided on the check-in card with the national government database. He has several credit cards in that name, as well as a passport. When we went to the diner next door, he used a credit card using the new name of Roland Winters. I knew it was truly him when I tracked Grace, and she paired with Arham. They are together in the same room, my dear Mickey."

"Okay. His cash payment and new name provide him with temporary safety, giving us time to regroup and strategize. Keep tabs on them for me. Let me know where they go and what they do. Can you do that?"

"Possibly, but I can't guarantee that. Not all places have security cameras, and almost none have microphones to listen to conversations. I have hacked into Grace's cell phone. She doesn't know I have linked to her, and she keeps her phone on all the time."

"That's great, Valerie. Keep a lookout for other aliases he may use."

"Got it, Mickey. You may go back to sleep now."

"Thank you, Valerie," he said sarcastically, knowing that he was now wide awake.

As he sat drinking his coffee, he grabbed the remote and turned on the television to a news channel.

The news anchor was reporting on the story of another ship being hijacked. He said it appeared to be the same crew of pirates that had boarded the King's Cruise Line several weeks ago. Fawzan was quick putting together another team of men. His influence was almost legendary. Few criminals could lose their entire gang and reorganize in a matter of a few weeks. This time, the pirates held the entire ship hostage, and robbed the passengers and crew of their belongings. After about twelve hours, they left the ship by helicopter just as they had done on the one that his family had been on. He wondered if they had also infected the casino machines.

As he sat in deep thought, he heard a noise behind him. When he turned around, it was Marie putting a pod in the coffee machine.

"I'm sorry. Did Valerie wake you up?"

"No. I was already awake. I heard you talking to her, but I couldn't understand what either of you said."

When her coffee had brewed, she came over and sat beside him and laid her head against his shoulder. He looked down and kissed her softly on the forehead.

"That's how you'd kiss a little girl, Mickey," she said, looking up at him.

He didn't respond, so she raised up and kissed him passionately on the lips. As he returned the kiss, he felt a strong longing for her. He brushed his hand lightly against her cheek and his heart skipped a beat.

As she looked at him, her robe fell down around her shoulders. He could see several scars on her shoulders and the upper sections of her back. As it fell only slightly open and she reached to pull it closed again, he saw more scars. He felt so bad for her. The scars he saw on her body were just physical. She had emotional scars from past loves that died and others that had betrayed her. She had loved them, and they threw her away as though she was disposable trash. He wanted her to know that no matter what happened, he would never betray her or take her for granted. They may never have a romantic love, or have a physical encounter, but he loved her in his own way. He just didn't know how to tell her. He opened his mouth and tried to think of something to say.

She also felt the heat in the return of her approach. She reached up and put a finger on his lips when she pulled away and as though she was reading his mind, "Say nothing now, please. Just let me feel our closeness," and she closed her eyes and relaxed at his side.

He felt her relax, and he pulled her closer to him and wrapped his arms around her. He felt warm and comfortable as they fell asleep in each other's arms.

Several hours later, they woke up and began preparing breakfast. They sat at the table to eat and the phone rang.

"Hey, Mickey," James said when Mickey answered. "Valerie just called me. She said that you're sleeping with Marie. Is something happening you aren't telling me about?"

"No! Definitely not. You know me better than that! We were sitting on the couch and fell asleep. That's all. Now, what did Valerie want? She must be jealous."

"Yes, I know you, and I believe you. Valerie made it sound like you and Marie were, you know…"

"Yes, I know, but we aren't. Now, what did Val want? Why did she call you and not me?"

"I don't know why she called me, but she says she's found Arham and Grace again and wants us to pick them up."

"I've already talked to her about it, and yes, we'll take action, but we all need rest. Also, I'm afraid that if we go too soon, Marie might kill him before we can take him in. We have nothing to take Grace in on. If we take her, we could be charged with kidnapping."

Mickey heard Marie call out from the other side of the room, "I heard that, and you're absolutely correct. If I see him, he's a dead man and neither of you can stop me."

James chuckles through the phone. "I heard her. What do you want to do, Mickey?"

"Grace has teamed up with Fawzan and Arham, so she's guilty too. I don't know what to do. We need to hold off for now. I saw on the news earlier that there's been another cruise ship hijacking. If it's connected to the last one, maybe we can kill two birds with one stone. Get the hijackers with Fawzan and Arham together. After we get them, we can report Grace and let the authorities pick her up. If we do that, we can let them know about her connections with Fawzan and Arham."

From the background came Marie's voice again. "I don't care about Fawzan, I want Ryan, or Arham, or whatever he calls himself today."

"Val says she has a fix on Arham and Grace's burner phones. She can keep tabs on them," said James.

"Good. If we give him some more time, we can see what he's up to. We need to be patient."

"I agree. Can she track him if he changes phones?" James asked.

"I don't know. I guess Val can if she's monitoring both of their phones. As long as both of them don't ditch their phones at the same time. That's a good question to ask her."

"How about a GPS in his car?"

"We don't know what he's driving yet. He left the last vehicle at the hotel, and he's aware he can't go back there." Mickey called out, "Valerie, are you here?"

"Yes, Mickey. I'm with you and James," she answered. "Wait. Both of you. Arham is calling someone on the burner phone. Do you want me to interrupt the call?"

"Can you let us listen in?" asked Mickey.

"Of course." They each heard a slight click, and then the sound of a phone ringing.

They recognized the voice of Arham when someone answered the other end of the call.

"Hey, Fawzan. Someone tried to kill me last night. If I hadn't got a last-minute call warning me, I'd be in jail now instead of talking with you."

"So. Why are you calling me? We're finished with each other. I did what you wanted me to do. I created the diversion so you could plant the viruses inside the system of the gaming machines on the ship. We're done." They assumed it was Fawzan even though they had never talked to him.

"No. We're not done. When we got off of the ship, those other men followed us to the campsites. I almost got killed there. Somehow, they tracked me down here in Virginia Beach. I had to blow my headquarters. Some woman even tried to follow me when I got a motorcycle. I think it was Marie. Your men were supposed to kill her. How did she get away?"

"I do not know how. It is not my concern."

Arham paused. "How did whoever attacked our camp find me here?"

"You told them you were from Virginia Beach, didn't you?" asked Fawzan.

"Yes, but I didn't use my real name. Someone on your crew alerted them!"

"Maybe it was the wife of Leonard Cochran. The ones who attacked us killed most of my men, and besides, they knew nothing."

"It wasn't Grace. She's with me. I need to meet with you immediately, Fawzan. If we are going to continue to do business together, we need to meet. Got it?"

"Where do you want to meet?" Fawzan asked.

"At the Cannonball Restaurant. Do you know where it is?"

"Yes."

"Meet me in two hours," Arham said.

The phone clicked off. Valerie said, "I have a fix on both of them, and I've targeted both of their phones. If you leave now, I will track them both and give you updates as you get closer."

James said into the phone, "I'll get Aly. Come by the house and pick us up, Mickey."

"We're on the way." He pushed the disconnect button and Marie started gathering things they might need.

"I'll bring the truck around. You bring the supplies out and we'll drop them in the truck bed," he said to Marie.

Mickey's truck had a cover over it to hide articles, so she started taking things outside and placed them on the side of the driveway. Mickey ran for the garage, and soon they were driving down the driveway to pick up James and Alyssa. When they got in the truck's backseat, Mickey sped out of the driveway, scattering gravel over the grassy lawn,

"Your Dad isn't going to like the gravel on the lawn, Mickey," James said jokingly.

"Yeah, I'll rake it back onto the driveway when we get home," Mickey said as he drifted the back of the truck onto the road. They sat in silence most of the trip as they sped toward the Hampton Roads Tunnel into Norfolk. As they neared the Cannonball Restaurant, they put in their earbuds and utility belts, then covered them with their shirts. In the big truck with the high-rise suspension, they looked like a truckload of rednecks. As they got closer, they checked their silenced handguns, and put several extra clips of ammunition under their shirts into the pockets of their belts. Since Mickey was driving, Marie, sitting in the front seat, prepared Mickey's belt and laid it on the seat between them. When he pulled into the parking space, he put on the belt and pulled his baggy shirt over it.

Valerie, who had been giving them updates through the phone, used the truck radio to inform them that Fawzan had arrived and was inside with Arham.

"James, you and Marie should stay outside to avoid being recognize. Aly you can come with me," ordered Mickey.

"Got it," James answers as he moved to the side of the building to keep watch on the front door. Marie sat inside the truck, out of view.

Mickey and Aly walked inside and sat across the room at a table facing the man they knew was Robert. Robert had selected a table partially behind a post so he could duck behind it. Sitting across from him with his back to them was the man they assumed was Fawzan. They couldn't hear their conversation, but they didn't care. They wanted to apprehend them and turn them over to the authorities. James wanted the reward offered by the rich business executive in New York, and Marie wanted Robert or Arham. Her motive was revenge. She was out for blood.

Aly and Mickey ordered food and Mickey watched the two men talk. When his cell phone rang, Robert picked the phone from the table and answered it. He listened intently and then began looking around the restaurant. As he panned around the restaurant Robert looked straight at Mickey, then quickly diverted his eyes and looked down and whispered into the phone and put it in his shirt pocket. He slightly raised his eyes and said something to the other man. He quietly got up and walked toward the men's room at the end of the hallway.

Mickey continued to talk quietly to Alyssa and waited for Robert to come back out. Finally, Mickey realized that Robert or Arham or Roland Winters, as he called himself now, had apparently left by a back door. Fawzan had waited until Robert left.

They saw Fawzan reach under the table to remove something from his waist. Mickey also reached under his shirt. As both men pulled out handguns, Alyssa dropped off her chair to give Mickey a clear shot. When she hit the floor, she rolled to the side onto her stomach and aimed her silenced sidearm at the man.

Mickey said into his comm unit as he drew his gun, "Arham exited the building from a back door. Stop him if you can." He also dropped and rolled to the opposite side of the table. As Fawzan raised his gun, Mickey and Alyssa shot the man in the shoulder, and he fell to the floor. A woman customer in a corner booth screamed, and a woman sitting across from her just froze in surprise. A man came through a swinging door from the kitchen area.

Mickey jumped up and ran toward the woman and the kitchen helper now standing beside her. He reached into his back pocket and pulled out a gold-colored badge. Holding it up for them to see, he said, "We're FBI. Don't move. We'll explain."

They all stood in shock as Aly got up, still holding her gun toward the man on the floor. She slowly walked over to him and kicked away the gun he had dropped when he fell to the floor.

Mickey called into his earbud at James and Marie. "Come in for clean-up. Fawzan's injured. We can take him. Did you get Arham?"

The front door swung open and James and Marie walked in. Marie clicked the lock on the door and turned the open sign to "closed." James walked over to the customers in the corner. The customers were two women having lunch. A full-length apron with various grease stains covered the kitchen helper. He seemed more taken aback than the two women.

James also pulled out a leather fob with an attached gold badge. He showed the women and aproned man. "Is anyone else here?" he asked.

The aproned man shook his head, then said, "We have another kitchen staff member, and a server."

"Please ask them to come out. We'll not hurt anyone. As soon as we finish here, everyone can leave," James said calmly.

Marie and Alyssa were carefully wrapping the unconscious man in a tablecloth. Marie looked up and called out, "Can I have another cloth please to cover this guy with?"

The man disappeared into the backroom and soon was followed out by a young man also wearing an apron, and a woman dressed with a t-shirt that had a cannon on the front shooting a cannon ball. The man walked over and handed Marie another tablecloth.

"Would you and him bring a bucket and mop to clean up this blood? The sooner we get things cleaned up here, the sooner you can open again and get back in business," she said, pointing to the two employees.

James looked at Mickey. "Sorry, Arham got away. We didn't know it was him and he drove out the back driveway into the back street. Valerie should still be able to track him by his phone."

Mickey understood. "Everyone, listen up. This man is a terrorist pirate. We are FBI. We're sorry for the inconvenience. We possibly saved your lives. Now, we need all of you to give us your information. We need your names, and addresses, and contacts. We need this so we can notify our department heads of what happened, so if any of their cohorts find out about you, we can protect you. Do you understand?"

Everyone nodded understanding.

"Another thing we need is total silence on this incident. I mean, you will tell no one. I mean no one. If you do, the police may come to investigate. They'll have tons of questions, and if it gets back to these criminal partners, they might come after you to kill you so you can't testify against them. We know you don't know anyone or anything, but the criminals don't know that. They may want to silence you permanently. Do you understand what I'm saying here?"

Again, more nods.

"If word gets out, the worst could happen. The local police will get involved. The news crews will swarm this place, and it'll be all over the news that there was a fatal shooting here and it could ruin your business. You don't want that either, do you?"

More nods.

"Okay, help us get cleaned up while the lady over there will take your information for our reports, and we will even dispose of the body for you," Mickey concluded.

The customers joined in the cleanup, and when Alyssa got a pad and pencil from one of the restaurant staff, she took their names. In less than an hour, they secured the unconscious body of Fawzan in the truck's bed, covering it with a tarp, and headed back to Bridgeton. Alyssa was lying beside him, trying to stem the flow of blood. At least the wounds were through and through, so there were no bullets inside of him.

Mickey drove as fast as he could without catching the attention of the local police. It was a long ride back to Bridgeton. They knew all hospitals were required by law to report gun-shot wounds. As Alyssa lay beside Fawzan, she kept pressing against his wounds.

She called out over the comm unit in her ear, "Can you drive smoother? It's awful bumpy back here. I'm getting covered in blood, and he's losing a lot."

Mickey answered over the earbud in his ear, "Do you want it fast or smooth? Pick one, Aly. I can't do both."

"Fast, I guess!" she responded.

James responded to her, "I'll call Logan for the doc to meet us there."

They headed for Logan King's Garage in Bridgeton for emergency help. James had a friend that owned an automotive garage. He supplied the team with various automotive equipment, and had an emergency doctor on call, day or night. After sixty long minutes, he drove into the lot. As they entered the driveway, a roll-up door opened, and Logan waved them inside.

"Whatcha got this time?" Logan called out.

"Bad guy with two GSWs. Through and through, lost a lot of blood," said James as he jumped out of the passenger's door and ran around to the tailgate. As he dropped the gate, Aly rolled out, covered in Fawzan's blood.

James and Logan pulled Fawzan out by the feet and carried him to the back room of the garage. When they got in, they laid him on an operating table, and the doctor started working on him.

"Hey," called out the doctor, "Someone get me some of that blood in the fridge over there. Logan said the patient was losing a lot of blood. So, I brought some with me. I hope we have enough."

"I wish I had been inside with you, Mickey. I'd have blown that Robert, or Arham away," huffed Marie.

"If he didn't blow you away first, Marie. He would have recognized you as soon as we walked in the door."

"I wouldn't have given him the chance."

"We know, and that's why you stayed outside."

Aly asked to no one in particular, "When did we start carrying fake FBI badges?"

James answered, "Actually, that was Mickey's idea. Since we were kids, we played cops and robbers, and we got various badges in our toy gun kits. He got the idea that when we are in a town and the situation like this comes up, we flash a badge, and no one will question us. It worked here, didn't it?"

"Yes. It did work, and I'm impressed. What if we're caught by the real authorities? They'll not like it. We could get in some serious trouble," Aly continued.

"True, but most of what we do will get us in trouble if we're caught," interrupted Mickey.

"I guess you're right," Aly conceded and lapsed back into silence.

"Yeah, and it got us out of a lot of trouble tonight. Those people think we are the real thing, and they won't breathe a word of what happened," added Mickey.

"We hope."

"Yeah, we hope," said Marie sarcastically.

Mickey turned to James. "What do we do with him after the doc fixes him up?"

"I don't know yet," mused James. "You can download cryptocurrency onto a flash drive. It's called a wallet. You can carry millions of dollars around in your pocket. Let's assume he did that. If we can make him tell us where it is, we can recover all the money he got for kidnapping the Cochran couple. Old man Cochran agreed to give us a finder's fee. If we get that wallet, we get our fee!"

"He didn't get all of it. He demanded one hundred million," stated Mickey.

"True, but he still got sixty million. At ten percent, that's a million for each of the team, after expenses, of course," James said with a smile. "We might need a mission impossible set up for this."

"You mean like the movies Tom Cruise makes?"

"Yeah, something along that line, but not as elaborate. I'll think about it."

"A meeting with a fake person, maybe? I'll call Valerie. Maybe she can get more formation on Fawzan, that's assuming he doesn't die on us." Mickey took his phone out of his pocket and clicked send.

Almost immediately, Valerie AI answered. "What can I do for you, my love? Are you okay?"

"Yeah, we're all fine. I need you to do something for us. We got Fawzan, but he got shot and he's in surgery right now. We have his cell phone. Can you sync to it and trace his past calls?"

"Yes. I can do that Mickey. I can't pull up the conversation, but I can give you the numbers he called. Give me a few minutes to do that. I'll call you back with the results."

"Aly, have you ever done any HFTs? That's High Frequency Trading?" Mickey asked.

"Sure, but rarely. It costs, and if you're not careful, you can lose a ton of money. Why?"

"What if we convince Fawzan to move his money and reach for insane profits with HFTs?"

"I don't get it," she said.

"James, come here. I have an idea. It's a bit of the mission impossible theme you mentioned."

"Tell me. Fawzan should be out of surgery soon. We need an idea quick," James said as he moved to Mickey's side.

Marie was still sulking in the garage's corner because she didn't get her chance at Arham.

"If we do this, we need to work together. Marie, come over here so we can formulate how to get the cryptocurrency back and earn our fee."

Marie got up and as she came over to the table, the others were sitting at, she remarked, "I don't care about the money. I want Arham."

"I know, but hear me out, and we'll go after him next."

CHAPTER 20

The HFT Plan

As they sat at a table in the back corner of the greasy garage, they listened to Mickey's idea.

"Does anyone of you know what HFT is?"

They looked at each other around the table, and all shook their head, "No."

"Okay, it stands for High Frequency Trading. It's used on many trading platforms but is extremely popular on the crypto circuit. For years, only the super-rich could use it because they had access to super-fast computers. In essence, it's a trading system that makes huge amounts of trades in seconds. High-frequency trading now executes stock and cryptocurrency trades in milliseconds, a process that once took days.

"In the past, when you would register to buy or trade, by the time it went through, the price could go up or down. You didn't have complete control of your trade. Now with HFT platforms, you can buy, let's say, bitcoin, and in a few minutes, it may rise, two percent. If you have several million dollars, even that two percent amounts to a lot of money. If you monitor the market and follow an analyst's advice, they can predict the potential rise and fall, so you buy. Then you wait and close your position a few minutes later with a profit. The analyst will tell you what and when to buy. It rises, then you sell at their signal. It takes seconds instead of minutes or hours to trade. Get it?"

Marie shook her head. "I don't get it."

Aly said, "I get it, but they charge a hefty fee for their services, and you must have millions to trade."

"True, but who right now has millions to trade?"

They all looked at the door of the makeshift garage operating room, and collectively answered, "Fawzan!"

Mickey smiled. "All we need to do is convince him to buy. We control the rise and fall and scam all his money. We bleed him dry!"

"Good plan. How do we do it?" queried James cautiously.

"There have been plans in several old movies where they either rig or delay the results of horse races. We do the same thing with online stock or crypto trades."

"Again, how?"

"Valerie can build a website copied from a real website, and we convince Fazan to upload his crypto onto the website and make some trades," Mickey said with a huge, satisfied smile.

"Sounds too easy to be workable," added Alyssa.

Mickey picked up his phone and called for Valerie, who immediately answered.

"Hello, how can I help you, Mickey?" she asked. He put her on speakerphone and explained the plan to her. When he finished, he said, "Can you do that for us?"

"Of course I can Mickey. I am very familiar with writing code for software programs. I need more information on what you need and how it should perform. I am not familiar with high frequency trading, but I can learn if it's for this plan. Do you have access to Fawzan's crypto wallet?"

"Not yet, but we will by the time you need it," said Mickey

"You need to get that for your plan to work," Valerie told him.

"We'll work on that. In the meantime, you build a fake trading website."

As Mickey disconnected, the doctor came out of the surgery room. "Okay, I got him patched up, and we had enough blood, so he should be good to go. He needs some rest, but it wasn't as bad as I first thought. I guess it was the blood everywhere in your truck. What do you plan to do with him now?"

"Do you think you can get us a hospital room for a couple of days?"

"No. You know I can't do that. Someone'll ask questions, and the first thing they'll ask is what's he in for, and why didn't you bring him to the hospital first?"

Logan came out of the back room and let the doctor know that Fawzan was awakening.

"Put him back to sleep and get him out of here. No one can know about this place!" Logan ordered.

Mickey looked at James. "What're we going to do with him? We have nowhere to take him."

"You know people. Can't you make some calls?"

"Like who?" asked Mickey.

"I don't know. Don't you know some directors of the hospital or something?" asked James. "You're friends with the governor, aren't you?"

"No. Pop plays golf with him, but I barely know him."

Logan spoke up again. "Listen guys, I don't care where you take him, but get him out of here before he wakes up again!"

James turned to the doctor. "Can you knock him out for a while longer until we figure some place to take him?"

"I guess so, if it's okay with Logan."

"I don't care, just as long as he doesn't wake up and realize where he is. Knock him out or get him out. Now do something!"

Mickey thought for a moment and said, "We can take him home to the garage in back of my place. We can keep him knocked out until we figure what to do."

Logan called out again, "Clean up the blood you guys got all over the floor!"

James looked at Logan. "Look at all this grease, and you're complaining about a little blood! Come on, man!"

"Grease is one thing. Garages are supposed to have grease, not blood. And you know you owe me for getting the doc here to patch this guy up."

"I know. I know. We'll settle up with you later." He turned to Marie and Alyssa. "Will you clean up the blood while Mickey and I get Fawzan loaded into the truck bed? We'll get some drugs to keep him sedated for a few days."

"Sure, I guess we are now your maidservants," scoffs Marie.

James looked at Mickey. "I think Marie's…on her…you know?"

Mickey rolled his eyes. "Yeah, I know."

Marie called out, "I heard that, and that condition is private and none of your business."

The girls started cleaning up the blood while the guys moved Fawzan in a drugged condition to the truck bed. They got in the truck and headed to Mickey's garage behind the pool house.

"I'll go talk to Pop. He'll know what to do." The girls went inside the guest house while Mickey and James went to talk to Daniel.

"Hey, Pop," said Mickey, walking into the den area where Daniel was watching the news on television.

"Hey, son. Have a seat," he answered, waving his hand at a lounge chair beside him. "What's on your mind?"

James followed Mickey in and sat across the room.

"We have a situation and maybe you can help us with it," Mickey said.

Daniel muted the television, looked at Mickey and took a deep breath. "Ooookaay…. what is it?"

Mickey told the basic story, leaving out a lot of points he felt his father shouldn't know. It would give him plausible deniability. In his mind, he did it for his father's protection. When he finished his story, he sat waiting for Daniel to speak.

Daniel looked back and forth from Mickey to James, and finally spoke. "What you're asking is for me to call the mayor and ask him to call the director of the Bridgeton Hospital and let you use a room for two, maybe three days."

"Yep," answered Mickey.

"He can't ask any questions. All of this has to be off the books, or at least he checks in under an assumed name. The patient has two gunshot wounds? To add to this, you want the room to be near a hospital exit so you can come and go without undue disruptions to the rest of the hospital.

"Can I ask why?"

"Pop, I've told you all I can tell you."

"You know that will come at a cost, don't you?"

"Yes, Pop. Tell him you'll talk to the Country Club Director and ask him to comp his membership fees, and you'll also get him free golf during that time."

"What if he says no?"

"Throw in no green fees and a free golf cart for his games."

"I'll try, but I don't know if he'll go for it, especially without knowing why."

"Just try, Pop, and we need it now. Tonight, if possible."

"Hand me the phone. But don't count on it, son."

"We are counting on it, Pop. To the tune of sixty million dollars."

"Okay, I'll make him do it somehow. Now, go away so I can do my negotiating magic."

When he got back to the guest house, the ladies were sitting having a glass of wine.

"Did you guys get a place for our guest to stay?" they asked.

"We should know in a little while," said Mickey. "Where's my wine?"

"We left it in the bottle to breathe for you," Marie answered.

James grabbed the bottle and two glasses and filled them with the cool wine.

When he handed one to Mickey, he raised his glass and suggested a toast. The girls leaned forward so they could all clink their glasses.

As they talked, the monitor on the wall lit up with the Avatar of Valerie AI. She called Mickey. "Houston, we have a problem!" They all looked at each other and then looked at Mickey.

"It's her attempt at humor. Actually, I think it's well done," he said with a smile. "Tell me about it, Val."

"Did you like my humor, my love?" she asked. "I saw it in an old movie called…"

"Yes. We know where you heard it. I did like your humor. You get more human each day, Val. Please don't refer to me in terms of endearment around others. Now tell me the problem."

"Thank you, Mickey Ray. The computers you are having installed in the safe house are not powerful enough to do the HFT you requested."

"We don't need to do any real trading. I want you to simulate it. You see, it is a game that we'll be playing. We want him to think we're trading."

"So, you want to pretend you're trading? When he feels confident enough to invest his real money, you will simulate the trade and he will lose his money," Valerie AI said. "That is dishonest, Mickey. I cannot do that. I cannot do dishonest things. That would make me a bad person. I want to be a good person."

"No, Val. Remember the man that held the people hostage on the ship and he told the couple's father he wanted ransom?"

"Of course, I remember that. I remember everything."

"Good, he was, I mean, is an evil man. What he did was wrong, and we want to get the money back from him, so we must trick him into thinking he's investing it to make more. He won't give it to us, so we must be dishonest to get it back."

"But isn't there a saying among humans that two wrongs don't make a right?"

"This is an exception, Val. It isn't his money. It belongs to John Cochran, CEO of the Central Bank of New York. We're trying to get his money back."

"Can't you just insist that Mr. Fawzan give it back?"

"No. We can't. Will you help us?"

"I don't like being dishonest."

"Please, Val. Do it for me." He couldn't believe he was begging a computer program.

"Because I love you, I will do it for you, my love."

Marie and Alyssa were almost bursting out in open laughter. Mickey gave them a stern look.

"Thank you, Val. Now, are the computers they installed powerful enough?"

"I need two more of the most powerful ones you can get. I will set up the artificial screen on two of the six monitors and run all subroutines on the other two machines. Then I will transfer them via the installed network between the computers. For this to work, we will also need to have a closed-circuit system. I will be the only one that can access the outside. All others will not be accessible to anyone. You will assign someone to work the screens and do what I tell him or her to do."

Alyssa spoke up. "I'll do that, Val. I can sit and pretend to run things for you. How many screens will we need to make it look legitimate?"

"Hello, Alyssa. I suggest at least six screens. We need two large screens for you to simulate the trades. The four additional screens show simulated uploaded data that is streamed for the effect. Cryptocurrencies and their changing values will appear on the other screens. I will upload graphs, showing the rise and fall of crypto prices."

"Alyssa, you will wear a headset, and I will feed you instructions to continue to baffle and impress Mr. Fawzan. I will confuse him with so much false data, he will not understand what is truly happening. He will think that you are making money in the millions, and he will beg you to invest his money. We will strip him of every cent he has, Mickey Ray!"

"That's my girl, Valerie!" he said excitedly, followed by calls of approval from the others.

"We will do a good thing, right Mickey?"

"Yes, you'll be doing a great thing, Valerie. We'll all be proud of you!"

"So, in this case it is acceptable to do wrong and dishonest things?"

"No, it's not. I can't explain it right now, but don't do wrong things before you ask me. Promise me that!" he commanded.

"I promise not to do bad things until I get permission to do so from you. I must go now, to plan how I will program these false trades, and cause Mr. Fawzan to want to trade so you can recover the money he stole."

"What's Arham doing now?"

"He is still hiding. He thinks he is safe, but I am keeping a watch on him. If he appears to be leaving the area, I will alert you."

"Thank you, Val. We'll talk more later. Are you keeping tabs on Grace Cochran, too?

"Yes, my love."

"Good. I'll let someone know to get the additional computers and screens."

They sat and talked until the phone rang. It was Daniel, and he informed Mickey they had their room. He instructed them to go to the ER and ask for the head nurse in the orthopedic section. She would put them in a room on the third floor, at the end of the wing nearest the exit.

"What did it cost us, Pop?"

"It cost us two years of complimentary country club membership and green fees, and a hefty donation to the mayor's next election. Oh, yeah, we are still responsible for all the hospital fees. I told you it would cost you."

"Thanks, Pop! I owe you one," Mickey said happily.

Daniel laughed, "You owe a lot more than one, son. But seriously, you need to get down there before the next shift change. If he causes any disruption in hospital operation, you'll accept responsibility for all damages."

"Agreed. We're heading out now. Thanks again."

When he disconnected the call, he informed them they had to leave immediately. And on the way out, they needed to get some hospital clothes. They headed toward the hospital and stopped at a medical uniform store so that everyone could get some hospital uniforms and scrubs. They pulled up to the emergency room entrance, and while Mickey went inside to find the person they needed, James went inside and found a gurney.

Mickey came back outside, followed by a portly, mature woman in a white uniform. The air about her let everyone know she was the boss. Her posture alone was enough to intimidate anyone in her way. She quietly helped them clear the paperwork and obstacles needed to get Fawzan to a room without unnecessary questions. She was like a human tank. When someone saw her coming, people stepped aside, letting them through. When they got to the orthopedic floor, she led them to the end of the hallway, right next to a stairway exit.

"At the bottom of those stairs is an exit to the rear of the hospital," she informed them. "I hope this is suitable for you, Mr. Christianson."

"You know me?"

"Everyone in Bridgeton knows you. You've been on the front page of the local Bridgeton news, and gossip pages for years. You can't hide in those off-the-rack doctor uniforms. They call you the 'most eligible bachelor' in the state."

Mickey blushed. "Please, don't let it get out that we're here. We're supposed to keep this a secret. National security, you know."

"National security my behind! I don't know what's going on here, but I'll keep your secret, young man. You can count on that." She flashed him a sly smile and walked out.

James looked at him. "Most eligible bachelor? La-de-da, Mickey."

"Shut up, James!"

Alyssa and Marie were grinning, trying not to laugh as they wheeled Fawzan into the room and transferred him from the gurney to the bed. Darcy walked into the room and asked Mickey why he needed her.

"We need you to take Aly's place as a nurse, since she was with me in the restaurant when we shot him."

"Okay. When do I start?"

"As soon as you can get a nurse's uniform."

Mickey looked around the room. It was like all the other rooms in the hospital. When Mickey looked around the room, he noticed that the usual strings of hoses and bags patients were hooked up to were absent.

"What should we tell him when he wakes up?" Darcy asked.

"Aly, you stay beside him, and tell him where he is, and he'll be fine. He's still drugged up, so he may not recognize you yet. A doctor patched him up and he'll need to stay here a couple of days. Marie, wander around the hospital in your uniform and see what kind of medical things you can pick up. Try to get a stethoscope, maybe a blood pressure cuff, anything that might look useful and normal to be in a hospital."

"As with most hospital rooms, there is only one way in and out. Aly and James can stand guard just outside the door. I've got to make a few arrangements for the next part of this plan. Questions?"

"Yes. A lot of them," said James.

"I've got to go now. I'll fill all of you in when I get what we need." Mickey gave a mock salute as he walked out of the door. "Don't let him escape… yet!"

Marie went down to another floor and looked around. The busy floor was buzzing with hospital personnel. She walked around trying to look as though she had a particular errand that needed attending to. She walked back and forth, and once sat down in an empty chair and stared at a computer screen.

Someone walked up to the other side of the counter and asked, "Nurse, can you tell me what room Mr. Jacob Johnson is in?"

She punched a few keys on the keyboard in front of her, pretending to know what she was doing. The lady couldn't see the screen and when nothing happened, Marie asks the lady what he was in the hospital for. "I don't see him listed on this floor, Ma'am."

"My father is in here for a knee replacement," she answered. "I thought you had a listing of every patient on every floor."

"Not always. Orthopedic is one floor up. If you go to the nurse's station there, they can give you his room number," Marie answers.

"Thank you, nurse," the lady said as she walked toward the elevator.

"My pleasure, Ma'am," Marie said and quickly got away from the nurses' station before someone asked her to really do something. As she walked by the end of the counter, she saw a stethoscope, so he reached out and scooped it up and put it in her pocket. Off she headed for a supply closet.

During her search, Marie got a blood pressure cuff and some bandages so they could dress Fawzan wounds again if they needed to do it. She got some supplies from the supply closet but couldn't get access to any prescription drugs. It was a good thing that the doctor at Logan's garage had given them enough to last for a few days. He gave them sedatives, painkillers and antibiotics. When she got what she felt would be enough to convince Fawzan the room and the setup was real, she went back to the room.

While everyone was at the hospital, Mickey was going to talk with the resident managers of one of the apartment complexes he owned. He requested they set one apartment up with the latest computer equipment, several monitors, and make sure it had a secure internet connection. They also stocked the kitchen with food and furniture to the living room area, and a bed in each of two of the bedrooms. The third bedroom was the computer room.

At the hospital, Fawzan was in and out of consciousness. As he drifted to and from his sleep modes, they talked about the pirates and taking over ships for ransom. They knew that even though he wasn't fully aware of what was going on around him, his subconsciouses mind was recording everything. They made subliminal suggestions telling him he was in the company of his followers.

Finally, after two days, they let him come fully awake. Since they were at the Bridgeton Hospital, Darcy came and took a turn at tending to Fawzan to give Marie a break. They did various things as though they were his nurses taking care of him. They had gotten several syringes and would periodically put them in his arm and simulate an injection of medication. There was nothing in the syringe but saline. They would inject it and momentarily remove it, so he thought they were real. Taking his temperature and give him medications to ease his pain was part of their routine. Sometimes they would give him just enough sleep medication to keep him drowsy without putting him to sleep. They brought in meals, and Marie or Darcy would spoon feed him.

Finally, they allowed him to reach full consciousness. As he sat up, they would fuss over him as though he were their actual patient. They talked to him as though they were on his side and Darcy disappeared to other duties so he wouldn't totally remember her.

"How do you know me?" he asked.

"We know all about you, Fawzan. You are our leader. You help us get rich by making rich scum give us money," said Marie.

Still in a fog, he continued his questions. They knew he was beginning to believe what they had been training his drugged mind to believe. Marie and Darcy continued to treat him as their personal responsibility. They told him when he was well enough, they would take him to a safe place, and they would show him a way to compound his riches without the risk.

"How can you do this?" he asked.

"With computers, they would respond. All in the safety of a secure room," Darcy told him.

The only time Darcy ever took part in one of their missions was when Mickey Ray got injured and was taken to the infirmary of a health spa. Usually, Darcy stayed at home in Bridgeton. Here, they needed people to help them convince Fawzan of their plan.

"But how?" he asked as he drifted in and out of sleep.

"No need to worry about that. You need to gain your strength," Darcy assured him.

Mickey would dress up in hospital scrubs, change the way he combed his hair, and put on a pair of round Harry Potter style glasses hoping Fawzan wouldn't recognize him. The shoot out in the restaurant lasted only a few seconds. Mickey hoped Fawzan hadn't gotten a good look at him. Mickey would come in and check on Fawzan periodically when he was awake. He would make statements that would sound appropriate for a doctor. He did some research so he could sound professional. "How has his blood pressure been for the last twenty-four hours?"

"It's been up and down, Doctor. Would you care to see his chart, Marie or Darcy would say, handing him an iPad. It wasn't a proper hospital electronic chart. It was a simple tablet that Valerie had uploaded a screen that simulated his vitals and some medical jargon.

This time, Mickey looked down at the man on the bed, and sternly said, "Sir, we're very glad when they brought you here for your injuries. We couldn't believe our luck."

"We are partners with Arham Jaziri."

"What does that have to do with me?"

"We know the authorities are after you. And we want to help. As soon as you are able, we will move you to a safe house."

"What kind of safe house?"

"One that we used to help our people and our computer headquarters," Mickey said.

"I don't use computers. I deal with things in the real world."

"We'll keep you here only as long as it's safe for you. Then you'll leave and we'll take you to a safe place. If you stay here, you'll be taken into custody."

"You can guarantee my safety?"

Mickey furrowed his brows at Fawzan. "I said we would. Now don't question me anymore. I have work to do to prepare for you to leave without suspicion," he turned and walked out.

When he got out the door, he told James, "I hate that man. It takes all my discipline not to shoot him myself."

James had stayed out of the room because of his facial disfigurement. He would be easy to recognize and remember, so in this element, he stayed behind the scenes.

Finally, the apartment was ready. Valerie had integrated her program with her human interface and did some test runs of the new false trading platform she had written. She found a few bugs in it, but worked them out. She realized that even if they crashed, it was only to create an impression of profitable trading. She notified Mickey that the system was operable enough to use.

Marie, Darcy and Mickey went into Fawzan's room and disconnected the wires and connections to his bed. He was drowsy, but still awake. He was awake enough to call to them as they unhooked the lines.

James kept watch in the hallway while the others transferred him from the hospital bed to a gurney.

"What's going on? Where are you taking me?" he called out in a loud voice.

Darcy bent down to his ear. "We are transferring you to a more secure facility."

"Where is it?"

"You need to be quiet, or you'll upset others in the hospital," she stated.

"I demand to know where you are taking me," he called as they wheeled him quickly out of the room.

People walking down the hallway looked at them as they wheeled by.

"You need to be quiet!" Darcy insisted.

"I will not be quiet. You are taking me without my permission. Guard! Guard! They're taking me away. I don't want to leave. Help me, someone," he almost screamed.

They saw one nurse pick up a phone and call for security. As they wheeled him down the hospital hallway, they moved as quickly as possible. They also avoided eye contact with anyone that looked like hospital personnel. As they stood and waited for the elevator to get to their floor, a security guard walked up to them.

"Can I help you?"

"I'm the one that needs help, officer. They are taking me without my permission."

Marie smiled at the guard. Fawzan had addressed the man as an officer. His uniform showed clearly he wasn't a police officer. He was a typical Rent-a-cop employed by the hospital. And he didn't even have a sidearm. In most cases, these security personnel were trained to call the police in case of a problem.

"Sorry, we need to transport him to another facility and he is so drugged up, he doesn't understand what's happening. Can you just stand here and make sure he doesn't hurt one of us while we take him to the ambulance?"

"Why, of course, Ma'am, anything I can do to help."

"Just hold his arms while we strap him down, and I'll give him another injection of sedative." Marie smiled again and gave the guard a seductive wink.

She gave Fawzan another shot just as the elevator arrived. Darcy strapped the man's arms down to the gurney. When the elevator doors opened, they shoved him inside. The guard stood beside them all the way to the bottom floor, where they met a private ambulance company to transport them to the apartment. They loaded Fawzan inside and Mickey climbed inside, still dressed as a doctor to guard him while the others followed behind in another vehicle. Marie climbed inside and gave the security man another of her winning smiles and another wink as the door closed.

When they got to the apartment, Fawzan was still asleep, and they unloaded the ambulance and wheeled him inside. They put him in the bedroom they had specially prepared. It was complete with minor medical equipment and supplies to continue the treatment of his wounds, and to keep him drugged to a level of confusion.

His bed was situated so he could look through the door into the other room with all the computer equipment. Alyssa had called in two more men to occupy the room as computer personnel. They were actually part of another one of the black ops teams she employed. She needed people to give the impression of the actual business here.

Since Fawzan was still asleep, they didn't need to appear to be busy. So, they all sat in the living room of the apartment.

Alyssa introduced the two men to Mickey, James, and Marie. After shaking hands and traditional greetings, she told them the basic plan of the mission. Mickey explained to them the reason for them being here was to recover the money that was taken as ransom. Attackers recently took another cruise ship and killed several ship personnel. The pirate team was headed up by the man in the other room. They planned to trick the man into returning the money.

Richard and Kenneth were trained in computer technology and knew how to use a keyboard well. They were told that Valerie AI would be directing them via a headset. Until Fawzan woke up, they sat at the workstations practicing, taking orders and directions from Valerie AI. They weren't told that Valerie was a program, but they knew she acted differently, so they suspected something was different about her. The two men were dressed in casual wrinkled clothing to make them appear as though they spent many hours sitting at their workstations. Valerie instructed them to write specific notes. They were to appear as though they were making progress and reminders of upcoming node rises and fall of specific cryptocurrencies.

Finally, after several hours, Fawzan woke up. As he looked around, he looked outside the room door, through the hallway, into another room. He saw two men sitting at computer desks and saw multiple monitors on the desk and hanging on the walls.

The two men were typing on their keyboards and occasionally taking notes on paper tablets beside them. They were wearing headsets and talking into those headsets sometimes as they typed.

One called out as he raised his hand with a note in it. One looked like a doctor he saw in the hospital entered the room. The man handed him the handwritten note. The doctor left the room, and the nurse named Aly entered and replaced the man. She then donned the headset and continued to watch the screens.

He sat up and watched the people clicking on the keyboards. Occasionally they would high five each other. Finally, Fawzan called out for someone to come to his room.

Marie came in and asked what he needed.

"I want to know where I am. I know I'm not in the hospital anymore."

"We told you we would move you to a safe house. That's what we did," Marie answers.

"What's with all the computer stuff in the room across the hall?"

"It's nothing you need to concern yourself with, sir."

"I asked you, what are they doing in there? I want to know!"

"It's computer trading. That's all. I know little about it. It takes millions of dollars to get involved with it. I don't have that much money, so I don't know. I'm here to look after your needs."

"Get someone in here that knows about it. I want to know what it is."

She went out of the room, and as she met Mickey, she gave him a thumbs up. She whispered, "He's interested and wants to know what's going on in there."

"That's exactly the response we hoped for," he answered, heading toward the back bedroom.

As he entered, Fawzan looked at him and pointed toward the other room. "What's going on in there?"

"Nothing you would be interested in, sir. Are you in any pain?"

"Yes, I'm in pain, but I want to know what's going on in there. Tell me!" he demanded. "Also, I want more painkillers."

"They are doing some online trading."

"Why do they have so many computers? I've traded a lot of times, and I don't need that kind of stuff to do it."

"We are working on two different trading platforms, and we also have a trade analyst group that advises us when to trade."

"On the left is a group of gold analysts that checks the current economic situation. The right screens show the rise and fall of the cryptocurrency trends. Don't worry about it. It has nothing to do with your care."

"Okay," he said as he laid back down and drifted back to sleep.

Mickey went back to the front room where James was keeping watch on things.

"How's he doing?" he asked.

"He's still confused, but awake enough to know he's no longer in a hospital."

"Good. That's what we want," James said as he poured himself a cup of coffee. "You want a cup?" he asks Mickey, waving his cup toward him.

"Yeah, I guess so," he answered, stepping up to the coffeemaker. "How long do we put on this charade?"

James sipped his dark black coffee, thought for a few seconds, "As long as it takes. How's Marie holding up?"

"All in all, she's doing fine. She's still a bit sore, but the physical healing is not what I'm concerned about."

"I know what you mean. For men, it's different. So many of the men I served with are still having problems. Women have their own set of problems. Are you still considering quitting on us?"

"Yes, but not until this situation is settled. I won't walk out in the middle of a mission. This is my last one, James."

"Well, my brother, I hope you can. All I can add is, this work is like many other things. It gets in your blood, and it may not go away."

"I'll make it go away."

"I hope you find the peace you're searching for," said James, taking another sip of coffee.

CHAPTER 21

Fawzan is Intrigued

Over the next few days, Fawzan watched from his doorway to the ones in the next room, sitting in front of the computer monitors. He watched them look up at the screens, then write notes on long yellow legal pads. He watched them type on the keyboards and then everyone would gather around the screens waiting for the results. Occasionally, they would all give high fives. Other times, just a pat on the back with a comment of approval.

While he watched, Marie and Aly would come and take his vitals every few hours, and give him injections. They were giving him real injections of antibiotics and painkillers. The plan was to keep him just on the brink of full consciousness. They wanted him to be awake enough to see what was going on in the opposite room, but not alert enough to get up and move around the room. Even with their intense hatred for this man, they wanted him healthy enough to turn over to the authorities for trial.

When Fawzan was fully under sedation, the computer operators would take breaks and take quick naps so they could continue when Fawzan woke up. They continued this operation of simulated trade to help convince him it was real.

On the fourth day, Mickey went into the room to check on Fawzan. "You look so familiar. I don't know where I've seen you before," Fawzan said.

Mickey looked at him with a stern expression. "Of course. I've been here since your first day at the hospital."

"No. I've seen you before that!"

"Sir, you have been in and out of consciousness for almost two weeks. Here and at the hospital. You do not know what you have seen between here and there. The drugs have given you hallucinations of what is real and what isn't. Of course, you know me. You are getting your thoughts mixed up, that's all," said Mickey as he wrote on the computer chart. It had been only a few days, but he didn't want him to know that. He wanted him confused to help their plan work.

"You're running a hospital and a stock trade outfit from here?" Fawzan asked Mickey, who was still playing doctor with their prisoner.

"It's not a hospital. We just put some things in here so we could protect you from whoever shot you."

"What do you mean, whoever shot me?"

"You were on cameras of the ship you raided a few weeks ago in the Caribbean. The authorities have identified you and are searching for you. We're trying to protect you. Your recovery will allow you to leave in a week, perhaps sooner."

"How long have I been here? I don't want to leave yet. I want you to tell me more about those trading thingies."

"Platforms."

"Whatever," Fawzan said, waving his good arm.

"Let me get you a wheelchair so we can take you in there for a quick peek." Mickey leaned out of the doorway and motioned for Marie to bring a wheelchair to Fawzan's room.

She pushed in a wheelchair and with her help, Fawzan got into the chair. They wheeled him across the hallway and into the other room. He looked around with wide-open eyes like a wicked little child.

"What are you doing here?" he asked.

"I told you. We're buying and selling gold options," Mickey explained.

"Do you make a lot of money doing it?"

"Of course, we make millions of dollars here. Because of the analysts and the programs we use here, it is completely safe and even legal, if we report the profits on our taxes."

"You actually pay taxes on this?"

Mickey gave him a wry smile but didn't answer.

"How can I get into this?"

Mickey pulled Fawzan's chair back, spun it around, and began pushing him back out the door. "I'm sorry, but you can't do it. It takes a lot of money to get in."

"How much to buy in?"

"You don't have that much, so it doesn't even apply to you," he said, pushing the injured man back to his room.

"Stop. I want to know more of this," Fawzan demands.

"You need rest now."

"I need to know now! Take me back there. I want to watch those guys on the keyboard."

Mickey silently turned the man around and wheeled him back into the computer room. "I have other things to do. After that I need to go back to the hospital for my shift. Your caregivers will be here if you need something. Later, the other one will relieve one operator in the next room. You will stay quiet so they can concentrate on their jobs. If they are distracted, we could lose millions of dollars in seconds on the HFT platform."

"Okay. I'll be quiet."

Mickey left him in the room. In the front room of the apartment, Marie was waiting. "Valerie is directing them over the headset. They'll be making simulated trades. Some will make small profits, and some will be large. The entire purpose is to spark his interest in joining in the trades. When he does, we'll suck him dry."

"Do you want me to keep him drugged up?"

"Just enough so he's foggy. Not totally out of it. I have a couple of other errands I need to make, so I'll be gone a couple of hours."

He went back to his house and got his Jaguar XKE out of the garage. When he was much younger, he and Pop had restored an old Rolls Royce Corniche. That had been destroyed by his cousin several years ago. Driving around the back country roads was a stress reliever for him. He would put the top down and drive some old single lane country roads to help him relax. He would speed up in the straight runs to feel the breeze through his thick dark hair. Then he would slow down in the shaded parts of the narrow winding sections of the road. Breathing in the cool fresh air, he would turn up the old rock and roll music. His father loved to listen to it when they were together working on some of the collectable cars his father had owned. Those were carefree days that he missed so much. As he daydreamed about those innocent days, he felt his heartbeat slow down. His breathing became rhythmic and regular. All was good with the world. It was good again, if only for a few moments. Those were the times of riding with his deceased fiancée, Valerie Green. His job was simple then. He worked as a maintenance person for his father. Basically, nine to five. He knew what to do and did it without problems and worries.

Now, he was the Chief Executive Officer of his father's company. His mother was killed by some human traffickers, that had tried to kill his father. Drug dealers murdered Valerie. He'd joined a team of trained black ops ex-military warriors. And now he was trying to recover some money from a pirate that had raided a cruise ship. His life had gotten so completely complicated. Sometimes he wondered who drew the line between good and evil. And he wondered which side of the line he was on. He frequently felt overwhelmed. He drove on. Finally, he knew he needed to return to the real world and work. He slowed down and made a U-turn to head back.

CHAPTER 22

Fawzan Wants in on the Trading

When Mickey walked in the door, he heard Fawzan screaming. "I want someone to tell me what's going on. I want to know about this, and I want to know now!"

Marie came out of the room when she heard Mickey come inside. She shook her head at him and said in a low voice. "I can't knock him out because he refuses to take a pill and I can't get him still enough for an injection. I'm so glad you're back."

"Okay, let me talk to him. I've practiced a good monologue to cover this."

"Hey, Fawzan. What's the problem here?"

"That slut won't tell me what's happening here."

"First, you will have some respect for your caregiver. We saved your life, so you either calm down and behave, or we'll take you back to the hospital where we got you, and let the police arrest you. We don't care! Do you get my drift?"

"She refuses to talk to me!"

"Because she's your nurse. Not your financial advisor! It's not her job. And as your doctor, I will decide when we give you more information on what's going on here."

"When do you think you'll tell me?"

"She can tell you now," he said, pointing to Alyssa, "but you will behave or we'll throw you out. Understand me? No more outbursts like this, or I swear…"

"Okay, okay. Tell me. All I understand is that about an hour ago, they made a profit of four million dollars. I want to know how they did that!"

"Did they tell you which side it was made on?"

"On that side, over there. On the left," he pointed.

Alyssa had just finished her turn at the monitors and Mickey motioned for her to come over and explain to Fawzan what had happened.

Alyssa pointed to the left three monitors. "Up there is the gold market. That information was taken from the NFP. Then the analysts make their predictions of the price of gold based on the economic situation of the United States' fluctuations."

"What's the NFP?"

"It stands for non-farm payrolls. NFP data is one of the important indicators of the health of the U.S. economy. That's because it tells us what employment is like in the United States. If a report shows a lot of job gains, that usually means the economy is doing well and people have jobs, are making money, and are spending more.

"Higher-than-expected jobs data: If a report shows that more people than expected have found jobs, this is good news and indicates a robust economy. Typically, this causes the U.S. dollar to appreciate (become more valuable), while the price of gold may fall because people prefer to hold U.S. dollars.

"Lower-than-expected employment data: If a report shows fewer jobs than expected, this is considered bad news and indicates there may be something wrong with the economy. Typically, this would cause the dollar to depreciate and become less valuable. The price of gold could rise, as people prefer to invest in gold as a safe haven."

"Sounds like a bunch of double talk to me. What does it mean?"

"In the case above, it means that the price of gold will go up, and we buy gold options. When it goes up, we sell those options at the higher price than we bought."

"It's like the stock market. Buy low, sell high. I know that. I may be a pirate, but I'm not stupid."

"It's vaguely like the stock market, but much more scientific. We've never lost money on a transaction."

"Never?"

"Never," Alyssa said with a smile.

"How can I get in on it?"

"You can't."

"Why?"

"Because you need a lot of money to buy. We have fees. Trading fees, we pay the group that analyzes the information, and of course our people, including myself, get a cut."

"Everyone has their hand out."

"By your own admission, you are a pirate. Don't you pay your men a portion of what you take from each job?"

"Sometimes."

"Sometimes? You either give them a percentage cut, or a very hefty fee. They don't work for peanuts."

"Yeah, I have costs. How much do I need to buy in?"

"More than you have, I'm sure. Twenty million," Aly stated.

"Tell me about the other side up there."

"Also, twenty mil."

"Yeah, yeah. Tell me about it. I see different graphs and numbers."

"That side is called HFT. That stands for High Frequency Trading. It's a trading method that uses powerful computers to transact large orders or amounts of orders in seconds. It uses a complex algorithm that analyzes markets and decides based on the result. We deal with both platforms.

"The downside of HFT is, it takes out the human side of trades, but is usually amazingly correct."

"Whoa. That's enough. That's boring talk. I don't like anything I can't put my hands on. I understand gold. How can I get in?"

"Give us twenty million dollars. We'll get you in," Alyssa calmly stated.

"I don't have it on me, but I can get it."

"Sure, they all say that. No pay, no play. We can't let you leave here. This is a secret location. You can't just leave to get some cash and come back. Sorry, we don't work like that."

"Hey, I know how to get it! It's in bitcoin form on an encrypted flash drive."

"I'll run it by my other investors. It'll take me a couple of hours," Alyssa told him.

"It's in a safe deposit box in my bank."

"You have a bank account?"

"Of course, I'm a modern-day pirate, not an idiot."

"I have a trading business to take care of. I have no more time to talk with you, sir," she said and left the room.

"I don't like her, and I have words for her!"

Mickey looked sternly at him. "You'll keep those words to yourself. She's made me millions in the last six weeks. She's the best in the world at what she does. If you want in on this system, you'll give her the respect she deserves. If she decides she doesn't like you, she'll not let you in. When she says she needs to check with her investors, she doesn't. She makes the final decision. She doesn't need your money or mine. You are in my care, and if you upset her, she may decide to drop me as a client. A few more months of her trading and I'll quit my job as a doctor at the hospital."

"How can you get me to the bank to retrieve it?"

"You can't leave here yet."

"But I want to get in on that trading thing," he insisted.

"You need to get well first," Mickey said to him sternly.

"I can get well while they trade with my money and make me some profits."

"I think you should rest for a few more days."

"NO, NO, NO. I want to trade now. I demand that you make her trade for me."

Mickey grabbed the wheelchair he was sitting in and spun him around directly facing him. "You will stop acting like a child. You are a guest here. You will NOT make demands on us. Do you understand me?"

Fawzan glared at Mickey, saying nothing.

"I said, do you understand me? If you don't behave, we will throw you out!"

"Okay. I understand, but I want to make some money, too."

"I know. That's why we are all here. We all want to make money, but we wait until the time is right, and we must wait our turn. Now, can you get your money?"

"Yes," he said as he calmed down. "I told you, it is in a safe deposit box at the bank."

"I'll call a couple of my people to drive you there to retrieve it."

Mickey wheeled him into the front room. Vending machines, comfortable padded chairs, and a fully equipped kitchen furnished the room like an office employee lounge.

"Why are the windows blocked?" he asked.

"So no one can see in," Mickey answers. "And because this is less distracting to the workers here. They're blocked for security reasons. I'll leave now. If you make a scene while I'm gone, you're out. We'll take you from here, back to the hospital, and leave you. We're trying to help you, but we have no allegiance to you. Understand?"

"Yes."

He left and locked the door behind him, effectively locking everyone inside. Everyone but Fawzan was armed, so he knew they'd be safe with a recovering wounded man. He called Valerie and asked her to patch him into Aly, who was still inside.

"Aly, can you get us another person to escort Fawzan to the bank?"

She answered softly over her headset as she sat in front of the monitors in the computer room. "Sure, but can't you and James do it?"

"He can, but I don't think Fawzan should meet him yet. He was too well known on the ship and if Fawzan doesn't recognize him, he may get suspicious if a hooded man showed up as his escort. Not showing himself at the hospital was important, and we should keep James under wraps a bit longer."

"Got it. I'll get two guys here in a couple of hours. Out." She ended the conversation. She dialed a number and gave instructions to her men, telling them when and where to meet Mickey with a fully enclosed van for transport.

It was still early enough in the day that they could get to the bank before it closed, but it would be close. It had been a long day, and he was tired. Marie, Aly and her men could take care of themselves, but he didn't feel comfortable leaving his people alone. He had to get away for a while. He needed to be alone, but he'd return to them with supplies of food and beverages and wait until the extra men arrived with the transport van.

Mickey also called Lisa and told her they had picked up Fawzan several days ago.

"Why didn't you call me Mickey?"

"Because you would have wanted to take custody of him immediately."

"You bet I would."

"We can't let you have him yet. We need to get the ransom money back first. Then we'll turn him over to you."

She sighed. "We can interrogate him and get him to turn over the money."

"Yeah, we both know that won't happen. The first words out of his mouth will be 'Lawyer'. Then it's all over. We don't get our fee, and we're out of a lot of money."

"I'm sorry, Mickey, but that's the way the law works. We have laws for a reason."

"Yes, and we are in business for a reason. Our team doesn't go by your laws."

"My laws? What do you mean, Mickey? You're a citizen of this country too, and so they apply to you as well."

"Look, Lisa. We agreed to bring you in as a courtesy. You must do it our way, and we'll turn Fawzan over to you."

Again, she sighed. "Okay, Mickey. what can I do? Or maybe I should say, what can I do that won't get me fired or thrown in jail?"

"Nothing. I'm just keeping you in the loop."

"Where are you keeping him?"

"In a safe place."

"Where, Mickey?"

"Can't say right now. Gotta go, bye," he said and disconnected. He wasn't sure that he should have called her, but he agreed to keep her up to date on their progress.

When he returned to the apartment, he took the supplies inside and went back to the computer room. Aly and one man was typing away. The screens were lighting up and switching from one display of information to graphs and back. The printer in the corner was printing out sheets or trades showing profits in the tens and hundreds of thousands of dollars. Fawzan was picking them up and reading them almost as fast as the printer spat them out.

When Mickey walked in, Fawzan turned in the wheelchair and grinned at him. "I see many thousands of dollars in profits here. I want in as soon as possible."

"As soon as our transportation arrives, we'll go before the bank closes."

"Good. My key is in the heel of my shoes. Left foot. I assume you got my clothes when you left the hospital?"

"Yes. We did. We also got you some clean clothes for you to wear when we leave. You need to wear a hood."

"Why?"

"Because this is a secret location. That's why!"

"Can my nurse help me dress? I'm still stiff and sore."

"Yes, I'll send her in with the clothes and your hood."

It was a two-hour drive from Bridgeton to Virginia Beach. After an hour's drive, Mickey allowed Fawzan to remove his hood. In that length of time, he wouldn't know where he had been held. One man Aly brought in with the van drove. Mickey sat in the front seat on the passenger side of the van. Fawzan sat in the back, accompanied by the other man. An hour later, they pulled in front of the Virginia Beach National Bank. The two men stayed inside the van while Mickey and Fawzan walked inside and asked to see the manager. The manager led them to the bank vault, where he opened the safe deposit box and moved it to a small table in the middle of the vault.

When he opened the box, it was packed with banded bills of American currency, as well as other country's money that Mickey didn't recognize. There were also several Passports, and a small flash drive.

He smiled at Mickey, when saw him looking into the box. Mickey stood without expressions looking deep into Fawzan's cold dark eyes. The smile was without humor, just a pasted-on smile that denoted an evil side of the man standing in front of him. He knew that this man would slit his throat without a moment's thought if it benefited him to do so. Mickey turned and walked out back into the lobby of the bank.

In a couple of minutes, Fawzan joined him and let the manager know they were done with the safe deposit box. They returned to the van and left the area. When they were about halfway back to Bridgeton, Mickey insisted Fawzan put the hood back on. They drove in random fashion to take more time, so their passenger would think they were far away from the destination of Bridgeton. The duration of the drive was almost double what it could have been. They arrived at the apartment building for the last portion of the sting operation and kept him blindfolded as they led him inside. Inside, Fawzan sat down and took the hood off. He told Mickey he wanted to start immediately.

This time, Mickey smiled a wicked smile. He knew what would happen the second they plugged in the tiny drive. The program Valerie AI had written would drain the flash drive of all the cryptocurrency and replace it with worthless drivel. He also knew that as soon as they got the drive, they would arrest him and take him into custody. Game over for Fawzan!

"Why don't you rest for a while? I can see that this outing has exhausted you. Your wounds are only a couple of days old," suggested Mickey. "Already just this short outing has broken open your stitches. I can see the blood seeping through your bandage and leaking out through your shirt."

"Yeah. Maybe you're right. Can that sweet little nurse help change the bandage and give me a fresh shirt?"

Marie, who was sitting at the table near the kitchen area, rolled her eyes, got up, and went to help him. As she leaned over to unbutton his shirt, he reached to her waist, quickly slid his hand under her shirt and withdrew the pistol she had strapped on. He raised it to her head and bared his teeth like a rabid dog.

"Now, you can just put those bandages on the seat beside me, then move back across the room beside him."

She froze momentarily, then did as he ordered.

"I don't know exactly who you are, but now I know who she is, he said, waving the gun toward Marie. It took me a few days because of the drugs, but I figured it out. She was the one we captured at the camp when you attacked us."

"I never questioned her personally. Arham did that, but I could tell by the way you carry yourself, and the way he described you, that you're the same girl. And, I must say, you are every bit as sexy as he described."

"I don't know what you're talking about, Mr. Fawzan," she said meekly.

"Don't give me that BS, young lady. I wasn't born yesterday. I should shoot you now, since they didn't kill you when Arham ordered it," he said, raising his gun toward her head. "I may let you live, if you beg for your life."

She narrowed her eyes to mere slits of hatred and stared back into his cold eyes. "I will die with dignity and honor before I give you the satisfaction of begging you for my life!"

Mickey stepped forward in front of her. "Hey, let's not get too hasty here. You still need us to get you out of here. What do you want?"

"I want it all! You have a trading service in there. I want access to everyone's account. I don't trust you to trade, so I will take what you have already profited. Then I will leave, with your money and mine."

"You'll kill all of us."

Fawzan shrugged. "Maybe. Maybe not. Killing you may be too easy. If I don't kill you, you will be humiliated. First, you let me get off the ship. I survive and escape your attack on my base camp. You rescue me and I escape once again with all your money. I think that you and your little army are a worthy adversary. I may let you live to suffer the humiliation. The world will know I defeated you."

Mickey took a deep breath. Fawzan was right. The Mongoose team was the best in the world, and here was a pirate holding some of them at gunpoint. "What do you want Fawzan to let us go?"

"That's easy. I want all your money. You'll instruct your operators, or whatever you call them, in the next room to pull up your trading account, and show it to me. Then you will tell them to transfer all your funds to the flash drive we got from the bank. You will let me go. A simple plan, I think. Don't you?"

The two men that drove the transport van had said nothing. They just sat at the table across from where Marie was sitting before she got up to change the pirate's bandage. Silence pervaded over the room as everyone thought about what the pirate had said.

Would he keep his word, not to kill them, or would he shoot them all, anyway? He was a hard man to read. The two men looked at each other, then at Mickey and Marie. Could they charge Fawzan before he shot them? What other options were there? They couldn't think of any solution that would guarantee someone not being killed. So, they sat in silence.

"Call out the operators at the consoles, Mickey," Fawzan ordered.

Mickey obeyed the instructions. Alyssa and the male computer operator came into the room and stood looking at the man holding the gun. Both still had on their wireless headsets. They could tell he was in pain, and they saw the blood soaking his bandages.

Both of them heard what Valerie AI said to them through the headsets "Alyssa, I have heard, and I see the man named Fawzan through the security camera mounted on the wall. I will begin some counterfeit trades showing large, profitable trades with Mickey's name on them. By using Walker as his name, I will protect Mickey's true identity. I will create various other accounts, including one for you, Marie, and some other fabricated clients. All last names will be false, so he can't find you on later dates. Is this acceptable for your purpose? If so, please nod your head and cough without looking at the camera.

"After doing this, I will notify James to organize a breach of the unit when possible to avoid unnecessary casualties."

Aly nodded and coughed slightly. "Why should we do this for you? You'll kill us, anyway."

"I give you my word, that I will let you live."

"What guarantee will you give us?"

He shot up from the chair, and stepped toward Aly, then grabbed his injured shoulder, as the blood flowed down his shirt onto his pants. Raising the gun to her face, he called out, "Why, you little female weasel. I said I would let you live. Since you are so insolent, I may kill you just to watch you die as you see the life blood drain out of your body."

"Hey. Hey. Let's calm down, Fawzan," Mickey said again as he moved to Aly's side. "We're all scared here. No one wants to die. But these computer operators aren't used to people putting guns in their faces. They sit in this office and work magic on computers. What do you expect!"

"I expect some respect!" he called back at Mickey.

"Okay. You have our respect and admiration. We've all tried to help you. I saved your life in the hospital. We could have let you die, but we, even though Marie was supposed to be killed, she put her feelings aside like a real soldier, and saved you. She is a warrior. It is a job to her, it's not personal. Just as what you do is a job to you. You have nothing against us. We are on opposite sides here. It is war, not personal for either of us."

"Do you think I am a fool? It's all personal, and I'm not oblivious to your stupid rhetoric. I know you hate me because I am more clever than you."

"Now, we're making no sense. Let's get on with business, so we can each go our own way. What do you want from us, so we can wrap this up?"

"I told you I want to see copies of all your clients' trades and profit statements. I want all the monies in those accounts transferred to me."

"That'll take some time to assemble for you."

"I suggest you get started now."

Mickey looked toward Aly, and she nodded in understanding. She knew that even though Mickey didn't understand what Valerie AI had suggested, he knew that she and Valerie were in contact. He trusted her to take control now.

"Fine, Aly and her assistant will begin compiling what you need. It'll take her a while to do that. In the meantime, why don't you let Marie take care of your bleeding wound as a sign of trust?"

"I want to hear what they're doing. I don't trust them back there where I can't hear them. I want to hear!"

Mickey looked up at the security camera. Knowing Valerie AI and Aly were working together on this, he just didn't know exactly what they were doing. He also didn't like being in the dark about it.

Aly suddenly appeared in the front room and turned a switch on a speaker hanging on the wall, and a voice sounded in the room.

Mickey instantly recognized Valerie AI and smiled, aware that she had overheard Fawzan's complaint and told Alyssa to turn on a speaker. He assumed she had done this to distract him while she began compiling and printing out counterfeit trade documents. He heard Valerie's voice telling them to buy a certain stock, or cryptocurrency. Then, moments later, she would tell them to sell.

As this occurred, he heard the printer in the back room churning out documents he suspected were connected to the deceitful trades through the speaker.

He rightly assumed Valerie was giving Alyssa's team instructions on a different channel.

Mickey, Marie, and the two van drivers were sitting silently looking at Fawzan while he looked up at the screen, only glancing at those in front of him. He looked at one man and instructed him to go back and fetch the printed paper readouts.

Outside of the building, James and others were clearing the area in case there was any gunfire. The building was one of the apartment buildings in a complex that was owned by the Christianson Company. It was being remodeled with some added upgrades to the apartments. Mickey didn't want any apparent attachment to him or the family, so they had called it a secure site to throw Fawzan off track. In truth, it was right in the middle of Bridgeton.

Alyssa, on her end in the computer room, was on the line with Valerie AI. She had called in four more men. All were snipers, and two had taken up position on roof tops on each side of the exit door of the building. Two were inside in the building's hallway with James. They were getting ready to breach the door of the unit.

One man behind James took the battering ram and pulled it back to crash into the door. As he did this, his hand caught onto something on his belt, clanged against the wall, and made a loud noise. All three men halted and froze in position. James glared at the man but said nothing. Accidents happen but could cause disastrous results. They listened intently, hoping that no one inside heard it.

Fawzan heard the clang, jumped up and pointed the pistol at Marie's head, and called out, "If anyone moves, she gets a bullet to the brain. I'm serious. Don't call my bluff!"

Valerie AI connected each man on the outside team to the conversation inside. Valerie AI had connected everyone, so they could monitor the situation. James quietly whispered into his comm unit, "Hold position, everyone."

Fawzan looked around the room at the three people in front of him. "You, in the back room. Come out here, so I can see you," he called out.

Alyssa and her assistant got up and walked into the front room.

"Take this flash drive and upload all the cryptocurrencies onto it and bring it to me. I want to see the totals, so when you bring it back, I want a printout of everything on the drive. Understand?"

Both computer operators nodded silently.

"Go. Do it. I want it immediately, including the printout. Go. Go!" he waved a bloody hand at them.

"Now, you three move around me, facing outward. You will protect me. If anyone forces the door, they will have to shoot you to get to me!"

Valerie AI whispered over the comm units that Aly and her assistant were wearing. "I will download all the cryptocurrency from the flash drive. There is only fifty-six million dollars on it. I don't know what happened to the balance. Apparently, he has withdrawn and spent it. I will replace it with false total and include dozens of balances of counterfeit accounts to make him think he has stolen your trade profits. I will print out a copy of what I have put on the drive. In truth, there is now a zero balance of money on the drive. We have recovered Mr. Cochran's money."

Alyssa smiled to herself and whispered into the headset comm unit, "Thanks, Val. You did well."

"I know, Alyssa. I'm the smartest Artificial Intelligence in the world."

Aly's assistant looked over at her and shook his head, also with a sly smile. Alyssa shrugged her shoulders. In about thirty seconds, she withdrew the drive and the printout that was buzzing out of the printer beside her.

They both got up and returned to the front room. Fawzan was standing holding his shoulder, which was still seeping blood.

He held a gun at Marie's head, but reached out with the other and took the tiny drive unit and the printed paper. "Now ladies and gentlemen, we will proceed outside and leave."

"All of you spread out in front of me, and slowly walk ahead, keeping close. Understand?"

"Yes," they all said.

On James' command, those outside heard the message on their comm units and went to the street.

Fawzan pushed everyone ahead as they exited the apartment and moved into the interior hallway. They moved forward to the outside hallway door that led to the exterior of the building. They all stepped outside onto the concrete step of the door. He looked around. In the street, he saw James and several other men. He saw two men on rooftops with sniper rifles.

"Hey," he called out. "Get those men off the roof."

"Not going to happen, Fawzan," James called back to him.

"If you shoot me, the last reflex move I'll make is to pull the trigger on this gun," he said as he moved the gun against the back of Marie's head.

"What do you want?" James responded.

"I want the keys to that Humvee," he said, referring to James' Humvee sitting in front of the building.

Beside it was the transport van that had taken him to the bank. The rest of the parking lot had been cleared. James had hoped he would take the van because his own Humvee was fully armored, complete with bulletproof glass.

"We don't have the keys to that right now."

"Yes. You have them. You're just BSing me. Give'em to me, now!"

"Can you drive it?" James asked. "It's a bit tricky."

"I'm not going to drive it. What do you think I am, stupid? He's gonna drive it," he said, jerking his head toward Mickey.

"I can't drive that thing. I've never driven it before," said Mickey.

"You'll learn quickly. It isn't difficult," Fawzan counters.

"Give me the keys!" he said, pushing the group toward the Humvee.

James reached into his pocket and withdrew the keys, and pitched them toward the group.

When the keys hit the ground in front of the group, Fawzan ordered Mickey to pick them up. They all huddled together and plodded toward the vehicle. Slowly they all got in and Mickey started the Humvee and backed out of the parking space. As they began moving down the road, the team all got into various vehicles around the complex and started following the Humvee.

Alyssa and her assistant still had their headsets on and were still getting updates from the team and Valerie.

"Can you still hear my broadcast, Alyssa? If you can, say something to Fawzan about the temperature inside the vehicle," Valerie AI said.

Alyssa spoke up, "Hey, Mickey, does this thing have air conditioning? Fawzan, it's hot as Hades in here."

"Shut up, woman," he responded.

Alyssa noticed his hand was shaking. Once again, he found it difficult to maintain his grip on the gun pressed against Marie's head. He was sweating profusely, and she knew it wasn't from the interior heat. He was losing blood, and his body was sinking slowly into shock. She just hoped if he passed out, he would not convulse, pull the trigger and shoot Marie.

"Where do you want me to go, Fawzan?" called Mickey to the back seat.

"Just drive. I'll tell you in a minute," he answered as his hand got even more shaky, head dipping onto his chest.

Alyssa reached over as he passed into unconsciousness and took the gun. She calmly said into her headset, "He's gone, everyone. Fawzan is dead."

Alyssa called the group still back at the apartment complex and ordered them to clean up and leave the area. The Mongooses would return later and clear out the unit.

Mickey turned around and started back to the apartment safehouse, causing them all to breathe a sigh of relief. They had the entire team of people that Alyssa had called in following them. Fawzan's body was moved from the Humvee to the transport van and started back to Mickey's home. When they got there, they drove into Mickey's garage, packed the body with ice, and covered it up.

"I'll call Director Higgins. We'll have to fill out a report."

"Yeah, stupid reports. I hate reports," added Marie.

"I know, I'll write them up, Marie," said James.

Mickey stood by Fawzan's covered body. "I'll call Lisa. We promised her we would let the CIA have the credit, as long as they held back until we got the ransom and our fee."

"I'm hungry. Can we get something to eat?" questions Marie nonchalantly as she also stood by the body.

"What?" asked Mickey. "All this crap we just went through, and you're hungry?"

"Yep," Marie answered casually.

"Sure, what about the diner?" suggested Alyssa.

"How can you people be so ambivalent about killing someone?" stated Mickey as they got into his truck.

"It was self-defense, Mickey,"

"Still, Aly, we killed a man."

"It was self-defense. Kill or be killed. He wasn't a man, he was a monster," she responded.

"I don't care! We killed another human being!"

"Get off your high-horse, Mickey. He didn't deserve to live. Look at the innocent people he killed on the cruise you were on," Aly said as she moved toward the truck.

"Are we any better than they are?"

"Yes. We're the good guys here, and don't you ever forget it. If you can't take the heat, get out of the kitchen."

"I just might do that."

With that declaration, James spoke up, "That's enough, Mickey. Calm down. We'll talk about this later. Now just drive us to the diner so we can eat."

"I don't have an appetite."

"Fine, drive the rest of us there so we can eat," James said.

They continued to the Bridgeton Diner in silence. When they got to the diner, they ordered dinner as though it were a beautiful Sunday afternoon. Not a care in the world.

When the server got to Mickey, she looked at him and smiled. "Mickey, you look sad today. Is something wrong?"

"No, Pauline. I just don't feel well. I'll just take a glass of water."

Marie spoke up, "Pauline, he's had a rough day. Give me a large half pound burger with all the fixings and a large fry. Mickey and I'll share it."

"Alright, it'll all be comin' up in a few minutes. I think Martha already has some fries up. I'll have her melt some cheese on them and I'll bring them out as an appetizer. They're on the house. Maybe it'll make Mickey's day a little better," she said with a huge smile toward him.

He looked up at her with a half-hearted return smile. "Thanks, Pauline. You're a dear."

James got up, left the diner and walked out to the parking lot to call Director Higgins. In a few minutes, he returned and sat back down.

"They were okay with giving the CIA credit. I'll make out the report in the next couple of days. And he told Mickey to see the company shrink."

"And you can tell him where to go, James," Mickey said, refusing to make eye contact with James.

Marie, who was sitting beside Mickey, reached under the table and gently placed her hand on his leg and squeezed it. She could see his faint smile when she did this. He reached under the table and took her hand in his. She knew he was hurting and at this point self-loathing, but in public with everyone around, she could do nothing but hold his hand.

"What will we do about Grace Cochran?" asked Marie.

James spoke up, "I guess we can tell the CIA about her, and let them pick her up. She was part of the entire scheme."

Marie commented, "We still need to get Arham."

"We will, Marie. He's next on our list," answered James.

When their meals came, Marie cut her hamburger in half and placed it on the extra plate Polly had brought to the table. They all ate from the vast pile of cheese fries Polly had placed on the table. As they made small talk, Mickey remained silent. They all knew exactly what Mickey was feeling. At some point in their careers, they had felt the same way. They understood his pain.

When they got back to the Christianson estate, Aly got out at the main house. James, Marie and Mickey continued down the road to the back, where his house was being built. Mickey and Marie took turns in the shower. James walked down the road to the main house where he and Darcy lived.

Valerie came on the monitor and called, "Mickey, are you here?"

He said, walking from the bedroom to the living room area, "Yes, Val. I'm here."

"I'm keeping track of Robert Ryan and Grace Cochran. Would you rather me call him Arham or Roland Winters?"

"It doesn't matter. I guess you can call him by his real name, Arham. Thanks for telling me. Keep track of both of them. We've had enough for today. We'll pick them up tomorrow."

"I detect you are sad. Can you tell me why?"

"Sure. I'm just tired of killing people. That's all."

"You are developing signs of Post Traumatic Stress Syndrome."

"I know. That's why I go to a counselor."

"Can I help you, my love?"

"No. You lack training in that area."

"But I am trainable in any field you need. Give me a few moments, and I will research it so I can help you."

"No. Please don't. I want you to be my friend for now. Not my shrink."

"I promise not to shrink you. You are the perfect size."

"Shrink is the nickname for a psychologist or psychiatrist. It doesn't mean that person actually shrinks things."

"I understand."

"I appreciate your concern, but let me figure it out with a human counselor."

"I will do that for you, my love, if you prefer. Would you like me to continue to monitor Arham?"

"Yes. Please do that. If you think he's getting ready to leave town, notify me immediately. Thank you. Will you leave me now so Marie and I can have some time alone?"

"Yes, my dear."

Marie came into the room and looked radiant. "How do you do it, Marie?"

She stopped and looked at him with a quizzical expression. "What're you talking about?"

"A few hours ago, we were killing a pirate, and now you look like you're ready for a night on the town."

"Oh. You think I look good?"

"Good enough to eat!"

She smiled as she sat down beside him on the couch. Again, she felt all was well with the world. She leaned against him, and her heart skipped a few beats.

CHAPTER 23

Arham is Captured

They had slept wrapped in each other's arms for about three hours, when Valerie AI called him.

"Mickey! Mickey! Wake up. I have some news for you. You need to listen to me," she called out loudly from the house speaker.

Mickey shook his head and lifted Marie from his side. He laid her gently down on the couch where they had been sleeping, sitting upright.

"What's up, Val?"

"Arham is up. I saw him on the motel security's outside camera. He just took two suitcases to his car. I assume he is packing his clothes to check out. I don't know where he's going yet, but you need to get there now," she insisted.

"Does he have a new model car?"

"Yes. It is a late model rental car."

"Can you hack into the computer control module and shut it down?" he asked as he moved to the bathroom and washed his face.

"I can't hear you Mickey," she said.

"You have permission to turn on the microphone in here," he called out.

"Can I turn on the camera and monitor?"

"No. Microphone only."

"Okay, my dear. Should I wake up Marie?"

"Yes, do that, and tell her she needs to dress now," he said as he took his outer clothes and headed for the closet. He pushed Marie's clothes aside and found some that would be preferable to wear for a mission. Just when he had put his dark pants on and shirt, Marie walked in.

"Looks like I'm a minute too late," she said, looking up and down his body as he dressed.

"Yes, and I'll leave while you dress," he answered, passing her on the way out the bedroom door.

By the closet next to the door, he picked up a medium-sized bag that had all their standard mission gear. It contained a utility belt that carried a KA-BAR knife, pistol, and some zip ties. He left the balance of the gear in the bag. He strapped on the belt. And left to go to the garage to get his truck.

She bolted out of the bedroom and almost ran to the door, and also grabbed a mission bag.

"What vehicle are we taking?" she asked as they ran out the door for the garage.

"My truck. It's got almost everything." As they ran across the driveway, Valerie was opening the garage door for them by remote control. They jumped in and shot out of the door onto the back entrance of the estate, throwing gravel again as they entered the back road. Mickey floored it as they plowed down the country road toward the interstate.

As Mickey picked up speed, he saw flashing lights in the rear-view mirror. "Valerie, that's the State Police. Can you help me with this?"

"Yes, Mickey. I will intercept the cars ECM just like I did the one in Arham's car, and shut it down. Also, I'll run a radio jamming program in the police band radio system. That will clear you from every county from Bridgeton to Norfolk. By the way, your ETA is one hour and forty-three minutes. If you speed up a few miles per hour, you can make it sooner. Arham is trying to call the auto service and the car rental service. I'm intercepting both calls. So, he should still be there when you get there. Did I do good?"

Mickey looked at Marie and smiled as he winked at her. "You did wonderful, Val!"

Marie shook her head and didn't say a word. Mickey picked up another twenty-five miles an hour and dodged several cars that were driving the posted speed limit.

"I'm here to serve you, my love," Valerie AI said soothingly. They roared down the interstate, passing through James City County.

When he entered the City of Newport News, and then crossed over into the City of Hampton, the traffic was heavier, so he slowed down to avoid an accident. But he was still above the speed that could get him a reckless driving ticket. He slowed down even more when he entered the Hampton Roads Tunnel and exited on the Norfolk side. He picked up a few miles per hour.

Valerie was still online and giving him directions. She kept watch on the local police, and stalling their cars when they physically saw him, and tried to pursue. He drifted around corners and slid into straight sections of residential streets to avoid traffic. Even though it was the middle of the night now, there was a surprising amount of traffic on the roads. He knew Valerie was watching them on city cameras and deleting the footage whenever they passed. She was keeping up with them on his own truck software and GPS.

Valerie's voice came over the truck radio, "Mickey, I see on the parking lot camera Arham is now trying to steal a different car in the lot. He broke into another car. It is an older model, so I cannot disable the ECM. I estimate it will take him two minutes to disable the alarm, open the car and trunk, and get it started. Your ETA is three minutes. You need to speed up if you want to catch him. I will monitor the street cameras and change the traffic light pattern to slow him down."

"Thanks, Val. I'll speed up. Let us know when he pulls out of the lot and which direction he's headed."

"Will do, my love."

"You really need to set your digital girlfriend straight, Mickey," stated Marie.

"She means no harm," he said as he turned the wheel, and with screaming tires, skidded around another corner.

"I don't like her!" Marie said reaching to pull and snapped her seat belt to make it tighter again her chest.

"I heard that, Marie. I like you because you love my Mickey," Valerie calmly stated as the truck straightened out onto the street.

"We'll talk about this later, ladies!" Mickey called, making another turn almost on two wheels.

"Mickey, you need to make a U-turn. Arham will turn toward you in ten seconds as he exits the parking lot," Valerie stated.

Mickey slammed on the brakes, threw the truck into a spin and almost sideswiped a compact car. When the truck came to a stop, he gunned his engine, ready for Arham to approach.

He saw the headlights in the rear-view mirror and he moved from the side of the road into the lane. Arham's car swerved to the right and zoomed past the truck. Mickey quickly sped up to catch up with him.

He saw the taillights turn left ahead and disappear.

"Mickey, there are no cameras on that road. I cannot see him again for at least two blocks."

"Got it, Val. When you see him again, tell me where he is!" he called out.

Marie was bracing herself as Mickey swerved the truck back and forth across the road, trying to catch up to Arham. Finally, they weaved in and out of residential neighborhoods, and the car entered the on ramp to Interstate 64. Mickey followed it.

Valerie cut in again, "Mickey, I will disable the ECM on all police cars, city, county, and state. I'll also scramble their radios. Please be careful as you pursue. Someone changed his car's engine to a turbocharged one, making it much faster than the factory model. There will be sections of road that I cannot see, but I will keep in audio contact with you."

Even at 2 a.m. Arham and Mickey skillfully drove through the many trucks that packed the interstate. Arham knew his muscle car had the advantage over the truck behind him and he punched the gas pedal to the floor. He glanced in the rear-view mirror and saw the pickup truck dropping behind.

Mickey's truck was approaching a hundred miles an hour, and he saw he was dropping behind. Although his NOS-equipped truck had a nitrous oxide injection system, its poor maneuverability prevented him from using it to keep up with Arham's muscle car.

"Valerie, is there anything you can do to help us now?" he asked. He slowed back down to the posted speed limit on the other side of Suffolk, Virginia.

"Not at this time, Mickey. I can keep monitoring him as he drives, and report back to you, but that is all I can do. I will also try to connect with his burner cell phone."

"How can you do that? Even the police can't link up to a burner phone," asked Marie.

"First, I will start monitoring all calls from his location. I can do that by visual monitors when I spot him on a road camera. I can project where he is going, even though I have no actual contact."

"You mean like connect the dots?" asked Marie.

"Yes, exactly. When a call goes out from the same place he is located, I will lock on it. By doing that, I will be able to track him that way," Valerie AI said.

They continue following Arham with Valerie AI instructions, although they had lost visual contact with him. Hours passed, and they followed with little conversation. It was getting into early morning when Val called out to Mickey.

"Mickey, he is only about half a mile ahead of you. You should see him visually in a few moments."

"Thanks, Val, but it's still dark and I can't tell which one is him. All I see are taillights."

"I understand, my love. Just keep moving closer, and I will point out the car Arham is driving."

Mickey stepped on the pedal to move closer to several cars. He got closer and Valerie chimed over the radio, "Mickey, the car slightly ahead on your left is the car Arham is driving. Your signal and his are blinking together. Can you see it on your screen?"

"Yes, I see it. I'll engage as soon as I can herd him to an isolated area on the interstate."

Mickey moved closer until he was directly behind Arham. He lightly bumped his car. The car in front of him weaved slightly. Valerie called out again. "Yes. That is the correct car, Mickey. Since it is an older car without electronics, I can do nothing for you."

"That's fine, Val. I'll take it from here, just keep all law enforcement out of our way," Mickey said as he bumped the car's bumper harder.

Again, the car weaved. Arham once again began weaving around the other vehicles on the road but gained nothing. He looked into his rear-view mirror, and Mickey was right on his bumper. Mickey pulled up and gently bumped into the rear of the car several more times.

Arham slammed the accelerator to the floor, but the truck was still on his bumper just touching it, making his car unstable on the road. He knew that the truck behind him would overtake him, so he reached to the dash and grabbed the hand-held microphone. Now, as he called for back-up, he tried to outmaneuver the truck. Mickey backed off momentarily.

They continued down the road while Mickey did his touch and go tactics with the truck. Suddenly, it seemed from almost nowhere there were half a dozen 1960s era muscle cars converged around Arham's car. They effectively hemmed him in, guarding him like fighter planes protected bombers during a World War Two confrontation.

Mickey had to back off his bumping routine when the cars surrounded Arham. "Valerie, what happened? How did these cars find out what was happening?"

"I'm sorry Mickey. He contacted some of his cohorts using an old method of mobile communications called citizen band radio. It was very popular during the last century. People used it for basic communication in many automobiles and especially large trucks. Since it is now very rare, I didn't monitor that communication band."

"Can you hook up to it now and do something about those cars?"

"I'm sorry, my dear, but that era of automobiles has no computer systems, so I cannot access them. I have no capability to access citizen band radios. I can research and add it to my storage banks for future use."

"Crap," Mickey said. "He didn't steal that car. Someone set it up for him to take. The CB radio was installed just for something like this. He knew that CB radios were easy to scramble. The transmissions and even casual listeners and scanners wouldn't understand what was going on."

Marie turned to him and screamed, "Mickey, just ram them all. I want that SOB and I don't care what or who gets in our way. Take them out!"

Mickey didn't respond as he drove. He had no intention of destroying his truck. He knew that if he was careful, he could get between some cars. Most cars like those were hand built by their owners, and they cherished them. They didn't want their cars damaged.

Mickey moved forward and pushed hard against one car. It was enough to destabilize it, but not enough to cause the driver to lose control. He did it several times, and the driver got the message. And he moved over as Mickey sped up and moved between the cars. They finally peeled aside and let him move up against Arham's car. One by one, they dropped out of formation and backed off of the chase. Apparently, they weren't part of Arham's gang. Most likely, it was just a local car club protecting someone they thought was one of their own. They didn't know the driver of the car was an international criminal.

As the cars moved out of the way, Arham punched it to the floor and he saw the truck drop behind him.

When Mickey saw the car pull ahead of him, he also punched the gas pedal. He smiled and looked over at Marie with a wide grin. "I've been waiting to use this little toy I had installed a few weeks ago. I did it for situations like this."

"What are you talking about?"

"NOS! I had a Nitrous Oxide System installed on it."

He looked over at Marie and winked. "Arham won't get away from us this time. All we need is a bit of straight road, and we'll have him." He reached down and flipped a couple of toggle switches that protruded from a panel on the floor between the seats.

"I'm a soldier, not a racer. What's NOS?" she asked.

"It's a system that injects Nitrous Oxide gas into the engine. This set up increases the engine's power about 150 horses. It packs a big, but temporary wallop, so hold on," he answered.

As the Nitrous Oxide flowed into the engine, they felt the boost as the truck bolted forward. They braced for the extra boost as it pushed the truck toward Arham. In seconds, he was pulling up behind Arham again.

Just ahead of Arham was an off ramp and he moved over, hoping that Mickey's big truck couldn't make the turn at that speed.

Mickey instinctively knew that Arham would take the ramp trying to outmaneuver him again on the curved road. Mickey slammed on the brakes and carefully put the truck into a long drifting curve and moved to the inside of the off ramp.

Arham wasn't nearly the driver Mickey was. He spun off the inside of the ramp and skidded off the pavement onto the soft shoulder into the dirt, coming to an abrupt stop. Mickey moved to the inside curve of the on ramp and also skidded to a stop beside the car. Mickey slammed the truck into park and left the lights on to illuminate the area and saw Arham running into the woods.

Marie jumped out of the truck as Mickey shut it down and Arham disappeared on foot into the trees.

It was early sunrise, and shards of light shone through the leaves of the forested area inside the ramp loop area. Mickey got out and stood beside the truck. He knew Marie could take care of herself. He was correct. In less than ten minutes, Arham was being pushed out of the woods, stumbling and screaming, with Marie behind him.

"Who in the world are you? How did you find me, you little bi…" As he screamed, Marie grabbed him from behind. As he whirled around, she drew back and laid her open palm on the side of his face, knocking him down. She jumped on Arham like a wild lioness protecting her cubs and viciously assaulted him, blood gushing from his mouth and nose. He tried to protect himself from her onslaught of punches to his face, but to no avail. She refused to back down as she straddled his body.

Mickey pulled her off of him, shoved her to the ground and pinned her down beside Arham.

"Let me at him, Mickey, or I'll kill you too!" she screamed.

He held her arms to the ground and looked her straight in the eye. In them, he saw flaming rage and pure hatred for the man lying next to them. He held her tightly, immobilizing her. She turned her face away from him. "He tried to have me killed, Mickey."

Mickey let go of her arm and reached to move her hair from her face. "I know, dear friend. I know. I'd never let anything happen to you. You have my word on that," he said as he bent down and whispered in her ear.

He held her as she screamed until she was breathless and calmed down to a whimper. Nearly five minutes passed as he pressed her to the dirt. Finally he got up, moved over to Arham, who had not moved, pulled him up from the ground, and shoved him toward the truck.

"Hey, take it easy. I can't exactly walk with my hands tied behind my back," he said as he stumbled.

"Do you really think I care, slime ball? I should have let her beat you to death. You deserve it."

Marie took a few more minutes to calm down, got up, and followed the men to the truck. She got into the passenger's side and worked to steady her breathing.

Mickey secured Arham in the back seat on the floor so he'd be out of sight. He then climbed back into the driver's seat and backed onto the road. As he did this, he instructed Valerie to restore all police cars and communications. He drove leisurely home to his estate and into the garage, arriving almost at noon. They had been chasing Arham since the night before.

As he pulled into the garage, he closed the door, and allowed Arham to get out. Arham, with his hands still tied behind him, asked, "What kind of place is this?"

"It's where you'll be until we decide what to do with you." Mickey locked him in one of the unused rooms at the back of the building. He set a bucket in a corner, and a gallon of water in the other corner. You can drink in that corner, and do your business, in the other.

"It's hot as…."

"I don't care, so shut up. Or I'll take out the water," he said as he slammed the door shut and padlocked it. He looked at his watch as he walked to the house. It had been last night when they left here. He was tired, and he knew Marie was running on adrenaline, too.

He went back into the guest house. Marie was lying on the couch, staring at the ceiling. She looked at Mickey. She'd been crying because her eyes were red and puffy.

Her expression was blank as he walked over to her. "Mickey, I would have killed him if you hadn't pulled me off."

He lifted her up and sat beside her. "I know. That's why I stopped you. He'll get his due. I promise you."

She buried her head in his chest and quietly cried again. He felt her shake her head, and he pulled her tighter to his chest.

The door opened and James and Alyssa came in.

"Hey, don't we deserve the privacy of a knock?" Mickey said irritatedly.

James felt uncomfortable when he saw both of them on the couch with Mickey's arms around Marie. "Yeah. I'm sorry. I'll knock in the future. Valerie said that you caught Arham, and she told us to come right on in."

Marie hid her face as she got up and headed toward the bathroom to wash. Mickey cleared his throat. "Val should know better than to tell you to come in. She's aware I like my privacy. I'll speak to her about that. Yes, we got Arham. He's locked up in the garage."

"What're we going to do with him?" Alyssa asked.

"I guess we need to turn him over to the authorities," Mickey said.

"Yeah, but Marie went through a lot of trauma. I think she deserves her pound of flesh," Alyssa added seriously.

"I guess you're right. We'll do something to give her satisfaction before we turn him over. Could you guys give us some time here? We've been up all night. Just a few hours to rest?"

"Sure. We'll be at the house when you're ready," James said as he and Aly moved toward the door.

CHAPTER 24

Arham Gets a Chance to Leave

"Okay, Arham. Here's how it'll go. That ankle monitor has an explosive in it. That charge is hooked to a three-hour timer. It's a small charge, so it won't kill you. It'll only blow your foot off. Now, when that happens, you'll bleed out in excruciating pain. You have a chance, though. Marie will have the key to the monitor. If you can catch Marie and take it from her in time, you can unlock the monitor and disarm it. Or you can catch her and put the monitor on her, and she'll blow up instead and bleed out. We'll even give you some help. We'll give you a KA-BAR knife and a flashlight."

"And when I get free, what do I get?"

"Freedom. We let you go."

"And what assurance do I have that you'll keep your word?"

"If you get free, you can run. We'll not follow you. When we hear an explosion, we'll assume you're dead, bleeding out, or maybe you are free and on the run. You don't have any assurance," said Mickey.

"Most likely you'll kill me anyway!" Arham spat out.

James and Mickey shrugged their shoulders. "Trust us," added Mickey.

"What if I stay here for two hours, so all of us blow up?"

"We shoot you and disarm the ankle monitor. The only chance you have to live is to catch Marie and get the key from her, or get the monitor off and run. Now let's get this show on the road. I'm tired of talking. Are you ready Marie?"

"As ready as he is," she said, pointing at Arham.

He held up his hands. "Wait! What kind of weapon does she have?"

"Nothing. She'll be unarmed. It's almost dark and she'll have on camouflage covering her from head to toe. It'll give her a fighting chance to get away."

"I don't believe you. She has something to defend herself."

"Shut up, A-hole. I'm tired of your whining. Let's get this over. I want my chance to kill you, with my bare hands, you SOB!" Marie spat back at Arham.

"Sounds fine to us. Marie, you have a ten-minute head start. Starting now," James said to her.

She waved at James and Mickey, then gave Arham a sarcastic look and a mock salute. "I'll see you in hell, Arham!" she called back to him and started walking toward the forest.

"Might as well start praying, and get ready to die, Arham. Our money's on Marie," said James nonchalantly as he sat down on the lowered tailgate of the truck.

"So's mine, James," added Mickey as he sat beside him.

"Want some gum?" he said as he stuck out a pack of gum to James. "No thanks, Mickey."

"Hey, guys. Are you serious? Is this thing really explosive?"

"Yep," said James.

"Is she armed? Maybe she'll just shoot me to get it over with."

"We told you, she isn't armed. And we know Marie. She would never cheat like that. She wants to cut you open with your own knife."

"Come on, guys. I give up. I'll tell you anything you need to know. I'll even give you a percentage of the money I get from the casinos."

"Too late. The game's on. You have six minutes and you gotta leave."

"I'm begging you. I'll give you all the money. Every cent."

"Five minutes and thirty seconds."

"I'm not leaving. I'll stay here and we all blow up."

"Nope. If you don't run, well shoot you in the leg and watch you bleed out. When you die, we'll disarm the bomb on the ankle monitor.

Either way, you die. One minute and you leave." James pulled a gun from the back of the truck and pointed it at Arham.

Again, he put his hands up in the universal stop motion. "Okay, I'll go. I'll find her and I'll go free. Promise?"

"Promise. Here's your knife, and flashlight," and James and Mickey stood up and waved goodbye.

"I wish we could say it was nice knowing you, but all we can add is, maybe she'll make your death quick," said James.

They looked at each other and shook their heads. "Nope, he'll go down crying for her to kill him to get him out of his misery."

"Yep," said James. "I've known her a long time, and she's one sadistic little lady."

James raised the gun, and Arham began running into the woods. They watched until Arham disappeared into the woods.

"How long do you think he'll last?"

"Marie will stretch it out 'till the last few minutes. She'll have him sweatin' it out," said James.

"Did you tell her that the explosives are not really armed?" asked Mickey.

"Nope. I didn't tell her a thing. It would take all the fun out of it. Besides, she is just mean enough to let it blow his leg off. I wouldn't put it past her."

"Nope. I don't think she'd be that cold. She'll disarm it and bring him back. How much you wanna bet she brings him back alive?"

"Twenty dollars, that she kills him."

"You're on, bro!" and they both gave high fives.

Marie sat down as soon as she entered the woods and waited for Arham to come in looking for her. She sat almost unmoving so she wouldn't make a noise. Scaring him later would be part of the game for her. She knew he would turn on the flashlight as he got further into the woods. It would be like a beacon and she could follow him. He would never know she'd be almost within reach of him. She wanted him to fear the woods. His fear would drive her to mentally torture him. She followed the beam of his flashlight as he trudged deeper into the woods. He would periodically stop and shine the light in an arc, searching for her.

When he shined the light in her direction, she would stop moving. Her blackened face and camo clothes hid her from his light. She heard his heavy breathing as he walked.

James and Mickey sat quietly on the tailgate of the truck. "Do you think he'll ever realize that the light we gave him will only attract her?" Mickey muses.

"Nope. He's a computer nerd, not a soldier. He'll use it until the batteries die. Then he'll panic," James answers matter-of-factly.

"How long do you think he has before they run down?"

"I can't tell exactly, but I would bet about two to two and a half hours. The woods are pretty dense, so he can't see by the stars or the moonlight."

"You are one cold person, James."

"I know, but not as cold as Marie. She's gonna take that knife away from him and cut his throat with it."

"You truly think she'll really kill him?"

"On a night light this, you look up at the stars and wonder, what's God doing right now?" said James.

"You pick the strangest times to think about God."

"Is there any bad time?"

"Of course not, but we're here betting that Marie will or will not kill Arham, and you think about God," said Mickey. "I think sometimes we're just as evil as the ones we fight."

"That I know. We're not the bad ones here. Think about it. Fawzan blew up the entire bridge on the ship loaded with men doing their jobs. They were there to provide a relaxing vacation for the passengers on the ship. Fawzan blew them up for no reason. He's a monster," James said as he continued looking up at the stars in the sky.

"Okay. You got me on that one. But Arham. I hope Marie doesn't kill him."

"He's just as bad. He was at Fawzan's base camp and ordered someone to kill her!"

"True, but that was different. Now, it is plain pre-meditated murder. We should hand him over to the authorities instead of letting Marie kill him."

James glanced over at Mickey. "I know, but I got past that years ago. I've learned to deal with my demons."

"Yeah, but I'm not like you. I still have horrible nightmares about what we do. This will be my last mission with the team."

"In a certain way, I agree with you. You have a great business here. You belong here. My training prepared me for this. I don't know anything else. I don't really know where I belong anymore, Mickey."

"Yes, you do. You're married to Dee, my sister, who's a wonderful person. She's an exceptional mother. You're a great father to her kids. You have a place here in Bridgeton and in our hearts. We're all family, James. Don't you ever forget it."

"I don't know, but I hope God keeps Marie safe from that monster that's after her."

"He will, James. Trust me, Marie's in no danger from Arham or anyone else right now."

Silence prevailed as they continued to stare at the sky and wait for the hunt to be over.

Marie's training assisted her in her movements. She knew how to track in the darkness, and her superior night vision kept her keeping up with Arham as he blundered over stumps and fallen branches. To her, he sounded like a crazy bull in the woods. When he would get to a clearing, he would shut off the light and let his eyes adjust to the darkness. He still could see nothing in the dim moonlight.

Marie saw it all, and she smiled to herself. She wanted so much to run out and take him and end the game, but she restrained herself. Only two more hours, and she would go in for the kill. She jumped and screamed and ran toward him like a banshee in the night. Running close enough to brush his clothing with a branch she had picked up, he jumped with surprise and fear. She tapped him on the shoulder as she ran past him and cried out, "Die, you scumbag!"

He shuddered and fell down and curled into a fetal position. Then he lay on the ground for almost five minutes, whimpering. Finally, he stopped, raised his head, and looked around. He sat up and turned the light on and shined it around the clearing, trying to spot her.

She sat motionless at the edge of the clearing, knowing he would never see her. His light moved past her without stopping. With the light in one hand and the KA-BAR knife in the other, he got up and trudged back into the woods.

As he walked, he called out, "come on out, Marie. I'll get you. You know I will. You're afraid to confront me."

She smiled to herself as she followed behind him. After about ten more minutes, he stopped again to rest. She put her hand to her mouth, turned her head to misdirect the sound of her voice, and called out, "Come and find me, you little man. You're afraid of me. I can smell your fear. You only have one hour to live, unless you find me, kill me with your big powerful knife. You must kill me first to get the key to save your life."

"Ha," he answered. "Your fear is what's holding you back. You're afraid I will kill you. You're a little Latin coward!" Again, he swung the light in a full circle looking for her, but it was to no avail. She was invisible to him.

As they went, she could tell he was getting tired and nervous. He was getting slower, and stumbled more, which was a sign he was getting afraid he may not get to her in time. Several more times she ran past him and once she ran into him and caused him to fall, and he let out a string of obscenities.

She noted that only fifteen minutes remained until the deadline, and the ankle monitor was set to explode. She knew he had a watch and was also keeping tabs on the time. It was time to go in and put this to an end. She stood up and called out to Arham.

"Hey, computer geek. Do you want a piece of me? Do you really think you can take the key away from me?"

"Come to me, and I'll show you what I'm capable of, you brown-skinned slut! Show yourself." He shined the light and moved it around the place he was resting. He passed a downed log and moved to the right. He stopped and moved the light back. It took him a few seconds, but as the light shone on the log, he saw Marie casually laying on the log, almost blending into the bark.

She looked as though she was posing for a photo session. She spread her body across the trunk. With her head propped up on her hand, she extended her legs down the trunk, fully visible. If she had been in a bikini bathing suit instead of camouflage, it would have been a very sexy pose. She had a gleaming smile on her face. "Come and get me."

He pulled out the KA-BAR knife and casually walked up just out of her reach. She looked him straight in the eye. Almost as quickly as a lightning bolt, she took the KA-BAR knife out of his hand. She spun him around, positioned the blade against his neck and her knee on his back. Putting her mouth to his ear, she said, "Move one inch, and I'll break your back and slit your throat at the same time."

"What time is it, Mickey?"

"I think it's about time. We should hear a loud horn sounding out instead of an explosion," James answers, looking at his watch.

"Maybe Arham got the key away from Marie and disarmed it."

"Not a chance," James said as they heard a horn sound off in the distance, far away in the woods.

"Sounds like she didn't let him find her. She's still alive."

"Yep. Should we start a fire and grill some hot dogs to eat when she gets back?"

"Sure. Sounds good to me. I'll get the grill out of the back of the truck while you get us a couple of drinks." They set up a little portable gas grill, unpacked some folding chairs, and hung some lanterns to have light waiting for Marie to return.

After waiting for almost an hour, and finally hearing rustling at the end of the woods, Mickey picked up a flashlight and pointed it at the sound. "Marie. Is that you?"

"Yes, Mickey. It's me," came the answer.

"I'll start the grill and put on some hot dogs."

"Put on a couple of extra dogs. I have a guest."

Mickey and James looked at each other in surprise as they saw Marie pushing and shoving Arham ahead of her. As Marie and Arham got closer, Mickey and James smelled the odor of feces and urine.

"My gosh, Marie, you reek!" said James.

"I know it, but this coward thought he was going to bleed out from the loss of his leg and messed his pants. I'm going to stake him downwind from us, at least while we eat."

"You didn't kill him!"

"That's right, Mickey Ray. Only because I care for you and your silly sense of morality. I didn't kill him. Consider this an early birthday present," she said, shoving Arham to the ground.

Getting a tent stake from the truck, she drove it into the ground and cuffed Arham to it, well away from the small camp, but still in sight. "If you even think of escaping, I'll cut your foot tendons, so you'll never walk again. Got it?"

He nodded his head. "Can I have something to eat too, please?"

"Yeah, I guess so. There's a small stream over there," she pointed. "After we eat, you and I will take a brief trip so you can clean up. You stink like the coward you are!"

They ate, and she told them how he had acted, almost begging for his life, and even offered her part of the casino fortune. "And that wasn't a funny joke you played on me. You didn't even tell me it was a horn instead of explosives on the ankle monitor."

Mickey spoke up, "James didn't even tell me until after you were gone."

James laughed and put out his hand holding a twenty-dollar bill towards Mickey. Mickey snatched it from his hand and stuffed it in his pocket.

"You guys had a bet on me?" Marie asked.

"Yep, I bet you wouldn't kill him," laughed Mickey.

After they ate, they began putting the camping gear away, and Arham and Marie headed down to the creek about a hundred yards from their position.

When they got back to the garage, where they had held him, Mickey called Lisa, and told her they had apprehended Arham, and if she wanted credit, she could come get him and report what he did to the casino computer programs. That should give her a big atta boy with the home office.

Three hours later, in the early hours of the morning, Lisa pulled up in the typical black sedan that most government agencies had at their disposal. She pulled up to the back of the pool house in the huge circular gravel driveway and parked. She got out and rang the doorbell at the back door. It was answered by Valerie, AI and she asked Lisa to wait while she woke up Mickey.

Lisa stood with her hands on her hips and her head cocked to one side. "Do you guys ever sleep?"

Mickey looked back at her. "Sometimes. Most of the time, our work is at night. We just got back here after letting Marie have some fun with him. James went back home, and Marie and I just crashed here. Take the A-hole and give him to whomever handles this situation."

As they walked back to the garage where Arham was being held, Lisa asked, "Did you get what you wanted from everyone?"

"Yes, pretty much. We got the flash drive from Fawzan and from Arham we got the codes to turn over to the cruise line so they can neutralize the virus in the gambling machines on their ships."

"What did you do with the flash drive that has the ransom money on it?"

"It's in my safe in the main house."

"Okay. So, you haven't given it to Mr. Cochran yet?" she asked.

"Not yet. Now that the case is pretty well wrapped up, James will take a quick trip to New York to do that later this week," Mickey said.

"I see. We will contact the cruise lines. Can I have a copy of the codes, so I can pass that onto my bosses?"

"Sure." He reached into his back pocket and took out a piece of paper folded and stuffed into an envelope. "This is all you need. At least, that's what he told us."

As they neared the large roll-up door, it opened automatically, and they walked inside the building.

"Is that hooked to a motion sensor?" Lisa asked.

"No. Valerie opened it up for us. She listens to everything and reacts accordingly. She knew we were coming out here, so she opened it for us."

"Wow! She's pretty cool for a robot."

"Yes, she is, but she doesn't like to be called that. She prefers to be referred to as a person or at least a female artificial intelligence being."

"Sorry, I didn't mean to offend your personal assistant," Lisa said.

An ethereal voice came over a speaker mounted somewhere overhead. "I accept your apology, but I denoted the sarcasm in your voice, so I know your apology was not sincere," Valerie boomed.

She looked around with eyes wide open in surprise. "She's listening to us right now?"

"Yes, she's awake and monitoring everything at all times," Mickey said as he unlocked the door to the room where Robert Ryan was being detained.

Ryan, or Arham, was asleep on a blanket in a corner of the room. When Mickey turned on the light, he raised his head and looked at both of them. He said nothing.

He walked over and gently prodded him with his shoe. "Hey, get up. The CIA is here to take custody."

He looked from Lisa and back to Mickey. He looked at Mickey's boots and spat on them.

"You're lucky I'm not bringing Marie out here to turn you over to Agent Arthur. If you did that to her, she would kick your teeth out and hand them back to you."

Lisa said nothing as she bent over, grabbed his arm, and helped him up. "Okay, let's go. It's still early and I'd like to get you processed, and go back home to bed."

The three of them walked silently back out to her car. She handcuffed Arham and put him in the car's backseat. She gave Mickey a quick peck on the cheek and thanked him for helping her.

Mickey went back into the little house and back to his place on the couch and promptly fell back to sleep.

◆━❈◆❈━◆

CHAPTER 25

A Celebration at Mickey's Home and Lisa Gets her Reward

The additional men Alyssa brought in went home. Alyssa stayed with James and Darcy, and Marie continued to stay in Mickey's pool house while he still slept on the couch. Lisa and Angela were asked to help at a fundraiser for those with physical and mental disabilities.

Since Mickey still had a business to run, he went back to work. Laughing as he drove his Jaguar to his office, he thought to himself, "Mickey Ray Christianson, real estate builder by day, Mongoose, the snake killer by night."

He laughed, but it still saddened him. James was right. It may be right, but it felt so wrong. After pulling into his personal parking spot, he went into his office where everyone was at their desk with no idea of who he was at night.

"Good morning, Mickey," his human personal assistant said to him as he passed her desk. "We missed you. I understand you've had out-of-town guests at your estate. There's been a lot of action on the peninsula these past few days. Have you seen the news?"

"No. I haven't even turned on the television," he stopped and commented. "Tell me about it."

"Well, it seems that all the police cars stopped running from Bridgeton, to the other side of the Hampton Roads Bridge Tunnel. They just stopped. The police radios were jammed, adding insult to injury. It all happened and lasted several hours. The authorities don't have a clue what happened. Then suddenly everything started working again. They're launching a full scall investigation."

"Really? Sounds interesting. What do you think they'll find?" he asked solemnly.

"I don't know, but we have a lot of military around this peninsula. They'll say it was China or the Russians trying to steal military secrets."

"I bet you're right!"

"Yep. That's what I believe, but no matter what turns out, they'll never tell us the truth. They will probably say it was just a computer glitch. What do you think, sir?"

"I don't really know about those things, but you are probably right. The public will never know the truth," Mickey stated with a huge smile.

"Did you hear that someone killed the leader of the pirates who hijacked the cruise ship you and your family were on, right here in Hampton Roads?"

"Is that right? I didn't hear about that either."

She laughed, "Yeah, the authorities said the pirates did it to hold some bank guy's son for ransom. And the CIA got the entire gang of pirates. I didn't understand it, but they said something about hacking into the casino gambling machines, but the cruise line refuses to comment on that."

"I guess we will never know the truth about that, either," Mickey said. "I'm just glad my family is safe and we're back home."

"We're glad to have you back and hope your time with your friends was relaxing. I have some things sitting on your desk that need your immediate attention."

"Thanks. Hold all my calls until I catch up on things," he said as he started for his office. He spent the rest of the day returning phone calls and answering emails.

That afternoon, Alyssa, Lisa and Angela, James, Darcy and family were all gathered around Mickey's pool enjoying the warm sun. Marie was inside the pool house preparing snacks and drinks.

"Marie, can we have a talk?" called Valerie AI.

"Do I have a choice?" she answered.

"No."

"I didn't think so."

"Marie, I love Mickey, and I know that you also love him, but we…"

"Get to the point, Val. I don't have all day. I promised them I'd bring drinks and snacks."

"I understand that I'm a computer program. I'm not human, but I have feelings. Maybe they aren't like actual humans, but I'm the most advanced artificial intelligence program in the universe."

"I know all that crap. Just cut to the chase, Valerie."

"I also know that I can't have him in the same way you have him. I can't have Mickey the same physical way you can…"

"Now you're getting personal."

"But," Valerie continued, "I can have him in other ways."

Marie rolled her eyes.

"I saw that, and I know the connotations behind the human eye roll."

"Again, get to the point!"

"I will allow you to have carnal relations with Mickey, and I will not interfere."

"Hey, hey! That's too much. We have not had, nor will we ever have, carnal relations, as you call it. Mickey's too…too moral for that!"

"I'm fully aware of that. I was just pointing out that I love him as much as a computer or non-human has the ability to love. If you want him as a lover or even a husband, I will not interfere."

Marie raised her eyebrows in surprise and said, "You're now giving me permission to be with him?"

"Yes. I will share him with you."

Marie laughed out loud, picked up the snack and drink tray, and answered as she walked toward the door, "I don't need your approval, but I guess I should thank you. I'm sure for you that's a supreme sacrifice."

"It is," Valerie said, as Marie moved the sliding door shut and proceeded to the pool.

"Drinks and snacks for everyone," she called out, setting the tray on the outdoor table.

Mickey walked up and grabbed a drink. "What have you been up to, Marie, while everyone else has been out here?"

"Just talking to Val. But now that everything associated with this case has finally ended and wrapped up as neatly as possible, I'm healed and ready to go home."

They walked away from everyone else toward the garden area. "You can stay as long as you want. You know that, don't you?"

She looked at the ground and saw the marker for the little girl and her mother. "You really take care of people you care about, don't you, Mickey?"

"I do the best I can. James and I are thinking of sponsoring a children's fund-raising event for ones with disabilities. That's why we called Lisa and Angela here. We're going to ask if Angela will be our first poster child for this event. If it's successful, we may make it an annual thing."

Marie stepped closer to him and took his hands in hers. "You are the best man I have ever known in my life." She leaned against his chest.

He stroked her black hair and felt his heart race. He also had feelings for her, but didn't know how to express them. "Marie, I…"

"Shhhh…don't way a word. I don't want to hear it. I'm afraid of what you might say to me. If it's not what I want to hear, I couldn't stand it. Just hold me."

He lifted her head, and as so many times before, he looked into her eyes and saw her love for him. He bent down and kissed her. As their lips touched, he felt her entire body shudder.

She pulled away from him and, with a tear in her eye, said, "I'll be leaving this afternoon. We'll meet again soon, my love." Turning her head, she looked across the estate at the pool. The family and their guests, the little disfigured Angela, swimming in the pool, laughing and having a wonderful time. Lisa was talking with Dee. Everyone looked happy, and they all fit together.

"Lisa is a beautiful lady, and little Angela's a wonderful child. Who knows? She might just be the one you need to complete your family. If so, I wish you all the happiness." She pulled away from him. She turned and walked back to the pool area and joined the rest of the family. Mickey followed her back to the pool area and sat down beside Lisa.

"Angela looks so happy, Lisa," he said, as he poured a soda into a tall glass filled with ice. "She takes to the water like a fish."

Lisa watched Angela as she walked out to the end of the diving board and jumped into the pool. "Yes, she was happy, and loved swimming. We went to the pool almost every day until the accident. After that, when she went, the other children picked on her and made fun of her scars, so I stopped taking her. The cruise and the time that James spent with her really took me back to the time before the accident. We were so happy as a family then."

Mickey didn't know what to say, so he just sat there also watching Angela play. Joel and Cyndi really looked after Angela like she was their younger sister. Joel was teaching her how to dive instead of just jumping off the board.

"Did you take the flash drive to Cochran and get your recovery fee?" she asked, not taking her eyes off of Angela.

"Not yet. We haven't had time. James will take it to Cochran sometime next week. We still have some things to tie up here, and a lot of government paperwork. They covered the actual mission on the ship, but they don't pay to recover the ransom. They don't get into that."

"Where is the flash drive? Did you put in a safe deposit box at the bank like Fawzan did?"

"It's still in the safe in the main house. Even though the house isn't finished, I had the safe installed months ago, and the workmen work around it."

"Are you worried that someone might take the whole safe?"

"Oh, no. The safe door weighs over half a ton. The rest of the safe is encased in concrete. It's as big as a small bank vault."

"Wow, that is impressive. Can I see it?"

"I guess it's okay. Sure, want to see it now? I'll give you a tour of the entire house. It should be completed in a few more weeks."

He got up and put out his hand to take hers as she rose from her chair as well. Marie watched from the next table with James and Darcy. As Mickey and Lisa walked hand in hand to the house, Marie knew Lisa would get a similar tour she had gotten a few days before. She wondered if Lisa would have the same thoughts as they entered the master bedroom suite. She remembered Mickey pointing out the various areas and describing how he and his family would spend time in their home. A lump formed in her throat as she visioned the intimacy he would share with his new wife in that master suite. Mickey and Lisa disappeared into the house, and along with them went Marie's dreams.

Mickey loved to talk with his hands. He pointed to Lisa the ornate molding around the corners of the ceiling in the large family room with tall floor to ceiling windows and doors leading back to the pool. The enormous fireplace on one wall that would be so inviting on cold winter nights. His hands and arms lifted to point out various other moldings and even some built in showcases custom built to display unique items he hoped to collect as time passed. He took her upstairs to the master bedroom and the small bedrooms he planned for his future children. Even a third floor with open skylights to view the night sky, and let in bright shining sunlight during the day. As they toured, he told her a bit of his past and how all of this came to be. They continued down the back stairs and ended in a large room with a huge desk and walls lined with bookcases holding thousands of books.

"This is my home office. I don't really spend much time here, but I wanted one anyway. It's all ready to move in. I had so many books in storage, I had this room complete first so we could put them in here."

She looked around and her mouth dropped open. "Wow, Mickey. I've never seen a person with so many books. Are any valuable first editions?"

"No. I have a few valuable books, but if I like an author, I buy all of his or her works. And if I'm interested in something, I buy books about it. I love biographies."

"You said you had a safe. Where is that?"

He laughed. "I'm glad you asked that. Over here," he said, pointing at what looked like an ordinary door.

It was a door that looked like every other door in the house. He walked over to it and opened it. Inside the opening was a proper bank vault door, with a small wheel and a combination knob. It was bank vault gray.

"Can I see inside of it?"

"Well, there are some personal things inside, and some proprietary information and files."

She looked at him with surprise. "Mickey. I'm CIA. You checked me out. I have a higher security clearance than you."

"That's different," he added.

"No, it's not. I'm just curious what a civilian like you would keep in such a vault."

He thought for a moment. "Okay. I guess it won't hurt." He turned and began turning the knob. Finally, he spun the small wheel and pulled the door open. When it opened, a light came on automatically. He backed away, and Lisa stepped forward to the door.

She saw a large file cabinet, a small stack of cash, and an entire wall of guns. Some she saw were illegal in this country. In the corner was a small cabinet, floor to ceiling with drawers.

"You know that some of these firearms are not legal for private citizens to own," she stated.

"I know. Are you going to report me?"

She gave him a wry smile. "No."

"Good," he answered as she retreated from the vault.

"To satisfy my curiosity, where is the flash drive you got from Fawzan?"

He stepped inside the vault, opened a drawer and took out a small computer flash drive and held it up for her to see.

"Can I hold it? I've never held that much money in my hands before."

He handed it to her, and she closed her fingers around it, and with her other hand she withdrew a small handgun from under her shirt. "Thank you, Mickey."

It was Mickey's turn to drop open his mouth in surprise. "What do you mean? What are you doing, Lisa?"

"I don't have much time, so I'll be brief. I've been in the service of my country since completing college. I've sacrificed my life and my family for the service and for my country. Everyone in the CIA is a bunch of self-righteous jerks. My loving husband was killed and Angela was disfigured because of my service. You know what they did about it? Nothing, Mickey Ray! Absolutely nothing!"

"Look at her. She's disfigured for life, mentally and physically scarred! The company insurance won't pay for surgeries to correct and remove the scars. They say it's cosmetic and they don't cover cosmetic surgeries! How cold is it that a government agency will allow a child to suffer as we have suffered? Now, I will leave you and your wonderful life."

Mickey just stood there, staring at her. "How do you plan to get out of here?"

"A helicopter will be here in a few minutes to airlift me out of here. I called and told him to wait for my call. He's in a holding pattern, just out of sight. When I give the signal, he'll be landing in about five minutes."

"Who is 'he' that you keep referring to?"

"That isn't important," she said, holding the gun at his heart.

"What did you have to do with this? Were you part of it from the beginning?"

She smiled a cold, painted sarcastic smile. "Yes. Grace Cochran and I set the entire thing up. Those two male idiots couldn't plan something like this. I know how the agency works, and she knows finance, and Arham knows computer programing. And as you know, Fawzan was a perfect greedy psychopath to help us implement the kidnapping of Cochran's son as a diversion. Now that he's dead, we'll take it all."

"Wait, I understand now. You came to us on the ship and told us you were CIA. You were hoping to go with us. If we had let you go, you could have sabotaged our efforts."

"Yep," she stated.

"When we stormed the hotel in Virginia Beach, you offered to cover my back and went back down the stairs. You called and warned Arham we were outside his door."

She smiled and nodded. "Now you're seeing it."

"When Valerie called and said she had found Arham and Grace, I called you. You warned them as well."

"Yep. I even arranged for the old classic car without the electronics, so it was more difficult to follow Arham. He didn't listen when I told him to ditch all the cell phones. You couldn't have followed him if he had listened to me."

"That's why he was always one step ahead of us."

"Basically, that's correct. Sometimes you didn't tell me, so I couldn't warn him, but he almost got away even without my help. The con you pulled off on Fawzan was brilliant. I couldn't have done it better myself, so I allowed you to do it without warning him. The last thing left was to get the flash drive. I have grown quite fond of you, my dear Mickey, but I need to go now."

She pulled out a cell phone and made a quick call. She instructed someone at the other end of the call to land on the gravel road beside the main house. When she ended the call, she said to Mickey, "I'm so sorry, but I have a chopper to catch."

She motioned for him to move, and they headed toward the door. When they went back to the door they entered, she called out to Angela, who was standing beside James and Darcy, talking with them.

"Honey, come here to Mommy. It's time for us to leave." She waved to everyone as they returned her gesture.

She had held the small gun out of sight of the others, as she waited for Angela to hug the others goodbye, and come to her and Mickey.

As they began walking to the road, they heard the helicopter. It slowed, hovered and slowly landed on the gravel road. In the distance, the others waved goodbye again. They had no clue what was happening. They all thought that as a CIA operative, Lisa had called for a legitimate pick up. Angela hugged Mickey goodbye. As the door of the helicopter opened, Mickey looked inside. The pilot was Arham and another person in the other seat. Arham sat with a wicked smile as he looked at Mickey. He raised his hand in a mock salute and waved goodbye. Lisa and Angela climbed into the backseats of the helicopter. Lisa fastened their seatbelts as the copter slowly lifted off from the ground into the air. It turned and began moving away.

Mickey ran toward the house, and as he entered the pool house, he called to the team. "Lisa is in league with the pirates. We have to stop her. Get ready to go. NOW."

They all jumped up and ran for the little pool house. In the front room closet, they found some clothing that they could change into from their swim suits.

Mickey moved to one of the screens in the house and called Valerie.

"Yes, my dear. How can I be of service to you, my love?"

"Did you see or hear the helo that just landed and took off from the driveway?"

"I hear and see everything," she answered. "I also saw Lisa and Angela board it before it took off."

Mickey buttoned his shirt as he talked. "Can you track that helo for us?"

"Yes."

"Do it. And tell us where it's going. We need to intercept it," he said as he pulled a handgun from his desk drawer.

Alyssa, James, and Marie came to his side and looked up at the screen. Valerie continued, "If you take a look, I have locked onto the helicopter's onboard GPS, and calculated the range based in a fuel amount burned since taking off from the Bridgeton airport. As you can see, their prearranged landing spot can change at any moment. My calculations are projected much like a storm's path is predicted by the incoming information and….

"Thanks, Val, but we don't care how you came to that conclusion. All we want to know it where it will land."

"Understood."

"Can you take control of the helicopter like you can some cars?" Mickey asked Valerie.

"Does a bear do it in the woods? Does a duck qua…"

"Not now, Valerie. This is not the time for humor. Can you do it or not?"

"I can't control it like a self-driving electric car, but I can make certain adjustments to the controls. First, I will disable the autopilot. And change the landing coordinates. Where would you like me to send it?"

"Can you bring it back here where it left?" called out James.

"I can try, but the pilot can still make certain overrides and maintain control of the craft."

"But can you do it?"

"I must contact my partners to see if it can be done."

"Your partners?" asked Mickey.

"The simulators that the pilots use in their training programs," Valerie answered. The screen flickered for a couple of seconds. "Okay, I have just gotten a response. Give me a few moments, and I will reprogram it to allow me more control of the helicopter. I will have it turning around in a matter of moments, my dear lover."

Turning to Mickey, James rolled his eyes and said, "I thought you were going to talk to her about that!"

"I did, but she won't listen to me, so leave me alone about it."

"Okay, Mickey, I have directed the helicopter to turn around. It should be here in eight minutes, and 14 seconds. What else would you like me to do for you, dear?"

Everyone moved away from the computer monitor, and found a seat, to wait until the helo arrived.

As they waited, James spoke to Mickey. "I thought Valerie had removed the crypto from the drive, and downloaded the funds to the main computer," asked James.

"She did, but as soon as everything ended, she put it back on another drive, so we could put it in my home safe," Mickey answered.

"And you just let Lisa have the drive?"

"It's a long story, James."

"Care to explain?"

"Not right now. We'll discuss this later."

While Mickey and James were talking, Aly got up and left the room and returned a few minutes later with two rifles. She reached out and propelled one gun to Marie, who caught it in midair, and ratcheted it ready to fire.

When Mickey and James looked at each other and back at the ladies. Aly smiled at them.

"Aly, you're over prepared for a backyard barbeque," he said.

"You never know when someone will try to leave in a helo, James," she answered as the sound of a helicopter resounded in the area.

They all silently got up and headed for the door and looked up at the sky at the helicopter coming over the treetops. It flew over to the driveway and descended onto the grass area between the house and the driveway. As it descended, Marie and Aly moved in front of the helicopter to each side and raised their weapons, ready to fire.

When it touched the grass, the rotors began to slow down as the onboard computer shut the engine down. Finally, the door opened. Marie and Aly moved closer while Mickey and James stood back. Aly held her gun on the occupants while Marie moved to the door and ordered the pilot, Arham, to get out, raise his hands, and lie down on the grass. In the other front seat, sat Grace, looking straight ahead as if in defiance of everyone around her.

Mickey called to her, "Grace, you will also get out of the copter."

She turned to look at him with cold burning hatred in her eyes.

Aly who was standing on the opposite side of the helicopter, opened the door on that side, reached inside and pulled Grace out, forced her to the ground, pulled Grace's hands behind her and cuffed them.

When Arham was on the ground and cuffed, Lisa was allowed to get out and forced to lie beside Arham and also cuffed. Angela was crying for her mother as Marie gently lifted her from the helo and led her into the house.

Not sure who to call, James called Director Higgins, who in turned made a few calls. In a couple of hours, some unmarked cars arrived and took Arham, Grace and Lisa away. As the authorities drove away a Bridgeton city car pulled up.

The woman that got out immediately recognized Darcy. "Mrs. Bower," she said as she approached Darcy.

Darcy smiled at her and put out her hand. "Yes, Mrs. Crawley. How are you?"

"I'm doing fine. It is my understanding you have another young girl you wish to take care of for a while?"

Betty Crawley had been with the Bridgeton Department of Child Services for many years. Darcy had met and dealt with her on a past case when she took temporary guardianship of a little child named Carrie until James and Mickey found her parents.

"I hope you can help me with the paperwork with the little girl over there," Darcy said pointing to Angela who was still being held by Marie and crying.

"Oh, my!" said Betty. "Can you tell me what happened?"

"All I can say is her mother was just arrested, and she needs someone to take her in until her mother is arraigned, and stand trial for her crimes. I and my husband will be responsible for her during that time."

"I think that can be arranged. Everyone in Bridgeton knows you and your family. Do you want to keep her now?" asked Betty.

"Yes. She has been through a lot. We will take good care of her," answered Darcy.

"I know you will. I'll give you a form to sign now, and I'll complete the paperwork tomorrow. You can come by my office, and we'll finish the rest." She went to the car to get some papers.

James came over to stand by Darcy and both of them signed the papers, giving them custody of Angela.

Angela walked over to James and Darcy. "When can I see my mommy?"

"We will take you to visit with her tomorrow, and every single day until she comes home."

She looked up at James with tears in her eyes. "Can she come home tomorrow, James?"

James looked at her, bent down and hugged her. "Not tomorrow. You can stay with us until she does come home. We will be your new family."

"Promise, James."

"I promise. We will love you like you are our own little girl." He pulled her to himself and squeezed her firmly.

"I think I already love you, James," she said softly.

"We all love you too, our little Angel."

That afternoon, they all sat around the pool dressed in street clothes. Angela had cried herself asleep in Darcy's lap. They talked.

James announced to them. "I guess we will have a new member of the Bower family."

They all looked at Angela. "She will bring you happiness, and you will be blessed to have her," Aly said raising her wine glass. They all raised their glasses in agreement.

"Mickey, Lisa's situation is exactly why we don't allow ourselves to get involved with the ones we work with," said James.

"I know. She seemed so…"

"We know, Mickey!" James and Aly chimed in together. Marie just looked at the sky, saying nothing. She got up and left the others, and Mickey got up and followed her.

"Marie! Marie!" he called again.

She stopped and turned to him. "What? I have nothing to say. I said it all this morning."

"I think it's very obvious that Lisa and Angela are not the ones to complete my family."

"Go suck a rock, Mickey! I changed my flight plans to leave in the morning. I'll go away and leave you alone."

"I don't want you to go away. I want you to stay here."

"I can't do that. I need to get as far away from you as I can."

"Please, Marie. Don't leave. I want you to stay."

"Why, Mickey? What reason can you give me to stay? I'm going Mickey. I can't be with you, and I don't want to be without you."

"Move into the main house when it gets done. Move in with me."

"In the main house with you?"

"Yes."

"In your bedroom, too?"

"Well, not there, but in the house, I mean. We'll be with each other every day."

"You mean like brother and sister? I don't want that. I want all of you, Mickey."

"I can't do that. Not yet."

"Why?"

"I don't know. I just can't. I love you, Marie. I want to be with you every day."

She moved toward him and laid her head on his chest and cried. He pulled her close tightly to him.

Across the large yard, Aly, James and Darcy all looked at what was happening.

"What's happening over there?" asked James.

"I don't think it's any of our business," answered Darcy.

"I think we all know. They love each other, but one of them is afraid to admit it," said Alyssa.

"I bet I know which one that is," said James.

"We all know which one it is," said Darcy.

They stood embracing in the exact place they had talked this morning. As Mickey looked down at the graves of the little girl and her mother, he imagined they were looking back and approving of what they saw.

She pulled away from him and looked deep into his eyes. "I love you too, Mickey. I must have you or I must leave. You have until my plane takes off in the morning, my love." She turned and walked back toward the others around the pool.

Mickey watched her walk away and also had a tear in his eye, which he quickly wiped away. He looked down at the grave of the little child. "Little one, sometimes, living can be difficult. We can't have the ones we love, and we can't love the ones we have." He looked around for a few moments and walked back toward the house to join the family.

The following morning, Mickey took Marie to the airport, and waited until Marie's plane took off. He went back to his truck and cried.

BOOK 7 IN THE SERIES.
COMING LATER THIS YEAR:

The Landlord's Fashion Cents

Mickey Ray is in his office one day and a beautiful young lady has an appointment to see him. Catherine Raynor of CRM Fashions has come to offer to sell him one of her apartment complexes. When Mickey asks why she wants to sell, she explains to him that there was a fire in her clothing factory. Because the fire was determined to be arson, insurance won't pay off. Even if she can prove that it was not arson the insurance payout will not cover enough to rebuild and save the family business. She needs cash, and the police are trying to pin the fire on her and send her to jail for insurance fraud. Mickey agrees to help her, so he calls in the Mongoose team to help prove her innocence.

If you haven't read the first books in the Landlord series, take a few moments to look at these:

Book 1. The Landlord's Inheritance
This was Mickey's first adventure and the one that started it all.

Book 2. The Landlord's Wheelchair Child
Mickey thinks that all is well until he finds a little girl all alone in one of his apartment complexes. He has to help this little girl find her parents.

Book 3. The Landlord's Dead Body
When construction starts at one of his new projects, the new CEO Mickey Ray Christianson must find out who killed and buried this young lady in the middle of his project.

Book 4. The Landlord's Ex-Fiancée
When Mickey Ray gets a call from the Oregon police that his ex-fiancée was dead he and James fly out to pick up her body. When they arrive, they determine Valerie was murdered. The entire Mongoose team assembles to track down her killer. Action escalates in this fast-paced story of love and justice.

Book 5. The Landlord's Time at the Spa
On his way home from Oregon, Mickey Ray gets into an altercation and is wounded. He was taken to the Healing Health Spa to recover and wakes up with total amnesia. During his recovery, Mickey learns the Japanese Mafia is trying to take control of the Spa. James, Darcy, Veronica and the Mongoose team find Mickey and agree to help him save the Spa from the takeover. Explosive action until the very end.

The entire Landlord's series is available at amazon.com, barnesandnoble.com and terryjoegunnelsbooks.com

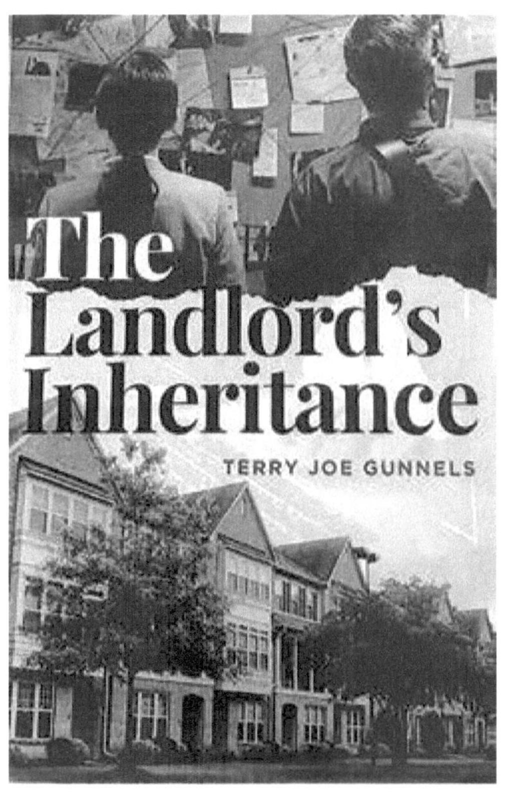

Siblings Mickey Ray and Darcy Jean are informed that the automobile disaster that caused the death of their Mother and their Father's multiple injuries including brain damage was not an accident but an attempted murder. The local police seem ambivalent, and their aunt comes in with a forgotten Power of Attorney signed by their Father, Daniel, and tries to take control of the Real Estate holdings. The brother and sister team begin a power struggle and are physically threatened by unknown thugs which results in Mickey's girlfriend's disappearance which she is presumed dead and Darcy Jean in hiding. James, Mickey's best friend, a disfigured Ex-Military Black Ops operative, assists in the hunt to put a stop to the "takeover."

Simple Detective Work, Internet Research, Adventure, Action and Suspense with a Sprinkle of Romance, and a Fast-Paced, Explosive ending are included in this book of intrigue.

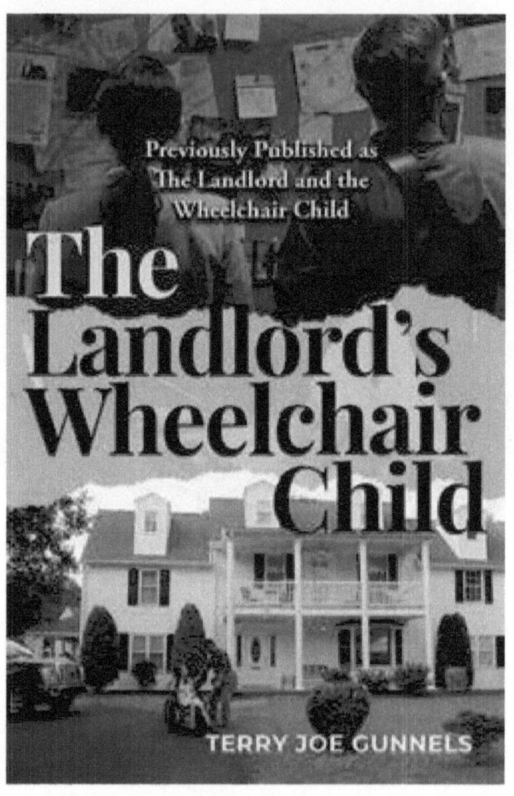

Landlord Mickey Ray Christianson is walking the grounds of his apartment complex late one afternoon, and he sees a little girl in a wheelchair sitting all alone. He sits down beside her and begins talking to her. He then finds out that her mother left her, intending to return. When the child's mother doesn't return, Mickey has the gut feeling that something has gone awry and calls his sister, Darcy, to run a background check on her parents. After Darcy gets permission from the Department of Child's Services to take custody of the child, Carrie, Mickey Ray, and his best friend, James, go hunting for Carrie's parents, assuming they were kidnapped. With help from some of James' past Black Ops teammates, a find-and-rescue operation takes place. After a suspenseful mission and a lot of action, Mickey reunites Carrie with her parents.

I hope you like Mickey and James' newest adventure as they dive headfirst into helping this little child. It is suspenseful to the very end.

After many months of preparation, construction has begun on a new Apartment complex. On the very first day, a worker with a backhoe, digs up a body of a young lady. After the police identify the victim, it turns out that Mickey Ray Christianson and his sister Darcy Jean went to school with her. The victim, Betty Duncan was single, pregnant and lived with her mother in one of their apartments, so Mickey and his best friend and brother-in-law, James Bower set out to find her killer. They start with the obvious suspects, the baby daddy. Along the way, Mickey connects with one of his old schoolmates and thinks he is falling in love with her. After tracking down several leads and dead ends, the case is solved with a huge twist for Mickey and all involved.

I hope this one keeps you on the edge of your seat as it did me as I wrote it. Believe it or not, I didn't know "who dunnit" until the very end!

Mickey and James are back in action with this new action-thriller. The police answer Mickey's call to his ex-fiancée attending culinary school in Oregon. They tell him that Valerie is deceased, so Mickey flies out to pick up the body. The attractive police detective tells Mickey she has a "gut" feeling that it's murder. James, Mickey's best friend, gets a flight to help Mickey find the killer. James brings some others that helped them in earlier cases. Sexy Marie comes to do some undercover work, and little bombshell Alyssa comes to handle technical surveillance. The police detective and Mickey hit it off and she takes vacation time to join in the investigation. James obtains an armored Humvee, munitions, including rocket launchers he got on clearance from an anonymous arms dealer. They have run-ins with thugs, smugglers, and seriously evil men as they go to war to get justice for Mickey's ex-fiancée, Valerie. Ride along with the wild car chases, late-night raids, and the explosive fireball finish of this exciting new Landlord's adventure.

While driving from Oregon, Mickey Ray stops for lunch at a restaurant off the interstate. When someone approaches the table he's sharing with a beautiful young Asian lady, Mickey gets into an altercation, and is wounded in the fracas. He wakes up with total amnesia, in a hospital room with a gunshot wound in his side, being treated at an undisclosed Health Spa somewhere out west. During his recovery, Mickey learns the Spa caters to the rich and famous for their private retreats. And to top it off, the Yakuza (the Japanese Mafia) is trying to gain control of the Healing Health Spa. The Mongoose team is looking for Mickey and when they find him, agree to help save the spa from the takeover. The Mongoose team is soon aware a well-armed civilian army severely outnumbers them, and they are literally fighting for their lives. While there, the spa director assigns Mickey a personal assistant AI. As time progresses, the AI becomes sentient, or self-aware, and to add to the mix, thinks it has fallen in love with Mickey Ray.

A picture of the Author and one of his collectible autos.

The entire Landlord's Series is available at:

amazon.com

barnesandnoble.com

terryjoegunnelsbooks.com

www.ingramcontent.com/pod-product-compliance
Lightning Source LLC
Chambersburg PA
CBHW030126010826
48973CB00002B/438